THE FOREST *of* ENCHANTMENTS

Praise for *The Forest of Enchantments*

'Chitra Banerjee Divakaruni turns the Ramayana around by telling it in the voice of Sita ... This inversion is a gift—it presents us with a way to know an already well-known story better and to love an already beloved story more'—**Arshia Sattar**

'Among the many, many Ramayanas there are now even—thankfully—some "Sitayanas", but I know of none with the special magic that Chitra Divakaruni ... brings to the telling'—**Philip Lutgendorf**

'This inspired evocation of the goddess Sita is an epic song of strength and solidarity told with joy and intensity. It brings to life the personalities and predicaments of the Ramayana'—**Namita Gokhale**

'A terrific read! Chitra Divakaruni has pulled off the near impossible by penning a story even more compelling than *The Palace of Illusions*' —**Ashwin Sanghi**

'Chitra Banerjee Divakaruni's Sita ... is an epitome of courage and self-respect, showing a path for all women. While weaving a familiar story, Chitra provides deep and surprising insights'—**Volga**

'A compassionate meditation on the thoughts and actions of its myriad characters, with Sita as a protagonist. Divakaruni ... has transformed

Sita's image from a meek, almost servile woman to a rebel, warrior and trailblazer'—*The Wire*

'[*The Forest of Enchantments*] brings Sita at the centre of the epic narrative and transforms an ancient story into a gripping, contemporary battle of wills'—*The Times of India*

'Chitra Banerjee Divakaruni does justice to the women of Ramayana ... *The Forest of Enchantments* is not just a retelling of a much-told epic, rather it is a book that tells it like it is—balanced and non-judgmental ... [It] reminds her readers that the Ramayana, besides being a morality tale, is a love story at its heart'—*Huffpost*

'Banerjee is markedly feminist ... Her spin on the most pivotal moment of Sita's life, the agnipariksha episode, is a moment of feminist brilliance. Her Sita answers all the questions we would have had when listening to the Ramayana while leaving us with plenty of food for thought' —*The New Indian Express*

'[Chitra Banerjee Divakaruni] has us racing to witness the inevitable convergence of Sita and Ravan—in trickery at first, then in violence, and ultimately in recognition'—*India Today*

'[*The Forest of Enchantments*] brings alive a great character' —*Scroll.in*

'In recasting the Ramayana as a love story Divakaruni accords Sita parity with Ram, revealing her innate strength. By giving primacy to her thoughts and feelings this also becomes the private tale of Shri and Shrimati Ramchandra Raghuvanshi, two wonderful people who loved each other but who broke up. To readers well-acquainted with that tragedy of modern times, the failed marriage, it will appeal. The ending, however, surpasses all expectations'—*The Sunday Standard*

'The success of ... *The Forest of Enchantments* hinges acutely on the skill with which Divakaruni deploys the narratorial voice'—*Mint*

'One of the simplest and most beautiful retellings of Sage Valmiki's epic'—*Jetwings*

THE FOREST *of* ENCHANTMENTS

CHITRA LEKHA
BANERJEE DIVAKARUNI

HarperCollins *Publishers* India

First published in hardback in India by HarperCollins *Publishers* 2019
HarperCollins *Publishers* India, Cyber City,
Building 10-A, Gurugram, Haryana – 122002, India
www.harpercollins.co.in

This edition published in paperback in India by HarperCollins *Publishers* 2019

19

P-ISBN: 978-93-5357-357-7
E-ISBN: 978-93-5302-599-1

Typeset in 11/14.2 Adobe Caslon Pro at
Manipal Technologies Limited, Manipal

Printed and bound at
Thomson Press (India) Ltd

MIX
Paper | Supporting responsible forestry
FSC® C010615
FSC
www.fsc.org

This book is produced from independently certified FSC® paper to ensure responsible forest management.

HarperCollins Publishers, Macken House, 39/40 Mayor Street Upper, Dublin 1, D01 C9W8, Ireland

To my three men
Murthy, Anand, Abhay
for teaching me love

Author's Note

TEN YEARS AGO, AFTER I published *The Palace of Illusions*, my novel on the Mahabharat told in the voice of Panchaali, many readers asked me what I would write about next.

Usually that's a question to which I have no answer, not for many months. I'm the kind of writer whose imagination must lie fallow for a while before it can come up with a topic into which I can throw myself body and soul.

But this time, I had my answer already.

I'm going to write the story of Sita, I said, because I've always been fascinated by the Ramayan. Just like Panchaali, my Sita (yes, with the presumptuous intimacy of authors, I thought of her as mine) will tell her own tale. She'll fill in the gaps between the adventures undertaken by the male characters in the epic, their victories and defeats. She'll tell us what inspired the crucial choices that directed the course of her life. What she believed in. What interested and moved her. How she felt when faced with the deepest of tragedies. And what gave her the ability to overcome them.

People thought it was a great idea. How long will it take, they asked.

Oh, maybe two or three years, I said blithely. I've already started on the research.

We'll be waiting eagerly for it, people said.

Two years passed, then three, then five, then seven. But my Sita novel didn't get written.

I wrote other books, contemporary novels set in India and America. They featured complicated women protagonists, some strong-willed, others downright stubborn, making waves wherever they went and suffering the consequences. I admired these heroines and thought of them as very different from Sita. Wasn't she, after all, good and meek and long-suffering, bearing her misfortunes with silent stoicism the way the perfect Indian woman was supposed to? Wasn't that why, when our elders blessed us, they said: May you be like Sita? And wasn't that why that statement always angered me?

The truth was, I didn't know how to write Sita's story. I wrote the other books because they were easier, and because I was afraid of tackling what I knew, deep down, to be the most challenging project of my life.

But I couldn't give up on her either. Sita's story haunted me. Because it was one of the first stories I was told, and because I sensed there was a disconnect between the truth of Sita and the way Indian popular culture thought of her. I sensed that Sita was more than what we took her to be. But who she was I didn't yet know.

Then, suddenly, a dear family member had to be rushed to the hospital and, as I waited by his bed in the ICU, the lesson that life is brief and fragile was brought home to me as never before. By the time we got back home, the incident had changed me. I knew I had no time to lose. I dropped my long resistance and returned to my research with a new urgency. I read the Valmiki Ramayan and the Adbhuta Ramayan and the Kamba Ramayan and, my favourite, the Bengali Krittibasi Ramayan from the fifteenth century. I discovered folk songs about Sita, or those addressed to her. I realized that there were many portraits of her, each different in a significant way. It gave me the courage to write my own version.

As I researched and meditated on my findings, I realized three important things.

One: Sita may be the incarnation of the goddess Lakshmi but, having taken on a mortal body, she is human, too, with human failings. As is Ram. The Ramayan is filled with instances of their human emotions. They love, they grow angry or confused, they weep, they miss each other to the point of heartbreak, they are afraid. They even joke about things. Sometimes Sita longs for what she can't have, or what's bad for her. Sometimes, like all of us, she says things she later regrets deeply. Ram loves Sita so much that, at a crucial moment, he can't say no to her even though he should. At other moments, he cares too much about what his subjects think of him. He becomes hostage to his desire to be the perfect king, which leads him into an action that will break his heart as well as his beloved's.

Two: Sita's choices and reactions stem from courage, though often it is a quiet courage, easy to mistake for meekness. It is the courage of endurance, of moving forward in spite of obstacles, of never giving in. It is the courage that has been reflected for centuries in the lives of women. Hers is the courage that speaks its mind at vital points in her journey, no matter what the cost—just as Indian women are now doing. In the final amazing and heartbreaking moments of her life, Sita demonstrates this courage that refuses to compromise, no matter how much is at stake.

Three: The story of Sita and Ram is one of the greatest and most tragic love stories—not just in our Indian culture but in the world. There was a time when I'd believed that, in order to care for Sita, the reader must end up hating Ram. But that is too simplistic. As I wrote *The Forest of Enchantments*, the novel became a meditation on the nature of love. I hope that, while focusing on the many wonderful, exciting and surprising layers to Sita's character, I've simultaneously been able to portray Ram as the complex being that he is: noble, earnest, devoted to his wife, but beset by challenges of his own and forced to choose between his public role of king and his private role of husband and lover.

As I send *The Forest of Enchantments* out into the world, I ask for the benediction of Sita, goddess, daughter, sister, lover, warrior, mother—and a role model for women all over the world. I pray that the novel lodges deep in the hearts of readers regardless of their gender; for Sita's story has much in it to inspire and console us all.

And, finally, I hope that it brings new meaning to that old blessing: May you be like Sita.

Prologue

TWO DAYS AGO, THE SAGE handed me the tome he had been composing for decades.

'It's my life's work,' he said, and a strange look flashed across his face, one I wouldn't have expected. It was part shyness and part desire for approbation. But why should the great Valmiki want approval from me, a queen bereft of her kingdom, a wife rejected by her husband at the height of his glory? I had come to Valmiki's hermitage having lost everything except the babies I carried inside me. I was forever in his debt for the refuge he'd given me at that most crucial moment.

'I'd like you to be the first to read it,' he said, 'before I give it to your sons to sing. After all, it's your story, too.'

I glanced down at the palm leaves in my arms, a hefty stack, reaching higher than my heart. A shudder went through me, sorrow and longing and fury and love, as I saw the title: *Ramayan*. The story of the glorious king Ram. My husband.

I stayed up through the night and the next night in my thatched hut at the edge of the ashram, reading. The oil in the lamps burned away without my noticing. In the next room, my fourteen-year-old sons awoke at the smell of scorched wicks and came to ensure that I was safe.

Lav, always protective of me, took me by the shoulders and said, 'You must sleep, or you'll make yourself ill. What's so urgent that it can't wait until morning?'

But Kush, the perceptive one, touched the dried salt on my cheek with a gentle finger and said, wonderingly (for it had been years since they'd seen me so distraught), 'Ma, why are you weeping?'

I kissed their heads, my boys balanced on the precarious edge of manhood, and sent them back to their beds with words of assurance, but I didn't lie down. Morning came. Wind whispered in the trees—mango, coconut, jackfruit—that I had planted around the edges of the ashram in the early years, when I needed work to distract me from my grief. On the riverbank, I heard the voices of the ashram dwellers greeting the sun with prayer. The purest notes were those of my sons, for they were adept at both weaponry and song. I waited until the assembly was dispersed, each to his or her task, and then I took the manuscript back to Valmiki.

The sage looked at me, curious.

'It's very good,' I said. 'The poetry is superb, the descriptions sublime, the rhythm perfect. You've captured the histories of earth and heaven both, the adventures and the wars, the weddings and the deaths, the betrayals and the farewells, the palace and the forest.'

'But?'

'But,' I said, and I couldn't keep the anger from my voice, 'what occurred when I was alone in the darkness, under the sorrow tree, you don't know. You don't know my despair. You don't even know my exhilaration, how it felt—first in the forest and then in Ayodhya—when I was the most beloved woman in creation.'

'I wrote what the divine vision showed me,' he said.

'It must have been a god that brought it to you, then, and not a goddess,' I said drily. 'For you haven't understood a woman's life, the heartbreak at the core of her joys, her unexpected alliances and desires, her negotiations where, in the hope of keeping one treasure safe, she must give up another.'

I expected anger, for he'd lavished a lifetime on this book. But not for nothing is he called maharshi, great sage.

'You must write that story yourself, Ma,' he said, 'for only you know it.'

He took out a new sheaf of the pounded leaves, a set of quills—items precious and hard to come by in our forest retreat. He called to an apprentice to carry his writing table to my room. He rummaged in a chest and handed me a sealed bottle of ink.

'Hurry,' he said. 'Time grows short.'

I walked to my room, shaky with possibility and trepidation. Time was, indeed, short. All these years my husband—yes, to my chagrin I still thought of him as such—had left me alone to raise my sons, allowing me, if not happiness, at least a tenuous peace. But now the planets were shifting. Everything was about to change again.

I barred the door and sat cross-legged on the ground, and arranged the palm leaves on the table. Outside, I could hear Valmiki teaching my sons how to sing the epic, where to raise their sweet silver voices in affirmation, where to whisper dark and shiveringly of the treachery of rakshasas, of human failings. They'd be performing it soon, if his vision was true—and I both feared and hoped that it was—in front of Ram, King of Ayodhya, the father they'd never met. The man who had banished them to the forest for no fault of their own even before they were born. If Valmiki's vision was true, soon I, too, would be facing him. Ram: monarch, father, warrior, husband. The beloved who abandoned me when I needed him most. My greatest joy and my greatest despair.

But I had a task to complete before that. I took a deep breath and touched the first palm leaf to my forehead, invoking Saraswati, goddess of creativity serene on her white swan, though a part of me wondered what she could know of my very human tribulations. I unplugged the inkpot and was startled to see the colour the sage had chosen for me. Red. But of course. How else could I write my story except in the colour of menstruation and childbirth, the colour of the marriage mark that changes women's lives, the colour of the flowers of the Ashoka tree under which I had spent my years of captivity in the palace of the demon king?

I picked up the quill and closed my eyes. I knew what I must do: travel back to the beginning, to the moment I met Ram. Become again the girl I'd been on that day, burnished with innocence, believing that goodness and love were armour enough. That was where I had to start.

But as I dipped my quill into the inkpot, they rose inside me. Voices. Some clamouring, some tentative, some whispering, so that I had to still my breath to hear them. Kaikeyi, second queen of Ayodhya, who wrested our throne from us out of blind devotion to her son, only to be hated by him for it; Ahalya, her beauty turned to stone by a husband's jealous fury; Surpanakha, wild enchantress of the forest, whose gravest crime was to desire the wrong man; Mandodari, wife to the legendary demon king, forced to watch her kingdom fall into ruin and her beloved son perish because of her husband's obsession with another woman; Urmila, my sweet sister, the forgotten one, the one I left behind as I set off with blithe ignorance on my forest adventure with my husband.

Write our story, too. For always we've been pushed into corners, trivialized, misunderstood, blamed, forgotten—or maligned and used as cautionary tales.

'Yes,' I said to them. 'Yes, I'll write your stories as best as I can, for without them, mine can't be complete.'

I set quill to leaf. In red ink I began to write—in crooked, effortful lettering because it had been so long since I'd composed anything—the Sitayan.

One

THE DAY THAT WAS TO change my life started like any other. I walked through the extensive gardens of my father, King Janak, revelling in the feel of the soft grass, beaded with the dews of dawn, on my bare feet. I was accompanied by the chief gardeners, for I was the overseer of the palace arbours, an unusual duty for a princess. They pointed out problems they'd been unable to solve: a gnarled champak, refusing to flower; a rare harshringar, shrivelling up no matter what they tried; a copse of bamboos with black rot creeping up their stalks.

I stroked leaves, dug around roots, breathed prayers. Behind me, I could hear the awed whispers of the gardeners. *Amazing; miraculous; look, they're already healing; I tell you, she's the earth-goddess herself, appeared straight out of the ground just to bless us.*

They exaggerated, of course. And although I'd told them clearly that I'm human, just like them, their veneration seemed to increase every year.

ALL THIS WAS BECAUSE of how my father found me. Yes, found. Though by virtue of my upbringing I was a princess, Sita, eldest daughter of the house of Mithila, in the kingdom of Vaideha, no one knew who I was by birth.

Father told us the story many times. It was one of my favourites, and my sister Urmila's as well.

The morning I was found, he'd gone to till the field beside the palace, to level it for a yagna that was to occur soon. He was fond of holy ceremonies and liked to participate in their preparation. If destiny hadn't placed upon him the duty of governing his people, he would have happily spent all his time at the feet of a rishi, listening to a treatise on the nature of the Supreme Reality.

That day, however, only a few steps into his ploughing, he was forced to a standstill. A baby lay in his path, naked and newborn, glistening in the young sun as though it was a mirage. He was amazed that I didn't cry, regarding him instead with unblinking eyes. I'd kicked off the cloth that swaddled me, a gold fabric finer than anything our Mithila weavers could produce, with strange and intricate designs the likes of which no one had ever seen. Believers said the gods had gifted me to the good king, who was childless in spite of years of effort. Sceptics wondered which cunning person had placed me there, at just the right moment, to be discovered by Janak. It must have been someone who knew my unworldly father well, they whispered. Other kings would have had the child removed without considering her fate. At best they would have ordered for her to be brought up in a servant's home. But my saintly father picked me up and held me to his chest. And as he did so, a great hunger within him was assuaged, and he was at peace.

This was my first lesson on the nature of love: that in a moment it could fulfil the cravings of a lifetime, like a light that someone might shine into a cavern that has been dark for a million years.

The power of love. It fascinated me from an early age. I thought about it often, even though I didn't quite understand what it was.

My strange gift with plants was a mystery to me. Perhaps it was because, like them, I was earth-born. Maybe for the same reason, when I touched a plant, I knew its healing properties. I could tell which grasses cured headaches and colds, which seeds fended off infections, which herbs to give women when their monthly blood flowed too long, and which potions healed the shaking sickness or gladdened a long-depressed heart.

And so, after my garden walk, I made my way to my other responsibility: the healing house adjoining the palace.

Our servants were the first to learn of my abilities and to seek my help. My queen-mother Sunaina, who was more concerned than delighted, tried to keep my skill a secret, but news travelled. Soon, people suffering from diseases deemed incurable would drag themselves across the country to the capital, begging to see me. They needed a place to stay, and finally my mother, accepting defeat, built the healing house.

Today I examined many of the sick, and instructed the physicians on the administration of unguents and potions. Finally, I moved to the hall of the dying, which was always difficult. At my touch, they grew quiet and breathed easy, and some did not open their eyes again. Only one man, who had been in unbearable pain because the karkat disease clutched him with its dread claws, grabbed my hand and touched it to his forehead, whispering that word again. *Goddess*.

'I'm no goddess,' I said to him sadly. 'Otherwise I would have saved you.' But he was gone already, a faint smile lingering on the edge of his lips. I closed his eyes, sighed, and turned to leave. I was late for my secret lesson in the martial arts.

Though I never would have confessed this to my family for fear of hurting them, I often wondered where I'd come from. Because what called to me most powerfully were the forests that I could see from the palace turrets. Raincloud-coloured, mysterious, full of stories, they pushed up against our kingdom from every side.

No one in my family felt the way I did about forests. Shatananda, my father's chief advisor, distrusted them deeply: the forests—and the rakshasas who lived in them. He was a little obsessed by rakshasas, our Shatananda. He spoke often about how fierce and wild they were. Not like humans. They bred in darkness and practised dark magic. They loved to feed on human flesh. They were watching us, he claimed, watching and waiting to take us over. He was always trying to get my peaceable father to line our borders with sentinels, to cut back the woods.

'Have you even seen a rakshasa?' I once asked him.

He refused to dignify my disbelief with an answer. Instead, he sent my father a telling look: this is what happens when you don't discipline girls as they ought to be.

I wasn't sure whether Shatananda was right about rakshasas, but I was certain he didn't understand forests. I wanted to visit a forest someday, though I didn't think I'd ever be granted the opportunity. It wasn't something that women did. Even my mother, the most intelligent person I knew, would have been baffled if I confessed this desire to her. So I satisfied myself by standing on the terrace on monsoon afternoons, watching the silvery rain bathing the tops of distant trees. Lightning cracked open the sky, spilling its longing into me. Sometimes I dreamed that I was walking the wilderness with its swaying grasses, its leaping, golden beasts, the earth-mother the way she'd been before people bent her to their desires.

The forest dream wasn't the only one I had. At other times, a wide expanse of water came to me in sleep, stretching to the horizon, filled with tumultuous waves. Wind roared over it, and beneath its surface, huge, amphibious monsters waited, ready to pull anyone who ventured close into its dark depths. The scene terrified and excited me at the same time.

Once when I told my mother about it, she said I must have dreamed of an ocean.

'Did you ever take me to see one when I was little?' I asked.

'No,' she said. 'There aren't any oceans near Mithila. Even our songs don't mention them. I've never seen one myself, only read of them in books. I wonder where that dream came from.'

She kissed my head and sent me off to play, but I could feel her watching me, perplexed. I knew the real question in her mind: *I wonder where you came from.*

MY MARTIAL ARTS LESSONS, which I loved, were secret because my father abhorred violence of any kind, even when it was necessary. My mother had to force him to rally our troops when, every once in a while, our neighbours took advantage of his peace-loving nature and encroached on our territory. She was, in some ways, the real ruler of Mithila, sharp of intellect, clear of vision, balancing kindness with justice. Often, my father brought particularly thorny problems of state to her. They would discuss the issues in their bedchamber late into the night, and the next day he would do as she counselled. But she never let anyone outside the immediate family know this.

Soon after I'd told her about my ocean dream, my mother asked if I'd like lessons in self-defence. I was surprised but delighted. I loved the idea of being a warrior. I asked if Urmila would be joining me. I was very fond of my sister, though she was quite different from me, always wanting to play with dolls and dress up in Mother's jewelry, and entertain the daughters of our ministers or visiting dignitaries.

'No,' she said.

'Why me, then?' I asked.

'I sense that your future's going to be different from that of most princesses,' she said. 'It might take you to dangerous places where you'll need to defend yourself. But let's keep it a secret.'

I happily agreed. Every day for the next few years, mysterious women from the hills that surrounded our city came, one by one, veiled against curious eyes, to my mother's personal courtyard to teach me. They didn't train me in the use of weapons, but what they taught was better: how the body itself could become a weapon, and how the opponent's body—its weight, its awkwardness, its ignorance of your strategy—could be used against him. I learned to move like a panther on the hunt, to run and leap and climb in silence, to fall the right way, without injury, to accept pain when it came. The women didn't spare me, and I often ended my lessons with bruises and aching muscles and sometimes a sprain. But they would massage me with unfamiliar herbal oils afterwards so that my hurts disappeared, and as I grew older, they taught me how to make these oils. My mother was our only spectator. She watched in silence, neither praising nor chiding nor expressing concern.

But today when, after a strenuous fight, I backed my teacher into a corner and kicked out her feet from under her, forcing her to raise her hands in surrender, Queen Sunaina smiled. She hugged me to her, sweat and all, and said, 'Now I'm as much at ease as a mother can be, sending her daughter out into the wild world.'

Her words sent a shiver through me, part excitement, part fear.

'I'm not going anywhere, Ma,' I said, hugging her back, letting the smell of the jasmines in her hair wash over me. 'I'm going to stay with you always.'

But we both knew that was wishful thinking. Girlhood was as ephemeral as a drop of water on a lily pad. Soon I'd have to leave all that I loved—parents, sister, palace, garden, the healing house—to take my place in another family, which I must then call mine. That's the lot of daughters, commoner or princess.

Two

IT HAD BEEN A GOOD day, busy but productive. Now I was enjoying a moment of rest on the palace terrace, watching the shadows from the hills grow long on my father's terrace, glad to have a little time to myself before my next task.

Evening was a time I both loved and hated. It was the time when the old stones of the terrace were comfort-cool underfoot, and the breeze carried the alluring fragrance of unknown forest flowers. But it was also the time when my sister Urmila and I had to go to the temple to pray to the goddess for husbands.

We'd been doing this for years now. So far it hadn't helped.

In preparation for my reluctant temple visit, I was filling my basket with flowers. I didn't like plucking them. It was a kind of murder. But if I refused, the priest would just make one of the maids do it, and they'd hurt the plants. At least I was careful to pick only the blooms that had spent most of their lifespan already.

Now I held a wilting mandara blossom in my palm and blew on it gently. Its petals grew strong and vivid red again, and I smiled. My small magic, which never failed to please me.

MY BASKET OF PRAYER flowers was almost full when I heard an impatient patter of footsteps and recognized them as my sister's. Princess Urmila, born to my parents—in one of life's ironies—just a year after they'd adopted me. Urmila, merry and mercurial, the baby of our family, who would pout until she got her way. Whom I loved dearly and who loved me back with her whole being. Who never said, not even when we had our spats, that she was the real princess and I the foundling.

Today she ran up the stairs, anklets jingling more insistently than usual, so I knew something important had happened. But when she told me, I shrugged.

'Another suitor. What's so special about that? Tell me, what does that bring the tally to?'

'One hundred and sixteen,' she said.

'I don't know why you're so excited. We both know what's going to happen.'

'No, Didi.' Urmila's eyes shone and her breath was uneven with excitement. 'He's—they're different.'

'They?'

'His younger brother has come with him. His name is Lakshman. The younger brother's, I mean. The older one is called Ram. They're from the west, a kingdom called Koshal, down in the plains. Very important. Bigger than ours. I overheard the courtiers talking.'

'You mean you were eavesdropping.'

Urmila's dimpled smile was mischievous. 'It's the best way to learn things people don't want you to know, sister. You should try it sometime. And here's why I think they're special: they killed a lot of rakshasas on the way. Even though they're only a little older than us.'

I must have looked surprised, because Urmila twirled around in glee. She loved it when she knew things I didn't. Then she grew serious.

'Do you think he might be the one?'

I could feel the yearning rising from her like shimmer-heat off the fields before the monsoons.

'Don't get your hopes up!' I said. 'You know how people love to exaggerate. How can a mere youth be a match for Shiva's bow?'

'You're right,' Urmila said in a flat voice, her excitement evaporating. She walked to the edge of the terrace, looking down on the pathway that I'd designed to wind elegantly through the red earth of the mango grove to the palace temple. Her shoulders drooped. She didn't sigh, out of love for me, but I felt her impatience, and even worse, her hopelessness. Because the unfortunate rule of our royal house is that the older daughter must be married before the younger one.

I'd tried many times to convince my father.

'Why can't you arrange Urmila's marriage first? She wants it more than I do.'

He never argued. He didn't need to—he was the king. He only smiled, but I knew the answer. It was tradition; thus he would follow it. That has always been the way of the Janaks.

'At least you could have chosen a more reasonable bridal contest for me, instead of demanding that the man string a sacred bow. Why, not one of my suitors has even been able to raise it off the ground!'

My father smiled again, this time sadly. He'd had no choice in designing the contest—and I knew that. I knew this also: it wasn't because of its weight that the kings had failed to lift the bow.

The bow was waiting for the right man.

I WAS SECRETLY HAPPY that my one hundred and sixteen suitors had failed, and that the news of this failure had travelled the length of the land, dissuading others. If my spinsterhood had not been a rock obstructing Urmila's happiness, I would have joyfully lived out the rest of my life beside my saintly and affectionate father and my keen-witted, elegant, laughing mother. I loved Mithila, its cool, crisp breezes that came down from the mountains, its fragrant gardens that bloomed year-round with white and purple flowers, its gentle people who loved to sing and dance. When the time came, I would have ruled the kingdom well. I was confident of that because I'd observed my father in court and learned from his goodness. And, more importantly, in our private chambers I'd listened to my mother advising him.

But when I confessed these wishes to my mother, she shook her head. 'Even if you were a goddess among women,' she said, and from her face I could see that she'd heard the whispers, too, 'it wouldn't be possible. The kingdom of Mithila can be ruled only by a man. This has been the custom of the country since before the scribes began to write its history.'

'Why can't customs change?' I asked angrily. 'Especially ones that don't make sense?'

'Not this one. Because it's built upon an age-old belief the citizens of Mithila hold: no woman is strong enough—or wise enough—to guide them.'

'I don't believe that!' I cried, outraged. 'Nor do you.'

'It doesn't matter what I believe,' she said. 'A good, caring monarch—and your father is certainly that—doesn't toy with the deep-rooted beliefs of his people. Not for the sake of personal happiness. Not even to prove a point.'

I thought about that for a while. Then I said, 'But actually, you're the one who decides what happens in Mithila. Aren't you as much a ruler as he?'

Mother smiled. 'Let's say your father and I share the royal duties—just as I hope you will, with your husband. But in the eyes of the populace, he's the king. And I'd never do anything to upset their belief in him, for in that lies the stability of the kingdom.'

This bothered my sense of fairness and I started to argue further, but my mother changed the subject.

'Listen carefully,' she said. The unusual seriousness in her voice silenced me.

Soon, she told me—for he was aging—my father would have to send out the royal elephant, who knew how to choose from the populace an appropriate male with the twenty-four auspicious signs on his body. He would be trained to become the next Janak; ultimately he would be crowned king. Our father needed to perform the marriages of his daughters before this happened because our futures would grow uncertain afterwards.

'Maybe I can just marry the next Janak and remain here as queen,' I suggested. Visitors to my father's court often remarked on how beautiful I was. I felt fairly confident that I could charm this nameless heir to the throne into accepting me as his wife.

My mother smiled sadly. 'I'm sure the next Janak would be happy to do that—but what if he can't pay your bride-price?'

So there was nothing more for me to do except join Urmila at the Parvati temple in dutiful, if tepid, prayer. I wasn't surprised that the prayers hadn't borne fruit.

'LOOK! LOOK!' URMILA SAID, pulling me behind a sprawling tulsi bush on the terrace so we wouldn't be seen.

Below, four people walked along the garden path that led to the temple. In the lead was Shatananda with his measured, self-important gait. His presence surprised me. The fact that he had been sent to personally escort these young guests suggested that my father considered them special. Beside him walked a tall man, whiplash-thin in white, his hair tied above his head in a severe manner that proclaimed him to be a sage. Even in this sleepy corner of Bharatvarsha, we knew of Vishwamitra, whose temper was legendary. Though born a prince, he'd set his heart upon becoming a brahmarshi, the highest of sages—a title reserved only for brahmins—and had, after innumerable struggles, achieved it. His was a colourful and cantankerous history. That he'd chosen to accompany these fledgling princes on their adventures hinted further at their uniqueness.

I watched the two brothers with interest. They walked behind Vishwamitra, looking around curiously at the trees my father had gathered from all over the continent to please me. I couldn't make out their features—the setting sun was in my eyes—but somehow I knew which one was Ram. He was slighter than his brother and darker in complexion, but he walked with a serene confidence. When Lakshman reached out to pluck a mango, he shook his head slightly, and Lakshman fell back at once.

There was something strangely, deeply familiar about the way Ram held himself, graceful and comfortable in his body and in the world.

How could that be? This was the first time I was seeing him, in waking or dream.

I felt a great need to discover more. I gripped Urmila's hand.

'Isn't it time for our prayers?' I said, though it was clearly too early.

For a moment Urmila looked startled. I'd never displayed this much interest in any of my suitors. Then mischief danced over her face.

'Indeed it is,' she cried.

I snatched up the basket, and arm-in-arm we ran down the stairs, careful to avoid our mother, who would have been rightly suspicious.

BECAUSE URMILA INSISTED UPON combing our hair and applying kajal to our eyes and sandalwood paste to our throats, we almost missed Ram and Lakshman. They'd completed their prostrations and were already leaving when we hurried up to the temple. Shatananda bowed to us—but curtly—and maintained a telling silence. His pursed lips made no secret of his displeasure. He's a wise minister, one my father rightly depends on, but overfond of propriety. If he had his way, we princesses would have been kept confined to our rooms, decorously draped in silks and gems like ceremonial dolls.

When custom dictated that we appear in public, he would have us seated at the women's end of the sabha, as far from the male gaze as possible. Instead, here we were in thin summer-cotton saris that barely hid our curves, tendrils of hair coming loose from our hasty braids, our bodies giving off the mingled scent of sandalwood and excitement and female sweat. He ushered the young men past us as rapidly as possible, without introductions. He was probably hoping they'd think we were maidservants.

But he couldn't stop us from looking.

Ram was young, as Urmila had warned me, far younger than my other suitors. I guessed him to be seventeen or eighteen, only a little older than me. He was indeed darker than Lakshman and slimmer, but his body was strong and wiry. A hefty bow was slung over his shoulder. He didn't seem to feel its weight. I'd assumed that he'd be exhausted from all the fighting he'd done, but he moved with lithe grace. Even in his travel-stained garments, he was unmistakably royal. His aura was calm and peaceful, quite unlike someone who had recently killed a host of rakshasas.

As he passed us, Ram looked at me. His eyes were large and very dark, and shaped like lotus petals. Pulled into them, I felt like I was falling. No, it was more like I was whisked away to a distant place that shone with a light that was at once brilliant and cool, to a time when I'd been someone else. There was an ocean, undulating gently around me, white-foamed as innocence, so beautiful that for a moment I couldn't breathe. In this world, too, Ram stood in front of me, though there was a great shining around him so I couldn't see his face. This ethereal light that filled the huge space where we seemed to float emanated from a giant gem at his neck. I took a step forward. Inexplicably, shockingly, I longed to rest my head on his bare chest.

Then I was back in the garden, blinking in confusion. Perhaps Ram had felt something similar. He had stopped, brow wrinkled as though he was trying to figure something out. He stared at me until a scowling Shatananda took hold of his elbow and drew him away, leaving me to suppress a sigh and enter the temple.

THE TEMPLE OF PARVATI was smaller than one might have expected to find in a palace: a single, windowless room built of rough-hewn stone. But the plain spire thrust itself unapologetically into the sky, demanding to be noticed by the heavens. No one knew when it had been constructed. Perhaps it was built by one of the earlier Janaks, or perhaps, as certain tales claimed, it rose fully formed from the earth. Whenever I stepped into it, I felt I was entering a space of power where the relationship between men and gods remained intimate and primeval. Where destinies could be shaped or, at the very least, revealed.

Today the black walls of the sanctuary gleamed in lamplight. The goddess's eyes, too, gleamed as though the statue were alive. I watched the priest decorate the onyx image with mandara flowers, which are supposed to be her favourite. He placed the largest one—the one I'd revived—upon her head. But I was distracted. I couldn't stop thinking of the vision I'd had, Ram and I together in the other world, the sweet intimacy we'd shared. Urmila's mind must have travelled with mine, for as the priest waved the arati lamp and chanted, she whispered to me that she thought Lakshman was a fine-looking man. The plaintive longing in her voice resonated in my heart. And suddenly I was sure, like never before, that Ram was the right mate—the only one—for me.

I prayed with more intensity than ever before, holding my breath until the room swam around me. *Holy Mother, you know what love is. They say that you went through many troubles and penances to win Lord Shiva as your husband. You even defied your parents to follow him into the wilderness. Please help us. I've never felt this way about a man—nor has Urmila, from what I can tell. Mother, guide Ram's hand tomorrow as he strings Shiva's bow so that Urmila and I can marry the two brothers.*

After I finished praying, I waited hopefully. I'd heard that sometimes the goddess presented a sign. But there was nothing.

We were halfway back to the palace when we heard rapid footsteps behind us, the priest calling our names. He hurried up, out of breath.

'The flower I placed on the idol's head,' he said, 'has fallen.'

'What does that mean?' Urmila asked.

'You must have asked for a boon. The goddess is willing to grant it.'

Urmila gripped my hand, her face afire with excitement, but the priest looked uneasy. 'The flower fell to the left of the statue,' he said. 'You'll get what you want, but it will not be what you expect. Success in the beginning will be followed by a thorny path.'

'What about the end?' I asked.

'Unclear,' the priest said. I could tell from his face that he wished the portent was better. 'There may be joy. But equally, there may be disaster. And in between, heartbreak.'

'I DON'T CARE,' URMILA said defiantly as we walked on in the dusk. 'I want to marry Lakshman. I'm willing to walk through innumerable koshas of thorns for him.' She ignored the warning about heartbreak. That was my sister—she only heard what she wanted to hear. She grasped my hand and held it hard against her chest. 'I'm tired of waiting. I want to live—now! Don't you?'

Her blood beat, rapid and erratic, against my palm. As though in answer, my heart lurched with longing. Suddenly I, too, was ready for marriage, along with any adventures it might bring.

But I couldn't let go so easily of the priest's warning. I wanted Ram. I desired him more than I'd ever desired anyone. But I wondered uneasily what price the gods would exact in exchange.

As we walked back to the palace, Urmila enumerating Lakshman's many heroic attributes for my benefit, I was distracted by another thought. The feeling I'd experienced when I saw Ram—this was not the first time I'd been shaken by such a sense of familiarity. I'd felt it on the day, several years ago, when Ravan, the famed demon king who was loved by many, hated by more, and feared by all, came to Mithila to try for my hand.

I REMEMBERED THE DAY well. Though they'd said nothing, I sensed my parents' nervousness. Ravan's reputation was a dark and paradoxical one, clouded in mystery. He came from an island in the faraway southern ocean, inhabited by monsters. No one at my father's court knew where it was. He'd spent decades in austere prayer and received the boon of invincibility. He'd pillaged kingdom after kingdom, both earthly and celestial, and taken whatever he fancied: riches, women, slaves. Even the god-king Indra was terrified of him. The sun and the moon, taken in battle, served as doorkeepers in his palace, which had been built by Vishwakarma, the divine architect, out of Vajra, a celestial metal so strong that no weapon could harm it. He had wrested Kubera's flying chariot, the pushpak viman, from him, even though Kubera was part-god and related to him besides. Paradoxically, he was a devotee of Shiva.

I found Ravan's story both fascinating and troublesome. If he was Shiva's follower, might it give him the power to string the bow? And if so, what form would my life take?

When I entered the hall, Ravan was already there, standing in front of the bow. He was the tallest and most striking of all my suitors, at once fierce and handsome. In front of him, my stately father appeared little more than a child. There was a dark shining around him. I realized—though how I knew this I couldn't tell—that he'd thrown a glamor-spell over himself, and what we were seeing was not his true appearance, which was at once more majestic and terrible. My mother had surrounded me with her women, dressing us alike, all of us veiled in heavy silks of the same hue, but somehow he knew, right away, who I was. He bowed to me with a familiar smile, his teeth very white against his thick, dark mustache, as though he owned me already.

What if he succeeds? I thought, lightheaded with sudden terror. I'd heard that the island he lived on was invisible to all except those he allowed to see it. No one who went there ever returned. Nor did they wish to, for they no longer remembered who they were. If he took me with him, I'd never see my parents, my sister, my land. I'd lose myself in him.

This last thought pulled at me, cool and seductive as an underwater current.

But the bow had not budged, although Ravan had tried again and again to lift it, his muscles straining, the veins bulging on his forehead, his eyes turning red with effort and rage. Finally, he'd given up with a cry so loud and full, I feared the hall would collapse around us.

'Be thankful that it's the bow of Shiva, whom I hold in great reverence,' he said to my father, who stood pale beneath his kingly demeanour, not knowing what would happen to his people now. 'Otherwise I'd have destroyed your entire kingdom and taken your daughter by force.' He raised his hand and clenched it. A cloud belching thunder and fire materialized, and into it he disappeared.

I stood wordless and shaken, like the rest of the assembly. But the flash of a vision I'd had as he vanished distracted me.

Ravan and I had been together in that same great Elsewhere that I sensed today with Ram. In that shimmering, shifting place, Ravan had knelt weeping, except he didn't look like the Ravan I'd just seen. Who he was in that world I didn't know, though clearly he was a celestial being. I couldn't see his face. *Don't send me away from you*, he beseeched, his palms joined, his head bent low. *I can't live without you.* His voice shook with misery—and with love. But he wasn't talking to me.

To whom had he spoken? And what did all this mean?

Three

I WAS USUALLY INDULGENT TOWARDS URMILA'S chatter, but tonight as we lay in the bedroom we'd shared since we were girls, I felt edgy with impatience. I needed to do something this night, but I couldn't do it until she fell asleep. I yawned pointedly while she repeated the tales she'd heard of Lakshman's exploits. When she forced me to respond, I spoke in drowsy monosyllables. But she was too excited to sleep.

When she was this way, I'd learned over the years, only one thing calmed her down: my singing. So I made up a song, one I felt was appropriate for tonight, repeating it over and over until her eyes closed and her breath slowed.

The wind blows through the forest
And comes to rest on the branches
Of the pomegranate tree in our father's garden.
The day has come, it sings.
The heroes are on their way.
Faces of gold, eyes glimmering like mountain lakes,
Will they bear our hearts away with them
To our destinies?

I slipped out of bed and, carefully avoiding the night guards, went to visit Shiva's bow. Having come from the realm of the gods, the bow knew many things. Perhaps it would provide answers to the questions that troubled me.

To reach the bow, which was housed in the court-room of the old palace, a distance from our living quarters, I had to walk through the silent palace grounds, the night fragrant with gardenias and stars. The visitors' palace, in which Ram was sleeping, lay in my path. No. I confess: I chose a longer way so that I'd have to pass by it. Outside, I stopped for a moment—I couldn't help it, though I knew it would be a terrible scandal if anyone discovered me here.

I imagined Ram. He would have bathed and rubbed scented oil onto his travel-weary limbs before sleep. Now he lay stretched out on the bed, his body dark against the conch-white sheets, his chest smelling of musk. Beneath closed lids, his eyes flickered. Was he dreaming? *Dream of me*, I willed him before I forced myself to continue on to the Hall of the Bow. The doors to the hall were unlocked, as I'd hoped. And there were no soldiers on duty outside. By now, my father knew that people were too afraid of the bow to venture near it.

My mother had told me the story of how the bow came to us. A few years after King Janak had found me, the sage Parashuram, who in his notorious wrath had massacred seven generations of the corrupt kings of Bharatvarsha, appeared in my father's court in a flash of lightning. In his hands he held a bow.

'I've come to marry your daughter Sita,' the sage announced. 'Bring her to me.' His dreadlocks danced like snakes and there was a fearsome frown on his face.

At first my father was too horrified at the sage's demand to respond. He feared, too, the unleashing of the sage's anger upon Mithila if he refused. Finally he stammered that this was indeed a great honour. But perhaps a girl who had just turned five was a bit young for the venerable sage?

Parashuram had let out a roar of laughter. 'It's a joke, you gullible fool! I vowed lifelong celibacy long ago, don't you know that? Ah, but the look on your face! Priceless! Actually, I've come with a message from my lord, Shiva. And a gift. He's sent you his bow to guard Sita because you're too simple and trusting to protect her yourself. Soon she'll grow into a beautiful woman, and gaggles of suitors will flock around her. However, she must wait for a special being, a divine prince born to right a great wrong, to restore order to the universe. But he can only fulfil his destiny if Sita becomes his wife. No, don't ask for details. You wouldn't understand, even if I wasted my time explaining. Just get this into your head: Shiva has sent this divine mandate—you can give your daughter in marriage only to the man who can string his great bow, the Haradhanu. That should keep the riffraff away. Your job is simple: just wait for the right man to show up.'

My father eyed the bow with skepticism. It didn't look too different from his own bows, except for the unusual carvings along its length. Letters, perhaps, in an unknown language. 'But who is this man?' he asked unhappily. 'And how long will we have to wait for him?' Divine mandates were worrisome and inconvenient; they tended to upset human plans. And the window for a girl's marriage, even if she was a princess, was a small one.

The sage gave a great thundery guffaw. 'Stop your foolish fretting! Everything will happen at the right moment.' He beckoned to Shatananda. 'You look like a competent fellow. Send out a proclamation about the bride-price throughout the land. Be sure to emphasize Shiva's wrath. It wouldn't hurt to describe the Haradhanu's special qualities, either—you'll find out what they are as soon as I leave. You'll still get some fools who think too highly of themselves, but not nearly as many as would've overrun your court otherwise.' He laid the bow on the ground, paid obeisance to it, and disappeared in another flash of light.

When he recovered from the shock of these unusual occurrences, my father tried to pick up the bow, intending to keep it safe in our armoury. But it was impossibly heavy. An entire phalanx of soldiers failed to lift it. My father was forced to let the bow lie where it had been set and build another court for himself. Now the old palace sat empty except when a new suitor came.

I OPENED THE DOOR of the hall, and there it lay in the middle of the floor, the Haradhanu. A ripple of joy went through me, as always, when I saw it. The bow reciprocated: I felt a wave of warmth emanating from it, for the bow and I had a special bond.

The first time I came across the Haradhanu, I was nine years old. Tired of the noisy and elaborate game of doll-weddings that Urmila and my visiting cousins, Mandavi and Shrutakirti, were playing, I'd been searching for a space where I could be alone. Even at that age I loved solitude. But wherever I went, people jostled around me, wanting things, asking questions. Finally, exasperated, I'd pushed open the door of the cool, dark hall, intending to hide in a corner until it was time for our midday meal. The bow lay in the centre of the floor, compact and intriguing, dusty with fear-filled neglect. My parents had warned me to stay away from it, though they hadn't told me anything else about it yet. Generally I was an obedient child. Why, then, did I walk over to it and run my hands over its carved surface. It was made of a strange material, neither wood nor metal. Under my palm it thrummed and grew flesh-warm, and I felt its spirit. Without words, the bow began to convey to me mysterious truths. I sat there for hours that day, mesmerized, though afterwards I couldn't remember anything.

The next morning I told my mother that the bow required a caretaker: me. She refused. She told me it was a magical object, and such objects had strange and dangerous powers beyond an ordinary human's understanding. But I was unusually stubborn.

'I have to do it,' I kept saying.

She denied me—until I added, 'The bow wants me to.'

'How would you know that?' she challenged.

'It told me.'

My mother's eyes widened in surprise. I didn't know if she believed me, but she no longer ordered me to stay away.

I spent many afternoons polishing the bow, telling it my thoughts, singing to it. Although my voice was unremarkable, it seemed to please the bow. Some days it grew magically light in my hands, allowing me to lift it with ease. But after a while, it would grow heavier, so that I had to struggle to hold it aloft.

'I'm making you stronger,' it said, and that was true. Not only did my muscles grow more powerful, and my bones sturdier, but I felt a thrumming energy passing from it into my body. When I mentioned this, the bow sounded pleased.

'Good that you're absorbing it,' it said. 'You'll need strength of many kinds in the future.'

Once when I'd raised the bow to string it—because sometimes it instructed me to do that—my mother came into the room, looking for me. I put the bow down quickly, but it was too late. She'd seen me. I braced myself for her questions—and possibly a scolding. Was it forbidden to handle Shiva's bow in this manner? But she backed out of the room without a word and told no one what she'd witnessed.

I was thankful for that, but aware of this also: something changed that day between my mother and myself. She no longer saw me as her daughter—or at least, not only as her daughter. Sometimes I'd look up from my daily activities—painting a scroll, embroidering a shawl, grinding herbs for a potion, tying up a young shoot—and find her eyes upon me, a little anxious, a little awed.

To see awe in a parent's eyes—it is a strange, lonely feeling.

THE BOW, HOWEVER, WASN'T done with me. It would make me sit in front of it, eyes closed, touching it. Then the palace would recede, and I would find myself in a horrific place, a different one each time. I'd be imprisoned in a tiny dungeon whose stones pressed in upon me so that I couldn't breathe. Or I'd be buried chest-deep in quicksand and sinking further down each moment. Or I'd be in a cave, my back to the rough stone wall, while a raging fire got closer and closer. My challenge would be to remain calm and devise the best strategy to deal with my situation. Sometimes there was no escape, and I had to learn to withdraw within myself and find the strength to endure. These mental lessons were the most difficult of all. I was never sure whether I mastered them or not. If I asked the bow, it would only say, frustratingly, 'There's more to learn. Because a trained mind is your strongest ally—and an untrained one your worst enemy.'

The time I spent with the bow was not always hard work. Sometimes it was pure magic. Once, in a vision, it showed me the gigantic ice peaks of Kailash from which it had come, blue in the thin air, of this world and yet not so.

'How amazing that you've come from somewhere so far away, so magical,' I said, a little enviously. 'I've only taken day-journeys from our palace, and never alone. Urmila's always with me, and my nurse, and often my parents, not to mention troops of soldiers.'

'Don't fret,' the bow said. 'You have many journeys in your future, some of which you'll wish you didn't have to undertake. And as for coming from somewhere far away, you, too, have done that.'

'From where? Tell me. Please!' I held my breath, hoping the bow would finally divulge to me what I'd always longed to know. Who my mother was. My father.

But the bow replied that it was referring to a different kind of place, one which I must remember by myself. It added that I was no ordinary person but one with a complicated destiny. My great sacrifice, it indicated, would save the world. Or did it mean that I was the great sacrifice? The bow was often troublingly ambiguous.

Once it told me I wasn't a woman at all.

'What am I, then?'

'A goddess, obviously.'

There was that word, again.

It wouldn't explain further.

TONIGHT I'D BARELY ENTERED the hall when I was struck by an enormous surge of excitement and impatience emanating from the bow. It took me a moment to understand what it was conveying to me: its task on our mortal earth, Bhulok, was almost done.

'Are you so happy to leave me, then?' I asked, a little hurt.

'I've appreciated your care, princess. You are, as I've said, a special being. But I'm ready to be reunited with my lord, Shiva the auspicious. To be in his hand is a happiness beyond explanation. Perhaps you'll feel a little of it when you see him—for you'll do so one day. In the moment of your blackest despair, he'll bring you hope. No, don't ask me anything more. Already I've said more than I should. Watch carefully for him, though. He'll be disguised, as he often is.'

This was intriguing, and on any other day, I'd have tried to cajole more information from the bow. But, newly pierced with love, I was interested in a different question.

'Tell me about the relationship between your Lord and his goddess consort,' I said. 'I've heard that they are much enamoured of each other.'

The bow said, 'Ah, the relationship of Shiva and Shakti! It's the perfect connection of male and female, equal yet splendidly different. It's based on love and respect and knowing each other's strengths and weaknesses. Yes, the gods also have their weaknesses. It's part of the divine play. My Lord and the Goddess are ideal helpmates to each other. Sometimes they fight, too. It's like a huge tempest unleashed over the ocean. But always they forgive each other—for without forgiveness what love can there be? And when they come together afterwards, that union is the sweetest.'

I listened mesmerized, visualizing the goddess with her divine mate, wondering if it was possible for humans to replicate this perfect relationship. Would I be blessed with such a love in my life?

I forced myself back to present matters. 'Tell me,' I said, 'does Ram come from the same realm as I do? Is that why I feel this closeness to him? This sense of recognition? And am I going to marry him?'

The bow spoke in the oblique manner it favoured when it was reluctant to divulge information. 'Ram is the greatest of the great, the saviour of the good, the destroyer of demons. You've been connected to him since before the ages of man. Out of love for him you've taken on this human body and agreed to be the cause for the final battle of Treta Yug between the forces of light and darkness.'

I wasn't sure what the words meant, but there was a resonance to them that seemed to lodge deep within my body. Still, I protested, saying, 'It sounds like lines from a song, ancient and heroic, quite disconnected from my little life. Am I really going to fight the forces of darkness?'

The bow didn't dignify my query with an answer.

'But how?'

'Remain true to yourself—and to your heart. Be courageous and remember, even the blackest night must end in dawn.'

That was frustratingly vague, but I knew nothing would be achieved by asking the bow what exactly it meant. It would tell me what it always said: *all will be clarified at the right time.*

I decided to follow a different tack. 'Here's something really strange. You remember Ravan?'

The bow snorted. I gathered that it wasn't too impressed by the demon king.

'Yes. How can I forget? He tried to lift me three times before he gave up and rushed back to that island of his. He was so furious, I thought he might explode.'

'When I saw him, I felt the same way as with Ram—as though I recognized him from some other time. How can that be?'

The bow was silent for a while, as though weighing how much it might reveal. Finally it said, 'I'm telling you things I shouldn't, because I've become overly fond of you through the years. You know Ravan from the same divine realm. You're connected to him, too, but in a different way. He came to earth because of a curse. Now, trapped in his demonic body, as you are trapped in your earthly one, he's forgotten who he really is.'

My body. People often said I was beautiful, with a pale golden, glimmering beauty. At such times I knew to remain modestly silent, but I realized they spoke the truth. I'd never thought of my body as a trap.

'What do you mean, I'm trapped in my body?'

'Anything that makes us forget our true selves is a trap, princess—even something we love or define as beautiful. Our time is almost up, so I'll end with one last piece of advice: in the midst of darkness, remember this conversation, what I told you today. It'll help you see past the darkness. It'll help you endure.'

Then it was silent. I realized with a pang that it would never speak to me again.

BACK IN MY BED, I tossed, restless. I wanted to sleep but couldn't, and this distressed me in my girlish vanity. I'll have circles under my eyes in the morning, I thought. I don't want Ram to see me like that.

Finally, in the small hours before dawn, I fell into a dream. I was in a beautiful forest. Every leaf gleamed emerald. Every brook sang a heavenly, heartbreaking song. Ram sat beside me in a hut whose walls and roof were made from flowering vines I'd planted and nurtured: champak, juthika, malli. Around me rose an intoxicating smell. At first I thought it was from the flowers. Then I realized it was the scent of Ram's body, headier than any human-made perfume. I moved closer to run my hand over the warm, protective expanse of his chest.

He put an arm around me and looked at me with such tenderness that I thought I would melt to my core.

'You are mine,' I said, 'and I am yours.'

'But of course,' he said. His eyes were as deep as eternity. I parted my lips to kiss him, but there was someone outside the hut. It angered me. Who could it be, disturbing our idyll?

I saw the flash of gleaming gold. It was a deer, the most amazing deer I had seen in this world, or even in that other unnamed one that came to me in fragments. It stood in the open doorway and regarded me with intelligent, mournful eyes. How soft would its neck be if I stroked it?

'I must have it,' I cried.

'This is no ordinary deer,' Ram said. 'It has the power to destroy us. Forget it.'

I was shaken by a strange and sudden longing. An anger. I wanted the deer. I needed it. It would make up, a little, for the things I gave up to be in the forest. Kingdom. Queenship. The child that I couldn't have because how could I subject a child to this wild, wandering life of exile?

'If your professions of love are true,' I said in a cold, formal tone that surprised me because it wasn't like me to speak in this manner, 'bring me the deer. If not, I will understand that the words of the heir of the House of Raghu are worth less than the ashes that are left behind when a fire dies.'

At this, a stillness descended upon Ram's face.

'I will go to capture it, then,' he said. 'But know this: my going is the end of our happiness.' And his face filled with a sorrow so deep that I awoke weeping.

Four

THERE MUST HAVE BEEN MUSIC when Ram walked into the Hall of the Bow that morning, because there was always music when the suitors came: the great boom of drums, the baying of the long trumpets, slender flute-notes drawn out like silver wire. I didn't notice them. Strings of marigold must have stretched from pillar to alabaster pillar, auspicious yellows and oranges as was the custom. I didn't see them. Deafening cheers by the crowd—because the citizens of Mithila were always welcomed at these events, and they always came. I heard nothing. Which sari had my mother dressed me in that morning? Which jewels had she twined in my hair, which ornaments had she fastened with loving anxiety around my neck, my waist? I only saw Ram's face, those lotus-petal eyes. The lines of his lips were as tender as in my dream. *You're mine,* I whispered. *I'm yours.* He tilted his head as though he'd heard me, all the way across the great hall. I thought I saw him smile.

Perhaps time, too, was caught as I was in the dazzle of that smile. The next events seemed to occur within the slow glide of a dream. Ram picked up the bow and, leaning into it, pressed its lower edge down with his foot until it bent. Did he conquer it with his strength, that strength which had destroyed hosts of rakshasas, or did the bow aid him, turning light as a twig in his hand as it had in mine. Was this the man it had been waiting for? His arm moved in a sinewy arc as he looped the string over the other edge—and thus the Haradhanu was strung. How effortless it seemed!

A cry of astonishment rose up from the viewers, and then a roar of applause. I smiled and stepped forward with the victory garland in my hands and my heart beating a rapid rhythm of joy. But Ram wasn't done. There was an absorbed look on his face as though his thoughts were far away. He tightened the string further until the bow creaked in protest. Ram continued pulling at the string; a great groaning came from the bow. Suddenly there was an explosion of sparks, blinding us. By the time I could see again, the bow was on the floor, shattered into innumerable pieces.

I was so shocked, I almost dropped the garland.

The applause in the hall died abruptly, replaced by consternation. The wilful destruction of a sacred object was an act of blasphemy. The consequences would surely be dire. I looked at my bow, its broken body strewn all over the floor, and a great sorrow welled up in me. Why would Ram indulge in such a wanton deed?

I wanted to kneel and gather the pieces and hold them close to my heart in a last embrace. I wanted to say goodbye and thank you and sorry as well. But just as I gestured to an attendant to take the garland from me, a shard of light sped from the fragments, like a comet reversed, and disappeared through the ceiling. I thought I heard music, high and unearthly, a melody at once of farewell and joy. Hearing it, my sorrow fell away.

When later I mentioned this to Urmila, she said, 'You're always imagining things.'

'What have you done, Ram!' my father cried, aghast. 'You've broken Shiva's sacred bow.'

The stern abstraction was gone from Ram's face, and he looked young and confused, so that I wanted to protect him. 'I can't explain it,' he said. 'But I knew it had to be done. This happens to me sometimes. It's as though some inner voice guides me.'

I thought this fascinating, but I could see that my father was troubled at the thought of a son-in-law who acted according to the dictates of voices audible only to him. Would his daughter be safe with such a man? I wanted to tell him that I would be fine. The bow had explained to me already that Ram wasn't like ordinary men. Naturally, his behaviour wouldn't be ordinary. I accepted that. After all, I wasn't completely ordinary myself.

I did wonder, though, at what other times had Ram been similarly guided. What else had he destroyed?

I'd have to ask him that, I thought. A smile tugged at my lips as I imagined where and when such a conversation might take place.

Perhaps I should have been more worried, but I wasn't. I was in love, and love is wild and optimistic, especially in the beginning. Thus I did not think of this: what else might he destroy in the future?

NOW IT WAS TIME for the exchange of garlands, which would betroth us until the wedding could take place. My father called me forward. My breath came fast as I raised my garland, jaati and madhavi, while Urmila held up a second one, made of scented champak, one of my favourite flowers, for Ram to place around my neck. I smiled at my husband-to-be with a shy and tremulous love. *I am yours*, I said again silently, and it seemed to me that with this thought my heart left my body and entered his.

But Ram wouldn't meet my eyes. Nor would he take the garland Urmila held out to him. He turned, instead, to my father. 'I can't proceed any further without the permission and blessings of my father,' he said. 'It wouldn't be right. King Dasharath sent me with Sage Vishwamitra to destroy the rakshasas that were obstructing his holy rituals. He knows nothing of our journey to Mithila, nor of the events that have occurred since.'

I lowered my arms, my face burning. Ram's tone was respectful; I couldn't fault what he said. Still, I felt rejected and ashamed of my eagerness. Anxious, too. What if King Dasharath didn't agree to this marriage? He was a more powerful and important monarch than my father. Perhaps he would deem this alliance unsuitable. What then would be my fate?

And suddenly I was angry. Filial duty was important to Ram. Good. But what of his duty towards me?

My father looked concerned, his eyes clouding. But he spoke calmly. 'You're right to want your father's blessing. I'll send a messenger to King Dasharath at once. We're well acquainted, having fought side by side at the battle of Vaijayant. I'm sanguine that he will agree to this alliance.'

Vishwamitra, who had stood silently in a corner, watching the unfolding drama with his hooded eyes, came forward now. 'I will go myself,' he said. 'King Janak, begin the wedding preparations. I pledge that I will bring Dasharath back with me. This marriage must take place.'

Must? I was glad that the sage was on my side, but that was a strangely urgent word.

My father bowed his thanks, but Ram raised his chin stubbornly. 'There's one other matter. I've promised my brothers that we'll get married at the same time—and into the same family, so as to avoid the conflicts that occur so often among wives.' A darkness passed over his face as he said this, and I wondered at its cause. 'Therefore, before we ask my father's permission, I must make sure that King Janak can fulfil my vow.'

My father looked thunderstruck. In the women's corner, my mother's face was drawn and pale. Even Vishwamitra was taken aback. 'Be reasonable, Ram!' he barked. 'King Janak has a second daughter, Urmila. Let's marry her to Lakshman. Surely that'll be fulfillment enough.'

I heard the sharp, delighted intake of Urmila's breath. But Ram shook his head, and his face was stubborn as stone. 'I've given my word, Sage. It can't be broken for the sake of convenience. That is not the custom of the House of Raghu.'

His words, eerily echoing the ones I'd uttered in my dream, sent a shock through me.

Everyone began to speak at once, arguing, trying to find their way around this new hurdle. Their voices rattled like stones inside my head. Urmila was on the verge of tears.

I thought of what the bow had taught me. I retreated to a place of silence within. My distress fell away and I was able to pray.

Divine Mother, find us a way out of this mess.

As though in response, words rose up within me like a fountain, though I had no idea of what I was about to say.

Low but resolute, a voice—mine yet not mine—cut through the cacophony. My parents looked startled, but it was Ram I was addressing. I saw wonder in his eyes and realized that this was the first time he was hearing me speak. 'Your desire to avoid conflict among brothers is a good one, Prince of Ayodhya, but perhaps you should have informed us of this vow before you strung Shiva's bow? Surely you knew that once her bride-price is paid, a woman can't marry anyone else.'

I was horrified at what I'd just said. It was rude to reprimand a guest, no matter what he'd done. Additionally, for a woman to speak up about her own marriage in this way was considered shameless. Even if all Ram's conditions were met, would he want a wife like this?

But deep inside me someone—was it the goddess?—said, *It's important to speak your mind to the man you're going to marry. What kind of relationship would you have if you couldn't do that?*

Ram looked at me silently. Was that compunction in his eyes? Was it guilt? Or was it displeasure?

The goddess wasn't done with me. More words spilled out of my mouth. 'Fortunately, as it happens, there *are* two other unmarried daughters in the house of Janak. Father, send a messenger to my uncle, King Kushadhwaja. Ask him to hurry here with my cousins, Mandavi and Shrutakirti.'

My final words were again for Ram. 'Would that satisfy your vow, O prince of the great House of Raghu?' Underneath its politeness, my voice was laced with sarcasm.

Ram's brows drew together in a frown. Surely he was angry now.

O Goddess, I thought, I've ruined everything with my sharp tongue.

But after a moment he bowed and said, 'Indeed it will, princess. I thank you for finding such an excellent solution.' There was a flicker in his eyes. I wanted to believe that it was glad relief, perhaps even respect. But possibly it was only surprise that a mere girl could untangle such a knotty situation.

THAT EVENING, THE BROTHERS joined our family for a meal on our terrace, among the sleeping flowers. We sat on cushions on the cool stone. Lamps hung from alcoves around us, swinging lightly in the breeze. Nearby a musician plucked on the strings of her veena and the notes rose like longing into the sky. The food was simple, as it usually was in my father's house: rice cooked with ghee, lentils, a couple of vegetables, and a milk dessert prepared personally by my mother as a special welcome to guests who might soon become family. What spiced the meal was our anticipation—and, in my case, anxiety. Vishwamitra had departed for Ayodhya, and Shatananda had gone to bring Uncle Kushadhwaja and my cousins back with him. Would they be successful in their quests? My father was optimistic, already treating Ram and Lakshman like the sons he'd never had. But I set little store by his confidence that all would turn out well because it was what he always said.

Urmila, however, didn't share my doubts. Now that her marriage to Lakshman (in her mind) was only a matter of time, she dropped her shyness and reverted to her usual lively, chattering self. She was full of questions, and in answer, Ram told us stories of their adventures while on the road with Vishwamitra. Lakshman, visibly proud of his brother's prowess, added details of valour that Ram had modestly left out. In the lamplight that threw up shadows of enchantment around us, we listened as the brothers painted for us their travels through the forests and their encounters with the rakshasas. I was forced to admit to myself, with some chagrin, that Shatananda seemed to have been right. The rakshasas, according to the brother, were a ferocious species. They knew strange enchantments, shooting arrows of fire or raining blood down on their foes. They could grow to enormous sizes in a heartbeat. As she listened, Urmila gripped my hand—but surreptitiously. She wished Lakshman to think her brave. My own breath grew uneven as I heard of Ram's battle with the demoness Tarhaka, who liked to fashion her clothing from the skins of brahmins she had tortured and killed.

'She came at Ram brandishing a huge sal tree,' Lakshman said, 'threatening to make a meal of him. But he dispatched her with the Vajra Baan.'

'What's a Vajra Baan?' Urmila whispered.

'It's a divine lightning arrow. Much more than an arrow, really. Only great warriors are given the gift of invoking it,' Lakshman explained kindly. 'Ram has many such astras—some far more powerful. He was the best student at our gurukul, so our teacher passed on the secret knowledge of these astras to him.' The glance he sent towards his brother was one of pure adoration.

'He taught you the use of many astras, too,' Ram said with a smile, but Lakshman had moved on to the next part of his tale.

'When Tarhaka fell to the ground, the forest shook as though it was an earthquake. Her corpse was as large as a mountain. Her fangs—she'd opened her mouth for a death scream, so I had a good look at them—were like elephant tusks, stained red from all the blood she'd drunk. Ram went on to kill thousands of other demons—no exaggeration, you can ask Sage Vishwamitra—who were terrorizing the holy ones. Their magic tricks were no match for my brother!'

'You killed as many rakshasas as I did, brother,' Ram said mildly. 'And remember, our strength was enhanced by the blessings of the holy ones.'

'There you go, being over-modest again!' Lakshman said. 'Kings need to know their own worth, and to make sure that others know it, too.'

'It's our father who is king,' Ram's voice was stern. 'May he reign for many years more.'

Lakshman bowed his head in obedience, though the line of his lips was stubborn. It was clear that in all things his allegiance lay with Ram, that he saw himself at once as his brother's prime protector and follower. A small disquiet rose up in me. Even if all went well and the four marriages took place as planned, what kind of husband would he make Urmila? Was there any space left in his heart for a wife?

And for that matter, what of Ram? He hadn't spoken to me all evening, although I often found his eyes on me. Was he angered by my taunting words? And even if he wasn't, where did a wife fit in among all his responsibilities to his lineage, his family and his kingdom? Did he even need someone else to love, when Lakshman and he seemed like one soul in two bodies?

All too soon, dinner was done and servants brought us bowls of rosewater to wash our hands. My parents wished the brothers a peaceful night and started on their way to the royal chambers. Urmila and I weren't ready for the evening to end. There was so much more we wanted to know about the brothers. But decorum decreed that we follow them, so we did.

As Urmila and I walked across the garden towards our living quarters, we were surprised to hear footsteps hurrying behind us. My heart beat hard as I turned to see who it was. The brothers had followed us! Ram came forward, palms joined, and bowing formally, asked if he might speak to me in private. The sconces lighting the tree-lined path flickered so that light and shadow danced on his face. I nodded, suddenly shy. Urmila threw us a curious look, then asked Lakshman if he would be so kind as to walk her to the princesses' quarters. Lakshman hesitated, but Ram must have given him a sign, because he bowed and followed my sister. We heard their footsteps receding from us and my sister's laughter like a spring bubbling up out of the earth, and then we were alone in the garden, amidst fragrant vines that I'd nurtured. Ram looked away from me, towards the goddess's temple. He seemed uncomfortable. It struck me that, valiant warrior though he was, he hadn't had much experience in speaking to young women. The knowledge filled me with a kind of tenderness.

Finally he spoke, his voice stilted. 'Princess, I know I'm behaving inappropriately, speaking to you alone in this manner, without your parents' knowledge. But I must—because I need to apologize and explain myself. When I told your father of my vow, I know I distressed you. But I couldn't go back on my promise, or abandon my dharma. Only misfortune can come of an alliance based on broken vows.'

I watched him carefully. I wanted to understand everything possible about this man. Right conduct was clearly important to him, as was his word—more important than anything. Again, the question came to me: what of his wife? Would he ever consider her to be as important as his dharma? What would his dharma say about the importance of loving his wife?

Ram continued. 'I was tempted, though. For the first time in my life, I regretted that rash vow. I wanted to push it away. My heart longed to remain silent so that I could place the betrothal garland around your neck.'

There was an intensity in his gaze that made my pulse speed up. He loved me and wanted me! It wasn't just my imagination.

Ram continued speaking, his voice ridged with emotion. 'You asked me, rightly, why I hadn't informed your father of my vow in advance. I should have, but I was weak. I didn't want him to turn me away before I'd even had the chance to try and win you. I knew that if I left Mithila without you, there would be a great emptiness at the centre of my life. So, selfishly, I remained silent. Will you forgive me for the pain I caused you?'

I inclined my head in assent, my heart too full for words. I'd already dropped my anger—perhaps because I loved him. Now his confession plucked the sting of rejection out of my heart.

'And then, when the problem seemed insurmountable,' Ram added, 'you found the perfect solution, one that had escaped even the royal advisors.'

I basked in his admiration for a moment. Then I had to tell the truth. 'I prayed to the goddess. The answer came from her.'

Ram took my hands in his. I was surprised at how rough his palms were. From archery, I guessed. I hadn't thought a prince's hands would be so calloused. I liked them far better than all the manicured, scented princely hands in the world.

But what did I know of princes—or even of ordinary men? Ram was the first man to touch my hand. And in that fragrant, lamp-lit moment, I vowed he'd be the last.

'Then it's a sign that the gods smile on our love,' he said. 'Do you know, I dreamed of you last night?'

And I of you, I was about to tell him. But then I remembered how ominous the dream had been and pushed it into the black abyss in my mind, where I hid all the things that frightened me, things I didn't understand. I focussed instead on what he'd just said. *Our love.* I looked up at the sky through thankful tears, and it seemed to me that the gods were, indeed, smiling down at us.

I went to bed that night hoping for another dream of Ram. A joyous one this time, now that he'd declared his affections. A dream did indeed come to me, but it wasn't of Ram. Nor was it joyous.

In the dream I rushed through air, borne aloft though I didn't know how to fly. My hair streamed behind me. My tears blazed like a meteor's tail, furious and filled with loss. I wrenched my heavy gold bangles from my arms, my bridal necklace from my throat. I threw them down upon the forest far below. But who would find my trail in that wilderness? With all the hatred in my heart, I cried, *Hear my curse, trickster. You and your evil lineage will fall to perdition for this. Your land will turn to ash.*

A voice answered, laughing, *I don't care about the future. In this moment, I have you, my lovely. That's enough for me.*

But who was it I spoke to with such loathing? And who was it that responded with such dark elation?

Five

A MESSENGER ARRIVED FROM DASHARATH. THE delighted king, along with his courtiers and a large army, was on his way. The entourage would reach Mithila within the week. Dasharath wanted the wedding to take place as soon as possible. Could King Janak look for an auspicious date to prepare for the ceremony?

My mother was relieved, but also, suddenly overwhelmed with preparations.

It's an old belief in Mithila that a daughter's dowry shouldn't be amassed until the wedding is set; such presumption may tempt fate. Though in general she scoffed at superstition, this one my mother had observed religiously. When I'd asked her why, she said that she loved Urmila and myself too much to risk our happiness for the sake of her beliefs.

Her embarrassed smile made me realize something I hadn't considered before: even the strongest intellect may be weakened by love. This struck me as paradoxical. Shouldn't love make us more courageous? More determined to live according to our principles?

I needed to study this strange emotion further. In my father's house, love flowed like a calm and aged river, nourishing but predictable. In Ayodhya, I would have new situations to examine.

My mother's quarters bustled with coming and going: jewellers carrying caskets filled with ornaments to cover every inch of a woman's body; weavers bent low under the weight of iridescent silks embroidered with gold thread; perfumers preparing unguents of sandalwood and rose petals. The palace was awash with enthusiastic melody, the court musicians composing new tunes for the first—and only—royal wedding of this generation. Cooks rushed back and forth with delicacies for my father to approve. My cousins arrived, and the women's quarters filled with their excited birdcalls. At night, Urmila climbed into my bed and threw her arms around me, whispering—as though someone, overhearing, might snatch away her joy—'Is this really happening?' I smiled, because it seemed that I, too, swayed between the calm harbour of my past and a sweet and heady dream.

The days passed in a blur. Beauticians scrubbed us with turmeric and bathed us in milk. They perfumed our newly washed hair with incense smoke. They applied ash of pearl to our faces to keep our skin dewy and pristine. From a palace window, I watched messengers ride off through the shimmery green of the forests with invitations. But there weren't as many as one would have expected for a fourfold royal wedding. I understood the reason; too many kings had come to try for my hand, only to return to their homes in fury and shame, defeated by Shiva's bow. Obviously, they couldn't be invited to my wedding. Nor could their allies. I felt a twinge of guilt. Because of me, my sister and cousins would be deprived of a ceremony as grand as they deserved.

But in the end, it didn't matter. The retinue King Dasharath brought with him was large enough to fill the wedding hall. Additionally, holy men of every kind, from sleek brahmins to mendicants with matted locks, arrived from all over Bharatvarsha to bless us. How had they even known? My father, delighted and unquestioning, constructed giant tents for their comfort and sent his best cooks to fashion their meals. Urmila told me the gossip: it was believed that among them, disguised, were gods and demigods, come to observe the most important marriage of the century—no, of the entire Treta Yug, ordained by Shiva himself.

'Can such things be true?' she asked. 'And is our marriage that important?'

I had no answer for her. Ever since I'd been swept up by the currents of that strange other life, where Ram and I seemed to know each other, I'd felt unmoored from our everyday world. Reality swirled and changed colour each day, like a sky filled with fast-moving clouds. Only this was constant: I longed for Ram, for him to hold my hands again in his archery-calloused fingers and tell me that he loved me.

There was, of course, no opportunity for that. Ram and Lakshman had joined their father, who had been housed in a separate palace at the edge of the royal grounds because it was considered inauspicious for brides and grooms to meet in the days that preceded the wedding. I had to console myself with the fact that in a few days we'd belong to each other. We'd spend the rest of our lives together, and we wouldn't allow any of society's foolish dictates to separate us.

THE NIGHT BEFORE THE wedding, my mother summoned me to her chambers. I made my way to her through a maze of coffers filled with jewels and gold plate. She pushed aside a pile of shimmery silver cloth from a bench and beckoned to me to sit by her. She wound her arms around me and hugged me to her bosom, which smelled of lotus blossoms. A pang went through me as I realized what a big change this wedding would bring into both our lives. Would we ever see each other again? Perhaps she felt something similar, for her eyes were damp, and this was unusual in my pragmatic mother. Or was it some other fear that brought tears to her eyes?

After a moment, she took a deep breath. When she spoke, her voice was practical and calm as always. 'Don't mind me. Mothers always get emotional at their daughter's weddings. When you have your own daughter, you'll know. It's like a cord is being cut, a stronger one than the physical birth-cord.'

I laid my head on her shoulder. I told her that I would always remain close to her in my heart. Surely there were ways of keeping in touch? Letter carriers? Messenger birds? And didn't daughters, even royal ones, come to their mother's home when it was time to deliver a child?

'You're right,' she said with a sigh. 'It's just that I have a foreboding that we'll never meet again. But that's not the reason I called you here tonight. I need to tell you what I've learned about your new family. I wish it were more, but Ayodhya is far from us, and I had only a little time. They are a complicated bunch, the members of the House of Raghu.'

'Shouldn't we call the other girls to listen too?' I asked.

She shook her head, her forehead furrowed by a rare frown. I realized, with a sinking of my heart, that something significant troubled her. 'Urmila, as you know, is easily excitable, and your cousins—much as I love them—are worse. They'd become unnecessarily anxious and might say the wrong thing in the presence of the wrong person. But you're level-headed and know to keep your own counsel. And you're good at problem-solving. I noticed how you immediately thought about your cousins when Ram told us of his pact with his brothers. I trust you'll use what I'm about to tell you in the best and wisest way.'

My stomach churned with nervousness. What was it about the court of King Dasharath that worried my mother so? I didn't share her confidence in my wisdom. I wanted to confess to her that I couldn't take credit for my quick-thinking earlier—it was all the goddess. Who knew if She would ever speak through me again? But why worry my mother even more? Instead, I took a deep breath and nodded. As eldest, I knew it was my role to watch over the others, to shield them when I could. I was prepared to do it to the best of my ability—and willingly, too. Ram wasn't the only one who knew where his duties lay.

'Your dear father,' my mother continued, 'is a saintly man. He was never interested in expanding his kingdom, either through war or marriage alliances. Thus I have the good fortune of being his only wife, loved by him even though I failed to produce a male heir to whom he could pass on the kingdom. He cherishes Urmila and you as much as he would have cherished sons. You don't know how rare this is in royal families! Sometimes I regret that I sheltered you so, here in our peaceful little corner of the world, because now you're going abroad with little armour to protect yourself from the intrigue that is common in palaces.'

She looked unhappy and uncertain. It hurt me because she had always been so confident. I put my arms around her and held her tightly.

'You've taught me to defend myself,' I said. 'You've allowed me to learn to heal both plants and humans. You've inspired me to be kind and courageous. To not tolerate wrongdoing. I'd rather live my life by these strategies than any other.'

My mother looked unconvinced. 'They're good qualities, but not, unfortunately, the ones society values most in a woman. Nor the ones that will help you best when manoeuvring around palace politics. But here's one thing I want you to remember. Maybe it will help you in a hard time: If you want to stand up against wrongdoing, if you want to bring about change, do it in a way that doesn't bruise a man's pride. You'll have a better chance of success.'

Protests crowded my mouth. Was a man's pride more important than the truth? Why should I have to strategize if I was in the right?

'But Mother,' I began, 'isn't—'

My mother raised her hand to silence me. 'We only have a little time left together. I must use it to tell you about your in-laws.

'King Dasharath is the opposite, in many ways, of your father. Early in his life he decided that the boundaries of his kingdom, Koshal, must stretch farther than it ever had before. His ambition led him to fight many wars—with kings and demons. He won most of them because he was a great warrior. He was impetuous and wild-tempered and loved the excitement of combat. He had no qualms about throwing himself into the thick of battle. Twice he was so grievously wounded that people feared he would die. He was a great hunter as well, though he gave that up after he killed the son of a blind ascetic, mistaking him for a deer. They say the ascetic laid a terrible curse on him for that, but I couldn't discover the details. He's milder now, and a most indulgent father—over-indulgent, some would say—because his children were born in his old age, after many holy yagnas.

'He dotes particularly on Ram, who is his favourite among all his sons.'

Dasharath certainly didn't make any efforts to hide his favouritism. Arriving in Mithila, he had hugged Ram for a long time, kissing his brow and murmuring endearments, while Lakshman got a few pats on the back. Bharat and Shatrughna stood back, deferential and ignored, not seeming to mind the attention heaped on their eldest brother. They were clearly as proud of Ram as Lakshman was.

'The brothers looked like they were at peace with Dasharath's treatment of them,' I said. 'Do you think it's something I need to worry about?'

'Not yet,' my mother said. 'But things might change, especially when it's time for Dasharath to announce his heir. So keep your eyes open. Your immediate task will be a different one, but difficult in its own way, because I can see how deeply you've fallen in love with Ram. No, don't blush. It's wonderful and I'm happy for you, for not all princesses get this gift. Anyway, your first job is to make sure Dasharath doesn't feel you're coming between him and Ram. As long as you're careful about that, Dasharath will love you. Not because of who you are, but because you're Ram's wife. Though I hope that'll change as he gets to know you and to appreciate your qualities.'

I nodded. It wasn't the best of situations, but I could manage it.

'A greater challenge,' my mother said, 'will be the women of the palace.'

'Women? Are there many?'

'Yes, because Dasharath took numerous wives—several hundred, if my sources are accurate! Some he married for gain and others for pleasure. There's a great deal of rivalry among his queens, and much vying for his attention. Though on the surface all is cordial, hidden animosities run deep. The three queens that concern you most are Kausalya, Sumitra and Kaikeyi.

'Kausalya, the eldest, is Dasharath's chief consort—but not his favourite, even though she's Ram's mother. That's been a deep sorrow to her. She'll try hard to make you her ally, to support her in her battles against the other queens. Listen patiently to her complaints about the other wives, but keep what she says to yourself. And as far as possible, be polite and respectful to them all and don't take sides.'

I nodded, absorbing all this.

'Sumitra, the exquisite, is the youngest of the three. For a time, Dasharath was infatuated with her beauty, as a result of which she grew disdainful of the other queens. But then she, too, was unable to give him the heir he wanted and fell from favour.'

'How, then, did Dasharath get his sons?'

'Finally, he had the holiest rishis in the land perform a very special prayer ceremony, as a result of which all the queens became pregnant. Something happened during that ceremony that indebted Sumitra to the other two queens—I couldn't discover the details—but afterwards, she no longer gave them any trouble. Kaushalya gave birth to Ram—he's the firstborn—Kaikeyi to Bharat, and Sumitra had the twins, Lakshman and Shatrughna. But she gave them to Kaushalya and Kaikeyi to bring up.'

I was startled by this information. I'd never have guessed that the devoted Lakshman was only a half-brother to Ram. Was there another, deeper tie that bound him so tightly to his older brother? Could it have been forged in that ethereal world that I'd glimpsed?

'What matters most to you in all of this,' my mother continued, 'is that Lakshman worships his older brother. He wants—no, needs—to be close to him. He's probably worrying right now that marriage will affect their relationship, that you'll take Ram away from him.'

'I wouldn't do that!' I cried hotly. 'I'm not that kind of person.'

'But he doesn't know it. So you must make a special effort to welcome Lakshman into your heart and into your chambers, and allow his relationship with his brother to continue unchanged. He'll love you for it—as will Sumitra. And in Lakshman you'll find a powerful protector.'

'I'll make sure Lakshman feels included,' I said. But I couldn't resist adding, 'Though I hope he'll devote some portion of his attention to his new wife!'

Lakshman would require careful handling. From what I'd seen, the two brothers were inseparable. That would have to change somewhat after marriage—both Urmila and I needed it to. We'd have to put our heads together and come up with a plan.

As for protection, I believed that even I, inexperienced as I was, would be better at protecting myself from palace intrigues than the blunt and hot-tempered Lakshman. And if by some strange chance I did require protection of another kind, didn't I have Ram?

'I've left Kaikeyi, the second wife of Dasharath, until the end,' my mother said, 'because she's the most complicated. An accomplished and intrepid charioteer, she often drove Dasharath's chariot when he was at war.'

'I didn't know women in Ayodhya were allowed to do such things!' I exclaimed in admiration. 'Aren't they much stricter about rules and traditions there?'

My mother gave me a wan smile. She was less enthusiastic about Kaikeyi than I was. 'She's a healer, too. Twice she saved the king's life when he was severely wounded.'

'A healer!' I said excitedly, glad to find someone in Ayodhya who shared my interests. I pictured us becoming friends, spending long afternoons sharing plant-lore. 'I could learn so much from her.'

But my mother shook her head in warning. 'Don't trust anyone in your new home too soon—least of all Kaikeyi. To continue with my story: Having saved the king's life, Kaikeyi became Dasharath's favourite wife, his counsellor and comfort, the most powerful person—male or female—in the palace. Be careful with her. I've heard that she's as changeable as clouds in a windy sky. If she takes a dislike to you, your life could become difficult. But perhaps I'm worrying unnecessarily. I've also heard that she has a deep fondness for Ram…'

I left my mother's chambers with my head whirling. How many people I'd have to deal with in my new family, to cajole or appease, comfort or avoid, as the need arose! I'd need to tread carefully between the quicksands of ancient antipathy. I'd have to build my relationship with my husband cautiously, without encroaching on territory that his family felt belonged to them. Could I manage all that? I counted out the things I needed to do on my fingers: respect Dasharath; be sympathetic to Kaushalya; be affectionate to Lakshman; observe Kaikeyi and learn from her how power could be used—all the while keeping a safe distance.

But here's what was most fascinating: how much all these people, so different from each other, loved Ram. What enchantment did my betrothed possess that made even enemies forget their ancient rivalries in their desire to make him happy? I waited impatiently for an opportunity to discover it for myself.

Six

FINALLY, THE DAY OF THE wedding arrived. My father's priests, as well as the ones King Dasharath had brought, had interpreted the heavenly signs and discovered that, by great good fortune, for a brief while, the auspicious lagna of karkata would reign in the skies. Sage Vasishta, Dasharath's guru, declared that the exchange of garlands between the brides and grooms needed to take place at that time, because couples united under these stars never suffered the sorrow of separation.

All was readied in accordance. The four brothers waited on one side of the hall where once Shiva's bow had lain. We sisters waited on the other side. But as the priest held up the aruni with which to light the sacred fire, a man appeared in the hall. There was an ethereal, moonlit glow about him. My father asked who he was, but he didn't reply. Instead, he began to dance. The musicians in the hall struck up a melody to accompany him, though later they'd have no recollection of what they had played. It lodged deep inside us, music such as we'd never heard before. The stranger twirled and bowed and leaped into the air, an unearthly grace in his gestures. None could take their eyes off him. None knew for how long he danced. We only knew that when the performance ended, we found ourselves breathless.

As suddenly as he had come, the dancer was gone. My father questioned the guards and doorkeepers, but no one had seen him leave. The priests hurried to light the wedding fire, but it was already too late. The auspicious lagna had passed. Vasishta surmised that this was the doing of the gods. Perhaps the dancer was a god himself.

'But why would the heavenly ones wish our children ill?' my father cried in dismay. 'Haven't we propitiated them with ample offerings?'

I could see that Dasharath was even more upset than my father, though he said nothing.

Vasishta shrugged. 'The ways of the gods are strange, hard for our limited human minds to encompass. Remember this, too: sometimes our ill luck has consequences that bless others.'

I didn't disbelieve him, but I was troubled. It was unfair that one person should suffer in order for others to be blessed. If the gods were powerful enough to shape our destinies, why couldn't they just send us good fortune untainted by sorrow?

MY FIRST UNPLEASANT SURPRISE came as we were about to depart for Ayodhya. My mother had planned for our nursemaid Malini to accompany Urmila and myself to Ayodhya, to help us settle into our new home. Mandavi and Shrutakirti had also brought their personal serving women from home. But King Dasharath had surprised us all by announcing that he had retainers—personally chosen by him—for each of his daughters-in-law.

'Now you are princesses of Ayodhya,' he said. 'It's only proper that you should be served by your own people.'

Urmila had been distraught while Malini wept silently into her sari. I, too, was upset. We'd been counting on Malini, a good-natured woman who didn't take things too seriously, to provide comfort and counsel when we were homesick, to laugh away imagined demons as she had done throughout our childhoods. I was additionally troubled by the high-handed way in which Dasharath made his decision, not taking into account who might be hurt by it, or what we wanted. My mother tried to reason with Dasharath.

'Let Malini be with them for a few days,' she said. 'You can send her back to Mithila once the girls settle in.'

But the king refused, though he was polite about it, and called for the palanquins. 'It's time we started on our journey back,' he said.

When the first set of bearers rushed up with my palanquin, I was astonished because I'd never seen one this regal or ostentatious. Its panels were decorated in gold and inlaid with ivory; the curtains covering its doors were made of a shimmery cloth that would allow me to look out without being seen. It was laden with silken bolsters and frothy quilts and was larger than the bed I was leaving behind in the palace of my parents. *The palace of my parents,* I thought with a pang. Having been given away in marriage to the House of Raghu, I could no longer call it mine.

'Could I please have Urmila share my palanquin on the way to Ayodhya?' I asked Dasharath. I wasn't sure how many opportunities I'd have to speak privately with my sister once we reached our new home. Marvelling at wonders and laughing at follies together as we travelled would help us deal with our disappointment at not having Malini with us. Additionally, I longed to know if being a wife felt as wonderful and magical to her as it did to me.

Dasharath looked scandalized at my request. 'No need of sharing, my child,' he said. 'I made sure to bring palanquins for each of my daughters-in-law so you can all travel in the comfort that befits your position.'

'Please, Father…' I said, 'having my sister beside me on this journey would give me more comfort than—'

But Dasharath shook his head firmly. 'No, my dear. That's not appropriate. What will people think!' I started to argue further, but my mother pressed my arm hard, a warning to let the matter go. *Choose your battles,* her stern grip seemed to say. *This isn't the time.*

She was right. The cavalcade was lined up, ready to leave for Ayodhya, horses neighing and stomping, servants loading food and drink into carts, priests sprinkling holy rice, praying for a safe journey. I bit back my words, but I promised myself that once I was settled in Ayodhya, I'd make sure that King Dasharath didn't dictate my life.

Before we left, my mother managed to pull us apart for a brief private goodbye. Urmila hugged her tightly, weeping. 'We're going so far away. We'll be so alone. Why won't Father-in-law let Malini come with us? It isn't fair! It isn't right.' Her anxiety was contagious. I, too, felt my eyes fill with tears.

But instead of consoling us, my mother spoke sternly. 'Pull yourselves together. Surely I've brought you up better than this? We come into the world alone, and we leave it alone. And in between, too, if it is destined, we'll be alone. Draw on your inner strength. Remember, you can be your own worst enemy—or your best friend. It's up to you. And also this: what you can't change, you must endure.'

Urmila continued weeping, but I stopped and stared at my mother. She stood tall and regal, suddenly unfamiliar, like a queen out of a tale, and looked at me gravely. I knew it was mostly to me that she'd spoken. *Endure*. A word solid as a tree trunk. A good word upon which to build a life, I thought. I would learn it, and it would help me through dark times.

THE SWAYING OF THE palanquin, along with the rhythmic chant of its bearers, threatened to put me in a trance, but I resisted valiantly. I didn't want to miss a single moment of my journey. Who knew if I'd ever embark on another one as long or as adventurous? Most women from princely families, my mother included, didn't stray far from their husbands' palaces once they were married—and Ayodhya seemed like a land with many more rules and restrictions than Mithila.

Though I still smarted from my father-in-law's high-handed treatment, I had to admit that travelling alone had certain compensations. Urmila would have kept me occupied with jokes about the wedding. She would have prevailed upon me to curl up with her under the quilt and sleep, warning me that otherwise I'd look haggard and ugly by the time I arrived in Ayodhya, where our mothers-in-law were waiting to evaluate the wives their sons were bringing home. Now in my solitude, I'd be able to watch the forest, stretching on either side of me into infinity. I'd heard my father's huntsmen talk about the wildlife that inhabited the forest, gazelles and bears and talking monkeys. I didn't believe monkeys could talk, but if they did, I hoped I'd see one. Who knew, maybe I might even come across a stray rakshasa or two.

But my hopes were soon dashed.

Our procession was headed by enthusiastic heralds that blew on horns and beat on drums, frightening away all wildlife. Worse, the thousand soldiers that Dasharath had brought with him flanked both sides of the road, stomping and shouting, slashing back the undergrowth and lopping off branches and vines, even those that didn't intrude on our path, with a vigour that made me feel ill. After a while, I couldn't stand it any longer and called to one of the horsemen who rode by my side as my special guard. It was on the tip of my tongue to summon the commander of the army, but I kept in mind my mother's advice and requested instead that he carry to Ram the message that his wife humbly requested to see him.

In a little while, I could see my husband—that dazzling, looming word I wasn't used to yet—riding toward me. His rapid hoof-beats matched the speeding rhythm of my heart. In his jewel-crusted prince's attire, wearing a rather official-looking coronet, Ram seemed very different from the young man in our temple garden with his lithe and dusty grace. But his eyes were the same, flecked with that ancient recognition.

At this moment they were also concerned. 'Are you well, my princess?' he asked, moving the palanquin curtains aside to grasp my hand, not caring who saw him. 'Is the motion of the palanquin causing you discomfort? This is a dangerous part of the forest, but once we've crossed it, I can request my royal father to stop at one of the hermitages that lie beyond...'

I was distracted by the warm pressure of his hand on mine, and his smell, a perfume I couldn't quite place but which I knew I'd always recognize now. At our wedding, after the exchange of garlands, he'd held my hand just like this, and shocked everyone by vowing aloud that he would never marry again. *Sita will be my only consort and beloved, all the days of my life.* The words had hummed inside me like honeybees. I hadn't expected such a gift, that my husband would be mine alone. The hall had filled with murmurs as people discussed such a vow, unprecedented in a prince. My father looked delighted. Dasharath was clearly displeased—no doubt he had hoped for many more valuable marital alliances for his heir—but he controlled himself and inclined his head in gracious acceptance of his son's impractical wish.

I pushed away the memory—amazing, to think that Ram and I had already begun accumulating memories—and assured him that I was well. The only thing distressing me was the callous behaviour of the soldiers. Could he order them not to harm the trees? 'This is their home, and we are visitors,' I added. 'We should treat them with courtesy and not cause them needless pain.'

Ram's brows drew together in surprise. Clearly, he'd never considered that plants feel pain as we do. But he inclined his head. 'You are tender-hearted, my dear. I can't fault that. It's right and necessary that women should be so.'

I wanted to ask him, wasn't it as important for a king to feel the hurt of others as women did? Wasn't he responsible for the animals and birds and trees in his realm, as well as the people? Who would protect them if he didn't? But already I was learning that I had to carefully choose the time and place for frank talk.

Ram beckoned to a nearby soldier and said something. The man took off at a run—to inform the commander of the prince's strange order, I guessed.

Ram bowed to me. 'My heart longs to remain here with you—but I must return to my father's side.'

Ram's horse neighed impatiently. No doubt he sensed my husband's desire to be back—as was proper—with his father. I smiled at Ram and spoke the ceremonially appropriate words of thanks and farewell. There would be opportunity enough for ethical discourse regarding the duties of a king, and who he was supposed to protect. After all, we were going to be together for the rest of our lives.

My PALANQUIN MADE ITS way through the forest in relative quiet now, giving me a chance to observe the many kinds of greens around me, in places shot through with sunshine, in places deepened by shadows or punctuated by the bright exclamation of flowers. I watched them longingly. I wanted to climb out and run my hands over bark and stem, smell the sap. I wanted to walk barefoot through the tickle of grass, find bird-nests and fox-lairs, and rare and precious healing herbs. But such things were not allowed to princesses, especially those married into the royal family of Ayodhya.

Still, it was a small thing to set against all the happiness I was carrying in my heart. My thoughts swung back to the wedding. After his vow, Ram had kept my hand in his as though he'd never let go. From time to time, as the priests chanted countless prayers for peace, prosperity and progeny, I stole a look at his face. Though it was appropriately solemn, there was a smile in his eyes. Did it indicate that nothing was worth taking too seriously? That even the longest ceremony would come to an end? Or was it a smile of anticipation? Was he thinking, as I was, of the moment when we'd finally be alone in our own bedchamber? Of course, for that we'd have to wait until we reached Ayodhya and Dasharath's priests found us an appropriately auspicious moment, just in case a royal heir was conceived.

When the ceremony was over and the elders had withdrawn, the room filled with the boisterous games and jokes that are common to weddings. My women teased Ram, complaining that he was too dark, no match for my fair complexion. I could see the loyal Lakshman bristling, ready to defend his brother, but Ram joked back, saying that surely when we slept together some of my beauty would rub off on him. I was pleasantly surprised by his sense of humour, and the fact that he delighted in asking riddles. *If you have it, you want to share it. If you share it, you don't have it. What is it?* He played with strands of my hair as he spoke; a flame of delight surged up my spine. I held on to that feeling now as the jogging of the palanquin bearers lulled me into a half-sleep.

THE DREAM I FELL into was partly a memory and partly a vision. We'd just set out from Mithila after the wedding, amid music and dance and the joyful tears of the citizens who had come to bid their princesses goodbye. Suddenly, a huge thunderclap startled everyone into silence. Surging dust blinded us, and when we could see again, a man blocked our path, his matted locks dancing like serpents. The rage in his face was a fire. In his left hand he carried an enormous bow, in his right, an axe. When I saw that axe, its blade still rust-red from the blood of long-dead royalty, I knew him: the Sage Parashuram, who had long ago brought us Shiva's bow. My heart sank.

'Who among you had the audacity to break my Lord's bow?' he bellowed. 'I'm here to pay you back for that insolence. Twenty-one times I rid the earth of the evil of kshatriyas. Perhaps it's time to do it again.'

Lakshman, who was as usual next to Ram, took an angry step forward, his hand on the hilt of his sword. 'Ram and Lakshman weren't born when you killed those kings, sage. Perhaps you might not find it so easy to destroy the kshatriya race this time!'

A horrified Dasharath rushed forward, hands joined imploringly. 'Pay no attention to Lakshman, great Rishi. He's just a hot-headed boy. Doesn't know what he's saying. And please forgive Ram. I don't know how he broke the bow. It must have been an accident. Certainly he didn't mean any harm. I'll do anything you want in reparation —'

The words had no effect on Parashuram, who gripped his axe and swung it up, ready to bring it down full-force on Ram's skull.

I stepped in front of Ram. It wasn't an act of courage. Until it happened, I didn't even know I was going to do it. Wherever the impulse had come from, it certainly wasn't my conscious mind. I realized, right away, that it was a thoroughly stupid move. I had no power over the enraged sage. He'd probably kill us both with the same blow. A little part of my mind said, *That's all right. It would be better than living on alone if he killed Ram.*

My move had frozen the entire assembly into shocked silence. Parashuram was the first to recover from it. 'Little Sita?' he said in a tone of wonder, staring at me, letting his axe-arm drop to his side. 'The girl for whom Shiva sent his bow down to earth? Is it really you?'

Ram moved me aside gently and addressed the sage. He spoke with respect, but as though to an equal. 'The bow broke because its job was done—and so is yours, sage. Go back to your austerities. That is your duty now.'

For a moment there was a strange look—of recognition—on Parashuram's face. Then it darkened with rage again. He shook the bow he was holding. 'So you think you can tell me what to do, you—you pipsqueak? Let's see you string *this* bow, then. It's the pair to Shiva's bow—this one belonged to Vishnu and was given to my father for safekeeping. If you can string this bow, I'll let you go. If not…' He shook his axe menacingly.

'Give me the arrow, too, sage,' Ram interrupted. Parashuram thrust both at him. Ram smiled at the bow—a smile of familiarity, it seemed. Then, in a motion so swift that I almost didn't see it occur, he strung it, set the arrow to it, and pointed it at the sage. He said, 'Vishnu's bow can't be drawn in vain. What shall I use the arrow for, Parashuram?'

For a moment, Parashuram looked stunned, as much at being called familiarly by his name as by the arrow pointing at him. Then he knelt in front of Ram and said, 'I recognize you now, Self of my Self, and your divine consort as well. Use the arrow to take from me all my powers, for you will need them.' And it seemed to me—but perhaps I imagined it, for no one else mentioned it later—that a brilliant light shot forth from his chest and entered my husband's body.

I AWOKE TO THE touch of an unfamiliar hand on my arm, a voice whispering apologies. I struggled up, startled, but it was only my new serving-woman. In a heavy Koshali accent that was hard to decipher, she informed me that we would be in Ayodhya soon. Would I like to clean up? The palanquin bearers had stopped to rest. I stepped out, stretched my stiff limbs, shook out the folds of my sari and washed my face in the scented water the woman poured for me. I combed my hair and, as best as I could in the lowering dark, refreshed the sindoor on my forehead. I hoped I'd make a good impression on my mothers-in-law.

'Look,' the Koshali woman said.

We were on a hillock. Ahead of us lay a huge city, stretching beyond the limits of my sight. Ayodhya. My new home. I didn't hope to love it the way I'd loved Mithila. The land of our childhood is a special place, where we are cherished without question or expectation. But I was determined to do my duty by it.

Duty! The word brought an ironic smile to my face. Already Ram's ideas were influencing me.

As I watched, dots of light flickered to life all over the city.

'The people are lighting lamps to welcome you,' my maid explained.

The lights twinkled in the balmy evening as though a cosmic hunter had caught the stars in his net and brought them down to earth to greet me. The sound of a flute rose from somewhere, deepening the magic of the scene. I'll always remember this,

I thought, and was surprised at the sudden, powerful connection I felt to this land. Perhaps duty was a kind of love, after all.

I'll be a good princess for you, I promised Ayodhya silently, and when time comes, a good queen. I'll guard you and bring prosperity to you the way only a woman can. If needed, I'll sacrifice my life for you, and my happiness.

A wind rose around me, from where I didn't know. It was unexpectedly cold and made me shiver. *Sacrifice, sacrifice*, whispered the trees, carrying my promise across the valley.

Seven

I STEPPED OUT OF MY PALANQUIN in front of the palace, a monolithic structure of hewn stone that loomed against the night. In spite of my tiredness, I was looking forward to meeting my new family. When Ram took me by the hand and led me forward, I accompanied him eagerly, a little nervous but ready to do what I could to make them like me. I had no idea that I was about to be sucked into the whirlpool of palace politics.

Dasharath's three queens were lined up in front of the massive front doors to welcome their new daughters-in-law. Kaushalya, Kaikeyi and Sumitra stood side-by-side—the picture of amity—so that I wondered if perhaps my mother had been misinformed about their rivalry.

There was no time to think further, for Ram was introducing me to his mother. I noticed that Kaushalya was quite a bit older than the other two women, with a wrinkled face and dark circles under her eyes. But her smile was genuine as she pressed sindoor on my forehead and took my hands in hers.

Behind each queen waited a line of servants bearing gifts for the daughters-in-law. One of the lines, I could see right away, was much longer than the others. The queen at the head of this line was lithe and statuesque, and dressed in a splendid red sari. She was greeting

Bharat, so I guessed this was Kaikeyi. I glanced curiously at her face, but most of it was covered by jewels and a glittery veil. I peered past her to see how Sumitra was welcoming Urmila, but I couldn't see much.

As the servants came forward and offered gifts to the new brides, I understood that unlike the dowry items that Dasharath had brought to the wedding, these had been paid for by the queens out of their own coffers. The expense and quality of the gifts indicated how rich each queen was, and how powerful. Clearly, in this regard, Kaikeyi was far ahead of the others.

As Kaushalya's servants presented me with my gifts, I could see that they were in good shape but not new. My mother-in-law admitted as much, her voice apologetic.

'My own mother gave these to me at my wedding. I've saved them all these years, dreaming of the moment when I'd pass them on to my daughter—for that's how I think of you. I do hope you like them.'

I was a little disappointed, for they weren't to my taste, which ran, like my mother Sunaina's, toward the simple and elegant. These jewellery sets were too heavy, their stones dulled from years spent within dark chests. The thick cloth-of-gold saris were definitely out of fashion. The silk bolsters and curtains looked a little faded, and the platters and glasses were large and cumbersome.

To the side, Kaikeyi was lavishing all kinds of expensive presents upon Mandavi—saris newly woven in colours I'd never seen, jewels in settings of exquisite craftsmanship, boxes made of ivory and mother-of-pearl, glittering vials filled with perfumes, combs and mirrors made of filigreed gold, even a large purple parrot, unlike any I'd seen before, that had been trained to bow and say good morning. Hearing my mother-in-law, she looked at us and laughed. It was a sound that managed to be lilting, charming and disdainful, all at the same time.

Kaushalya's shoulders sagged and she seemed to shrink. I could see how afraid she was that I'd think less of her because these gifts weren't fancy enough. And that it would affect our relationship.

Impulsively, I stepped forward and gave her a hug. Speaking louder than I needed to, I said, 'I love everything you've given me, Kaushalya-Ma. Anyone can buy new things, but presents passed down the generations hold in them the blessings of the elders. I'm sure your saris will bring me luck. I look forward to wearing one of them for the next royal event. Maybe you'd like to help me choose it?'

'I'd love that,' Kaushalya said, her face transformed into a wreath of smiles, tears of joy glimmering in her eyes. With a spring in her step, she led me towards my quarters, chattering about the prayer ceremony she was planning for Ram and me, and how the red silk with the parrot-green border would be just right for the occasion.

Over her head, Ram threw me a grateful smile filled with so much love that I felt I was walking on moonbeams. But I could sense Kaikeyi's hard stare on my back.

I'd already failed to follow my mother's warning: *be polite and respectful to all and don't take sides.*

THE NEXT FEW DAYS were a blur of court ceremonies, prayer services and countless guests. All the neighbouring kings paid us a visit, curious to see the princesses that the sons of Dasharath had brought home all of a sudden. The story of the great bow had spread across the land, so I was of special interest to them. From their respectful manner and lavish gifts, I understood that Koshal was even more important than I'd realized. This scared me a little, because as eldest, Ram would one day rule this mighty land, and it would be my job to support him in being the greatest king possible.

I allowed Kaushalya to dress me the way she wanted for all the events, and her delight in seeing me wear her gifts was so great that I didn't mind being out of fashion.

'But, Sister,' Urmila protested, 'the clothes our mother chose for you are so much more beautiful! And Kaushalya-Ma, nice as she is, doesn't even know how to drape a sari to bring out the best in you.

I'm sorry, but this green sari makes you look like—like a tightly wrapped bottle gourd!' She herself was most elegantly attired in a pale pink sari with a shimmer of gold running through it, sheer enough to show off all her curves. Lakshman could barely keep his eyes off her.

But fashion wasn't as important to me as to Urmila. There would be time enough to wear my mother's saris. And in any case Ram's eyes were on me all the time, too. The appreciation in them went beyond mere admiration of my looks.

RAM AND I WAITED until after the fanfare had died down to consummate our marriage. Neither of our educations had touched on the matter of sex, so we had to figure it out for ourselves. But for all our ignorance we did very well, and because it was the first time for us both, it was special in a way that I knew I'd remember all my life. Ram wasn't shy about telling me what pleased him, and he asked me what I liked until I overcame my shyness and answered. Bedtime became at once exciting and joyful, a secret gift I looked forward to all day while we went about our separate duties—his as heir-apparent, mine as new bride. Even his evenings were spent with his father, discussing how to make Koshal more prosperous, and they usually had their night meal in the king's chambers.

Yes, my father-in-law had separate quarters, which no one entered unless invited. I suspected he retreated there when the drama created by his wives became too much for him!

Dasharath liked things done right, and he liked variety. So the cook would send in gold platters filled with numerous items, different each day. Ram described the food for me: a hill of fragrant rice, topped with ghee, surrounded by appetizers and curries and meats of many kinds, antelope or goat or boar. And finally, bowls and dishes filled with desserts from different regions of Bharatvarsha—laddus and kheer and milk-sandesh. The king had a sweet tooth. Ram, who was a frugal eater, would only sample things and end his meal with a bowl of yogurt while Dasharath shook his head and declared he needed to eat more. How, otherwise, would he have the strength to rule a land as vast and prosperous as Koshal, surrounded by greedy kings just waiting to grab a piece of it?

I didn't mind Ram's busy days. At night—every night—he was all mine. And always would be because of his one-wife vow, the importance of which I appreciated much more now that I was in Ayodhya and saw the king's complicated marital relationships.

What I enjoyed as much as the physical pleasures of love was the time afterwards, when Ram and I lay, limbs intertwined, heads on the same pillow, and conversed into the night. Darkness added a special intimacy to the moment. I felt I could tell Ram things I would have hesitated to bring up otherwise. He, too, must have felt the same, for he told me about sorrows and fears which, judging from his calm daytime demeanour, I would never have guessed.

I told Ram about how I often wondered who my real parents were, and why they had abandoned me. How much I wanted to find them, and how guilty and ungrateful I felt about this because King Janak and Queen Sunaina had been so good to me. For his part, he confessed his doubts: would he be ready, when the time came, to take on the burden of ruling Koshal? Would he have the strength to be a good king?

'What do you mean by *a good king*?' I asked.

'One who rules not by force but by example,' he said. His voice deepened and his diction grew formal, so that I could tell how crucial this was to him. 'One who follows the laws perfectly, even when his heart might beg him to do otherwise. No blame should ever attach to a king, for then how can he pronounce judgement on another? Our scriptures say, such a king blesses his kingdom.'

I told him it was most commendable, if a bit too idealistic. What I didn't tell him was that, as he'd spoken, a dart of disquiet had shot through me.

ANOTHER NIGHT, RAM TOLD me his mother's tragic story.

The only child of the king of Koshal, Kaushalya had been married to Dasharath amidst great jubilation. Although not exceptionally beautiful, she was a sought-after prize, because half the kingdom of Koshal came with her as dowry. Furthermore, her father promised Dasharath that upon his death, his son-in-law would rule the entire country. Dasharath was a handsome and dynamic young man then, and Kaushalya, a simple and good-hearted girl, fell deeply in love with him. She delighted in the importance of being the royal consort and accompanying him on all state occasions. Dasharath was kind and respectful to her, and she hoped that with time he would come to love her as she loved him.

'It wasn't a perfect marriage, by any means,' Ram said wryly. My father had an eye for women, many of whom ended up in the palace as concubines. This was a trial to my mother, but she'd been taught that queens were expected to accept such behaviour. So she did. It helped that she was far above them in birth and influence. My father spent his nights with them, but he always came back to my mother. He was genuinely fond of her and liked conversing with her. Though she didn't understand the subtleties of statesmanship, she admired even his smallest achievements and he enjoyed that. He allowed her to fuss over him—laying out his clothes, fixing his favourite dishes—and this gave her great satisfaction.'

A few years into their marriage, Kaushalya gave birth to a daughter, Shanta. Dasharath gave the girl to his friend, King Romapad, because of a promise he'd made earlier. Kaushalya didn't like this, but she took comfort in the belief that she'd provide her beloved husband with a male heir soon. But unfortunately, no other children came. Dasharath began looking for another wife, finally choosing Kaikeyi, daughter of Ashwapati, and forming an alliance with the powerful kingdom of Kekaya. That, too, Kaushalya accepted. Royal marriages were often strategic, and the kingdom did need a prince.

'But what wounded her to the heart,' Ram said, 'was that my father fell completely in love with Kaikeyi: her beauty, her intellect, her courage. All his nights—and many hours of his days—were now spent with his new wife. To make matters worse, Kaikeyi had been trained in the art of war. The next time there was a battle, she insisted on driving Dasharath's chariot. She performed superbly, and Dasharath won the battle—which further strengthened her hold over him. She drove his chariot in other wars too, and twice saved his life. Totally captivated and deeply indebted to Kaikeyi, Dasharath gave her the best chambers in the palace and sought her counsel in all matters. He spent all his time—except for a few minimal hours in court—with her.

'Demoted and forgotten, my mother felt her life was over. Even the servants, aware of her powerlessness, ignored her.'

'But Kaikeyi couldn't give him the son he wanted, could she?' I asked.

'No. Father made a third alliance, bringing home Sumitra, princess of Kashi. But Kaikeyi somehow managed to retain her position as his favourite queen.'

The problem was clearly with the king, but it was the queens who had to pay the price for it. Bitter words filled my mouth, but I prudently held them. What was the point of venting my outrage on Ram?

Finally, the desperate Dasharath managed to get the famous Rishya-shringa muni to perform a putra-kameshti yagna for him. Out of the sacrificial fire came a luminous being, carrying a vessel of kheer. Drinking this, he said, would make the queen pregnant.

'As royal consort, my mother sat beside my father in the yagna and received the kheer. But her delight was short-lived. My father insisted that she share it with Kaikeyi. My mother couldn't disobey the royal command, but she diluted it by giving some of the kheer to Sumitra. Thus, the four of us were born.

'You must have been a great solace to your mother,' I said, pleased that we were now entering a happier part of the story.

'Unfortunately, that wasn't the case.' Even in the dark I could hear the sorrow vibrating through my husband's voice. 'She thought my birth—and especially the fact that I was the eldest—would bring her what she'd always longed for, the love of her husband. But it didn't. Father gave her many rich gifts—and then went back to Kaikeyi, whose influence over him grew even stronger when she gave birth to Bharat.'

Ram, however, remained Dasharath's favourite. This was a two-edged sword for Kaushalya. She loved that the king cherished her son more than the other boys. Dasharath had little to say to Kaikeyi and Sumitra's sons when their mothers dressed them in their best and brought them over to offer pranams. But he'd sit for hours listening to the baby Ram babbling nonsense. This also meant, however, that Dasharath wanted him nearby all the time. Kaushalya got Ram to herself only to bathe and feed and sing lullabies. Her mother-heart was always hungry, but she had one solace: he slept in her bed. She'd force herself to stay awake at night just to watch the marvel of him breathe.

But things got worse.

'When I was a little older, my father decreed that I should live in his quarters. He took excellent care of me. Sometimes, waking at night, I'd find him personally covering me with the quilt I'd kicked off, or soothing a nightmare. Awed by this man, larger than life, who was not only my father but my King as well, I couldn't tell him how much I missed my mother.'

Soon Dasharath began to take Ram to court with him. I could picture Ram, a quiet and serious boy, listening to debates about law and justice, strategic meetings about wars, and long discussions of what was best for the kingdom. All of it sank deep, transforming him from a child into a prince.

'I was particularly struck by the complaints against the man-eating rakshasa tribes that were encroaching upon our kingdom from the forest-borders, terrorizing our people,' Ram said. 'I remember announcing to my father that I'd drive them away permanently. Failing that, I'd kill them. I remember how proud that made him.'

'You fulfilled your promise, didn't you, when you rid Vishwamitra of the rakshasas that were ruining the prayer ceremonies in his ashram?'

'Yes. I tried to run them off first, but Tarhaka and her people—foolishly brave—refused to retreat. They attacked Lakshman and me, and I was forced to cut them down,' Ram said. 'It gave me no pleasure though.'

For a while, we both silently contemplated what he'd said. I was surprised—pleasantly so—that Ram didn't revel in his victory over the rakshasas. Then he went on with his story.

'I was lost even further to my mother when I was sent to Sage Vasishta's ashram for my education. On my brief visits home, there were many demands on my time: attending events in the raj sabha so that the courtiers would get used to me sitting beside my father, offering my opinions on matters of state; riding in processions across Ayodhya, tossing coins at cheering citizens; and of course, spending time with my Father-King, who insisted that I eat and sleep in his royal quarters. I crept away to my mother whenever I could so she could cook me a favourite dish or two. But all too soon it would be time for me to go back to the ashram. My mother never complained, but I felt the heavy weight of her sadness.'

He sighed. 'Some people are born unlucky, possessing so much externally, yet destitute within. My mother is one of them. Thank you for listening. I've never shared this with anyone, not even Lakshman.'

I appreciated his trust, but I wasn't willing to let go of the story. 'Now that you're a man, can't you do something for your mother?'

'When I vowed to marry only one woman, I did it as much for her as for you. To tell her that I felt her pain and would never make another woman suffer as she did. I hope she understood. What else can I do without going against my father?' He shook his head. 'But enough of old sorrows. It's late. We must rest now.'

He pressed his face into the hollow of my shoulder and fell asleep in the sudden way he had. He never wasted time, Ram, especially on things he believed he couldn't change. But I lay awake for a long time, holding him, listening to him breathe. I didn't believe in giving in to fate, not without a good fight. Kaushalya had done everything possible, in her sweet and simple way, to make me feel at home in Ayodhya. In return, I was determined to do something to make her life better.

Eight

My plan was simple, once I convinced Ram to support me. He told Dasharath that, newly married as I was, I wanted my husband to have his evening meal with me in our chambers. I was homesick and lonely and needed his company. My father-in-law may not have been pleased, but how could he say no to such a request, especially when presented by his favourite son?

'Sita would love for you to join us, Father,' Ram added. 'She admires you greatly and longs to hear your words of wisdom. And she wants to cook for you with her own hands.'

At first Dasharath grumbled, pointing out that he had a weak stomach and that only his chief cook knew what agreed with him. But when I offered to let his cook instruct me, he agreed grudgingly. To his surprise, he enjoyed the evenings more than he'd expected to. I stayed in the background, allowing Ram to devote his full attention to him. I cooked the dishes that Dasharath wanted, introducing only one or two Mithilan delicacies. He tried them gingerly and found that he liked them. Over several nights, he grew comfortable enough with me to loosen his waistband after his meal and belch with loud satisfaction. He began to stay on after dinner, telling me stories of his battle exploits. The stories were repetitive and often bloody, but I did my best to look interested and asked questions. Apparently they were the right questions, for Dasharath told Ram approvingly that I had a warrior's brain.

The groundwork was laid. It was time to move forward.

For the occasion of Gauri Vrata, a festival particularly auspicious for couples, I asked my father-in-law if Mother Kaushalya could join us. He replied with a cautious yes. Next, Ram and I schooled Kaushalya. Dress with simple elegance. Be pleasant and cheerful and stay in the background. No intense conversations. No accusations or weeping. Cook a dish—just one—which you know he likes, but say nothing about it. Above all, enjoy the moment and have no expectations.

Kaushalya understood that it was her one opportunity. She did as we instructed. The evening turned out so well that at the end of it, Dasharath suggested that we do this again.

And so it was that Kaushalya came to dine with us each week, getting more of a chance to spend time with her beloved husband and son than she'd ever had. I was happy to let her instruct my maids or cook some of the dishes. Ram made sure the conversation remained pleasant. At dinner, I dismissed the servants and waited on them myself, so that Dasharath could relax without fear that his words or actions would be carried to the other queens. Slowly he began to talk more to Kaushalya and offer her compliments, mostly on her cooking, but sometimes on her appearance as well.

Happiness transformed Kaushalya. She seemed to grow younger and blushed prettily when the king's eyes rested on her. And although usually at the end of the evening Dasharath went to Kaikeyi's chambers, he now sometimes offered to stay with Kaushalya for the night.

One evening, after his parents had left together, chatting amicably, Ram held me close and kissed me. 'You're a miracle worker,' he said. 'I'd never have believed this could happen.'

'I couldn't have done it without your help,' I said, kissing him back. 'We're partners.'

'Partners for life—I'm certainly thankful for that. And of your kindness towards my mother. You didn't have to do this!'

'Well, I do owe her something. After all, isn't she responsible for the fact that I have a wonderful—and most attractive—husband?' And holding him by the hand, I laughingly pulled Ram to our bedroom and to another exciting night of discoveries.

This incident taught me that the more love we distribute, the more it grows, coming back to us from unexpected sources. And its corollary: when we demand love, believing it to be our right, it shrivels, leaving only resentment behind.

I TRIED TO DOWNPLAY our evening meals with Dasharath, but in this palace, rumours travelled like spores borne by summer winds, taking root everywhere. It didn't help that Kaushalya went around dressed in her best saris, looking radiant. Following our instructions, she didn't say anything to people who asked why she was so happy, but her smiling silence only gave rise to more speculation. It didn't help, either, that everyone seemed to know where the king slept each night.

Urmila, always good at keeping up with gossip, came over to my chambers, full of excitement. 'People are saying it's a miracle. Dasharath and Kaushalya haven't been on such good terms since they were newly married. They're whispering that you must have put some kind of magical Mithilan herb in the king's food, because everyone knows how good you are with such things!'

I grimaced. I'd been giving some simple herbal remedies to my maids. In their enthusiastic gratitude, they must have spread the word.

'In fact,' Urmila continued, 'Mother Sumitra's been badgering me to get her some of this magical substance!'

We were sitting on the balcony attached to my chambers. It was a large and spacious balcony that I was thankful for, as Dasharath's palace, built more for fortification than elegance, possessed few balconies. Knowing of my love for the outdoors, Ram had spoken to the appropriate officials and moved us to these chambers from the overly grand ones originally assigned to us. His efforts made me appreciate the balcony further. I filled it with plants and trees that I'd loved in Mithila as well as some of Ram's favourites—for each day I was learning more of what he liked—including a blue lotus that I grew in a stone trough. Everything had blossomed beyond my expectations. Sometimes I sat here alone, listening to the leaves rustle, and imagined I was in a forest. At the end of the day, Ram would join me, and together we'd watch the stars and breathe in the gentle fragrance of the night-blooming harshringar flower. He often told me that this was the most peaceful place in the entire palace.

'Sorry, all I have are these pakoras,' I said, handing Urmila a platter. 'They do have jeera and ajwain in them, along with ginger and fresh fennel from my terrace garden, so they might help Mother Sumitra's digestion. And if our stomachs are happy and healthy, the rest of us immediately feels a lot better.'

'Well, then, I could do with some of these pakoras myself,' Urmila said, and a shadow fell on her usually cheerful face. 'You're so lucky. Your mother-in-law lets you do whatever you want—plus you have your own quarters.'

She stopped because she wasn't a complainer, and didn't have a single jealous bone in her body, but I felt guilty. I did have my own chambers, where I was mistress, and my own servants. Here, Urmila and my cousins could visit me whenever they wanted. We'd order my cook to make our favourite childhood dishes. We'd confide or complain without fear of eavesdroppers, make silly girlish jokes, or even weep because we missed our parents. And at night, when Ram and I were in bed, I could let myself dive into the current of our passion without worrying about anyone hearing our love cries. Perhaps that was one reason our relationship was doing so well.

Bharat, too, had his own quarters. Kaikeyi, who—Urmila said—liked her privacy, had made sure of that. Bharat's chambers were spacious, and he asked Shatrughna to join him. Shatrughna agreed with such alacrity that Sumitra didn't have a chance to stop him. That worked out very well for Mandavi and Shrutakirti, who helped each other manage their little household without outside interference. Being together kept them from feeling lonely too. But it had made Sumitra more possessive of Lakshman and more determined to control Urmila.

'I don't mind living with Mother Sumitra,' Urmila said. 'But she wants to be with Lakshman all the time! She's waiting at the door when he gets back from helping Ram with governing problems. She's the one asking if he's tired and offering him a cool drink. She's the one serving him food, and asking if he wants second helpings. She sits with us after dinner, asking Lakshman about his day until we go to bed. It annoys him, too, I think. But I'm not sure. He's too filial to be rude to her, and I can't tell what he's thinking.

'By bedtime he's so tired that he's yawning non-stop. How can anyone be romantic then, or even have a conversation that means anything? I usually just rub his back and in a couple of minutes he falls asleep. Why, Didi, I don't know Lakshman any better now than I did on the day of my wedding. I certainly didn't expect marriage to be like this!'

Urmila was on the verge of tears. I thought long and hard, then said, 'You'll have to talk to Mother Sumitra.'

'She'll never listen to me!'

'What if you tell her that Ram and I are considering having Lakshman and you move into our quarters—like Bharat did with Shatrughna. But you're willing to stay on with her because you're fond of her—if some changes are made.'

Urmila made a face, but I was pleased to see that she was listening carefully.

I continued. 'If Lakshman and you can have three nights a week on your own, you'll stay.' Urmila's eyes shone with mischief. 'Maybe I'll add that otherwise she'll never get any grandchildren!'

Before I could answer, my maid entered apologetically.

'Sorry to disturb, princess, but I was told to hand this to you at once.' She extended a platter with a scroll on it. Surprised, I picked it up. The expensive cream-coloured parchment was heavy and soft to the touch and sealed with a red seal I didn't recognize, a tiger in mid-spring. I broke the seal and unrolled the parchment. It was an invitation from Kaikeyi to visit her in her chambers this afternoon.

It was the first time she'd contacted me, although I'd been in Ayodhya for months now.

Urmila, reading over my shoulder, sucked in her breath apprehensively. 'I bet she isn't happy about all the time our father-in-law is spending in your quarters—and with Mother Kaushalya instead of with her. I think she's heard the rumours, too, and wants to figure out what you've been up to. Careful, Didi, I've heard some scary stories about Queen Kaikeyi.'

I made a secret gesture to her to say no more. Although my maid seemed trustworthy, I sensed that in Ayodhya it was best to be cautious in front of the servants.

'The queen's messenger is waiting for your answer,' the maid said.

I wrote back that I'd be honoured to visit Kaikeyi. It wasn't as though I had a choice. Disobeying her summons would be a clear insult, and I didn't want to antagonize Kaikeyi any more than I already had on my first night. My handwriting wasn't as neat as usual—I think my hand shook a little, partly with excitement but mostly with nervousness. I wished I could have asked Ram for advice—after all, he'd known her all his life, and they seemed to get along well. But he'd been sent to oversee the repair of a fortress. I wondered if that was the reason Kaikeyi had chosen to meet me today, when I was unprepared and alone and easy to intimidate.

Well, I thought, taking a deep breath and sitting up tall, I might be alone and unprepared, but she wasn't going to intimidate me, at least not easily.

Nine

KAIKEYI'S CHAMBERS WERE FAR MORE elegant and opulent than those of the other queens, and filled with unique and expensive art objects fashioned in a manner very unlike the craftsmanship of Ayodhya, which tended to be solid and heavy. I was shown into a large room where, to my surprise, I found her practising sword-fighting with another woman—her trainer, I guessed. Both women had their saris tied tightly and tucked between their legs in a way that allowed fluid movement. Sweat beaded Kaikeyi's face like pearl drops. Slim and strong and nimble, she moved like a much younger woman. Something about her stance reminded me of the symbol on her seal, which she'd clearly chosen with care: the leaping tiger. Here was a woman who knew her power and allure and was willing to make the most of them. I could see why Dasharath was so attracted to her.

Kaikeyi wiped her face in a leisurely manner and nodded to her trainer to leave. It struck me that she'd planned the entire scene carefully. This is how she'd wanted me to see her: thrusting and parrying, dangerous and magnetic at once, her teeth bared in fierce jubilation. An opponent to beware of.

'So, princess,' she said, even before I could offer her my greetings, 'I was waiting for you to invite me to your chambers so I could come and bless you with a wedding gift. But you never did.'

I was taken aback by this sudden attack. Don't get flustered, I told myself. That's what she wants. I took my time and offered a proper obeisance to her, and then I said, 'Forgive me. I am not aware of the Ayodhyan customs. In Mithila it would be considered presumptuous of me to invite an elder before she has given me a sign. But please know that you are welcome in my humble rooms any time.'

I could see that Kaikeyi hadn't expected such an answer—polite yet confident—from me. There was a glint of respect in her eyes, but also a hardening of the jaw. Another test was coming.

'I hear you're a renowned herbalist—and perhaps a magician, too, one whose expertise is love-potions. Certainly it seems that you've made our king fall in love—finally—with his oldest wife,' Kaikeyi said, placing a slight emphasis on *oldest*.

I could feel anger rising in me, for Kaushalya's sake more than my own, but I knew that was what the queen was counting on: that I'd get upset and flustered and say something stupid. Instead I replied, in my most innocent voice, 'My skills are nothing compared to yours, Kaikeyi-Ma. Why, you've kept my father-in-law enchanted for many decades now.' On the surface, the words were a compliment, but they could be interpreted otherwise too.

Kaikeyi stared at me, eyes narrowed. Then she waved her hand, dismissing the topic. 'Since you're so skilled in healing, I want you to tell me what I should do with my maid, who has been sick for four days now with burning pains in the stomach and a bloody flux.'

Another test! I tried to deflect it with politeness. 'Please don't embarrass me, Kaikeyi-Ma. You are a renowned healer. Even in Mithila people speak with awe about how you saved King Dasharath's life when he was sorely wounded in war. Whatever solution I come up with, surely you'll have tried it already.'

When she insisted, I said, 'Flux may occur due to imbalances of different kinds, for which the remedies would be different. Perhaps I could see the girl?'

Kaikeyi hesitated for the tiniest moment, but that was enough. I knew there wasn't really a sick girl.

'She's too sick to stand,' Kaikeyi said. 'Tell me, and I'll try your remedy on her.'

'Since this is the height of summer, I'd advise something to cool her system,' I said. 'Ghee, though usually beneficial, is too heavy at this time. Perhaps a glass of light buttermilk, with a little cumin and fresh crushed mint. Sweet honey, mixed with the prabal pishti herb, might help, too. But mostly I would make sure she isn't stressed, with no one angry with her for being ill.'

Kaileyi threw me a sharp glance to ascertain if this last bit was a dig at her, but I went on innocently. 'Stress can inflame the ulcer further, as you know, and cause more bleeding. I'll be happy to send you some prabal pishti from my balcony-garden—'

Kaikeyi cut me off. 'Not necessary.'

I'd won again. I hid a smile and waited for whatever she had planned next.

'Enough of useless talk!' Kaikeyi said. 'I hear you've been trained in weaponry. I'd like to invite you to a duel with swords, to see how well a Mithilan princess fights.'

I stared at her in dismay. How did she know so much about me? And how was I going to get out of this one?

Finally I said, 'Your sources of information are truly thorough, great queen. So you must also know that I fight solely in self-defence. The only weapon I use is my own body, and I only use it when I'm in danger. Therefore, I beg you to excuse me.'

But Kaikeyi had already called for the swords.

Two swords, one with a golden hilt and one with a silver one, were brought to us by two women carrying a huge, heavy brass tray. Even in my nervousness, I noticed how unusually plain-faced they were—just like the woman who'd let me into Kaikeyi's quarters.

I filed that observation away and focussed on the swords. They looked sharp and dangerous and very long. Kaikeyi picked up the gold-hilted sword, hefted it, and looked impatiently at me. 'Take up your weapon! Or shall I let it be known throughout the kingdom that Mithilan women are too cowardly to accept a challenge?'

I sighed. She'd do it, too, I was sure. I had to uphold the honour of my homeland.

I tucked up my pleats between my legs and tied the sari end tightly around my waist, just as Kaikeyi had. 'I'm doing this since you insist,' I said. 'But I'll fight in my own way. If you draw blood, you win. And if I disarm you, I win.'

'Very well,' Kaikeyi said, but she was displeased. Even if she won, there wouldn't be much to boast of if her opponent was unarmed.

We circled each other, trying to judge each other's skill and style. Kaikeyi was older, and she'd already practised today. Thus she might tire easier. But she was more experienced, and because of the sword, her reach was much longer than mine. I guessed she'd try to rush me early on. She wouldn't wound me seriously, I was almost certain of that. But she wasn't above giving me a nasty nick that might leave a scar. I'd annoyed her and won our verbal battles, and she was ready to right that score.

Oh Goddess, I thought. *Why do you send me this challenge, just when things are going smoothly and I'm beginning to think of Ayodhya as home*?

The answer came to me in a flash so bright that it made me blink. *Because this is part of the dark fate that is unfurling, unknown to you. It will prepare you a little for the many battles you must fight.*

Fight? Me? What kinds of battles?

Kaikeyi must have seen that I was distracted. She thrust suddenly at my shoulder with her blade, and I had to jump back to avoid its sharp point. We circled each other some more, Kaikeyi switching the sword from her right hand to her left. She was ambidextrous. This would be an additional challenge. I moved light and fast, feinting this way and then that, trying to guess what she'd do. What her weakness might be. Her advantage was already clear: she wanted this fight, while I'd been pushed into it reluctantly.

Kaikeyi moved like quicksilver, her eyes focussed unblinkingly on mine, then pushed forward. I understood her strategy: she wanted to force me against a wall or into a corner. And here was her possible weakness: she'd try to do this fast—she knew I had more stamina than she did. Perhaps in her hurry, she'd make a mistake.

As I'd guessed, Kaikeyi pressed her advantage, slashing the air. Her sword-thrusts were different each time, but always vicious. Sometimes the blade flew straight at me, and sometimes it carved the air in a semi-circle or a figure eight. A couple of times, I tried to get behind her so that I could get her in a choke-hold. But each time she guessed my manoeuvre and blocked me with her sword. And always, she moved forward, pushing me inevitably toward the wall, moving her sword hand rapidly to keep me from slipping out from under her guard. One part of me said, *Let her have her victory. What did it matter?* I could always explain to Ram later that I'd allowed her to win. He'd understand and possibly applaud it as the more politic decision, for it would make Kaikeyi happy and she would leave me—and by extension, Ram and his mother—in peace.

Kaikeyi thrust at me again, teeth parted in a predatory grin. She'd surmised that I was intimidated by her expertise and that it would be a quick, easy win.

No! I thought. I won't give up. For the sake of my mother, who had pushed against tradition to make sure I learned to defend myself. For the sake of Kaushalya, who would have to bear Kaikeyi's endless taunts about her weak and cowardly daughter-in-law. And for the sake of Mithila, my motherland, to prove that its women, though normally peace-loving, were dangerous when provoked.

The wall was almost touching my shoulder-blades now. My only chance to turn things around lay in trying something risky and unexpected. Just as Kaikeyi pulled back her sword so she could thrust again, skewering me against the wall this time, I leaped high in the air with a yell and kicked, aiming for her sword hand. Kaikeyi's mouth fell open in shock as her blade went flying. She doubled up, clutching her wrist. I felt bad about having hurt her, but I couldn't waste time. I grabbed her from behind in a strangle-hold and kept my arm tight around her neck until she raised her hands to signify that she'd given up.

I'd expected Kaikeyi to be furious, perhaps to curse me out or order me to leave. But the first thing she did once she recovered her breath was burst out in a rueful, wheezing laugh. 'Bested by a slip of a girl!' she said, shaking her head. 'I guess I deserve it, for underestimating you. Oh, I'll never live it down!'

'No one needs to know,' I said.

She looked at me, eyebrows raised in surprise.

'I'm certainly not planning to tell anyone,' I said, 'except Ram, because I tell him everything. But I'll swear him to secrecy. I hope I haven't hurt your hand too much. I can bring you a poultice made from turmeric and guggul—'

This time she looked at me as though she were re-evaluating me. Was there a tinge of admiration in her glance?

'You're not like what I was told,' she said. Before I could ask who her informant had been, she clapped her hands and several attendants—all of them plain-faced, if not downright ugly—rushed up with bowls of hot and cold water scented with jasmine petals, thick, soft cloths to wipe our faces, and sandalwood to rub onto our bodies.

When we had cleansed ourselves, another maid brought a gold platter. From it Kaikeyi lifted up a beautiful pearl and gold necklace of unusual workmanship.

'From Kekaya, my father's kingdom,' she said, with a sigh that was proud but unexpectedly melancholy. 'How I miss it, though it's been decades since I left.'

'Do you never visit?' I ventured to ask.

'No. King Dasharath refuses to let me go. I guess it's the price I pay to keep him thinking that I'm indispensable. Fortunately, he doesn't mind if I send Bharat, so I do that often. Bharat's uncles and grandfather are very fond of him, and they always invite Shatrughna to go along too. The boys have a great time, and through them we're able to exchange news and gifts. Such is the life of a queen, filled with compromise. You'll know it soon enough.' She proceeded to clasp the necklace around my neck, where it hung heavy and regal, and complimented me on how good it looked on me.

The rest of my visit we ate—the attendants brought us dish upon dish of Kekayan delicacies, which I had to admit were very good—and chatted. We spoke of my upbringing in Mithila and hers in Kekaya, and about how life in Ayodhya was different. She told me about the women in the palace, whom to avoid because they were fools, and whom to watch out for because they were dangerous. Against my expectations, I found I was enjoying myself. Kaikeyi had a sharp sense of humour, which she often turned on herself, sharing funny stories about her follies when she was a new bride. She delighted in divulging embarrassing facts about people, and such was her wit that she made me feel that she and I were allied, in our superior intelligence and charisma, against them all. I could well understand why Dasharath was still captivated by her. Once in a while, though, she'd throw me a sudden, pointed question—about my relationship with Kaushalya, or what exactly we talked about when Dasharath came for dinner, or what Ram thought he might do differently when he became king, and whether he ever mentioned Bharat in his plans. I had to remain vigilant so that I could provide an answer without telling her things that I might later regret.

At the end of my visit, Kaikeyi walked with me to the doorway of her chambers, flashed me a singularly sweet smile, and gave me a hug. I smiled back. Even though I guessed she's set out to deliberately charm me, I found that I liked her.

'Finally, there's another woman in the royal family with brains and guts—and good looks, too,' she said as we parted. 'I look forward to many conversations with you. Tell Ram he's made a great choice. You'll be the perfect helpmate for him—and a perfect queen.'

I basked in the glory of that statement all the way back to my chambers.

When Ram returned to Ayodhya, I told him about the visit. He was immediately wary, and when I described the sparring, he grew downright angry. He examined my foot to make sure I hadn't hurt it, running his long, sensitive fingers over my arch, his lips tight with displeasure. I let him fuss over me for a while because I loved that, but finally I reassured him that I was fine.

'I'm glad it ended well,' he said. 'I don't know what Kaikeyi-Ma was thinking, to do something dangerous like that! She's a difficult person, hard to understand. She's always been nice to me, though she's caused my mother plenty of grief. She's very smart, and knows it. Maybe that's part of the reason she doesn't get along with the other queens. She prefers to spend her time learning about what goes on in court. Father built a special covered balcony for her so she can attend sabha sessions without being seen. And often, later, she gives him good advice about what needs to be done, and who to watch out for.

'In any case, it's best if you stay away from her.'

I agreed. I'd enjoyed my visit with Kaikeyi, but Ram was right. Kaikeyi oozed trouble from every pore of her beautiful, carefully maintained body—and I didn't believe in going looking for trouble. If the inner voice—the voice of the goddess?—that I'd heard just before our duel was to be trusted, trouble was going to find me soon enough.

That night, when we were almost asleep, I remembered something else and tapped Ram's shoulder until he opened his eyes. 'All of Kaikeyi's maids are so ugly. Why do you think that is? I know she can afford to hire prettier girls. Is it because she always wants to be the most beautiful one in the room?'

Ram laughed, but then he said, 'No. Kaikeyi's too confident about her looks and her hold over my father to care about such things. I think it's because of Manthara, her nursemaid, who came to Ayodhya with her when she got married. Did you know that Kaikeyi's mother died giving birth to her? Manthara was the one who brought her up. The two of them are very close, and where Kaikeyi is concerned, Manthara's as fierce as a lioness with a newborn cub. Manthara's a hunchback, so Kaikeyi makes sure not to hire anyone whose looks might make Manthara feel worse.'

'I don't remember seeing a hunchback,' I said.

'You wouldn't have seen her,' Ram said. 'She's too self-conscious to appear before newcomers. But rest assured that she saw you—probably from a peephole somewhere—and gave Kaikeyi a full report later of what she thought. And what she said will affect how Kaikeyi behaves towards you the next time you see her.'

I shivered, uneasy at the thought of being examined secretively. After a while I said, 'Manthara must really like you then, because Kaikeyi's always nice to you.'

But Ram had fallen asleep and didn't answer me.

KAUSHALYA AND I WERE on our way to the royal temple, an ornate marble affair officiated over noisily by dozens of priests. Ram's birthday was approaching, and she wanted to arrange a big prayer ceremony for him. We made our way through the courtyard, where rows of saplings were arranged in blocks according to colour and tied to stakes so they stood severely at attention. I sent forth some healing energy to them and felt their gratitude.

The palace gardens could do with some naturalness and spontaneity—and with a little strategizing, I could get it done. The next time he visited us for dinner, I'd ask Dasharath if I might add a few of my favourite plants to the landscaping. I felt confident that he'd agree. He wasn't particularly interested in gardens. What little free time he had, he preferred to spend indoors, in the sumptuous palace halls cooled by moistened rush-curtains and intricate air-tunnels.

Additionally, I was sure he'd say yes because, in the last few months, I'd learned the right way to approach him so that he didn't feel his authority was being threatened. As a result, he'd grown quite fond of me and often indulged me like a daughter. At the dinners in my chambers, he joked with me the way he didn't with anyone else, not even Ram. He brought me little gifts—sweetmeats, a songbird, a pair of earrings. Sometimes, after we'd eaten, he'd take off his heavy crown and ask me to massage his head. He was going bald, like my father, and as I worked warm almond oil into his scalp, I'd feel a surge of tenderness.

Walking with Kaushalya, I spent a few happy moments daydreaming. I'd have creepers growing over the walls, white madhavi lata or showers of pink coral vine to soften the forbidding lines of hewn stone. A spring could wind in-between the trees, splashing over stones. A jasmine bower with seats in a corner would provide privacy. And in little nooks here and there, I'd plant sweet-smelling Mithilan herbs, of which I was running out.

I was pulled out of my happy imaginings by a movement to my left, on the upper level of the palace. Behind the friezed passage that ran along the length of the structure, a shape scurried along, clearly following us. It was the size of a child, but it moved with a lurching, uneven gait. Was it an animal? Perhaps one of the queens had a pet ape? Then I knew.

I tugged surreptitiously at Kaushalya's arm.

'Ah, you've noticed Manthara the hunchback,' Kaushalya said, with a grimace of distaste. 'Our resident spy. She came with Kaikeyi from her father's house as part of her bride-gift. I don't understand what Kaikeyi's father was thinking! Manthara isn't of much use—why, she can't even stand up straight. She's very devoted to Kaikeyi, of course. But I don't think she's a good influence on her. She tends to encourage Kaikeyi's tantrums.'

Ah. Now I understood why Dasharath was so insistent that we not bring our own servants from our parents' home.

'Between you and me,' Kaushalya continued, her voice dipping low, 'King Dasharath would love to get rid of Manthara. But the last time he suggested that she be sent back to her village—with many gifts, of course—to enjoy her old age at leisure, Kaikeyi locked herself up in her anger chamber. Did you know she has an anger chamber in her quarters? I don't understand how Dasharath allows it. He certainly wouldn't have let me have one—not that I've ever wanted something so barbaric and unwomanly. Anyway, Kaikeyi threw off all her ornaments and silks and refused to eat or drink anything until he apologized and promised that Manthara could stay in Ayodhya as long as she wanted.' There was outrage in Kaushalya's voice—that a mere wife should be able to do this. But underneath that I heard a trace of longing.

So my mighty father-in-law, respected and feared by all the kingdoms that surrounded Ayodhya, had bent to Kaikeyi's will! Was it just her charm, or was there another reason she had so much power over him? I was fascinated, too, by the concept of an anger chamber. I imagined the beautiful queen pacing this room like a tigress, feeding her own fury, waiting to pounce on the hapless Dasharath, who she knew wouldn't be able to stay away from her.

In Mithila, on the rare occasions when my mother was angry with my father—mostly because people took advantage of his goodness—she told him so. Sometimes she raised her voice. Once or twice, she wept. But usually they went to their rooms and worked out their problems privately and without undue drama, and afterwards they seemed closer than ever. Growing up, I'd believed these peaceful interchanges were the norm. Now I knew how lucky both my parents were, and how special their relationship.

Love was full of contradictions. Sometimes the person you loved weakened you and sometimes he or she made you a stronger person. But under exactly what conditions did these very different changes occur?

And would Ram's love turn out to be more like my father's, or like Dasharath's? If we disagreed deeply about something, what reactions would it prompt in him?

I pushed the thought away firmly. I hoped never to have a reason to find out.

'Since that anger-chamber incident,' Kaushalya was saying, 'Manthara acts like her feet don't touch the ground! She doesn't even pretend to work. All she does is creep around the palace, watching and listening and digging up secrets and reporting back to her mistress. Gives me the shivers. Let's hope she gets tired of following you around soon.'

I hoped so too. Even though I didn't have any secrets I needed to protect, Manthara made me uncomfortable in a way I couldn't explain. I checked cautiously, not wanting to give away the fact that I'd noticed her. There she was, scurrying above us—though it must have been difficult and painful for her to keep up—until we passed beyond that wing of the palace.

For a long time afterwards, I heard inside my head the scraping, thumping sounds her body had made against the wall and felt her invisible eyes on me, assessing and cold. It sickened me. Then I felt guilty for feeling uncharitable towards someone to whom fate had been so unkind, so I said nothing of this incident to Ram.

Ten

EARLY IN THE MORNING, KAUSHALYA showed up in my rooms, flushed with nervous excitement. Dasharath had sent word. He would take his night meal in her chambers. Sage Vasishta, and Sumantra, the minister, would be accompanying him. He'd asked Kaushalya to make sure Ram and I were present.

'He told me that the other princes should be present,' Kaushalya was saying, 'so I'll invite Lakshman. He's a sweet boy, don't you agree, and so devoted to Ram. And your sister, of course. I think Dasharath forgot that Bharat's away visiting his uncle in Kekaya, and Shatrughna's gone with him, like he always does. They've taken their wives, too, so I don't have to worry about them. He didn't mention the other queens. I'll take that to mean that they haven't been invited.'

She threw me a brief, victorious glance, then went back to thinking aloud.

'His guru and his chief advisor—now why would Dasharath invite them to a family dinner? Unless—unless … No! It would be bad luck to speak it! I'm just going to wait for the king to announce what's on his mind.'

But both she and I knew what was on *her* mind. Ten years had passed since Ram's marriage—ten years during which Ram had ably assisted his father in ruling the kingdom. Did Dasharath now feel

Ram was ready to take over? Was he planning to step down and have my husband crowned? I saw a wild joy brighten Kaushalya's face. Apart from her adoration of Ram and her belief that he'd be the perfect ruler, she knew that as the mother of the king, she would—finally and definitively—be first among the queens.

As for me, I felt joy and excitement but also trepidation. As queen, I'd have many new responsibilities. For the last ten years, I'd been living in a comfortable limbo between girlhood and adulthood, enjoying an extended honeymoon, happy with fixing little problems here and there. Now I'd have to maintain harmony in the entire palace. I'd have to make sure everyone discharged their duties appropriately. If they didn't, I'd have to chide or even punish them. If anything went wrong, all eyes would be upon me. Was I ready for such a major change?

But it was too soon to worry. Though old, Dasharath was in excellent health. The transfer of kingship would take months, perhaps even years.

'What should I instruct Cook to make?' Kaushalya asked. 'My Ram is easy, and so are you, but Lakshman loves meat, venison in particular. The king's been having digestive problems recently, so he needs something light. Perhaps some mung dal with soft rice and a little ghee? Vasishta is vegetarian. He might like some jackfruit curry—it's in season now. Cook will have to send servants to the marketplace right away. I have no idea what Sumantra likes to eat. He's never come to dinner before this.' She wrung her hands. 'Oh dear, it's already late in the day. All the best things will be gone.'

'Don't worry, Mother,' I soothed her. 'I'm sure everything will turn out beautifully. I'll make the dessert, if you like.'

'Yes, yes, make some payesh,' Kaushalya said. 'Dasharath likes your payesh. The servant can stop at the palace goshala and get fresh milk. He can pick up a sack of the best gopalbhog rice from the palace granary. I'll ask Cook to bring you a big tile of jaggery. But make it early. I want you to have enough time to dress up as befits—' But here she clapped her hand over her mouth and hurried off to tell the maids to wash the floor of the formal dining chamber and fill the tallest lamps with oil.

THOUGH IN GENERAL MY father-in-law loved making an entrance, with the doorkeepers announcing his royal presence, today he was too excited to wait.

'My queen!' he called, pushing open the door of Kaushalya's quarters himself, 'I consulted the court astrologers. Tomorrow's an auspicious day, the star Pushya ascending. It'll be the perfect time for Ram's coronation.'

Kaushalya, who'd come running when she heard his voice, her hair only half-done because he'd arrived earlier than expected, was too startled to speak.

'Yes, wife, I've made my decision!' Dasharath boomed from the doorway. Today he didn't seem to care who heard him. 'Ram's going to be crowned king tomorrow.'

'Tomorrow!' Kaushalya's face was a mix of delight and surprise. And some consternation. She'd hoped and longed for this news for years—probably since Ram's birth. She'd confided in me that she'd been waiting for Dasharath to announce it ever since Ram was married. But she hadn't expected the coronation to follow so swiftly upon the king's declaration, nor, I think, had she expected to hand the reins of queenship to me so fast.

'Yes,' Dasharath said. 'I don't believe in dilly-dallying once my mind is made up. I know Ram's ready to be a wonderful ruler. After all, I've been preparing him for years—and now he has the perfect wife as well.' He beckoned to me with a smile. 'Come here, child.' I touched his feet in a pranam, and he kissed me on the forehead. 'You're to become queen of Ayodhya tomorrow! What do you think of that? Are you ready for it?'

There was a huge knot of nervousness in my stomach, but he looked so jubilant, I murmured, 'By your blessings and the grace of the goddess.'

Dasharath beamed. 'That's the spirit! Confident but not overly so.' He turned to Kaushalya again. 'And you—are you ready? As mother of the king, there are a lot of preparations for you to take care of!'

'But why are you in such a hurry?' Kaushalya asked.

I, too, was surprised. Dasharath loved ceremony. Surely he wanted the many kings who were his friends and allies to be present at this festive event, to bless his son, offer their support and fealty, and bring him lavish gifts?

We hadn't noticed Vasishta, who had entered the room silently behind Dasharath, his face gaunter than usual. 'The king had a dream last night. In it he rode southward on an ass, under a sky filled with falling meteors. We believe it is best not to delay the coronation.'

'What a strange dream!' Kaushalya exclaimed. 'What could it possibly mean?'

Dasharath turned away, but the sage said, 'South is the direction to the death-kingdom of Yama. The court astrologers have divined that it's a portent of destruction and dishonour.'

From Kaushalya's face, I could see that she didn't want to believe the omen, didn't want it to overshadow the most important event in her son's life. 'Perhaps the dream has some simpler cause,' she ventured. 'Last night, the king ate at Kaikeyi's. Her food is so spicy, it always gives him indigestion. Perhaps that's what caused the—'

Dasharath held up his hand, stopping her mid-sentence. 'Wife, you know I'm not one of those men who live their lives by the movements of the planets. But with Ram, I refuse to take a chance. He's too dear to me, too important.' He put an arm around her shoulders, an affectionate display rare to him, especially in company. 'I don't want you to worry. Focus on the things you have to get done by tomorrow. Vasishta will give you all the details.' He looked around, frowning. 'But why isn't Ram here yet?'

All of a sudden, his face appeared aged. Ah, what a chameleon thing love was, lifting us up one minute, casting us down the next.

Sumantra said, 'Remember, Sire, you sent him to the northern borders to settle a land dispute between tribes. I've sent a messenger to him to return post-haste, but it's a long distance. I'm sure we'll see him soon. There's no cause for worry.'

But Dasharath paced up and down, refusing our offers of a light repast or a soothing drink, until we heard a commotion at the door. Ram entered, dust-covered from his journey. His eyes sought me out first, a quick glance of love and concern, before he turned to his father and touched his feet.

'The messenger recalled me even before I could pass judgement on the tribes, Father, saying it was an urgent matter. Is all well in the kingdom?'

Dasharath raised him and held him in a tight embrace. 'All is very well, my dearest son, now that you're back safely. I have some news for you though: you are to be made king tomorrow.'

Ram didn't believe in displaying emotion, especially in company. He'd told me early on that self-control was the mark of a good ruler. Also that it was safer when people around you—rivals and even friends—didn't know exactly what you thought or felt. But today we could all read the astonishment on his face. 'So sudden? But my brothers Bharat and Shatrughna are still in Kekaya. Surely they should be present at the ceremony…' He didn't sound particularly happy.

'Oh, Bharat won't mind,' Dasharath said airily. 'He's always known you're going to be king, and Shatrughna follows Bharat's lead. And besides, I have a good reason.' He went on to describe the omen.

Ram looked concerned. 'Perhaps we should have a special puja done for your long life and continued health first. Then we can plan the coronation.'

Dasharath waved away the suggestion. 'Later, later. For the good of the kingdom, it's more important that you be crowned before anything else.'

He'd said the magic words. *Good of the kingdom*. Ram bowed. 'I'm at your command, my king,' he said. 'I thank you for your trust in me.'

'Oh, enough of all this formality!' Dasharath cried, holding out his arms. 'Come now, give your old father a hug.'

I looked at Ram closely as he embraced Dasharath, but he had his public face on. I'd have to wait until we were alone to find out how he really felt about this kingship, thrust so suddenly on him. I knew this much though: he'd be a great king. Greater than his father, because he'd never allow personal emotion to weaken him in his royal duty. The knowledge filled me with pride, and a small, strange disquiet.

THE EVENING FLEW BY. Vasishta instructed us all in the formalities to be observed between now and the coronation—prayers, rituals baths, fasts, the giving of alms, a fire sacrifice at night before we slept. Lakshman and Urmila joined us, Lakshman whooping when he heard the news and lifting his brother off his feet in an enthusiastic hug. Urmila, who was a lot happier since she'd followed my advice and had a talk with Sumitra, clasped my hand tightly and whispered in my ear that I'd surely be the best—and prettiest—queen to sit on Ayodhya's throne.

I whispered back that queens in Ayodhya didn't exactly sit on thrones. After the coronation, they returned to the women's quarters.

'Things change,' she whispered to me. 'Ram isn't like the kings before him. He loves and values you in a way this kingdom hasn't ever seen. Hasn't he declared, publicly, that he won't take another wife?'

Indeed, he'd done so—not only at the wedding, but again, a few months ago, when a royal messenger from the kingdom of Mahishmati had brought a request for a marital alliance. Although Dasharath had been displeased by his son's refusal, my spirits had soared because I occupied all of my husband's heart.

AS INSTRUCTED, RAM AND I spent much of the night in prayer. Rather, he prayed, and I watched him, yawning because I wasn't a particularly devout person. When I prayed—and I must confess it was only when I was in trouble—I did it in a busy rush of words, usually asking the goddess for a boon. But when Ram prayed, he closed his eyes and stillness filled his entire being. It was as though he retreated somewhere deep within himself. I wanted very much to follow him there, or, failing that, to at least know where it was. But when I asked him about it, he looked perplexed at my question.

'I go into my heart-centre,' he said, 'to commune with the Divine. Don't you do the same?'

I was too abashed to tell him that I didn't.

At last we lay down on the floor, on a bed made of scratchy grasses, because Vasishta had explained that before he was crowned king Ram must experience a little of the hardships of his poorer subjects. We didn't touch each other. Tonight we were supposed to keep ourselves pure and not indulge in bodily pleasures. Vasishta had said something about keeping an unsheathed sword in the bed between us, but I thought that was overly dramatic, not to mention dangerous, and vetoed it. I told Ram that surely we could hold each other and not go any further, but Ram thought we'd better not take a chance. He was probably right. When we were close, things happened to our bodies that we couldn't always control. As a compromise, we intertwined our fingers and talked into the small hours of the night. Tired though he was, Ram couldn't sleep, and I wanted to keep him company.

'Are you planning to change anything when you become king?' I asked.

'Yes, actually I am,' he said, sitting up in his excitement. 'Though I'll do it gradually so as to not offend my father. In my kingdom, every man will have a voice, no matter how humble he is. No one should feel his concerns are ignored, or that he doesn't receive justice.'

I wanted to ask, *what about the women*? But Ram was totally focussed on his vision, and I didn't want to interrupt.

'I expect that many people will be too afraid to voice their opinions. After all, they aren't used to doing it with my father. So I plan to have royal spies travel through the kingdom, watching and listening and asking careful questions, keeping a finger on the pulse of the city. They'll report to me, and in this way, I'll solve any problems that arise before they grow too large.'

He looked at me, his face intent and shining, waiting for my response.

'It's a very good plan,' I said, smiling at him. And it was. But I had misgivings. Did every man in the city deserve to have his opinion listened to, or his grievances addressed? If Ayodhya was anything like Mithila, there were bound to be many belligerent fools, and unfortunately they were the ones that complained the loudest, often for little reason.

I was worrying needlessly, I told myself. Ram is smart. He can surely distinguish between real problems and unreasonable demands.

'Sita!' Ram said. 'You aren't listening. I asked you twice what I can give you on my coronation day.'

'I have everything I need,' I said, smiling. 'And more.'

'That's what's amazing about you. I don't know any woman—my mother included—who would have said that if her husband offered her a gift.'

I shrugged. 'You've given me your heart. All of it. What more is there to ask for?'

'I insist!' Ram said. 'I must give you something special. Something to show my love. After all, you're the one who taught me what love is.'

'Then give me this gift,' I said. 'Promise that I'll always be your helpmate. That you'll share all your thoughts with me, the happy ones and the sad ones, the troubles as well as the victories.'

'That's not much of a gift,' Ram grumbled. 'Don't I do that already? But all right, I agree.' He pressed his lips into my palm. 'Do you think this violates Vasishta's injunctions?'

'I don't think the goddess would mind, because she, too, knows what love is,' I said.

I SLEPT FITFULLY THAT night, partly due to the scratchy rushes, and partly due to the overexcitement of the day. And sleeping I dreamt that I was in a room made of shining metal. The floors and walls, silver grey and seamless, looked as though they'd been forged in a giant's smithy. It was completely empty, except for the woman who sat in its centre. Her back, straight as a sword, was turned to me. Her hair fell around her, untied and wild. Her discarded jewellery was scattered around her on the floor. Her beautiful clothes were torn to strips. I knew, in the way dreamers often do, that she had ripped them herself, methodically.

There was an insistent knocking at the door. The woman ignored it.

'My dearest, dearest wife,' cried a voice, the abject anxiety in it so foreign that it took me a moment to recognize it as King Dasharath's. 'Please let me in. Tell me who has dared to anger you. I will surely punish them, even to death. I promise you this. Please, my best beloved, speak to me. Your unhappiness is like a sword twisting in my heart.'

I knew then what place this was. Kaikeyi's anger chamber.

Kaikeyi remained silent, forcing Dasharath to plead more and more desperately. When she finally spoke, her voice was cool. 'I do not need any new promises from you. You made two promises to me already, years ago. Do you remember them?'

'Yes, of course,' Dasharath said. 'How can I forget? You saved me twice, once in battle when I was grievously wounded, and once when I was ill, almost dying, and you sucked the poison from my body with your own lips. But you would not accept any gifts I offered you then.'

Kaikeyi opened the door to the anger room. Dasharath put out his arms hungrily to embrace her, but she pushed him away. 'It is time to redeem your promise, King.'

'Tell me what you want,' the king said, his face suffused with love—or was it folly? 'Whatever it is, I will give it to you, or die trying.'

Kaikeyi smiled, and her smile was beautiful and cool as moonlight in summer, or snow on a parched summer day. And dangerous, at the same time, as the shining edge of a dagger. It made me understand why the king was so infatuated with her, even in the autumn of their lives.

Then she spoke, but what she said the dream would not allow me to hear. I only saw the king fall to his knees, hands clasped in entreaty, face distorted by horror. I strained hard to catch his words. But the scene grew dim as though enveloped in smoke, and I awoke alone on my bed of rushes, for Ram had already left for the morning rituals that must take place before a coronation can occur.

My maids crowded around me, buzzing with excitement, getting me ready for my special day. They bathed me in milk and turmeric and dressed me in a special sari my mother had packed with my dowry, though neither she nor I had expected that I should wear it so soon. It was an unusual colour, like the sky before sunrise. But when it caught the light, it shone like a thousand opals. Embroidered all over with pearls, it was heavy, symbolizing, perhaps, that queenship was a serious responsibility. But after my talk with Ram last night, it was a responsibility I was ready for. I drew myself up to my full height as the maids settled the folds of the sari around me and secured it with a gold waistband. The room filled with the excited exclamations of the women as they rubbed sandalwood oil onto my wrists and tied my hair up high in a new style so it would support a coronet.

Urmila had come over to help. 'The royal messengers went out last night,' she told me as she clasped a necklace of rubies around my throat and stood back to eye me appraisingly.

'Don't tell me that even here in Ayodhya you have your informants!' I joked.

She quelled me with a serious look. 'And you should, too, especially now that you're going to be queen. How else will you keep abreast of all the plots hatched in this palace? Today, though, I only heard good things. All the neighbouring kings have been invited—I believe several are on their way already. Heralds have announced the news across the city. Sweetmeats have been distributed to every household, along with gold coins. The festivities will continue for a fortnight after the coronation. Can't you hear the people celebrating?'

Indeed, mixed with the noise of trumpets and drums outside the palace, I could hear the crowd's joyful roar. I recognized Ram's name and mine, repeated over and over so one wasn't quite sure who was first, or where one ended and the other began: *Ramsitaramsitaramsitaram*. The smell of marigolds and lotuses were everywhere. They made me giddy.

Urmila ran off to get herself ready for the ceremony—sister to the queen was an important role, she declared, for which she had to look appropriately grand. Fortunately, our far-thinking mother had packed her a deep blue sari that complemented mine and was perfect for the occasion.

I waved her goodbye with a smile—her enthusiasm was infectious—and started on my way to Kaushalya's quarters. Ram and I were supposed to break our fast with her before we all proceeded to the coronation hall. I was sure Kaushalya would have prepared a huge feast in honour of this special occasion, probably cooking several items with her own hands. My biggest worry as I walked towards her chambers was that I might offend her because I was too nervous to eat anything.

Eleven

I'D WALKED ONLY A FEW steps before I was forced to stop. Blocking my path was a tiny woman, bent under the weight of the hump on her back. I knew her at once though we hadn't met: Manthara. She was dressed in a gaudy red silk far above her station and wore around her neck a double string of luscious pearls. They looked familiar, and after a moment, I realized that Kaikeyi had been wearing them when I saw her last.

What did Kaikeyi's spy want with me?

'Greetings, Princess, and congratulations,' Manthara said. She gave me a bow that seemed exaggerated, almost a caricature. But perhaps I was imagining this because the hunchback made me uncomfortable. I tried to offer her a gracious smile. Her deformity—and the way people looked at her because of it, with disgust or fear—was not her fault.

'I bring you a message from Dasharath,' Manthara said.

I was surprised by the familiar way in which she said the king's name. It was disrespectful for a servant, no matter how favoured, to do so.

Manthara continued, 'You are to present yourself at Queen Kaikeyi's chambers, where he spent the night. Ram, too, has been summoned there. Come with me.'

The disturbing dream I'd had last night flickered in my mind.

I didn't want to follow Manthara. I didn't trust her. 'It'll make us late for the ceremony,' I protested.

'Don't worry, you'll have plenty of time,' Manthara said. The smile on her face was more like a smirk. Lurching from side to side, she moved with unexpected rapidity along a narrow veranda I hadn't noticed earlier. 'Ram's coronation isn't about to happen just yet.'

From the veranda, which ran along one edge of the palace, we could see the bordering street. The music was louder here. Men and women danced on the street, strewing flower petals. A ceremonial gate decorated with bright fabrics and coloured flags had been erected. I guessed that Ram and I were supposed to begin a chariot-procession from there. Manthara stopped for a moment, rising on her toes to observe the festivities. 'Ah, the stupid masses. They'll soon be dancing to a different tune. Truly, ignorance is bliss, is it not?'

Her words sent a chill through me. I wanted to ask what she meant, but I knew that was exactly what she wished me to do. I wouldn't give her the satisfaction.

I pressed my lips together and followed her in silence. The reason for this detour in our plans would become clear in a few minutes. Probably Kaikeyi wanted to give us a wedding gift. Forcing us to come to her chambers for it was her way of asserting her power, especially as she knew that her importance would diminish once Kaushalya became queen-mother.

But my dream kept coming back to me—Dasharath on his knees, that haunting look of horror and hopelessness on his face.

MANTHARA USHERED ME INTO a great hall. I hadn't been here before—Kaikeyi had received me in a smaller room the last time. This space was grand and formal. Kaikeyi had decorated it as though it were a royal court, with floors of polished, intricately designed stone, and massive, carved furniture. But today it appeared strangely dim in spite of the gleaming floors and walls, and the huge windows which opened onto the glorious day outside, echoing with celebration. Dasharath sat on the dais, on a golden throne. I bowed to him, but he seemed not to see me. I was shocked at how old he looked. The hair clumped around his face was greyer than before. An unkempt stubble dotted his cheeks, and his eyes were bleary and unfocussed. In one night, he seemed to have aged decades. Had he fallen suddenly ill? Suffered an attack of some kind?

'Father!' I called, hurrying towards him, but Kaikeyi moved with agility, inserting herself between us. In contrast to the king, she appeared young and invigorated, more beautiful than ever. Her face shone, and she wore a heavy gold sari and a great amount of jewellery.

'Sit,' she said, with a dazzling smile, leading me to a low chair, clearly inappropriate for the queen-to-be. 'Ram should be here any moment, and then we'll begin. Manthara, give Sita something to drink.'

I began a polite refusal, wishing only to finish whatever formalities Kaikeyi had planned and leave quickly. Vasishta had warned us not to be late. As at my wedding, the auspicious moment today was a short one. He didn't want us to miss it. But Manthara had already thrust a cold silver glass filled with pomegranate juice into my hand. Not wishing to appear rude, I took a reluctant sip of the blood-red liquid.

Then Ram was in the room. His presence made me feel better. Now that he'd arrived, he'd take charge. Whatever was wrong would be set right. I rose, smiling. But he didn't even see me. His worried eyes were focussed on Dasharath.

'I came as soon as I received your summons, Sire. What's wrong?'

Dasharath said nothing, but a spasm passed over his face and tears sprang to his eyes. He held out his trembling hands and Ram knelt in front of him and clasped them tightly.

'Kaikeyi-Ma, is my father ill? I know you're a gifted healer, and you must be taking good care of him, but maybe we should send for—'

The king's lips moved, though for a moment he was unable to form words. Finally he said, his voice low and harsh, 'Healer! She's the cause of all my ills. Rakshasi! She'll be the cause of my death as well. I curse the day I married her.'

'What's the problem?' Ram asked, his voice reflecting the shock that we both felt. 'No matter what it is, I promise that I'll help you take care of it.'

But the king hung his head as though in shame. He seemed to have receded into an inner world where none of us were present. Instead, it was Kaikeyi who spoke.

'Indeed, Ram, you alone can help Dasharath. Years ago, I saved his life twice, and he promised me two boons. Today I've claimed them—but they can only be fulfilled by you. The men of the House of Raghu have always prided themselves on keeping their word. Now their honour lies in your hands.'

Ram disengaged himself from his father gently and stood tall. I could see he was about to speak. His face had taken on a noble, detached look that frightened me. I rushed over to him and grabbed his arm. According to palace protocol, I should have remained silent, but I had a bad feeling about all this. 'Don't make any promises until you know what she wants,' I whispered fiercely. He laid his hand over mine, but he didn't look at me. Instead, he spoke to Kaikeyi.

'You needn't bring up the reputation of the Raghu-Vamsa, Kaikeyi-Ma, in order to gain your wish,' he said, his tone mildly reproving. 'I'll do anything I can to help my father keep his word.'

For a moment, Kaikeyi hesitated. Was it shame that flitted across her face? She glanced at Manthara, as though gathering her resolve. 'These are the two boons. One, that my son Bharat be made king of Koshala instead of you. That is his right. Because you might not know this—and your father has conveniently forgotten it—but when we were married, Dasharath promised my father that my son would sit on the throne of Ayodhya. And here's the second boon: that you be banished to the forest for fourteen years.'

Blood roared in my ears so loudly, I was sure I'd heard wrong. Kaikeyi loved Ram. I'd seen genuine fondness fill her face when she talked to him. Now, overnight, she was ready to wrest his kingdom away from him and throw him into darkness and danger.

'How can you do this?' I cried, my fury making me forget all the lessons in caution that my mother had taught me. 'It's wrong in every way. We all know that Ram would be a better king than Bharat. He's been trained for it his whole life, while Bharat's always away in Kekaya. He's rarely attended court sessions. Has he put down uprisings, like Ram, or—'

'If he hasn't,' Kaikeyi interrupted coldly, 'it's because his father never gave him the opportunity.'

Ram's hand tightened around my wrist, his grasp like iron. I knew I'd have a bruise later, but that was the least of my concerns. Stand up against this huge injustice, I wanted to say. But he shook his head, indicating he didn't want me to speak.

I obeyed, but in my mind I begged him. *Protest. If nothing else, remind your father of his kingly duty to the people of Ayodhya.*

But my husband didn't do that. Instead, without hesitation, he said, 'It will be as you wish.' He bowed formally to Kaikeyi, his face impassive. Only I saw the hurt that flickered for a moment in his eyes.

Kaikeyi smiled her triumph.

If love can change so quickly into hate, I thought, looking at her face, what are we to depend on?

RAM AND I MADE our way to Kaushalya's quarters. So many emotions swirled inside me, I could hardly breathe. But topmost was outrage. Ram and I had never fought, but I was ready for it now.

I said, 'I can't believe that you agreed to Kaikeyi's unfair demands without standing up to her! It would be a different matter if your father-king asked you to step down, but he clearly doesn't want that.

And for good reason. He knows you're the only one who can hold Koshal together after he's gone.'

Ram looked at me. I could see the stress on his face. 'And that's what I'm doing. Apart from honouring my father's promise, which is my duty as his son, I want Koshal to have peace. If I protested, strife would erupt all over the kingdom. Kaikeyi is powerful—she has her own faction here, her own guards. Riots could occur, maybe even civil war. Maybe worse, if she calls upon her brother to come and join her with his powerful Kekaya army. I can't be the cause of so much death and destruction.'

'But—' I began hotly.

He put a gentle arm around me. 'I know this is a shock to you, dearest one. I need you to be strong now, and calm. I need your support, my wife.'

I looked into his eyes and saw that, beneath all the resolve, he, too, was worried. He, too, didn't know how things would turn out. He, too, was reeling at this betrayal.

I pushed away my own sorrows and fears. *Later*, I said to them. *I'll deal with you later.* My duty was clear, and it was an easier one than Ram's. It consisted only of one thing: helping Ram get through this challenge. I held his face in my hands and kissed him. I didn't care who might see us. The calamity into which we'd been thrust had burned away my concern with social niceties.

'Whatever you decide,' I said to him, 'I'll support you. Whatever comes to you as a result of your decision, we'll handle it together.' I felt the energy flowing from my palm chakras into the whirling vortex in Ram's head. It didn't drain me as I thought it might. Instead, it invigorated me. Such was love's magic—the giver gained more than the receiver.

Hand in hand, we went to break the news to Kaushalya.

KAUSHALYA'S QUARTERS WERE FRAGRANT with incense and music and filled with women—her own companions as well as many of the minor queens who had come to pay their respects, now that they thought she was about to be elevated to queen-motherhood. They were singing good-luck songs and eating sweetmeats, but they broke off in shock when we entered, closely followed by attendants carrying the stricken king on a pallet. The gold bowl of kumkum, with which Kaushalya was about to mark our foreheads, fell from her hand, leaving an ugly red splotch on her sari. She, too, would have fallen if Ram hadn't caught her. In a few words, he explained to her—and to Lakshman and Urmila, who were waiting to accompany us to the coronation hall—what Kaikeyi had asked for, and what he'd agreed to.

Urmila was too stunned to move or speak, but Lakshman's face grew black with fury. 'What nonsense is this, brother?' he cried in a voice so terrible that all except Ram trembled. 'Why should you give up your right to the throne just because, in his old age, our father has lost his senses and become a puppet in our stepmother's hands? How could he even consider her ridiculous demands? I've lost all respect for him. You're the eldest and the best among us brothers—you're my king. Say the word and I'll single-handedly capture Bharat and drag him in chains to your feet. Whosoever tries to stop me—be it foot-soldier or mighty warrior or even Shatrughna, with whom I shared my mother's womb—I'll kill them all.'

I was looking at another of love's many faces. It made us ready to wreak havoc—even on people we cared for—in order to protect those whom we cherished more. Wasn't it the same force that impelled Kaikeyi to turn on Ram in order to guard her own son's interest? Wasn't it the same force that led Manthara—for the hunchback, I suspected, was the orchestrator of this entire disaster—to whisper directives to Kaikeyi, whom she still saw as the innocent child to whom she'd devoted her entire misshapen life?

I was learning more about the twisted paths along which love swept us humans along than I'd ever expected—or wanted. Looking at the terrible shining in Lakshman's face, I hoped that I'd never find myself standing in the path of such ruthless zeal.

'Silence, brother!' Ram said, and although he spoke in a soft voice, there was steel underneath. 'Never speak ill of our father. He's achieved more in his lifetime than we'll ever know—and as you can see, he's already suffering. Neither should you be angry with Bharat, who's the most blameless of all. He doesn't care for kingship—you know that. I suspect he'll be deeply distressed when he learns what has happened here.'

Looking unconvinced, Lakshman lowered his head like a bull about to charge. 'He'd better be,' I heard him mutter.

'Why even blame my father for what has transpired?' Ram continued. 'Hasn't our teacher, Vasishta, taught us that many strands of karma must come together for an upheaval like this to occur—yours, mine, the kingdom's, perhaps the entire earth's. The wise man accepts it calmly. Who knows why I'm going into the forest, and whom I'll meet there?'

'How can you be so philosophical at this time?' Lakshman shouted. 'That's what Kaikeyi's counting on—your overdeveloped sense of decency. You need to fight her. All you've ever wanted, since we were children, is to rule Ayodhya, and do it well. How can you let her take that away from you? Forget about yourself, but don't you care about our citizens who are waiting—no, longing—for you to become their king?'

'Brother, please,' Ram said. I could see in his eyes the pain of having all his dreams crashing around him. 'I don't have time to discuss this right now. All I can say is, don't make things more difficult for me.'

At that, Lakshman bowed his head and said no more. He, too—like me—was caught in love's shackles.

Now Kaushalya came forward, weeping, and clasped Ram's hands. 'Why are you scolding Lakshman? He only speaks out of loyalty to you. And he's right. Why should you be banished like a common criminal? What harm have you ever done? Even if you give the throne to Bharat out of some misguided sense of duty, you must not go into the forest! How can you possibly survive there for fourteen years, among all those wild beasts and rakshasas and black magic? No doubt that's exactly what that witch Kaikeyi is counting on.' She took a deep breath and continued, 'If you don't want to remain in this palace, that's fine. I don't want to stay here, either, not after all this. Let's go, you and I and Sita, to a little corner of Koshal far away from Ayodhya. We'll live in a mud hut, if need be. Or we could go to Mithila. I'm sure Janak would gladly take us in. There at least you'll be safe. There at least I'll see you each day. No, don't refuse me so quickly. As your mother, am I not your elder too? Isn't my request worth something? Don't you have a duty towards me, just as you do towards Dasharath?'

Ram held his mother close. I could see how much it hurt him to refuse her, but his voice was firm. 'Be calm and draw upon the strength and wisdom that I know you possess. As my dearly loved mother, you must help me now. Help me follow the path of right which—as you yourself taught me—isn't always easy. You know that my first duty—no matter how much I love you—must be to my father because he's also my king. He's your king too. That's why you need to put aside your own sorrow and comfort him after I'm gone.'

Such was the power of his voice that Kaushalya stopped weeping. Ah, what a king he would have made, my Ram! And now, instead, he'd struggle in the forest—and probably perish there. Kaushalya was right—who could last, alone in the wilderness, for fourteen years? A deep sorrow welled up in me.

'As for me,' Ram added—but this time his voice had changed and his eyes were unfocussed, as though he were seeing things beyond mortal vision— 'whatever befalls me in the forest, know that to be my destiny. I embrace it.'

'Well, you'll not be embracing it alone,' Lakshman cried. 'I'm going to the forest with you. And don't you try to tell me that it's my duty to stay here. My duty is to follow you—I've been doing that ever since I learned to crawl. You'll need someone to take care of you in the forest, to watch your back, to protect you when you rest. And I'll do that—or die trying.'

His words had pulled Ram out of his trance. 'Very well, brother,' he said. 'I confess, I'll be a lot happier in the forest if I have you for company.' And he smiled his first smile since our lives were turned upside down.

Watching that sweet smile that wasn't meant for me, I was stung by jealousy. Some of the jealousy was of the bond between the brothers, but mostly it was jealousy of the freedom given to men to go wherever they wanted in the wide world.

I allowed some of the outrage I'd pushed down to come back up. You're so concerned about everyone else, I said silently to Ram. Your father, your mother, Lakshman, even the absent Bharat. But what about me? Have you forgotten about me?

Of course he hadn't—I knew that. He was waiting until we were alone. I had a good idea about what he planned to ask me then. Well, it wasn't going to work! I'd make sure of that by fighting him with everything in my arsenal. But I'd fight smart, the way my mother had taught me.

Help me, Goddess, I cried silently. *Because my goal is not to win over Ram but to win him over.*

'What will happen to us now, Didi?' a small voice said. Cold fingers worked their way into mine.

I looked at Urmila, her face pale and frightened. 'I'm not going to give up so easily,' I said. 'And neither should you.' Quickly, I whispered my plan to her, what both of us sisters needed to do. I squeezed her shoulder to give her strength, pushed her towards her quarters and hurried to mine to confront my husband.

Twelve

I PACED MY BEDROOM IN A fever of impatience, but fortunately I didn't have to wait long. Although Dasharath and Kaushalya—and the sobbing Sumitra, for news had travelled quickly to her, as bad news tends to do—had begged them to stay at least one more night, the brothers decided to leave Ayodhya the very same day.

'I've come to get my weapons and say goodbye,' my husband said as he strode in. 'Please don't delay me.' He spoke rapidly, as though he'd rehearsed the words several times. I could see he was afraid I was going to indulge in histrionics. Well, he was about to be surprised.

'I'm depending on you to take care of my parents in my absence,' he added, his tone all business. But I saw the way his hand clenched his bow, the knuckles white. 'That will be your most important duty when I'm gone.'

'I'm sorry,' I said, very sweetly. 'I'm not going to be able do that. You see, I'm going to the forest with you.'

His brows snapped together. 'What folly is this? You can't possibly come with me. You're a woman. It's too dangerous. I won't allow it.'

I wanted to say, *not all women are weak and helpless like you think. For all you know, I might be of help to you*. But I remembered my mother's teachings, kept those thoughts to myself and chose my words carefully. If this was going to work—and it had to, because

I couldn't imagine living in this mausoleum of a palace without him—I had to appeal to Ram in the right way.

'You're a fine one to talk of duty!' I said, allowing just enough anger into my voice. 'If I'm not misremembering my wedding vows, didn't I state that my foremost duty as your faithful spouse was to follow you, even to the ends of the earth? To be with you in riches and poverty? To take care of you the best I can? Isn't that what you just told your mother to do for her husband? You can't deprive me of my wifely right.'

Duty. Right. Those are the terms that Ram understood best, so I used them. But beneath them I was saying, *I love you. I need you. Don't abandon me.*

Ram crossed the room and tilted up my chin so he could look into my eyes. 'Do you really mean what you're saying? Do you even realize what it means?' he said harshly. 'You have no idea of the kinds of dangers the forest holds. Fourteen years of hard living in the wilderness—why, long before our banishment ends, you'll start hating me for subjecting you to that.'

His face was thunderous, but I wasn't afraid. I put my arms around his neck and pressed my lips against the warmth of his chest, pushing aside his silken coronation garments to kiss the small, crinkly curls of hair that I loved. 'Do you really think I could ever hate you? I don't care how much hardship we face in the forest. At least we'll be together as we go through our troubles. It'll kill me to remain here alone—more surely than any wild beast or rakshasa might. Because I can't live without you. It's as simple as that.'

For a moment, Ram hesitated. Then his arms went around me, tight. He took a deep, ragged breath, burying his face in my hair, breathing in its scent. 'Oh God!' he cried, and there was a wealth of undeclared joy in the words. But in a moment he was back to his dutiful, pragmatic self. 'You'd better get ready, then. You can't wear all this finery in the jungle, you know. Luckily for us,'—here he gave me a wry smile—'Kaikeyi has sent over, most helpfully, several pieces of tree-bark cloth. Put one on. I'm afraid you'll have to take off your ornaments too. They'll only be a hindrance, perhaps a danger, as we roam the forest. Give them to my mother for safekeeping, or ask the palace treasurer to donate them to the poor. That's what I've done with my valuables. Be quick. We need to pass beyond the boundaries of the city before sunset so that we can find a safe place to sleep.'

But where love and sorrow bind people together, goodbyes are not so easily said. We were about to discover that.

KAUSHALYA'S CHAMBERS WERE DARK when we entered, all the windows covered with dark hangings, so that I had to stop and blink to accustom my eyes to the gloom. There was a sound, low, like the buzzing of bees. It took me a moment to realize that it was the soft keening of his wives who had, just a few hours before, been singing wedding songs. Dasharath himself lay unmoving on a couch. He seemed to have aged further in the little time that had passed since I saw him last. When I touched his feet and asked for a parting blessing, he laid his hand on my back, but didn't raise his head to look at me. I don't think he even realized that I was leaving. His thoughts seemed to wander, for he spoke of things I didn't quite understand, a hermit-boy he'd killed by mistake while hunting, and how the boy's father, dying of a broken heart, had cursed Dasharath that he, too, would suffer a similar fate.

Was he losing his mind? Could an excess of love do that?

Kaushalya, however, saw me wearing the tree-bark cloth that was already rubbing my skin raw and knew at once what was happening. She burst into new tears. It hadn't crossed her mind that I, too, might go with Ram. She tried her best to make me stay, pointing out the special dangers the forest held for women. Failing in that, she asked what she'd live for if I, too, left her. Finally, she used my parents. How could she bear to tell them that she'd sent off their carefully nurtured daughter to wander in the wilderness?

My heart ached for her, but my mind was made up. I reminded her that Ram and Lakshman had already killed many rakshasas and were sure to keep me safe. As for my parents, they had always impressed upon me the importance of a wife's duty. They'd be more upset if I stayed home in comfort, abandoning Ram to suffer alone.

But Kaushalya continued weeping, hiding her face in her hands. Ram paced up and down. He hated to see his mother unhappy. I was afraid that he might have second thoughts about taking me along.

I could only think of one more thing. 'If I go to the forest, Mother,' I said, 'I can take care of your son.'

Kaushalya paused in her crying. She didn't look up, but clearly she was listening. I pressed on. 'I'll cook for him and make sure he has the most comfortable bed possible to sleep in. And maybe my presence will give him a little happiness in his exile.'

Kaushalya looked up. Her face was still wet, but instead of sorrow, it was now suffused with tenderness. 'If you can make Ram happier,' she said, 'then of course you must go with him. Don't worry about me. I'll manage somehow.'

So this, too, was true of love: it could make us forget our own needs. It could make us strong even when the world was collapsing around us.

Now Kaushalya said, 'But I can't bear to see you, the daughter-in-law of Ayodhya—no, the rightful queen—dressed in this horrible tree-bark. Where did you get it? Ah, Kaikeyi, of course.' She took me to her inner chamber and dressed me in a sturdy silk and ornaments from her own coffer—for I'd already given all my jewels away. I would have preferred wearing the same thing that Ram and Lakshman wore, but I didn't want to argue. It was the least I could do for my mother-in-law.

When Ram saw my clothing, he shook his head in dismay.

'Mother, what are you doing? Our strategy is to travel incognito. It's a lot safer that way. If Sita's dressed like this, she'll attract all kinds of unwanted attention. Bandits, beggars, and God knows who—or what—else.'

Kaushalya squared her jaw stubbornly. 'It's an additional blow to my heart to see my only daughter-in-law leaving the palace like a beggar. Surely between you and your brother, you can protect your wife from a few robbers!'

She looked like she might start crying again.

'Very well,' Ram said hastily. But I could see he didn't like it.

All this time, Dasharath lay as though in a daze. I wasn't sure if he heard what we were saying, or realized what was about to occur in just a few moments.

'Time to go!' Lakshman called impatiently from the door. He too was clad in tree-bark and had his bow in his hand. But he was alone. Urmila was supposed to have persuaded him to let her accompany us—she and I had strategized about it. What had gone wrong?

'Where's my sister?' I asked Lakshman. 'Isn't she coming with us?'

He looked angry. But I knew by now that this was often his expression when he was uncomfortable about something, so I asked again.

'No,' he said. He didn't offer any information.

'Where is she?'

'In our bedroom, although she might be with my mother now. Ma's been crying a lot, so I told her to keep her company. Sister-in-law, we need to leave without delay, or else we'll be stuck in the marshes with no shelter when night falls.'

I didn't bother to answer him. I ran to Urmila's quarters, but her rooms were empty, the doors left carelessly open, as though she no longer cared who might step in and take her valuables. How would I find her? Where in this cavern of a palace might she be hiding? I looked in her usual haunts, but she was not in any of them. I stopped by Sumitra's rooms, but her maid said the queen had taken to her bed with a severe headache, and that she was alone. I could hear Ram calling me, his tones impatient. I felt torn in two. Was this a woman's predicament, always to be pulled between conflicting loves?

I was about to give up when I thought of one last place.

When I stepped out onto my balcony, I almost didn't recognize it, for all my flowers and herbs, which I had tended so lovingly all these years, had shrivelled and turned black. And there on the cold stone floor, among the dead blossoms, sat my sister.

I knelt down and held her tightly. I didn't ask for details. I could guess what must have happened.

'Lakshman refused to take me with him,' Urmila said. Her voice was calm and emotionless, and this frightened me more than if she'd been weeping. 'He said he had his hands full taking care of Ram, who was his first duty.

'"Didi's going with you," I said. "Why can't I?"

'At this he grew displeased and said that he hoped Ram knew better than to say yes to you because you'd be a burden on them. It was hard enough to survive in the wilderness without having to protect a woman also.

'"I'm ordering you to stay here and take care of the mothers," he said. "If you really love me, you'll do what I'm asking you. You'll do your duty."

'"Isn't it my duty to take care of you?" I asked him.

'"No," he said. "Your duty is to obey me."

'"What's your duty towards me?" I asked, barring his path.

'"I can't engage in philosophical discussions right now," he said. He set me aside and left.'

What could I offer as comfort to Urmila? I knew the dual causes of her pain: that Lakshman had refused her heart's offer, and that I, too, was abandoning her. I held her tightly. She smelled of sandalwood and female sweat, that long-ago smell from our father's garden on the day we first saw Ram and Lakshman. On that day, Urmila had blithely announced that she'd be willing to walk as many thorn-filled koshas as needed, if she could marry Lakshman. She was still willing, but it hadn't done her any good.

How innocent we'd been, thinking that if only we willed something hard enough, it would come true. I wondered what we'd both be like by the time we saw each other next time, or if we'd even meet again.

'I wanted so much to go with you,' Urmila said. 'I wanted so much to be with Lakshman. I told him I didn't care for comfort, that I didn't fear danger. But he wouldn't take me. He said he couldn't handle trying to take care of me on top of every other problem he had. That's all I am to my husband, Didi. One more problem.'

Anger spiked in me, but I tried to speak calmly. 'You know he doesn't mean it. You know he's not good at saying what he really means. He loves you, but there are many pressures on him now. You must forgive him.'

But my sister threw her arms around my neck and wept bitterly and wordlessly.

Part of me wanted to remain with her. Let the men go off to the forest on their own, I thought. My presence would comfort my sister, who had looked up to me all her life. Wasn't that my duty too? Hadn't my mother told me to take care of her?

These different loves and duties battled within me, but finally, my love for Ram won. Was it the right choice? I'd never be sure. But it was getting late. Ram was calling my name, his voice strained. There was no more time for debates. And so, guiltily, with a silent prayer to the goddess to watch over her and help her bear her sorrow, I pulled myself free of her arms and left Urmila.

Forgive me, Sister, I said silently, you who are the unsung heroine of this tale, the one who has the tougher role: to wait and to worry.

WE'D PLANNED TO WALK from the palace to the borders of the city, as was appropriate for mendicants, but there was a crush of people outside, men and women, and even children, weeping and begging Ram not to leave. How had they found out? Bad news, I guess, is like an infection, needing only air to carry it everywhere.

As soon as the palace gates were opened, the crowd surged forward, and it was hard for the guards to hold it back. Finally, Sumantra said he'd drive us in his chariot to the edge of town, and we had to agree. Even so, it was hard to get through the lamenters. Many tried to throw themselves under the chariot wheels to stop us, frenzied as they were with their fear of what would befall Ayodhya now that there was a change of regime. I closed my eyes. It was too painful to watch. Still, I could hear the women crying to me, 'Don't go! If you leave, the goddess Lakshmi herself will leave the city, along with you.'

Then, through the din, I heard Dasharath. 'Ram, Ram,' he cried, so loudly that I thought his lungs would burst. The abject desperation in his voice forced me to turn and look. But I wish I hadn't. Because there he was, running down the common road behind our chariot on faltering feet, crownless and dishevelled, his dhoti askew, his white hair streaming behind him. Attendants tried to stop him, but he shook them off with sudden strength. As I watched, he stumbled and fell on the dirt.

I pulled at Ram's arm. 'Please stop, at least for a moment,' I said. 'We can't leave him like this.'

There were tears in Ram's eyes. He gripped the edge of the chariot, but he continued staring ahead. Love and duty battled on his face. Then duty won.

'Stopping won't change matters,' he said. 'It'll only prolong his pain. Don't look at him. Leave him a little dignity. That is the only thing we can do for him now.'

I hid my face in my husband's chest, and the tears that I'd held onto for so long burst from me like a storm. Ram's arms came around me, and I felt, on my forehead, his own tears.

Thus we crossed from city to forest, from the known world to the unknown.

Thirteen

Days and distances rushed by us, grains of sand in a storm. Determined to move away as quickly as possible from Ayodhya, that ache in our heart, we left Sumantra weeping in his chariot. We crossed marshes and fens and rivers: Ganga and Jamuna, Sarayu and Falgu. We accepted the hospitality of many, not caring whether they were of high caste or low, for Ram loved all whose hearts were pure. We walked over rough ground until our feet blistered and bled and healed and grew calluses. Rain beat down upon us. Sun scorched us. And once we entered the woods, bloodsucking insects dived down, whining, to feed delightedly on our palace-fattened bodies.

My only solace in all this hardship was the company of my husband, and his sensitivity to my difficulties. He massaged my tired feet and wept when he saw their state. He padded the hard ground extra-thick with sweet-smelling rushes so that I'd be able to sleep better at night. Still, the punishing pace we'd set ourselves was too much for me. When we reached Chitrakoot Mountain, Ram looked at my exhausted face and announced that we'd stop here for a few days. I could have wept with relief.

'It's not safe,' Lakshman grumbled. 'This is one of the main routes through the forest. Anyone can find us here.'

It seemed that he was right. Just two days later, there was a disturbance in the air. The birds grew silent. The animals retreated into invisibility. In the distance we heard a faint roar, like a forest fire, that grew into the thud of hoofbeats and the clang of weaponry.

Lakshman narrowed his eyes and sniffed the air, but it was Ram who said, 'Bharat is coming.'

Lakshman pushed his brother behind him and stood at attention. 'Take care of Sister-in-law,' he said.

'It's only Bharat,' said my husband. 'Our own brother. You worry too much.'

'I have to,' Lakshman retorted, 'because you don't worry enough. Not everyone's as righteous—or simple—as you. When will you learn that? And tell me this: if Bharat's really coming in friendship, why's he bringing the whole blasted army of Ayodhya with him?' He strung his bow and held it steady as the cacophony of the marching soldiers grew closer.

Ram smiled and shook his head, but I shivered. What if Bharat was coming to make sure that he would be king not only now but forever? That there would be no one to come back after fourteen years and reclaim Ayodhya from him?

My husband, however, turned out to be a better judge of character than his suspicious brother and doubting wife. When Bharat finally appeared, he was dressed not as a warrior or even a king, but in the white cotton dhoti of a mourning son, barefoot, his head shaven. He threw himself weeping at his brother's feet, and Ram, lifting him up, also wept, because he knew that Dasharath was dead.

'He died just moments after you left, crying your name, his eyes darkening even before the dust had settled from the passing of your chariot,' Bharat said.

I learned a new fact about love that day: it could kill. Sometimes it could kill instantaneously.

Bharat begged Ram to return and take over the kingdom. 'That's why I brought the ministers and commanders of the army with me, and even our guru, Vasishta,' he said. 'So that we can crown you at once with all the proper ceremonies. The throne rightfully belongs to you, and no amount of plotting by my mother'—here his voice broke, and shame darkened his face—'will make it otherwise.'

I'd never paid much attention to Bharat. To me, he'd been a shadow planet orbiting around my husband's brilliance. But now I saw that there was an austerity in his bearing, a nobility. Not many men would have been willing to give up a kingdom that had fallen into their lap easier than a ripe mango. I couldn't help but admire that.

My thoughts were interrupted by Lakshman. 'Bharat's right, you know. As firstborn, the kingdom is yours. Also, you'll be better at ruling it than any one of us. You came away to the forest for Father's sake. You've fulfilled his promise, unreasonable as it was. Now that he's dead, your debt is cancelled. Now you must return for the sake of the people of Ayodhya. Isn't that your main duty as a king, to take care of your subjects?'

He'd spoken that magic word: *duty*. The duty of a king towards his people. I saw Ram stand up taller. A look of indecision flitted over his face.

Shatrughna, who'd been standing in the shadows, stepped forward to add his entreaties. 'Please come back, brother. Even Guru Vasishta agrees that with the king's death, your vow is fulfilled. What Kaikeyi—I can't stand to call her *mother*—made you do was totally wrong. You should have seen how angry Bharat was with her when he came back to Ayodhya and found what she'd done. He denounced her publicly in the court and imprisoned her in her quarters. She won't give you any trouble. You won't have to see her ever again. And as for that hunchback devil who was the real schemer behind all this, I beat her half to death and threw her out on the streets. If Bharat hadn't stopped me, I'd have killed her.'

Bharat joined his palms in imploration. 'Please come back, eldest brother. The kingdom is in turmoil. People are rioting. Many are leaving Koshal. Your return would help Kaushalya-Ma, too. She's so depressed that we're afraid for her life.'

Ram paced up and down in silence. I could feel the conflict raging inside him. Was he weighing his duty to a dead father against the love of a living mother? Was he thinking of what was best for his subjects—for that's how they still thought of themselves, Ram's people, no matter who sat on the throne? For a moment his eyes lighted on me. Was he thinking of his husbandly duty? To protect me from danger, to provide me with the comforts and dignities that were mine as the rightful queen of Ayodhya.

Once again, our fortunes seemed to be shifting. I tried to imagine returning to Ayodhya, which had receded, dreamlike, from my mind. It would be wonderful to enjoy again the luxuries I'd taken for granted all my life. To bathe in warm scented water instead of cold streams in which slimy creatures lurked. To wear freshly laundered clothes instead of the same mud-crusted sari over and over. To sleep on a soft bed and not on leaves which, no matter how high Ram piled them, didn't protect me from the ground, lumpy with roots and stones. To get away from the insects who whined around my ears day and night and preferred me to the men as their food source.

Most of all, it would be wonderful to be back with Urmila and Kaushalya-Ma again, to not have guilt well up in me whenever I remembered how I'd left them.

Yet strangely a part of me didn't want to abandon our adventure so soon. I had the feeling we'd only scratched the surface of what the forest had to offer, that so far it had been testing us. Once it was convinced that we were worthy, that we had truly chosen it over other options, it would open up untold treasures for our enjoyment. What these were, I had no idea. I only sensed that they were deep and intense, enchanting beyond anything I'd ever experienced. Sweet, but with an exciting aftertaste of danger.

Now I held my breath, watching Ram, wondering what he'd say. Whatever he decided would change the course of all our lives.

Ram spoke slowly. 'You make good points, brothers. Indeed it's important for a king to take care of his people. But I'm still—and foremost—a son bound by his father's pledge. I must respectfully disagree with Guru Vasishta: whether King Dasharath is alive or not makes no difference to a vow that was made in the presence of gods. Only after the fourteen years he promised to Kaikeyi can I be free to be king to my people and a son to my mother. Until then, brother Bharat, you are Ayodhya's only hope. Take care of Kaushalya-Ma for me, and try to forgive Kaikeyi-Ma. Remember, whatever she did, she did to protect you, the way a tigress protects its young, not caring if her claws slash anyone in the process…'

A closed look came over Bharat's face, and he spoke in a hard voice, 'I'm sorry, brother, but I'll never forgive her for how she destroyed our entire family.' He clasped Ram's hand, tears in his eyes, 'Please let me go to the forest instead of you. If the pledge requires that someone must be banished for fourteen years, that someone must suffer, let me be that person. Perhaps then some of the weight of Kaikeyi's sin, which I feel on my head, will be lifted.'

The hatred with which he said his mother's name shook me. Surely, all his life, Bharat had loved his mother dearly. Surely he realized that what she'd done had been for his sake alone. But today when he spoke of her, there was only disgust in his voice.

Could love, which I'd taken to be powerful and everlasting, be so frail as well? Could you pluck it out of your heart as easily as you'd pull a weed from a bed of flowers? I thought of my love for Ram—and his for me—which defined my entire being. It frightened me to imagine this happening to us. I'd never be able to survive such a loss.

I came back to the present with a start. Ram was speaking to Bharat. 'You should feel no such weight. Among us all, you're the most innocent. But we can't modify a vow to suit our convenience. That's not the way of the Raghu lineage—you know that. I—and I alone—must live in the forest for my allotted time. It's my destiny.

Perhaps I'm being sent to the forest to cleanse it of dark forces. Rule the kingdom for me until I return. I know you'll do it masterfully.'

Bharat didn't protest again. He must have heard the tone of finality in my husband's voice. He knew that Ayodhya could not remain unkinged any longer. He took back with him Ram's sandals, saying he'd place them on the throne. He himself would sit on the floor, governing Ayodhya as a regent in the absence of the true king.

Just before he left, I asked the question that had been eating at me all this while.

'What news of Urmila?' I missed her so much, it was hard to even speak her name.

Bharat seemed taken aback by my question. Enmeshed in affairs of state, he'd clearly given no thought to her. But Shatrughna, the quiet one, said, 'Shrutakirti told me that she's shut herself in her chambers since you left. Not even her cousins have been allowed to enter her room. She must have sworn her attendants to secrecy, for they won't say anything except that she is not ill.'

I stole a glance at Lakshman. He stared out at the shadows that had taken over the forest, his face devoid of expression. But I saw his throat constrict, and I knew he thought of his wife with sorrow. Perhaps he wished that he'd allowed her to accompany us.

That night, when Ram and I were finally alone, I said, 'If Vasishta, who knows the Vedas better than anyone in Ayodhya, says it's acceptable for you to be crowned king, no one will question it. You know that. You also know that you'd be a far better king than Bharat. It'll benefit so many people if you go back. Why don't you?'

Ram answered, 'I can't risk people thinking that I looked for a loophole in the vow because I coveted the kingdom. There can't be any stain on me when my kingship begins. Then the vision I have of a pure and righteous reign, Ram-rajya, will be ruined.'

'You're a king, not a god!' I exclaimed. 'No one expects you to be perfect. Why, even our gods do questionable things sometimes. A little gossip can't destroy a kingdom. There was plenty of gossip about your father, but he was still a fine king.'

But Ram only said, with that stubborn tilt to his chin, 'That may be so, but it's not *my* vision of kingship.'

I didn't argue. It had been a long, stressful day for us all, and I didn't have the heart to disagree further with my husband, to tell him that he was creating standards impossible to live by. I laid my head on his shoulder and tried to sleep, willing myself to dream of Urmila, to reach and comfort her in this way.

But dreams are fractious things and reveal only what they wish. I found myself in Urmila's room where she lay in bed, her eyes shut, a dim blue light misting around her. Her body was as still as death. My heart twisted with sorrow and guilt. I called her name and shook her shoulder. It was warm and pliant, but she didn't respond. Her spirit had receded somewhere far—perhaps in grief, perhaps in anger, perhaps, in abhimaan. I couldn't reach her, my sister whom I'd failed in her hour of need.

I AWOKE, WEEPING, TO find Ram sitting upright on the bed. There were traces of dried tears on his cheeks as well.

'Did you have a bad dream, too?' I said, sitting up myself. 'Was it of your father's death?'

'No. All beings must pass when their allotted time on earth is over—I know that.'

'What, then?'

At first he wouldn't say, but after I rubbed his back for a while, he told me, 'I was weeping for my father because he failed, at the very end, as a king. He held his personal honour higher than what was good for his people. He shouldn't have done that. I'm afraid I might grow weak like him.'

'I'm sure you won't,' I said.

Ram shook his head. 'I'm not so certain. After all, his blood runs in my veins.'

'Dasharath failed because his wife pushed him to the brink,' I said. 'I'll stand by you and help you the best I can. Surely, together, we'll succeed in creating Ram-rajya.'

He smiled then. 'You're the best wife a man could have. You've never caused me a single moment of sorrow, and I'm sure you never will.'

We lay down, holding each other as an antidote against all the worries plaguing us. Exhausted, I fell back into sleep, hoping for the healing blankness of oblivion, but it was not to be so. Another dream came to me.

I was in a chamber made of iron, windowless. It looked familiar and yet different. At first I thought it was empty. Then I saw the woman slumped against the shadowed wall, defeat and despair written clearly in her posture. It was Kaikeyi I was seeing—but Kaikeyi with the spirit gone out of her. Kaikeyi, banished to her anger chamber, which had now become her prison because there was no one left in her life to care if she was upset. Kaikeyi who had gambled everything for the love of her son, and lost it all because she hadn't understood one crucial thing.

This is what Kaikeyi failed to see: it's not enough to merely love someone. Even if we love them with our entire being, even if we're willing to commit the most heinous sin for their well-being. We must understand and respect the values that drive them. We must want what they want, not what we want for them.

Fourteen

EACH DAY WE TRAVELLED FARTHER from all we'd known, making our way towards Panchabati, which, Ram was told by sages we encountered, was the true heart of the forest, mysterious and unspoiled and beautiful, home to beings unlike any we had seen before.

'Are there rakshasas?' Lakshman asked, voicing the thought that was in all our minds. 'If so, we need to be prepared to defend ourselves. To kill them.'

The sages hesitated. One said, 'There are, though they call themselves by different names, and may even look different, depending upon the group they belong to. The rakshasas that live in cities are quite different from the ones that wander here in the forests.'

'Not all of them are ferocious, nor do they all eat human flesh,' another added. 'Many will leave you alone if they don't feel you are a danger to them.'

Ram nodded, though Lakshman looked sceptical.

'Do they practise evil magic? Like Tarhaka and her cohorts, whom Ram and I killed?' he asked.

'Each tribe is unique. Tarhaka belonged to a militant group that believed the forest was theirs—the last space left to them, since humans had taken over most of the cities—and thus they wanted to drive us out, through death if necessary,' another sage commented.

'Some of them know magic,' the leader of their group told us. 'Others are so good at witchcraft, they can become invisible whenever they want to.' With a smile, he added, 'Why, some could be watching us right now!'

I glanced around, half fearful, half excited. I saw nothing. The sage was probably joking with us. But sooner or later—I felt this in my gut—I would meet a rakshasa. Would he be anything like Ravan, the only rakshasa I'd seen so far? Somehow, I didn't think so. Even from the moment's glimpse I'd had of him, I could tell that Ravan was unique.

ONE EVENING, WE CAME upon a small hermitage. This surprised me. Most rishis who had ashrams lived on the edges of the forest, closer to civilization, partly for safety and partly for practical reasons.

I was further surprised when Ram said, 'I know this place. I've been here before.'

'How can that be?' I said. 'Didn't you say you've never been to this part of the country?'

'I haven't,' my husband said.

Lakshman, who'd been looking around carefully, said, 'It looks to me like the ashram of that sage, what's his name, the one who turned his wife into stone, remember? But wasn't that near Mithila?'

Mithila! My heart sped up when I heard that beloved name. Could we, by some strange twist of fate, have doubled back unknowingly towards my father's kingdom? Might I perhaps see my parents again?

Ram knew what I was thinking. He did that frequently nowadays, perhaps because we spent so much time together. Or was it because he loved me more? He shook his head a little sadly, his eyes soft with compassion. 'We aren't anywhere near Mithila, dear one. But sages have occult powers, siddhis they've garnered through years of meditation. Perhaps Sage Gautam decided to transport his ashram to an entirely new part of the land so that he and his wife could start life fresh.'

Distracted from my disappointment, I asked, 'Why would he want to do that? And didn't Lakshman just say that he turned his wife into stone? How would he be able to have any kind of life with her?'

'It's because Ram transformed her back into a human being,' Lakshman said proudly. 'I guess my brother has a few powers of his own!'

Astonished, I turned to my husband. 'You never told me this!'

Ram shrugged, modest as always. 'The subject never came up. And in any case, I didn't do much. We were walking along a forest path when Vishwamitra asked me to place my foot on a particular boulder. I was just as astonished as Lakshman when it changed into a woman.'

I stared at my husband, this man who could perform such amazing feats so matter-of-factly and then, without a trace of ego, let them slip from his mind. *Who are you?* I wanted to ask. But I knew he'd only say, 'What do you mean? You know who I am—your husband, Lakshman's brother, the exiled son of Dasharath.'

Intrigued by the story of Ahalya, I pressed Ram until he told me all he knew.

Ahalya, the beautiful, was created by Brahma himself, who then gave her in marriage to Gautam, the ascetic. Things went well—Gautam busy with his austerities, Ahalya devoted to taking care of him—until she came to the notice of Indra. As king of the gods, Indra believed that such a beautiful woman should belong to him. He approached Ahalya, promising her luxuries and pleasures beyond imagining, but she was a virtuous wife and rebuffed him. Indra wasn't ready to give up, however. He waited until a day when the sage went deep into the forest to perform a special yagna. Then he transformed himself magically and, in the guise of Gautam, came to the ashram and took Ahalya to bed. Returning late at night, Gautam sensed that something was wrong. The energies in the ashram were disturbed. Using his powers, he realized what had happened.

In his fury, he cursed Indra: a thousand vulvas would erupt all over his body. Indra went around like that for a while, until his wife Sachi, taking pity on his shame, intervened, praying on his behalf. Then they were turned into eyes.

Worse, Gautam was equally angry with Ahalya and cursed her too. For betraying her sacred marital vows for the sake of bodily pleasure, she would be turned into stone. Ahalya declared her innocence, pointing out that she was as much a victim of Indra's trickery as Gautam. But it was too late. The curse was in full force. Already her body was petrifying. All Gautam could do at that point was to promise her that a special being would soon be born, and his pure and powerful touch would restore her to life.

'And that's exactly what happened,' Lakshman added. 'I couldn't believe my eyes when a woman, beautiful but pale as a marble statue, rose up from the rubble. Her husband must have sensed the ending of the curse, because he appeared suddenly, out of nowhere and, thanking Ram, whisked her away. And my brother…'

'Enough, Lakshman,' Ram said, embarrassed as always by praise. 'Stop talking and move faster! We must get to the ascetic's hut before dark.'

AHALYA'S STORY FILLED ME with dissatisfaction. I longed to ask Ram a hundred questions. But there was no time. The sun had sunk low already. I followed my husband down a narrow path that wound its way through the trees, while Lakshman, as usual, brought up the rear.

In a little while we came upon a structure that was smaller than the other ashrams I'd seen, and more modest: a single thatched hut consisting of only a couple of rooms. Unlike in other ashrams, there were no other buildings to house students. Indeed, no students were in sight, making themselves busy sweeping or chopping wood or milking the single cow who stood, somewhat forlornly, under a tree.

Perhaps, after what had happened, Gautam preferred not to have any young men around.

Gautam was already at the door, looking quite unsurprised. He must have sensed our coming. He was gaunt and gnarled and severe-looking, though when he saw Ram, his face grew soft and affectionate. I thought at first that, as with many others, Ram had charmed him by his very presence. Then I remembered that they had a history. He owed a great deal to my husband.

But I was more interested in the woman who stood behind Gautam, straight and tall and, indeed, pale as a statue. The years had whitened her hair and etched wrinkles into the corners of her eyes, but Ahalya was still strikingly beautiful. She seemed pleased to see us but didn't add any words to her husband's welcome. Indeed, through the evening, as she served us a simple meal of fruits and milk, she was silent, as though the stillness of stone had taken over her being. Even when I thanked her for her hospitality she didn't answer, although she did smile.

'She has taken a vow of silence,' Gautam explained with some pride. 'It is a severe vow and will bring her much spiritual merit.'

Out of the corner of my eye, I caught a sudden movement. Ahalya, who was on her way to the kitchen, had stopped and turned. She was looking directly at me, and if I read her glance right, it indicated that her husband didn't know the truth. That he didn't understand her at all.

There was a mystery here. I hoped I'd have a chance to solve it.

Over dinner, the men discussed many things that affected the state of our continent of Bharatvarsha. Gautam was surprisingly knowledgeable about issues such as wars and alliances between kingdoms, who controlled the trade routes, the mountain passes and the river bridges—and rakshasas, which seemed to be the topic he was most passionate about.

'They've become dangerously strong lately, and better organized. Holy men can hardly live in the forest nowadays without being attacked and routed. Several have had to close their gurukulas and send their students home, after a few violent incidents. Even I had to use up my powers—which I gained through decades of meditation—to shift this ashram to a new place when rakshasas besieged it.

'They want the entire forest to themselves. To drive us back into the cities. But as you know, Ram, we rishis can't live in cities. We need to be in nature to teach and pray and follow our ancient customs and perform our fire sacrifices. So there's a conflict, and the rakshasas are winning because the rishis aren't fighters. You've got to help us get rid of them!'

Ram looked concerned. I knew he took the code of the warrior, honour-bound to defend the helpless, very seriously. It was doubly binding when someone asked him directly for aid, as Gautam had just done. 'A huge change seems to have occurred among the rakshasas,' he said. 'They seem much more organized and belligerent. Do you have any ideas why?'

'Oh yes,' Gautam said vehemently. 'I know exactly why. All this started happening ever since they banded together under one leader. They're very loyal to him because he lets them live independently in whichever part of the country they wish and asks little of them except fealty in case there's a major war. They send him tithes of their own will, but he never demands it. He doesn't have to. He's so rich that wealth matters little to him. If they're ever in trouble and appeal to him, he immediately sends an army to help them and to train them for the future. That's why they've been winning all the skirmishes.'

'This leader, what's his name?' Ram asked.

I waited eagerly to hear what Gautam might say, for rakshasa or not, this person seemed to be a better—and smarter—ruler than many of the human kings I'd come across. But at that moment, Ahalya beckoned to me from the alcove. Her arms were full of rushes, and I gathered that she needed my help. I had to follow her—it would have been rude to delay. I felt a pang of regret at not hearing the name of this special rakshasa king. But being alone with Ahalya would give me the chance to ask her something I'd been longing to find out.

Ahalya led me into the small room where Ram and I would sleep that night. There I helped her make a bed with the sweet-smelling rushes. Her movements were as graceful as a dance, and her eyes affectionate, and once she laid her hand upon my head as though in blessing. But when I tried to initiate a conversation, she remained silent. I'd hoped that perhaps when we were away from the men she'd let down her guard and speak. I didn't believe she was observing a vow of silence to gain spiritual merit—I'd seen the look she'd given me.

Meeting Ahalya had made me realize how starved I was for female companionship. Surely she hungered for it too? I missed Urmila terribly, our small, inconsequential, laughter-filled chatter, our outpourings of the heart. I'd been hoping for an opportunity for woman-talk, and, more importantly, an answer to the question that swelled inside me, troublesome as heartburn. But all my efforts to entice Ahalya into speech failed.

The simple bed was soon made. Ahalya turned to leave. It was my last chance. I didn't want to offend or, worse still, hurt her, but I had to know. I clasped her hand and, though her brows drew together in surprise and perhaps displeasure, rushed into speech. 'Forgive me if I'm overstepping my bounds, but an ethical question has been bothering me ever since I heard your story. May I ask?'

Ahalya's frown disappeared. She said, 'I know what you are about to ask. In general, I do not speak of that time in my life. But I will allow you one question because you made a great sacrifice for the sake of love, leaving behind the safety of the palace to follow your husband into grave danger.'

'Danger?' I whispered. The way Ahalya said the word made me uneasy. She seemed to refer to something beyond the usual perils of forest living.

'Yes, danger. I sense it looming ahead, appearing suddenly in a form you do not expect it to take. Perhaps my answer will help you when it strikes.'

Her tone sent a shiver through me. She seemed so sure of the calamity that was about to befall us. But how could it? Ram and Lakshman were great warriors, and always vigilant. I, too, had kept up with my martial arts practice, even though I knew the men regarded my exercises with amusement.

Pushing my misgivings aside, I said, 'Please explain to me why you were punished by your husband. Doesn't it go against the dictates of dharma? You did nothing wrong. You were tricked by Indra. Why should you be made to suffer for his sin? For being a victim? It was unfair.'

Ahalya smiled, a smile at once sad and sweet that transformed her face so that I caught a glimpse of the ravishingly beautiful woman she must have been earlier. 'I tortured myself with these same thoughts many times as I lay stone-bound. Yes, that was part of the curse—that I should feel every moment of my interment. Finally, an answer came. When you put your hand in the fire, knowingly or unknowingly, do you not get burned? Such is the ancient law of the universe. Of karma and its fruit. The idea of motive is irrelevant to it.'

I was shaken by her reply. I'd always thought motive was more important than action, more even than destiny. Could it be that I was wrong? But now another thought troubled me. 'Your husband—he condemned you even before he gave you a chance to speak. You'd been his faithful wife for many years. He loved you—and he knew you loved him. You'd never given him cause to doubt you. And yet he forgot all that in an instant and punished you so severely. I understand that he did it in anger, that in anger we can lose ourselves. But you—when you were turned back into a woman, you forgave him. Forgave him not just his jealous, blind fury, but also for not trusting you, for immediately thinking the worst of you. Or did you? And do you still love him? How is it possible to love someone after they do something like that to you?'

Ahalya turned from me, her face unreadable. 'I have answered one question, as I promised,' she said as she left the room. 'The answer to this one you must figure out through your own life's challenges—they will be upon you soon enough.'

When I came back to the main room, the men were still discussing rakshasas. 'Perhaps that's why destiny brought you to the forest,' Gautam was saying. 'To get rid of them for good. To wipe out their unholy ways. To spread the light of civilization. You must promise me you'll try your best to do that.'

Lakshman nodded in vehement agreement. Ram looked unsure, but then he, too, bowed in assent.

THAT NIGHT, IN BED with Ram, I whispered—because the walls of the ashram, woven of palm fronds, were thin, 'Gautam did Ahalya wrong. She was innocent—I'm convinced of it. But he never gave her a chance to tell her own story before he punished her.'

Ram said, 'Gautam is a revered sage. It's not for me to judge such a holy man's motives. I salvaged the situation, didn't I, the best way I could?'

I had to agree with that, but dissatisfaction still pricked me, a sense of justice left undone. It also bothered me that Ram was so deferential to the sages, so quick to accept whatever they did or wanted him to do.

That night I dreamed of Ahalya, the moment she turned back into a woman. I saw her emerge from rock limb by limb. I saw on her face not joy but the terrible pain of becoming human again. Sage Gautam reached out towards her. His face was suffused with love—and remorse as well. He spoke, and though I couldn't hear his words, I guessed that he asked her pardon.

Ahalya hesitated. I tried to read her expression. Was there hurt in it? Was there forgiveness, because when you truly love someone how can you not forgive them? Was there the realization that of all the imperfect choices open to her, going back to Gautam was the best one?

Finally she put her hand in his. But she didn't smile, and she didn't look at him. Was it then she made the decision that she'd punish him the rest of her life by never speaking to him again, so he'd always remember what he'd done? They receded into mist, leaving me with another lesson: once mistrust has wounded it mortally, love can't be fully healed again.

Fifteen

THE SAGES WE MET IN our travels had recommended we make for the part of Panchabati that bordered the Godavari river. Once there, I found the region wild and mysterious but welcoming as well, with its many banyan trees, its shrubs that sparkled with star-like blossoms, and its proliferation of mysterious species of animals and birds I'd never seen. When Ram said that we'd wandered enough, and that we'd make our home here until the end of our forest days, I agreed happily.

I'd been right about nature testing us. Now it seemed that we'd passed the test, and she showed us her kind and bounteous face. Here in Panchabati I saw brilliant sunsets spreading like a smile across the sky and molten-silver moonrises. I saw stars glimmering like shy eyes from behind veils of cloud. I saw birds and beasts, multi-hued, multi-pelted, so different from the creatures I'd known that I was struck with awe. The plants here were particularly attuned to me. Bushes would pull in their sharp thorns and burst into flower when I watered them or loosened the earth around their roots. Squirrel-like creatures, their long white hair smooth as silk-thread, would scurry up to take berries from my palm. Brilliant blue songbirds with curved beaks would land on my shoulder and allow me to stroke their plumage.

There were others who watched us from afar, only their glistening eyes visible through the thick foliage. I sometimes glimpsed, at a great distance in the sky, bird-like creatures with enormous wings and what appeared to be human heads.

I asked Ram what they were. He said that Vishwamitra had once mentioned descendants of the heavenly eagle, Garuda. They kept an eye on the forest and made sure all was going according to nature's dictates.

Lakshman didn't approve of my friendship with the forest creatures. Some of them, he warned me, might be shape-shifters, tricky, even dangerous. I nodded, mostly to keep the peace. (I'd learned by now that Lakshman didn't like being contradicted.) But I didn't believe him and often, when the men were away hunting, enticed the tiny black-skinned deer, who were my favourite and only came up to my knee, to eat from my hand.

What I loved most about Panchabati was that here, once the brothers had examined the area and found it safe, Ram was finally able to relax. For the first time since I'd known him, he could forget about being a righteous ruler. In this place that seemed apart from the world of cities and towns, he could be, instead, a lover. It transformed him.

He picked wildflowers and braided them, with inexpert tenderness, into my hair. He travelled for miles to find honeycombs for me to suck on, for he knew I had a sweet tooth. With Lakshman's help, he built a one-room hut right on the bank of the Godavari because I said I liked the view. Here Ram and I slept at night, lulled into dreams by the swishing of the river and the fragrance of the flowering vines that I'd planted around the posts.

Where Lakshman slept, or whether he slept at all, I didn't know. Wrapped in my own happiness-cocoon, I'm afraid I didn't pay him as much attention as I should have. On a few occasions when I awoke at night, I saw him standing at the edge of our clearing, bow in hand, listening with such still intensity that he could have been the carving of a warrior. He looked very alone. I'd feel guilty and think that tomorrow I'd cook him a favourite dish—whatever I could manage with my meagre culinary supplies. I'd ask Ram to take the watch so that his brother could get a good night's sleep. I'd insist that we build a second hut where Lakshman could rest in comfort.

Then I'd say to myself, Ram knows what he's doing. I shouldn't interfere. And, relieved with that decision, I'd snuggle closer into my husband's comforting embrace where I could suspend all concerns.

Such is the seduction of love: it makes you not want to think too much. It makes you unwilling to question the one you love.

Thus the years passed, as though in a happy haze. Ten, eleven, twelve, until I lost count.

Panchabati had its problems, of course. In the summers it was humid and airless in the shade of the banyans. In the rainy season, mud squelched underfoot. I'd learned how to pound and boil bark to keep us decent (our original clothing having disintegrated long ago), but the thick material was difficult to dry and we spent months draped in uncomfortable, damp sheets. The dampness attracted insects that whined and bit and seemed particularly fond of my flesh.

Recently, a new problem troubled me. Tired of our diet of fruits and roots, I'd planted a vegetable garden from seeds that Ahalya had given. The vegetables grew enthusiastically, and I was thankful to know that I hadn't lost my touch. But then something strange began to occur. No matter how careful I was, how diligently I constructed a thorn-fence around the garden, I'd wake in the morning to find the best things gone, or worse still, abandoned half-eaten. Sometimes entire plants were ripped out of the ground. It upset me more than it should have when I saw them lying in the mud, injured beyond my healing abilities.

Or perhaps it was something else, recently much in my mind, which was the real reason for my distress: the fact that I was growing older. Other women my age—perhaps even my cousins Shrutakirti and Mandavi back in Ayodhya—already had children. Sometimes I imagined them breastfeeding an infant. The milky smell of the child, the happy weight of him or her in their arms, the way he'd rub his sleepy face against their skin.

ONCE, AFTER WE'D BEEN in the forest for a decade, I asked Ram if we might consider having children. It was hard to speak of it, for it was my secret—and somehow, I felt, illicit—desire. But I forced myself.

'I'm lonely,' I said. 'And the years are passing. I'm not sure how much more time I have for childbearing. Think about it. How hard can it be? All around us animals and birds with far less resources and intelligence are bringing up their families. I promise, I'll take full care of him or her. You won't have to do a thing.'

As soon as I'd spoken, I felt stupid. I was sure Ram would point out that my analogy was flawed. We weren't animals. How could we compare ourselves to them?

But Ram only said, very kindly, 'Dearest, remember, we decided on this long ago, at the beginning of my banishment. It wouldn't be right to subject a child to the dangers of the forest. More importantly, princes and princesses must have a proper education so that they can fulfil their responsibilities as adults. We could never provide them with that here. That is why we've been so careful all these…'

'We can provide them with all the essentials,' I interrupted hotly, unwilling to back down. 'We have so many skills. I could teach them self-defence and cooking and gardening and healing and songs and stories and letters and even regal comportment. Lakshman could teach them hunting and tracking and wrestling. You could teach them all about royal duties and higher morals and the use of special astras, and—'

'Forgive me, my love,' Ram interrupted, his eyes sad. 'I'm sorry that my ill fortune has deprived you of one of the greatest joys of womanhood. But we can't do this until we go back to Ayodhya. I understand your longing, but—'

'You don't understand!' I cried. How could he? He wasn't a woman. Time didn't press on him as heavily. His body wasn't made to harbour another life.

His arms came around me, tight. 'Please be patient for a little while longer, Sita—the way you've been all this time. We only have two more years in the forest. It'll be over soon.'

I pushed him away and fled behind a thicket, where I wept scalding, angry tears. If Ram had scoffed at me, or said I was being unreasonable, I could have handled it better. I could have fought him back. But his kindness only made things worse. 'You *don't* understand my longing,' I whispered fiercely. I wrapped my arms tight around me, but they still ached with emptiness. 'And two years isn't *soon*.'

I never brought up the matter again. What was the point? Ram had already made a decision—based not on emotion or impulse, which I might have been able to change, but on the unshakeable pillars of rightness and duty. Talking further about it and realizing how deep my unhappiness went would only fill him with sorrow and guilt.

That's how love stops us when it might be healthier to speak out, to not let frustration and rage build up until it explodes.

'DEER,' RAM DIAGNOSED WHEN he saw my ravaged garden. 'And maybe rabbits.'

'Not possible,' Lakshman said. 'They wouldn't dare. I walk up and down here all night. Must be rakshasas. They can come and go in the blink of an eye.'

'You're always imagining rakshasas!' Ram laughed. 'Haven't we lived here peacefully for over a decade now? Set a trap—perhaps we'll have venison for dinner.'

Out of loyalty to him, I said nothing. But for once I thought Lakshman may be right. In recent weeks, I'd felt a presence. A sense of being watched—not in a menacing way, but with curiosity. A few times I'd glimpsed a girl, slim and brown as bark, peering from behind a tree. As far as I could tell, she wore no clothes. But she disappeared even before my heart had a chance to speed up, so I wasn't sure.

I didn't mention her to Ram. Before we had our last discussion about children, I used to tell him everything, but not anymore. Perhaps it was because I was still angry. Perhaps I just wanted to talk to the girl. Get to know her a little. If we became friends, perhaps I'd feel less lonely, less obsessed with the baby I couldn't have. I guessed that Ram—and especially Lakshman—would be suspicious of her. Who she was. Where she'd come from. Very probably Lakshman would drive her away. I didn't want that.

I WAS BATHING IN the river when the girl showed up next, popping up from behind a giant clump of elephant ears, startling me into swallowing a large mouthful of water. She watched with interest as I coughed and sputtered and grabbed for my bark-cloth, winding the unwieldy, dripping garment around me the best I could. Her teeth, bared in amusement, were very white and pointed, and her dark skin gleamed. Though I could only see her head and neck, I was quite sure now she didn't have any clothes on. Possibly the forest-people she belonged to didn't believe in clothing. How freeing that must be, to feel the cool, bracing wind on your skin, leaves and rushes brushing up against you like silk, instead of this stiff, fraying bark-cloth.

Even before I'd managed to catch my breath, the girl began to barrage me with questions.

'What's your name? Where are you from? What are you doing here? Don't you know it's dangerous? This lake, especially. There are crocodiles in the water.'

I told her briefly about Ram's vow and how the three of us ended up in the forest. 'I don't bother the crocodiles, so they leave me alone,' I added.

The girl narrowed her eyes. 'You shouldn't be here. This part of the forest belongs to my brothers, Khar and Dushan, and they don't like intruders.'

'We didn't know about your brothers,' I said. 'Nor have we seen them. Otherwise we'd have asked permission. What is the name of your tribe?'

'They've been keeping an eye on you,' she said. 'You'll see them when they want you to. Let's hope that never happens. They're not exactly the friendly type.' Ignoring the last part of my question, she went on to more queries.

'Where do you come from?'

I told her.

'Ayodhya, huh?' she said. 'Never heard of it. But then, I don't keep much track of cities. I prefer the freedom of forest life. Tell me again, are both the men with you your mates?

'Oh no,' I said, scandalized. 'The fairer one, he's my brother-in-law.'

'I like dark better too,' she said. 'My husband, he had beautiful dark skin. Day or night, it gleamed like someone had oiled it lovingly. But he's dead now.'

Before I could say how sorry I was, she disappeared.

Sixteen

We were sitting on the mud porch of our hut in the evening, enjoying a strong wind that had sprung up. It would probably rain later, and the leaf-thatched roof of our hut would leak, but for the moment the wind had chased the mosquitoes away, and that was a pleasant relief. Ram and Lakshman were discussing astras, while I was daydreaming about being back in Ayodhya. Dressed in queenly silks, I sat on my veranda, which was filled with more flowers than ever. I'd just had a long hot-water bath, and a maid was rubbing scented oils into my hair. A little girl with long hair, curly like Ram's, ran in, an apologetic nurse following at her heels, and clambered into my lap. When the nurse tried to take her away, she threw her arms around my neck and held me tight.

A movement at the edge of the clearing dissolved my pleasant daydream. It was the girl from the lake, but now she looked different. She wore garlands of white flowers around her neck and wrists, and against them her skin glowed like polished onyx. Flowers decorated her nose and ears and were woven so skilfully into her curly, unruly hair that they looked like they'd grown there. She wore a sari—if one could call it that. It was made of a pink fabric, at once sheer and iridescent, like nothing I'd ever seen, wound tight around her curves and reaching only to her knees. She pulled at it from time to time. I could tell she wasn't used to wearing it. Still, she walked with confidence, swaying her hips in a clearly sexual way, without inhibition. I wanted to feel offended. But there was something innocent and natural in her movements, like a peacock preening itself in mating season. In her own way she was beautiful, with a wild scent about her that I could smell even from this distance, like musk or rain.

I was eager to talk further with her, but this time I was clearly not the focus of her attention. She ignored me and made straight for the men—my husband, to be precise.

'Greetings, handsome one!' she said to Ram. 'Welcome to my forest. I'm pleased to see you. We don't get to see men too often, this deep in the wilderness. And when we do, they're usually ugly, woodcutter-hunter types, or rishis, who are worse, all scrawny and severe—which clearly you're not. So tell me, who are you, and what are you doing here?'

What was she playing at? I thought, annoyed. I'd already given her all this information.

As I stared at the girl, I noticed that a glittery film flitted over her face like a cloud. I wondered if she'd thrown a glamour over her true appearance. The thought pulled me back to the Hall of the Bow on the day the king of the rakshasas had come to try his luck. He'd had a similar glimmering around him, keeping us from seeing his true appearance. I wondered what this woman really looked like, and suddenly I was concerned. My heart began to beat faster. Was she a rakshasi? And if so, what did she want?

I tried to catch the men's eye and figure out what they were thinking. Lakshman didn't look up from the arrows he was sharpening, but I could see the frown on his face. Ram, courteous as always, told the woman briefly who we were and why we were here. I considered announcing that I'd already met her and given her all this information, but then I thought I'd wait and see what she was up to. Besides, Ram would be displeased that I hadn't told him about our meeting.

'Ayodhya,' the woman said. 'It sounds very grand! I know I've heard of it, even though I live so far away.'

Indeed you have, I thought. Because I told you just this morning.

'I came up here from across the ocean,' she continued, 'to visit my brothers. I'm from a royal family, too. An asura family.'

A shiver went through me. I'd gleaned, from listening in on the men's conversations with the sages, that that was what the more militant rakshasas liked to call themselves. *Asura. Not-god.* Implying they were better.

Lakshman's head had jerked up and he was now watching the woman carefully.

She didn't seem to notice. 'Not to brag,' she continued, 'but we're probably the most famous asura clan. My oldest brother—he's the king—is feared even by the gods. We live on a magical island in the middle of the ocean. My brother's built a palace there. I'm not much for palaces, but even I can see how fine it is. Me, I prefer roaming in the forest. Living the natural life. Plus I like to speak my mind—and that can get you in trouble in court. Wouldn't you agree?'

Lakshman threw her a sharp glance, but Ram only smiled noncommittally. That was encouragement enough for her to continue.

'You're probably wondering what my name is. I've quite a few, depending on who I feel like being. Minakshi. Surpanakha. My family called me that because they thought I had beautiful nails. You can call me Kaamarupini, the desirable one.'

Now even Ram was getting impatient. 'What can I do for you, lady?' he asked brusquely.

Kaamarupini lowered her head bashfully. Or was that part of her act? 'I know I'm talking too much. It must be because I'm nervous. I haven't done this before, and certainly not with a human. I know my family won't approve, but I don't care. They never approve of me, anyway. What I wanted to tell you is that I've been watching you for a while, and—' here she stammered a bit, then spoke in a rush—'I really like you. So I'm asking you to be my mate.'

I was outraged. Wait just one moment! I wanted to say. Can't you see he has a perfectly satisfactory mate already? But I remained silent, trusting that Ram would know the right way to defuse this situation.

Later I'd wonder, was that my first mistake with Surpanakha? Could I have defused the situation if I'd intervened before things escalated? Do we women trust too much when we love? Do we expect our men to solve every problem that comes up?

'I guarantee you,' Kaamarupini continued, 'I'll make you happy. I know all kinds of magic. I can fly halfway around the world with you, take you to beaches filled with silver-white sands where no man has ever set foot, or to mountains so high that from their peaks you can see the entire world. We can frolic in lakes filled with heavenly lotuses. Or if you prefer, I can build you a palace filled with every comfort you can imagine. And should you ever get tired of my looks, I can change them and become slim and tall, or soft and curvy, or golden-haired like the pale women of the north. In fact, I can fulfil every fantasy of yours.' As she spoke, she made a gesture with her hand, and her hair grew straight and turned pale and silken, like corn fibres.

Ram smiled. But I noticed that though his lips quirked up charmingly, his eyes were cold.

'I'd love to take you up on your generous offer, fair maiden, but as you see,' here he gestured toward me, 'I have a wife, and I've sworn an oath not to take another mate.'

The girl looked confused, which was understandable. Plenty of humans, too—Dasharath included—had been confused as to why Ram had sworn to such an unnecessary and inconvenient vow, particularly when no one had asked him to. In any case, I was glad that matters had been clarified. I waited for Ram to say goodbye and for the girl to leave so that I could go back to my daydreams.

But Ram threw me a quick smile as though sharing a private joke, though I didn't exactly grasp what it might be, and continued. 'Why don't you talk to my brother, Lakshman. He's better looking than me—fair-skinned, more muscular. Most important, he's all alone in the forest and would surely appreciate some female company.'

I was shocked. True, Lakshman hadn't taken the one-wife vow. Still I felt outraged on my sister's behalf and upset at Ram's insensitivity. And confused as well. It wasn't like my husband to joke like this. What was he thinking of?

The girl, too, looked confused. She glanced at Lakshman, who looked thunderous, and then back at Ram.

Surely now Lakshman would lose his temper and send her off with a cutting comment or a threat, I thought.

Then I saw a lightning glance pass between the brothers. Lakshman's expression changed immediately, and I realized that the two brothers were in perfect synchrony, like a single soul in two bodies. Would I ever be able to reach that kind of understanding with Ram, no matter how much I loved him?

Probably not, I thought, a bit sadly. Loving someone didn't necessarily mean you understood them. In fact, remembering Dasharath and Kaikeyi, I wondered if loving someone too much prevented you from seeing them less clearly than an objective bystander.

Lakshman was bowing to Kaamarupini, palms joined.

'With all due respect, beautiful one, I am but the servant of my brother. Why would you wish for a servant to be your mate, you who come from such a glorious lineage, when you can have the master himself? Ask him again—I am certain he can't withstand your charms for too long.'

The girl paused, uncertain, then took a step towards Ram.

Couldn't she see that the men were mocking her? I thought it cruel of them to do so. Admittedly, the girl had gone beyond the norms of maidenly behaviour, offering herself in this manner to a man she barely knew, but perhaps the rules of conduct were different for asuras. In any case, she didn't deserve to be taunted. I gestured to her from behind Ram's back to leave with dignity before things went any further.

But my gesture had a very different effect from what I'd intended. The girl's head snapped up as though she were noticing me for the first time. A look of rage took over her face.

'You puny human female!' she cried. 'You're the reason for this whole problem, isn't it? You're the only thing standing between Ram and me. If you weren't here, he'd fall in love with me right now. Well, I can take care of that!'

In the blink of an eye, she changed again, swelling to twice her size. Now her face was black and monstrous, and her eyes pulsed red. Her hair writhed like snakes. Her teeth grew into fangs. Her nails, too, grew until they were curved and sharp as scimitars. 'I am Surpanakha, your doom,' she screamed as she rushed at me.

I flinched, more startled than afraid, the way I'd be if a slender, pretty chameleon had suddenly puffed itself up to scare off predators.

My movement had caught Ram's eye, and his face turned dark with anger.

'It's all right,' I called to him as I braced myself in warrior stance, knees slightly bent, hands fisted. Asura or not, I was confident that I could handle her, turning her strength against herself. The girl had probably used magic to appear fiercer than she really was, and in case I got into trouble, Ram was there to help me.

But Ram's words cut through the air like a knife. 'I will not have my wife terrorized in this way. Lakshman, take care of this immoral, unnatural creature.'

Before his words had stopped echoing in my ears, before I had a chance to cry out *no*, Lakshman picked up his bow and, in one swift motion, released an arrow that corkscrewed through the air and chopped off the girl's nose and ears.

I watched, frozen with shock, as blood cascaded down Surpanakha's face, staining her shimmery pink sari. She looked at my husband, her eyes full of disbelief that someone could do such a thing to her when all she'd offered him was love. Then, screaming her pain and outrage, she vanished in a swirl of red mist.

From a distance we heard her final words, 'You'll be sorry. Ah, you'll be sorry. All of you. My brothers shall know of this—and then you'll be sorry you were ever born.'

THAT NIGHT NONE OF us slept. Lakshman paced around the hut, as alert as a panther on the prowl. Ram sat at the door, his bow and arrows ready. His muscles gleamed tautly in the dappled moonlight. I lay on my bed of leaves, trying not to toss and turn. Ram had sent me inside and instructed me to sleep, saying I had nothing to worry about. The two of them would protect me. I didn't doubt that part, though I would have preferred to sit beside Ram, helping him keep watch. Sleep was an impossibility, anyway. What kept me awake, though, wasn't fear. It was the vision of the girl, her gashed, bleeding face, the shock in her eyes.

That, and the conversation I'd had with the two men afterwards.

'Did you need to be so harsh?' I'd asked, once Surpanakha's screams had died away. 'To mutilate her so horribly? She was just an infatuated girl—you could've easily scared her off.'

'We were protecting you,' Ram said. He sounded hurt. He was right. It was his concern for me that had made him react so quickly and harshly. Knowing that made me feel worse.

'You don't understand, Sister-in-law,' Lakshman said heatedly. 'They're not human like us. They're rakshasas. They can't be treated with human courtesy. They don't understand it, and they certainly don't appreciate it. If we'd done anything less to her, she would've just thought we were weak. She would've come back with her whole horde to attack us when we were sleeping.'

'Lakshman's right,' Ram added. 'You can't trust a rakshasa. They'll turn on you any moment like a venomous snake—that's just how they're made. In fact, they're worse than snakes because they're devious. You haven't heard the horrifying stories the rishis told us that time when we went to fight Tarhaka. How they'd take pleasure in skinning the sages alive. The best thing you can do with a rakshasa is to kill it as quickly as possible.'

I stared at him, surprised at his vehemence. In earlier times, Ram had expressed regret at having to kill rakshasas. What had made him change?

'In fact,' he continued, 'Lakshman was being kind to this one, sparing her life because she was a female.'

I didn't think that living with a mutilated face was any easier than a clean death, especially for a woman who had so badly wanted a mate. But saying this would have led us to a confrontation, and at this time, particularly, we needed to stick together.

I blamed love, too, for my silence. How it makes us back down from protesting because we're afraid of displeasing the beloved, or because we're afraid that our disagreement is the symptom of a greater disease: incompatibility of values.

So I said—though I couldn't keep the shrillness from my voice, 'Don't you think she'll come back with her whole horde, anyway? Doesn't she have even more reason now?'

Ram misunderstood my tone. 'Don't be afraid, dearest. No matter how many rakshasas this Surpanakha brings back, we're ready for them.'

Lakshman added, 'Ram probably never told you—you know how modest he is—but the rishis blessed us with a special boon after we killed Tarhaka and her horde. Our quivers will never be empty of arrows. Those rakshasas don't have a chance!'

'Can't you see, we'll be doing them a service,' Ram said. 'Helping to bring peace to the forests, making them safer for the rishis.'

I didn't argue further. I could see the men wouldn't change their minds. Their belief in the superiority of their own ways was too deeply ingrained in them. But I wasn't satisfied. We were visitors to the forest, which already had its own rules, its own rhythm, its own savage beauty. It belonged more to the rakshasas than to us. What right did we have to cause destruction to those who had been here long before we came?

THE RAKSHASAS ARRIVED SOON, as the men had predicted, waves of them, camouflaged by darkness because the moon had disappeared. Perhaps that was part of their magic, or perhaps they just knew nature's cycles and made use of them. Lakshman shot a fire arrow into a tall pipal tree, which burst into flame. I gasped, feeling its burning pain. And then we could see them all: wave after wave, white war-paint swirled over their dark skin, mouths distended in outrage as they yelled their battle cries, their vengeance for their sister.

Mingled with fear and disgust, I couldn't help but feel sympathy. In their place, wouldn't I have done the same?

They died, of course, every single one, screaming their pain as their souls left their bodies. Because whatever the rishis might have said to Ram and Lakshman, I refused to believe they didn't have souls. Stepping out onto the porch in the morning, I was horrified by the carnage confronting me. The expressions on the faces of the dead were not so different from what one might see on human soldiers: fear and desperation and pain. Their blood, which I'd expected to be a monstrous black, was red as ours, staining the entire forest floor as far as I could see. But everything it had come into contact with—plants, grass, even hundred-year old trees, had shrivelled up.

'We'll have to move from here,' Ram said. 'When their bodies decompose, they let out poisonous fumes.'

He was right. I was already feeling a little dizzy, and the stench was overwhelming. Still, I felt we needed to do something.

'I understand that you had to kill them. They attacked us, after all,' I told Ram. 'But shouldn't we do something for the bodies? Cremate them, maybe, like you would have with human enemies?'

'They don't deserve such respect,' Lakshman said. But Ram, more practical, explained that their decomposing bodies were highly flammable and might cause a forest fire if we tried to cremate them.

I capitulated, but before we left, I walked around the piles of dead, my sari pressed against my nose, searching. I was looking for Surpanakha's body. I was determined to give her, at least, a burial. But she wasn't there.

We moved upriver, where the wind blew clear. We found a suitable spot and built another hut. I planted new flowers. Soon the entire roof bloomed sunrise-orange with trumpet vines, and the porch was overhung with curtains of jasmine that filled our nights with fragrance and gave Ram and me all the privacy we could desire. For a while, the men watched carefully for rakshasas, but maybe they'd killed them all, for no others disturbed us.

Except in my dream, one that kept coming back. In it, the mutilated Kaamarupini knelt in front of an enormous, jewelled throne in a courtroom whose roof receded into stars. On the throne sat a man whose face I could not see. He didn't raise his voice. Still, it cut through the entire hall. It was distorted with tears and fury yet strangely familiar.

'Tell me who has done this to you, sister. I will personally make sure they are punished—and I will choose the revenge that will hurt them the most.'

Seventeen

TIME PASSED. THE DAYS FELL on us like gentle rain; the nights wrapped us in gauzy arms embroidered with stars. Only a few months, and then we'd be making our way back to Ayodhya.

Ayodhya! After so many years in the forest, the city seemed unreal to me, a place out of an old tale. If someone had asked me what the palace had looked like, or even my quarters, I wouldn't have been able to answer. Thoughts of returning there filled me with turmoil, worries and elation jostling one another. All the people I'd known there—how much they must have changed by now! And in their eyes I'd see how much I'd changed. I thought of Kaushalya. Had grief aged her? I longed to see Urmila. She'd be upset with me for having abandoned her for so long. I'd have to work long and hard to cajole her out of her well-deserved anger. And what would happen when we finally came face to face with Kaikeyi? Ram may have forgiven her, but Lakshman had not, and of my own feelings I was unsure.

I knew I'd miss the forest in spite of its hardships, for I'd known a kind of freedom here, a lightness that I'd never experience again once I was crowned queen of Ayodhya. Most important, here I'd had Ram all to myself. In Panchabati, he had shed his responsibilities as son and prince and become, foremost, my friend and lover. Though we'd been married for so long, we still played courtship games, I pretending to be upset over little things, he wooing me back into good humour with a small forest-gift. Sometimes he sang to me, making me smile because he was always slightly off-key, my husband who was so perfect at everything else. For me, that was part of his charm.

Lakshman probably felt we were being silly, but uncharacteristically he kept his thoughts to himself, giving us as much privacy as possible. In turn, I allowed him to have his own special time with his brother to go hunting or fishing, promising not to venture outside the hut on those occasions.

We both knew that once Ram became king, he'd grow distant from us. He'd belong, first and foremost, to his people. We accepted that that was how it had to be.

There were no more attacks by rakshasas. Ram and Lakshman must have killed them all. Or perhaps news of their battle-prowess had sped through the rakshasa tribes, and no one else dared to face them. My dreams of Surpanakha had ceased, too, so I didn't bother to tell Ram about them.

The deer appeared soon after that.

From the first, I sensed there was something unusual about the animal. For one, it was larger than any of the other deer I'd seen, and its skin wasn't spotted but a clean, shining gold. Everything about it gleamed—its antlers, its hooves, the lake-black eyes it solemnly regarded me with as though it had things it wanted to tell me. For another, it wasn't afraid of me. It watched as I walked towards it with a handful of the fresh spinach leaves I grew in my garden, emerald green and dewy, but unlike the other deer, it wouldn't take them from my hand, nor from the ground when I lay them down and backed away. When I approached it again, it allowed me to reach a certain closeness, and then it moved away, stepping elegantly, quite unafraid. Its strangeness, of course, was part of its appeal. But the most unusual thing about the deer, though I wouldn't realize it until later, was that I couldn't stop thinking about it.

When I told Ram about the deer, he smiled indulgently, as though I were a child to be humoured. I could see that he didn't believe me when I insisted that it was different from all the other deer I had seen. This annoyed me. I decided that I would conquer the deer. If charm did not work, I would employ subterfuge. I felt a strange desire to throw my arms around its neck, to hug its silkiness. I would weave a rope of dry grasses, tie it around its neck, and lead it victoriously to Ram. When we went back to Ayodhya, I would take it with me.

But the deer was a wily creature. It allowed me to approach closer each day, but every time it shied away just before I could touch it. It was as though it were teasing me. My need for the deer grew like an ache, an addiction. It merged with my hunger for a baby, which I'd carefully kept secret from Ram.

AFTER A WEEK OF this, I was feverish with frustration.

'I want you to catch this deer for me,' I said to Ram. 'I've got to have it.'

Ram looked at me in surprise because it wasn't my habit to make demands. But I wasn't myself. That's what happens when we crave something so much. I made Ram hide inside the hut while I waited outside with my usual offering of spinach leaves until the deer appeared. Then I whispered to Ram to take a look.

The deer appeared even more beautiful, if that were possible, on this day. Its large, expressive eyes were fringed with thick lashes. Its antlers sparkled as though studded with jewels. When Ram stepped out from the hut, I tensed, afraid that it would flee into the forest, but it only retreated to the edge of the clearing. Even when Lakshman arrived, lugging a load of firewood, it didn't disappear. From the shadow of the trees it watched us, unblinking. For a moment, I thought its eyes glimmered with tears. But I was only being fanciful.

Ram was watching the deer intently. He hadn't responded to me.

'Isn't it beautiful?' I whispered again. I waited eagerly for him to agree, a little indulgently, as he usually did when I got excited over something I came across in the forest. But he only said, 'I don't have a good feeling about this animal. Something about it isn't right. It makes me uncomfortable.'

Lakshman had come up to us by this time. 'I feel the same way, brother,' he said. 'Maybe it's a rakshasa in disguise, here to spy upon us. The best thing to do is scare it off. Shall I do that?' He reached for his bow, and the deer stepped backward warily until only the tip of its antlers showed through the bushes.

I was suddenly furious with Lakshman and his continuous talk about rakshasas. What right had he to spoil my innocent pleasure? God knows I had few enough in this wilderness.

I turned to Ram, sure he'd honour my request. In such matters, he was always a most indulgent and loving husband. But today he said, 'Better you forget about this creature, Sita, whatever it is. I'll get you something else—another deer, if you wish.'

Anger throbbed inside me, cold as iron. Did he think I was a child, to be distracted, to be fobbed off with a toy, a replacement to suit his convenience? What was wrong with him? Why was he being so insensitive today, siding with his brother? Couldn't he feel how achingly lonely I was? How much I longed for something to hold in my empty arms and cuddle and take care of? Something that depended upon me for its happiness, maybe even its survival, the way a child might. The way a husband never would.

The words flew from my mouth before I knew what I was saying. The language I used was formal, my tone more suited to the royal court than the leaf-thatched hut I was standing in front of. 'Did you not, at the time of our marriage ceremony, promise to provide for all my needs? I think you will agree that I have rarely asked you for anything all these years, and even then only small things. But today I am asking. I wish for that deer and no other, however difficult it might be to get. If you refuse, I will understand that the words of the heir of the House of Raghu are worth less than the ashes that are left behind when a fire dies.'

My voice reverberated in the clearing. The deer took a step forward, as though drawn to it. The whites of its eyes glinted. The look in them was strangely human. I shivered. Why did my words sound so familiar—and so ominous? I longed to take them back, but my pride wouldn't allow me.

Ram looked into my face, his eyes filled with so much love and sorrow that I wanted to throw myself at him and embrace him with both arms. To say, *Forget the deer. I have you. That's enough.* I even took a step forward. But it was too late. He'd already shouldered his bow and was turning away. His last words to me before he disappeared into the dark tangle of trees where the deer had fled were, 'Since this animal matters so much to you, I'll bring it back, alive or dead.' To Lakshman, he said, 'Brother, guard Sita until I return.'

And Lakshman's voice, resolute: 'Don't worry, brother. I'll guard her, I swear it upon my honour.'

TIME PASSED. BUT AH, how slowly it passed, the moments like grains that ants were carrying from a mountain of sugar, one at a time. The sun tilted past its zenith. The shadows lengthened and turned purple, though it was too early for them to do so. The forest grew unnaturally cold. Far above, I thought I saw a strange shape soaring and wheeling, disappearing in and out of clouds. I couldn't tell what it was. Lakshman paced up and down wordlessly, curtly refusing food when I offered it to him. He wanted me to know he was displeased with me for sending Ram on this stupid errand. And therefore I couldn't share my unease with him, nor my mortification at having allowed anger to get the best of me, to have parted from Ram with such bitter words.

How entangled love is with expectation, that poison vine! The stronger the expectation, the more our anger towards the beloved if he doesn't fulfil it—and the less our control over ourselves. Why else couldn't I stop myself when I knew very well that I shouldn't bring up the House of Raghu, and their pride in keeping their word? I was well aware that it was the chink in Ram's armour. I shouldn't have used my knowledge, born of intimacy, against him. But I did.

After a while, my mortification was overshadowed by worry. Ram was never gone for so long when he went hunting. Even on the rare occasions when he'd come across tigers or lions, he'd dispatched them with ease. And this was just a deer! He should have caught it already. I knew he had special astras that turned into nets or ropes and bound his target effortlessly. So why hadn't he come back yet?

Finally, I couldn't stop myself. 'I'm afraid for Ram,' I told Lakshman. 'I wish I hadn't sent him after that deer. What if he's in danger?'

Lakshman, plain speaker that he was, said, 'That's right. You shouldn't have nagged him to go. We both told you something was very wrong with that deer.' Then, seeing the distress on my face, he added, kindly, 'But you needn't worry about Ram. There's not a creature in this forest, beast or rakshasa, that can hurt him.'

The conviction in his voice calmed me. But just then I heard a cry. It was Ram's voice, though I'd never heard it distorted like this with pain and anguish. 'Sita! Sita! Ah, I'm wounded. Ah, treachery. Brother Lakshman, I need you. Come to my aid, brother.'

My entire body began to tremble. 'Lakshman, get your bow and arrows! Didn't you hear that? You must go. Go right now! Ram's in trouble. He needs your help. Maybe that deer was a rakshasa, after all—'

Lakshman shook his head. 'That's not Ram. Can't be. I know it for sure. Sister-in-law, you've got to believe me. You haven't seen Ram fight the way I have. He's a match for even the king of rakshasas. Besides, he wouldn't be wailing and begging that way, like some coward weakling. That's not his style.'

The voice came to us again, borne over a shuddering wind. It seemed fainter this time. 'Brother, help me. Come quick—' It broke off mid-sentence.

'Go, Lakshman,' I cried. 'Clearly, he's in trouble of some kind. Go for my peace of mind, even if you don't think Ram needs you—'

But, infuriatingly, Lakshman didn't move. 'I promised Ram that I'd guard you. No matter what happens, I can't leave you alone. You're a lot more vulnerable than he is. I'm sure all this is rakshasa magic. Ignore it. Have more faith in your husband!'

I heard the voice again. It was clearly Ram's. How could Lakshman claim it wasn't?

'Lakshman!' it said. It sounded more distant now, as though Ram was being dragged away even as he called to us. 'Sita!' There was a horrible choking, gurgling sound. Then an ominous silence.

'Lakshman,' I cried, weeping. 'As your elder sister-in-law, I order you to go!'

Lakshman shook his head. 'With all due respect, Sister-in-law, my elder brother's order takes precedence over yours. He told me to take care of you, and by my honour, that's what I'm going to do.'

I paced up and down, wringing my hands, crazed with worry. What could I say to Lakshman to shake him up? To force him to go to my beleaguered husband's aid? Then it came to me, the greatest insult I could think of.

'How dare you speak of honour!' I cried, pouring all the taunting rage I could summon into my voice, regretting the words even as I formed them. 'I understand now why you're refusing to go to help Ram. You want me for yourself. You're hoping that, if Ram dies, you'll make me your wife. Ah, why not? After all, he's only a half-brother. My poor Ram! Bharat has taken his kingdom. Why shouldn't you take his wife? But it won't work, I tell you. I'll kill myself rather than let you lay even a finger on me.'

Lakshman's face went white with shock at my words. I braced myself for his rage, but he only said, with great sadness, 'You know full well that I respect you like my own mother and want nothing more than to protect you. But after what you've said, questioning my honour, I can't remain here. I'll break my promise to Ram, something I've never done in my life. And I'll go in search of him, though I know he's perfectly safe. But you, left alone—you're in grave peril. I feel it in my bones.' He took his bow and, with its sharp edge, inscribed a large circle around the hut. I think he whispered a mantra while he drew it, for the line began to glow like it was on fire.

'Don't step outside this rekha on any account,' he said to me as he left. 'I hope it'll keep you safe. I pray to the gods to watch over you.'

But his voice was bleak, as though he didn't expect much of them.

Eighteen

ONCE LAKSHMAN DISAPPEARED DOWN THE same forest path that Ram had taken, I sat down heavily on the threshold, covered my face with my hands and wept in regret and despair. How beautifully the day had begun—and look where we were now. It was all my fault. Why had I wanted that deer so much? Thinking back, I couldn't understand it. It had been like a fever, that strange desire that had gripped me, as though I'd been bewitched. And though I didn't regret forcing Lakshman to go to Ram's help, I cringed when I remembered the cruel tactics I'd used. The hurt, and then the disgust, in his eye, that I could say such things. *Just let Ram be safe*, I cried over and over. *Please, Goddess, let him come back to me quickly. I promise, I'll never ask him—or you—for anything again. And I'll apologize profusely to Lakshman. I will! I'll explain to him that I never meant any of those harsh words. I'll let him spend as much time with his brother as he wants, and I'll stay out of their way.*

Often when I prayed fervently for something, there was a sign. But today, nothing. Clearly, I'd angered the goddess—and who could blame her, when I'd been so selfish and stupid?

I WAS STARTLED FROM my entreaties by a gentle voice. 'Good day, lady. The blessings of a sadhu upon you and your house.'

A man stood in the clearing, just outside the boundary Lakshman had drawn around me, its fiery contours now faded into dusty ordinariness. He was dressed in the orange robes of a holy mendicant. He must have been on the road for a while, because his robes were tattered and his hair, falling about his face, was matted and unkempt. We'd come across wandering sadhus like him as we traversed the forest, though recently, as we went deeper into Panchabati, we'd seen less of them. I always enjoyed their description of their journeys and their words of wisdom. It was a special pleasure to see their hungry eyes light up as I offered them whatever simple meal I'd prepared.

I was particularly thankful to see this sadhu today and decided to ask him to keep me company until the men returned. Talking to him would keep my mind from the horrific images my wild imagination kept conjuring up: Ram injured; Ram fallen into a pit, perhaps, or stuck in a bog; Ram lying alone, close to death. When my husband returned safe and sound—as surely he would, by divine grace—the sadhu's presence would temper some of his anger. Ram was rarely angry, but this time, when he learned of the unforgivable things I'd said to Lakshman, I knew he'd be furious.

I greeted the sadhu respectfully and asked him his name.

'You may call me Dashaanan,' he replied.

It was a strange name, one I hadn't heard before. The sadhu must have seen my surprise, because he gave a wry smile and said, 'Ten headed—it refers to the many weaknesses that make me stumble on the spiritual path. But enough of me. Who are you, maiden, and why are you alone in this dangerous forest?'

Speaking was a welcome respite from worry, so I told him my name, and how I'd been found in the earth of Mithila, so that no one really knew where I came from, and how Ram had married me by lifting and stringing Shiva's great bow.

'Sita,' he said, 'Sita.' He spoke my name slowly, meditatively. I thought I saw a glint in his eyes, but I must have been mistaken, for when he looked at me, his pupils were old and dull and glazed over with cataracts. 'Fascinating story, your marriage. How many wonders there are in this creation! Tell me more about your adventures.'

That was all the encouragement I needed. I described my beloved Ram to him in great detail, and his loyal brother Lakshman also. I explained about Kaikeyi and the boons she'd been able to claim because men from the House of Raghu never went back on their promise. I described our thirteen years of difficult wandering, and listened with some satisfaction to his words of sympathy and his praise because he thought I'd been such a good wife and put up with so much. Finally, I told him of the golden deer and confessed—a little shamefacedly—how I'd fought with my husband and forced him to go after it. I even voiced my fear that it might be a wicked rakshasa in disguise.

'It might, indeed,' the sage said, and a strange look, akin to sorrow, passed over his face. 'In which case it would have led your husband far into the wilderness, for rakshasas are wily creatures. That's too bad, for I would have loved to meet your illustrious husband—such a brave warrior, a veritable scourge to evil rakshasas everywhere. But I can't delay any longer. There's a holy cave some distance from here, and I must reach it before nightfall.'

'Please rest awhile in the shade of our porch,' I entreated. 'Ram and Lakshman will be back soon. Lakshman will bring you fresh fruits. Ram will fetch water to wash your feet. I'll gather the wild rice which grows by the river and cook it for you, along with the vegetables from my garden. I'm a fast cook. There will still be plenty of time for you to reach your cave.'

But the sadhu shook his head. 'My vows of monkhood will not allow that. Already I've spent too long with you, a woman and a householder, and I'm afraid this has reduced my merits. I'm not supposed to even step onto the shadow of a house, let alone take comfort on its porch. If you wish to give me alms, you may give them now. But I can only accept them from where I'm standing.'

It would be a great shame if a holy man left our home—makeshift though it was—empty-handed. I ran inside and gathered, in the pallu of my sari, whatever food I had—just a few fruits, unfortunately. But when I came out, I realized that the sage stood too far away for me to reach him without crossing the boundary Lakshman had created for me. I didn't quite believe that staying inside the line would keep me from all harm. But having spoken so many cruel words to Lakshman, I didn't want to further upset him by disregarding his dictum.

'Please come a little closer, sage,' I said, a little embarrassedly, pointing to the line. 'I'm not supposed to cross this rekha.' Even as I spoke, it seemed a silly thing to say.

The sadhu drew himself up. I could feel indignation rising from him, shimmering like heat waves on a summer day. His face grew dark with anger. I resigned myself to a tongue-lashing. Why was it that our holy men who made a big deal of giving up so many things—comfort, fame, family—couldn't seem to give up their tempers?

'Are you trying to tempt me, woman?' he cried. 'Are you trying to lure me near you so that I'll break my vows? Didn't I just tell you, I do *not* set foot in the compounds of householders? Forget about your alms! I don't want them. One more day of going hungry will not kill me. But I must say, this isn't the kind of hospitality I expected from the House of Raghu—or from the daughter of Janak and Sunaina!'

His words sent my mind spinning. Living with Ram, I'd taken on some of his sensitivities. I knew how mortified he'd be if he learned that a sadhu had left our home complaining that he was disappointed by Raghu hospitality. But worse: by calling cleverly on my father and mother he'd made me feel personally guilty. How did he even know their names? I hadn't told him anything about them. Clearly, the sage had occult powers.

It had been a prime rule in my parents' palace that no one—holy mendicant or common beggar—went away hungry. My mother had impressed upon me that it was our duty as householders to take care of the guests that landed at our door, invited or otherwise. By failing in that duty, might I bring a new spate of bad luck down on us? Holy men often possessed strange siddhis. Might his ill-will obstruct our safe return to Ayodhya, to Ram's long-awaited coronation?

I swayed between my two choices: breaking my illogical promise to Lakshman or failing in my duty to my guest, who was additionally a holy man. Which was worse? What would Ram have wanted me to do?

At this moment, the face that rose in my mind, strangely, was that of my father-in-law. For the first time, I felt a deep sympathy for King Dasharath and the options he'd been faced with, far more difficult than mine, complicated further by the bonds of love: to break his word to his favourite wife, or to unfairly banish his dearest son.

There are no easy answers, Dasharath's voice said inside my head. *Especially when we want to please the one we love. That same love clouds our eyes and doesn't allow us to see what's right in front of us.*

There was no more time to debate the issue. The sadhu had stomped off towards the same thicket where, seemingly a lifetime ago, the golden deer had vanished.

'Stop, sage,' I cried. 'I'm coming.'

AS SOON AS I stepped over Lakshman's rekha, I knew I'd made a huge mistake. It wasn't only because of the pain that went through me, as though a thousand thorns had pricked me at once. It was also the sage.

One moment he was half-hidden in forest foliage, and the next he was beside me. I didn't understand how he could move so fast. In fact, I hadn't seen him move at all. He had my arm in a hot, vise-grip and was twisting it so that pain ran up all the way to my neck like a wave of fire. His face had changed, the gaunt mendicant features transformed into a handsome, proud and triumphant visage. There was a crown on his head. Gold-woven robes covered him and the jewels in his ears and on his arms dazzled me. Even as I stared at him in horrified disbelief I understood that everything I'd seen before was a glamour spell. Rakshasa glamour.

But where had he come from? Ram and Lakshman had been certain that they'd killed all the rakshasas in the Panchabati forest.

'Shall I chop off your nose and ears, like your husband and his brother did to my sister?' he asked. 'Or shall I torture and kill you, and leave your mutilated body for them to find—as I found my brothers?' The anger that quivered in his voice was cold and controlled, his accent elegant but unfamiliar. I should have been too terrified and distraught to notice these things, but I did. The mind works in strange ways. Yes, indeed, because my mind was busy figuring out who this stranger was and why he had come here. Why he'd chosen me as his prey. It was saying, *Of course*. Because even through my anguish and anger, how could I blame him for what he was doing—exacting retribution for the disfigured Surpanakha, and for his brothers, who'd fought to death in their efforts to avenge her.

This must be the other brother Surpanakha had mentioned, the one who ruled a beautiful, distant land across the ocean. I tried to remember if she'd told us his name, but my heart pounded so loudly, I couldn't think.

I listened for Ram and Lakshman, hoping against hope to hear the crunch of leaves under their footsteps. But there was nothing. The deer-rakshasa that Surpanakha's brother must have brought with him had led Ram far away indeed. I was alone.

I had only myself to depend on.

I ignored the burning pain in my arm and shoulder and aimed a sudden kick, with all my strength, at the back of my captor's knees. It was one of my favourite martial moves, guaranteed to make an opponent lose his balance and fall on his back. I was ready to leap on him and gouge out his eyes in an instant, as I'd been taught. Sometimes the move made an opponent fall face forward—in which case I was prepared to bring down the side of my arm like a blade on the back of his neck, paralysing him.

But the rakshasa didn't even flinch. Instead he laughed and put me effortlessly into a choke-hold so tight that it cut off my breath. In a moment, things were swimming in front of my eyes. In another moment I'd be unconscious—or maybe dead from a broken neck.

'Go ahead and do what you will,' I gasped while I still had the strength to speak. Surpanakha's bleeding face rose in my mind. 'You have the right,' I added.

Inside, I prayed he'd kill me quickly. And if he tortured me, cutting pieces off my body slowly, and eating them raw, in front of my eyes, as some sages had told us rakshasas liked to do, I prayed I'd have the fortitude to not beg for mercy.

THE RAKSHASA DID NEITHER. Instead he loosened his grasp on my throat. I bent over, wheezing and coughing. But I kept my wary eyes on him, partly to be ready for what he'd do next, and partly because there might be another chance to attack him.

The rakshasa gave me a long, considering look. There was, I think, some admiration in it. Then his face hardened. 'Death would be too easy for you, and I'm not the kind of person—unlike your husband—who disfigures a woman and abandons her to a lifetime of sorrow and shame. Nor do I eat human flesh. Most asuras don't. I bet the rishis didn't tell you that, did they?

'This is what I'm going to do instead: I'll take you away to my kingdom and leave your husband to a lifetime of searching and mourning and regretting, knowing that he brought this fate upon you.'

To be taken captive, to spend years—perhaps my entire life—in some faraway rakshasa kingdom as a slave. To know all the while that my beloved husband was looking everywhere for me, crazed with sorrow—for that's the kind of man Ram was, never to give up. To fear that he might not ever find me—or that, even if he knew where I was, he'd be unable to rescue me. How could he—with only

Lakshman to help him—even if he was the best warrior in the world? I imagined the two of them searching vainly in the wilderness, never returning to Ayodhya—because how could they return, admitting in shame that they'd allowed me to be abducted? Sorrow lanced me sharper than any fear I'd had for myself.

Truly, this was a far worse punishment than a swift death.

I struggled mightily, giving up on the elegant moves I'd been taught. I kicked and clawed and bit at the rakshasa, and in between I yelled for help. By now I knew I couldn't defeat him, but I was hoping I could delay him until Ram returned. My nails raised welts on his dark, smooth skin, and my teeth drew blood. Even for a rakshasa, it must have hurt. But he only smiled a wolfish grin—I could see he was enjoying my futile efforts—and whistled. It was a high, wild sound, and in response, something came hurtling down from the sky, some kind of giant glittering bird. No, it was a chariot unlike anything I'd ever seen or imagined, huge and silver and thrumming, with metal wings and gears shaped like flowers. I was so amazed, I couldn't help staring in open-mouthed wonder. For a moment, I even forgot to struggle.

'You might want to close your lips,' the rakshasa said kindly. 'A bug might wander in.'

I snapped shut my jaws and glared at him.

'This is Pushpak,' the rakshasa said with pride, 'the best flying chariot in the world. I wrested it from my half-brother Kubera because he thought he was so much better than us asuras. I think it likes being with me better. Don't you, Pushpak?'

The machine made a purring sound.

'Come along now,' said the rakshasa. 'There'll be plenty of time for chatting later. We've got a long way to go, and I'd like to be back in my palace by dinnertime. I *am* rather hungry—that part of what I told you was true.'

I kicked and screamed with renewed vigour, but he grabbed me unceremoniously around the middle and threw me over his shoulder. I tore at his back, screaming for help. Only my echoes answered me. Only the vines I'd planted around the hut reached out and wound themselves around my wrists and ankles to hold me back. The rakshasa cut through them easily with his sword, leaving them slashed to pieces, dying on the ground. I could feel their pain as life drained out of them.

This made me so furious that I forgot to be afraid.

'Tell me your real name, you coward,' I shouted, kicking at his shins as he pulled me onto the chariot. 'For clearly you're a coward, you shameless creature, to steal a man's wife when he isn't around.'

If I'd hoped to make the rakshasa lose his temper, I failed. He flashed me another grin, sharp and triumphant and a little wry. 'Not a coward. Merely a strategist with a penchant for justice. Your husband has already killed so many of my kinsmen. It wouldn't be right to endanger more of them. And what could be a more fitting punishment for a man who has destroyed a woman's chance at finding love than to snatch from him the woman he loves? For him to know she's a captive in an asura king's palace, the latest object of his kingly affections?'

His last words made me shudder. What did he mean? He was looking at me, a hot glint in his eyes. I couldn't tell if he was serious, or if he was trying to frighten me.

'As for my name,' the rakshasa continued, raising his voice as though in a challenge, 'I am Ravan, ruler of Lanka-across-the-ocean. Let Ram come there—if he can even find it—and rescue you if he dares!'

RAVAN! A JOLT WENT through my brain. That same asura king who had come to Mithila—a lifetime ago, it seemed. His face was different now, his handsomeness grown heavy, with harsh lines around the mouth, a weariness in the eyes. Had he not told me his name, I wouldn't have guessed him to be the king who had strode into the great hall with such confidence, wrapped in a gold-glittering spell. When he failed at lifting the magic bow that was my bride-price, how furious he'd been. How afraid my parents were that he'd create mayhem. But because of his love for Shiva, he'd controlled himself and left peacefully. As though it was yesterday, I remembered the strange feeling of recognition I'd had when our eyes met for a moment. An odd closeness, a bond from some other world.

Perhaps if I felt it again, I could appeal to the better part of him. Perhaps he'd listen.

I forced myself to look into Ravan's eyes, trying to call up that mysterious closeness again. But there was no sense of recognition this time, no feeling of being wafted into another world. It was like looking into an opaque pool, one which, if you fell into it, would pull you into its drowning depths.

If Ravan noticed me staring, he gave no indication of it. He whispered a word. His tone was affectionate, and the chariot hummed in reply. We shot up into the air at a speed I hadn't previously imagined possible. Below us, my hut and the clearing in which it sat shrank into a dot, then into nothingness as it was swallowed by the forest. The forest, too, shrank until it was no bigger than a bedsheet, pocked by peaks. Rivers glinted here and there in it, thin threads of silver. Somewhere deep inside, a part of me marvelled at the sight even as I flailed and screamed and tried to gouge out the rakshasa's eyes. Ravan held me off easily, the corner of his mouth lifting in a small, mocking smile. He didn't try to stop me.

When my voice grew hoarse and my arms too tired to punch him, I prayed to the goddess to save me. When she was silent, I prayed to the rest of the gods, anyone who came to my mind.

But the sky above me remained empty. The gods—if indeed they even existed—had their own plan, and it didn't coincide with my distressed need.

For a moment I thought I'd throw myself out of the chariot. It would be worth it, just to foil the demon king's plan. But I didn't. It wasn't that I was afraid of death. How could I be? I knew nothing of it. Still, I didn't want to die. Not without seeing Ram one more time. That's how the bonds of love tie us down.

TIME SPED BY US, roaring like a horde of beasts. How far did I travel? How long did it take? I don't know. I think I was in a trance. Perhaps it was rakshasa magic. Perhaps it was shock. Vaguely, I remember a giant bird flying at the chariot, cursing Ravan in a human voice, declaring his name: Jatayu. He tried valiantly to rescue me, but he was old, and Ravan chopped off his wings without even a moment's hesitation, leaving him to spiral down to his death, spewing blood, while I stared in guilty horror because he'd died in his efforts to save me.

Elsewhere, on a mountain peak below, a group of hairy men—or were they monkeys?—sat clustered, conferring. I threw down my jewellery to them. Necklace, bangles, anklets.

'Give them to Ram,' I cried. 'Tell him that Ravan of Lanka has stolen his Sita. Tell him that she'll be waiting for him to come and rescue her.'

But we were too high up for them to hear my words. The jewellery fell through the air, glinting like teardrops, and was lost in the dense foliage.

Time tightened around me like a whirlpool. I think I lost consciousness. Maybe it was because Ravan spoke to me in an amorous tone that was more frightening than all the threatening he'd done earlier. It seemed to me we swooped low over an ocean froth-white with waves beneath which churned tentacled monsters. Then we soared upward into black clouds edged with lightning until my hair crackled with the currents. When I woke up, groggy as though I'd drunk many cups of bitter wine, I was inside a walled city made of gold, situated atop a mountain. It shone so bright, it almost blinded me. The walls were many storeys tall, and heavily armed guards patrolled atop them constantly. The main gate was attended by shining, noble beings that seemed to be gods. I recalled hearing tales that Ravan had defeated the celestials and forced them to wait upon him in Lanka. Even if my poor husband managed to get this far, over the churning, monster-infested ocean, what chance did he have to overcome them? How would he ever enter this city, fiercely guarded as it was? What hope, then, was there for me?

Nineteen

RAVAN AND I DESCENDED FROM the chariot, he leading, I following with docile footsteps. This was because he'd asked me, very politely, whether I'd prefer to do as he instructed, or be carried over his shoulder like a sack of rice.

As I set foot on Lankan soil, it was as though my mind split in two. One part was still in shock at how rapidly, because of just three wrong decisions, my life had plummeted into calamity. The other part—perhaps to keep myself from going mad with fear—observed everything around me with a cool and critical eye.

A great cheer went up as soon as we descended from the flying chariot—clearly, the crowd of rakshasas waiting there had known of Ravan's quest and could see that he'd been successful.

Ravan was surrounded by felicitators, male and female, bowing and applauding. A little distance away, a chorus of youngsters burst into a song of welcome. I'd wanted to believe that he was a tyrant, but I could see that he was dearly loved. And he was a good leader, equally gracious to all, acknowledging greetings whether they were offered by the aristocrat or the more humble citizens.

Ravan's people were handsome and tastefully attired—no clothing made from human skins were to be seen. Subtle contrasts in their attire suggested differences of social class. Though we humans had lumped them together, these asuras were so distinct from the forest-dwelling rakshasas that they hardly seemed to belong to the same race. Under other circumstance, I'd have been interested to learn more about them. But now they were my enemies. All I could think was that if Ram ever made it this far, they'd do everything they could to kill him.

A LITTLE WAY BEHIND the crowd, two people stood silently. I could feel disapproval emanating from them. The male rakshasa was younger than Ravan, with a strong facial resemblance to him. The other was a female, slim and tall and regal, dressed in rich, shining garments and many ornaments. But her beautiful eyes were dark with anger—and sadness.

As Ravan walked over, the male said, 'Brother, it's an evil, heedless thing that you've done.'

Ravan smiled wryly. 'And here I thought I'd achieved something special, avenging our sister without losing a single soldier!'

'This is no joking matter,' Ravan's brother said. 'I consulted the astrologers. They claim that this action of yours will bring about the ruin of our beautiful Lanka.'

'You pay too much attention to the influence of the heavenly bodies, Vibheeshan,' Ravan said. 'Have you forgotten that they obey my commands? Even the sun and moon are gatekeepers at my palace!'

Vibheeshan put a hand on Ravan's arm. 'Please return her, brother—it's not too late. If you like, I'll take her back to Panchabati myself—'

'I'm not returning her,' Ravan said. 'Can't you just enjoy this moment of victory instead of thinking up the gloomiest possibilities?'

Throwing off Vibheeshan's hand, he brought me over to the woman.

'This is Mandodari, my chief queen,' he said. 'Of all the women in my life, she is the wisest. Though I, being less wise, don't always listen to her counsel.'

'My Lord,' Queen Mandodari said in a strained voice, 'I need to speak with you urgently. I have important information regarding this woman that I need to—'

'You shall tell me all about it,' Ravan said, cupping her face affectionately in his hands. 'And I will give you my full attention. But first I need to take care of some state matters—and then some personal ones.' Pointing to me, he said, 'As you can see, this is Sita, my prize. I wrested her from her husband for Surpanakha's sake, but now I've decided to keep her for my own purposes. Take her to my pleasure-palace. Have her made ready. And have the yakshini guards keep an eye on her. She can be a handful! I'll come for her soon.'

His words sent a chill through me. *My own purposes. Have her made ready. I'll come for her soon.*

What did he mean to do with me? And how was I going to stop him?

WHILE RAVAN WAS ESCORTED by his entourage towards a huge, glittering building that I guessed to be the royal court, Mandodari pulled me along to a chariot that was waiting for her. Her grasp on my wrist was rough, and she didn't speak. Her beautiful, chiselled face was schooled to show no emotion. But I could feel anger emanating from her, as well as shame. I could imagine how insulting it must be for her—she who was the daughter of a great king, I was sure—to have anything to do with Ravan's latest conquest. Beneath them I sensed something else: a shimmer of fear.

Why should Mandodari be afraid of me, a powerless captive?

The charioteer brought us to a gigantic palace glittering with gold and precious stones. The architecture was intricate, with features I'd never seen in the human world: musical fountains sang a welcome as we approached them; flowering vines carved into the columns released heady perfumes; walls of sculpted dancers came to life, bending and leaping, when I turned my eyes towards them.

The palace was guarded by stern and beautiful females, twice as tall as I was. I guessed that they were the yakshinis that Ravan mentioned. They must have once been the guardians of Indra's court. Forgotten tales from Mithila, from the time when Ravan came to try for my hand, rose in my mind. He had battled the king of the gods and won. He had probably brought the yakshinis here after that victory. Did they long for their celestial home as I was now longing for my earthly one? Their impassive faces gave nothing away.

How many females were captive here in Lanka? Had they all resigned themselves to their fate?

I set my jaw defiantly. I didn't know how I'd stand up against the enormous might of the asura king. But I knew this much: I was going to resist him with everything I had.

MY FIRST TEST CAME as soon as we descended from the chariot. Mandodari gripped my arm once again. 'Come,' she said, 'there's no time to waste. The king will be here very soon. You must go to the inner chambers.'

'Why?' I asked, though I feared I knew the answer already. 'What's going to happen there?'

Mandodari's nostrils flared with distaste. 'The maids will bathe you in perfumed waters and arrange your hair in the latest style. They'll dress you in the very best silks and jewels, whatever you want, so that when the king comes, you'll look your best. If you please him, you'll become one of his consorts—perhaps even his favourite for a while—until he tires of you.' She shrugged. ' Then—'

I'd heard enough. 'I refuse,' I said, cutting her off. 'Drag me into the palace, if you must. I refuse to go in of my own will. I love my husband—and only him. Ravan may force me shamefully and take my body against my will—I'm only a mortal woman, after all—but he'll never touch my heart. That belongs to Ram, forever and ever.'

Mandodari ignored me and clapped her hands. Two of the female guards came forward, each grabbing one of my arms. They began to drag me forward. In a few moments, they would pull me over the threshold. That, I sensed, would be the end. I guessed that the buildings were constructed magically—within them, people could no longer exercise their own willpower. They did whatever Ravan wanted them to.

Goddess, I thought frantically. Is this my destiny?

From inside me an answer rose, powerful as a volcanic eruption. Was it the goddess or my own inner strength? I couldn't distinguish them anymore. *You are meant for greater things.*

Words poured through me then, mine and the goddess's together. 'Hear me, spirits of the island, the sea and the forest. O Gods above, be my witness. I hereby curse Ravan and his entire lineage. When Ram comes for vengeance—as he surely will—this entire city will be filled with death and burning. The smoke will cover even the sun. The stench of bodies will spread beyond the boundaries of Lanka. Only vultures will be here to attend to the dead.'

Mandodari let go of my wrist as though I'd scalded her. Her face was stricken. Turning to the charioteer, she said, 'Inform the king that he needs to come here at once. It's urgent.'

ALMOST IMMEDIATELY, RAVAN ARRIVED. How he came, I did not know. One moment he wasn't there, and then he was. He was dressed resplendently in royal robes of silk, with a gem-encrusted crown on his head. Mandodari, who had retreated some distance from me, hurried to him, wringing her hands.

'The woman made a prophecy that Lanka will be destroyed by her husband. You will die—our sons will die—no one would be left even to cremate the dead. That's exactly what I dreamed last night. I was trying to tell you about it earlier, but you wouldn't listen. I saw the entire city in flames. I saw on the ground the severed head of my beloved son, your heir Meghnad. I saw the goddess Chamundi who protects our city ascending to the heavens, her face turned away from my pleas.

'Send back this witch, this bad-luck creature, before she brings ruin on us all. Please, husband, I never complained when you brought other women to Lanka. But this time, I'm begging you.' Weeping, she knelt in front of him.

Ravan picked her up gently and whispered consolations to her. He spoke for a while. What he said, I didn't know, only that she looked as sad as before and newly hopeless.

Ravan beckoned to one of the guards, who helped her into the chariot, which took her away. All through, she kept her eyes averted from mine.

Ravan must have gestured to the guards, for now they stepped back far enough so that we could have a private conversation. I tensed, fisting my hands, considering a sudden attack. But I knew it would be useless. He was too strong, and additionally, his magical powers had grown to their fullest now that he was home. Better to conserve my strength and my dignity. I looked around, checking if there was a place to flee to. But there were guards all around, and beyond them the greatest guard of all: the ocean.

For the moment, I was trapped. I was afraid Ravan would take advantage of this and lay his hands on me. But surprisingly, he didn't do this. Instead, he maintained his distance and spoke in measured tones.

'As you know, Sita, I captured you for the purpose of vengeance. But having watched you since the time I took you from your dwelling, I'm filled with admiration for your fiery spirit. I no longer want to keep you imprisoned in my dungeons, as I'd originally intended. Nor can I bear to kill you, as my ministers are advising me, and send your corpse back to the forest so that your husband stops searching for you. And I refuse to return you, as my brother Vibheeshan counsels.

'Instead, I want you to become my chief queen, raised above all others, to reign supreme in my palace. Anything you ask will be given to you—all comforts and luxuries, all wealth, all pleasures you can imagine, here on earth, or even in the court of Indra, which he yields to me whenever I decide to go there. Only say yes to me, my beloved!'

These entreaties were far worse than the threats Ravan had flung at me earlier. The husky desire in his voice at once sickened, frightened and angered me. His hot gaze burned my skin until my body trembled with disgust. Only Ram was entitled to look at me in this way, to say these things.

I covered my face with my sari. I curbed my longing to rage against Ravan. It would do no good to engage with him, which, I guessed, was what he wanted. Keeping my voice neutral, I said, 'I love Ram with my whole heart. With my last breath, I'll be faithful to my marriage vows, no matter what you say or do.'

Ravan said, 'I could take you against your will, you know. I'm no saint, I've done it with other women. But in your case, I don't want that. It's not your body I crave, but your heart. I'll give you a year to change your mind. At the end of that time, either you'll become my queen, or I'll turn you over to Surpanakha, who will love the opportunity of designing for you whatever kind of death she thinks you deserve.

'Ram will never be able to reach Lanka. You might as well accept that. And even if he does, how will he destroy me? I who have defeated even the gods, to whom Brahma himself has given the boon of indestructibility!'

He clapped his hands and the yakshinis glided forward. 'Take her to my pleasure grove. Make sure she's comfortable but surrounded by the fiercest guards. Here are my orders: they're not to cause her bodily harm, but they're to do everything they can to break her spirit.'

With this, he threw me a final, fiery glance of mingled hatred and desire and disappeared into a swirl of light, much as he had done, lifetimes ago it seemed, in King Janak's flower-bedecked marriage hall in Mithila. The memory of that innocent, happy time was like being pierced with a sword.

Two yakshinis took me by the arm with rough impassivity and led me forward. Their fingers were hard as stone and as cold. The chill penetrated my entire body as I stumbled through the dark, for with the disappearance of Ravan, the sunlight had suddenly fled. More rakshasa magic, no doubt.

Ram, beloved, I cried silently, *where are you in the hour of my need*? But I already knew where he was: very far away, hacking his way through the wilderness, searching frantically for me, moving farther away with every step because he had no idea where I'd vanished to.

ON, ON WE WENT through a blackness deeper than night. Sometimes it seemed we climbed up a hillside, though in the mirk no vista was visible. Sometimes we waded through muddy swamps, where unseen slimy creatures brushed up against me, making me flinch. Once or twice I was certain we walked, single file, through narrow underground tunnels. Where were we going? How large was this island? Or was this more rakshasa magic? When I was sure that in my fatigue I could not walk another step, we came to a stop. We were among trees whose leaves whispered in the wind. *Sita, Sita, Sita.* Or did they say, *Sorrow, Sorrow, Sorrow?*

One of my guards produced a torch, and in its smoky flame I saw that I was in a grove of enormous trees laden with large red flowers. I recognized them. A hysterical laugh spiralled up inside me at the irony of the universe, for they were ashoka trees, a name that meant *joy*.

A guard pushed at me roughly, causing me to fall to my knees. 'Eh, you, what are you laughing at?' She cried in a guttural voice. I looked up to see that at some point of my journey, the yakshinis had melted away and been replaced by the ugliest rakshasis I'd ever seen. They must have come from a very different tribe, for they were as unlike as could be from Mandodari or Kaamarupini-Surpanakha, or even the crowd that greeted us when Ravan and I landed in Lanka, with fanged teeth, long, curved nails, red eyes and hair that spiralled wildly from their heads, waving like serpents. Lakshman would have felt vindicated to see them, for they were everything he believed rakshasas to be.

The thought of my dear brother-in-law twisted inside me, bringing tears to my eyes. If only I hadn't maligned him and forced him away from me, and then disobeyed him wilfully. I pictured him accompanying Ram in his futile search, doubly distressed because of worry for me and sorrow for his brother. *Oh Lakshman, can you ever forgive me?*

'Crying now, is she?' Another of the rakshasis spat. 'She hasn't had anything to cry about yet, the stupid creature! But she will. Oh yes, she will!'

The rakshasis crowded around me, examining me in the light of more flaming torches.

'This pale, puny human,' one said. 'Why does our king consider her so important?'

'For her I was taken off citadel guard duty and brought here?' another said, hissing in disgust.

'Is she a traitor? A spy?' A third asked. She poked at me with her toes. 'Why don't we just make a meal of her? That'll keep her from causing any further trouble! Though scrawny as she is, she won't make more than a couple of mouthfuls.'

'Now, now, girls,' said a tall, muscular rakshasi, whose matted grey hair attested to her age and experience. She was clearly their leader. 'The King has told us what to do. It's not for the likes of you to be questioning him.' She gestured at me to sit up. 'I am Trijata, the chief of the guards. Make yourself comfortable, dearie. There's a nice little bower behind this grove. Our king said you can stay there. I recommend it. From what I gathered, you'll be here a long time, and the mosquitoes in the grove are no joke! Of course the best thing would be to change your mind and accept our king as your mate and save us all a lot of trouble.'

'Never!' I said, putting every bit of strength that was left in me into my voice. 'And I refuse to accept any comforts offered by that despicable monster.'

The rakshasis muttered angrily, displeased with this show of disrespect to their king. Some moved forward threateningly, baring fangs. But Trijata stopped them with her upraised hand.

'We shall see,' she said philosophically. 'Let me just tell you this much—I've lived a long time, and I've never seen a woman resist our king. Sooner or later, they all give in.' She clapped and ordered one of the guards to bring me some food.

A rakshasi brought a hank of roasted, charred meat. I turned from it in disgust. I was afraid she might try to force-feed me, but she shrugged and muttered something about did I think I was too good for food like this, and ate it herself.

Trijata said, 'No matter. She'll eat when she's hungry enough.'

I lay down under a large ashoka tree, using its root as a pillow. I turned away from the rakshasis and begged it to protect me. The tree rustled and sighed. I felt its flowers drop on me like tears, for it was as helpless as I was.

Suddenly there were bright lights around me, and a musical voice asking, 'Where is she?'

I turned warily and opened my eyes. A rakshasi stood in front of me, not as beautiful as Mandodari, but clearly of the same class. She was dressed with restrained elegance, and there was kindness in her face. Behind her stood several attendants carrying trays and boxes.

'Lady Sarama!' Trijata exclaimed in surprise. 'What are you doing here?'

'The queen sent me with some proper food for Sita,' the woman said. 'She can't possibly eat half-cooked flesh, like you guards do!' To me, she said, 'I'm Vibheeshan's wife. I'm sorry to meet you under such circumstances, but I want to make your stay in Lanka as comfortable as possible—even though I see you've decided not to stay in the bower.' She looked at me more sympathetically than anyone had in this place.

Sarama gestured to her maids, who came forward with quilts for me to lie on, and silver platters on which were arranged many delicate dishes, both sweet and savoury. My mouth watered at the smell, for I was very hungry. I appreciated Sarama's gentleness to me, but I forced myself to turn away.

'I thank you for your trouble,' I said. 'I'm sorry to reject the queen's gifts, but I've taken a vow not to eat or drink anything while in captivity, nor accept any comforts. The best help you can give me is to persuade Ravan to return me to my husband.'

Sarama sighed. 'I'd certainly do that, if it were within my powers—for my sake as well as yours. But the king is infatuated with you. He chastised my husband severely for suggesting that you be sent back, and he refuses to listen to the queen as well. I'll come back tomorrow, in case you change your mind about eating. At the very least, I hope we can be friends.'

After she left, I turned my back to my captors and lay down. Sympathetic though Sarama was, I didn't think I could be friends with anyone in this prison. How I longed for Urmila's arms around me, or my mother Sunaina's lips on my forehead. But thinking of them only made me feel more alone.

I pressed my cheek into the ground and spoke to the only one who remained with me in this hellish place. 'Give me your strength in this place of sorrow and fear, Mother Earth, you who protected me when I was a helpless infant,' I whispered. 'Give me the courage to bear my imprisonment until Ram comes.'

But how long would that take? And how would I be able to keep my fasting-vow, against which my body was already rebelling, until then?

I TOSSED AND TURNED for a long time in spite of my exhaustion. When I finally fell into a troubled sleep, a dream came to me. In it, a god appeared, carrying a small golden bowl.

'I am Indra,' he said. 'I bring you sudha, the nectar of the gods. Drink. It will keep you from starving. Be strong and patient. Ram is coming, but it will take time.'

Even in the dream, I knew enough to be suspicious. 'Why should I believe you? Perhaps this is more of Ravan's magic, aimed to trick me into breaking my vow. If you're really Indra, show me a sign.'

Indra bowed his head. His body shimmered, and a thousand eyes appeared all over him. I believed him then, for the eyes were a mark of his shame, a remnant of the curse of Sage Gautam. I took the cup.

The sweet liquid spread a fiery warmth through my body, but my heart was still troubled. 'I know what a great warrior Ram is, but how will he know where I am? And even if he manages to find out, who will have the courage to aid him against Ravan? How can Ram cross this ocean, filled with monsters whose goal is to kill intruders and protect Lanka? And hasn't Brahma given Ravan the boon of indestructibility?

'So many questions!' Indra sighed. 'Here's one answer: Ravan's not as indestructible as he thinks he is. Brahma tricked him, making him list all the beings he wanted to be invincible against. Ravan left out a couple of species that he didn't think worth worrying about.'

'What species?'

'Men and monkeys,' Indra said. Before I could ask him any more questions, he hurried on. 'Have faith. Forces are aligning in the heavens and on earth. But such things don't happen overnight. I'll try to appear in your dreams from time to time, but it's difficult to pierce through the asura magic that shrouds this island.'

I wasn't pacified with this vague answer, but Indra was already fading. 'Wait!' I cried, asking him the question that had bothered me for a long time. 'Did you ever love Ahalya? Were you sorry that you'd ruined her life?'

Indra disappeared without answering, which didn't surprise me. The gods are slippery beings. I awoke to a heavy grey morning, filled with the taunts and jeers of my guards, who were even uglier—if that was possible—in daylight than they'd seemed the night before.

Twenty

IN CAPTIVITY, DAYS AND NIGHTS blurred for me. Some of this was my own disorientation, and some was rakshasa magic, which kept me from seeing the sun for weeks on end. I figured Ravan had decided that the constant darkness would demoralize me and break me down sooner, so I decided to fight it with all I had.

I wasn't allowed to leave the pleasure gardens, but Trijata, whom I'd cured of a bad toothache by making her a poultice out of liquorice paste, let me walk around the grove sometimes. The walks brought me a little solace. The plants and trees were innocent and beautiful. When I touched them, I could feel their sympathy for me. If they were ailing, my touch cured them. And thus we grew to love each other. I was particularly fond of the ashoka tree under which I slept. When no one was watching, I cleared the dead leaves that piled up around it, and when I lay down to sleep, I placed my palms against its trunk to draw in comfort. But all this I did secretly. I was afraid that if my guards knew how much I cared about the tree, they'd harm it just to cause me pain.

The rakshasis had many ways of tormenting me. They made a game of poking at me with sharp nails that bruised my skin just when I fell asleep, or suddenly transforming themselves into horrifying monster-shapes to startle me, or rushing at me, teeth bared, as though to devour me. They couldn't injure me seriously because of Ravan's orders. But they did their gleeful best to break me down.

This unending barrage of attacks demoralized me. I was constantly tense and exhausted, and it was hard, under those conditions, to maintain hope. It was hardest when they boasted, in detail, of how they'd torture and kill my husband if he ever made it as far as Lanka. At times they used rakshasa magic to create images of an injured and bleeding Ram, collapsed on the ground in front of me. Surpanakha must have described to them, in detail, what he looked like, because the images were horrifyingly realistic. It was all I could do not to break down weeping.

At these painful moments, I would place my attention in my heart centre, as I'd been taught, and mentally practise my self-defence exercises. I visualized Ravan as my opponent. *Allow him to pursue you and at the last moment, step sideways and bring up the knee in a sudden movement to the opponent's groin; when he doubles over, press your thumbs into his eyes to blind him. Or step back as though retreating, and when the opponent lunges at you, hit his windpipe with your hand, held straight as a knife. At the right angle, the impact will break his neck.* I didn't know if I'd ever have the opportunity to do any of this, but if so, I wanted to be ready. Meanwhile, concentrating on the exercises helped me to remain calm.

When the rakshasis tired of their sport and their snores filled the night, I prayed for a dream—as Indra had promised—that would let me know what Ram was doing. But sleep came to me blind and grey, or filled with nightmares. Each morning I told myself, *I will not give up*. But how long would I be able to keep my resolve? I didn't even know if time was passing, or if in this place of evil enchantment, Ravan held day and night, week and month, in his control.

SOME MORNINGS I'D WAKE to find Surpanakha standing over me, muttering. The hatred flowing from her was so palpable, I could taste it. Trijata kept a tense watch nearby at those times to make sure she didn't injure me seriously. I'd sit up, steeling myself for an attack, certainly verbal, sometimes physical: a slap, a shove, a kick. Sometimes she'd grab my face and force me to look into hers, which was difficult because there were gaping holes where her nose and ears had been. More importantly, something had gone out of her eyes, a joyful trust I'd noticed in the Panchabati forest. They looked opaque and dead now. I couldn't help continuing to feel guilty about that.

'Ugly, aren't I?' she said to me once. Her voice, which I remembered as musical, came out in a croak. 'The court physicians wanted to fill in the holes, but I said, no. This way, every time my brother sees me, he'll remember what was done to me. It'll keep his loathing of your husband fresh and strong.' She looked me up and down. 'Well, you don't look that great yourself; more like a scrawny crow. I don't know how you've managed to keep my brother captivated.' She spat. A greenish glob landed on my foot. I forced myself not to jerk away. 'But time's running out on you. Ten months of the year he's given you have passed.'

Had it been so long already? And still there was no sign of Ram, no word from him. My rakshasi guards had stopped mentioning him. Clearly, they didn't consider him a threat any longer. An appalling thought snaked through me: had my husband given up?

Surpanakha narrowed her eyes as though she could read my mind. 'There's no way Ram can rescue you, even if he dared. But frankly, I don't think he's trying. I think he's gone back to Ayodhya and taken another wife. Why would he want anything to do with a woman who'd been abducted, who'd been touched—or worse—by another male? So you'd better make your decision—Ravan's queen, or my slave.' She threw me a snarl of a smile. 'I hope you choose me. That way, I can keep you alive for a long time—long after you beg me to kill you.'

ONCE IN A WHILE, Sarama came to see me, and we walked around the gardens together. She tried to distract me from my sorrows by telling me stories about Lanka, how it had been magically constructed. How Ravan had won it from Kuber. The rakshasis watched her suspiciously and tried to eavesdrop on our conversation, but Sarama's magic was stronger than theirs. She constructed a veil around us that they couldn't pierce. They would have loved to stop her from visiting me, but they couldn't—she was royalty, after all. But her power was waning, they knew that.

Sarama had every reason to hate me—I was the cause of all her troubles—but strangely, she didn't. Perhaps it was because I was the only person with whom she could share her worries. She told me that Ravan had accused Vibheeshan, in open court, of not being a proper asura because he kept entreating Ravan to send me away. Of being too sympathetic to humans. Of worshipping the enemy gods in secret, with the vain hope of taking over the kingdom with their help.

'That is so unfair,' she cried. 'All Vibheeshan cares for is the good of Lanka. I'm terrified that Ravan will exile him one of these days. Vibheeshan is quite sure war is coming.'

My heart leaped with hope when she said that, but I remained silent, for Sarama was very distressed.

'I don't know what'll happen then. Our son Taranisen—I worry most about him. He's just a boy, though on his way to becoming a fine warrior. He's very attached to Ravan, very loyal to him. If war comes, he'll definitely volunteer to fight.'

The anxious love in her voice resonated achingly in my heart for the children I didn't—and probably would never—have. I thought of love's contradictions, how it fills us with joy but also with worry for welfare of the loved one and pain for his suffering.

I loved it most when Sarama asked me to tell her about Ram. I'd whisper to her what a great warrior he was, what a caring, considerate, indulgent husband. I'd describe our adventures in the forest, and how much I loved and missed him. Just being able to speak his name aloud consoled me greatly. I think Sarama knew that.

My most unexpected visitor was Queen Mandodari. She always came alone and never spoke, only watched me from a distance over the heads of the rakshasis who bowed deferentially to her. After my initial rejection of her gifts, she didn't offer me any others. But sometimes I saw her looking at my earth-bed and my tattered bark-cloth sari with sadness. At other times I felt she was examining my face carefully, but what she was looking for I couldn't tell.

One night, after she'd been staring at me for a long time, I decided I'd speak to her, though I wasn't sure what would be the appropriate thing to say to a woman who clearly saw me as her nemesis.

'Mother Mandodari,' I started.

She flinched and interrupted me sharply. '*What* did you call me?'

I was surprised at how agitated she was. *Mother* was a common enough courtesy-term used for older women. I hoped she didn't mistake my intentions, didn't think I was taunting her by pointing out that she was older and thus less desirable. Or did she think it was presumptuous of a human to address her thus?

Mandodari clapped her hands. When Trijata ran up, she said something, and all the rakshasis retreated until they were lost in the night mists. Then she came close to me, and bending, whispered in my ear, 'Is it true that the king and queen of Mithila are not your real parents? Is it true that they found you in a field?'

'Yes,' I said, mystified by her question. How could the circumstances of my birth be of interest to Ravan's queen? Was she perhaps planning to use my uncertain—and therefore suspect—ancestry to dissuade Ravan from wanting to marry me? If so, I was definitely on her side.

In the dim light of a single flickering torch, Mandodari's eyes shone. It took me a moment to realize they were filled with unshed tears.

'Did anyone ever tell you what kind of cloth you were wrapped in when you were found? What colour it was, what material?'

Strange questions. But I answered them readily enough, 'I don't remember a particular colour, but the cloth was a fine silk, unlike anything people wove in Mithila. I remember my mother Sunaina telling me that they'd never seen anything like it.'

Silence weighed down upon us as Mandodari considered what I'd just said. Finally, she lowered herself heavily to the ground in front of me, unmindful of her expensive clothing, and said, still in a whisper, 'I want to tell you a story. It's a dangerous story which, if known, could destroy me. But I feel I must tell it to you. Can I trust you? Will you promise to keep it to yourself?'

Intrigued, I nodded, and she began.

'MANY YEARS AGO,' MANDODARI said, 'I gave birth to a baby girl. It wasn't a normal conception. I won't go into the details, but let me just tell you this much: my husband was gravely displeased with me. And when the asura priests who examined her stars foretold that the child would be the cause of her father's death and the ruin of his kingdom, he was livid. So he ordered the baby to be killed.

'I begged and pleaded, but Ravan wouldn't listen. Finally, the night before the baby was to be taken away, I managed to bribe the rakshasa who was given the duty of killing the baby. It was a huge bribe that depleted my coffers. But I didn't mind, especially when he promised me that he would leave her somewhere far away and safe.

'I wrapped the baby in a beautiful yellow silk into which I'd woven a good-luck symbol and handed her to him. Ah, even after all these years, I remember how it hurt—as though someone was tearing out my innards. He took the infant to a distant land and left her there. Where he went, he never told me—for my own safety and his, he said. But he did tell me that he'd made sure it was a good place, a place where a good man would find the girl and bring her up.

'I never mentioned this to anyone. I held it in my heart, my dark, cold, dangerous secret, my small consolation. Ravan was certain the baby was dead. The old retainer who'd taken the baby passed away soon after. I relaxed a little, certain that now no one would find out what I'd done. I resigned myself to the fact that I'd never see my daughter.

'I thought about her all the time, though—what did she look like, how was she doing, was she married now, did she have her own children? Let her be safe, I prayed every day. Let her be happy. Sometimes I told myself, Stop! For all I know, the baby was left in a forest or by a river. She was just a newborn—she must have died.

'But when I saw you, I began to wonder. The stubborn way you have of tilting your chin. The bravery with which you've refused to obey Ravan and enter his palace, even though he could have killed you—or worse, tortured you—for it. I used to be like that a long time ago, before living with Ravan drained away my spirit. I began coming to the ashoka grove at night to watch you, and the more I watched, the more I became convinced that you are my daughter. Even the way you sleep, turned to your left with your legs drawn up towards your chest—that's how I sleep, an old habit I can't seem to get rid of although it's annoyed Ravan for years.'

I didn't believe one bit of this farfetched story, though I could see how badly Mandodari wanted it to be true—because if so, it would assuage some of her guilt.

'Each day I'm torn in two,' Mandodari continued, 'both delighted and terrified. I can't decide if I should tell Ravan—'

'Why don't you do that?' I said. Maybe it would get Ravan to look at me differently. There were risks in it, of course. If he became convinced that I was the cursed daughter, he'd probably kill me. But wouldn't that swift end be better than this endless torture? And there was a chance that he might believe Mandodari and send me back to Ram. An infinitesimal chance—but worth trying for.

Mandodari looked down. 'I'm too frightened of what he'll do to me in retaliation for such a great crime—going not just against him but endangering the whole country. You haven't seen Ravan in one of his rages. When it happens, even the earth trembles and the gods hide their faces. If he punished me with death, I could endure it. But he'd consider that too easy. He won't care that I'm his queen. He'll put me in his dungeons. You haven't seen them, or the dungeon masters who devise the most infernal, drawn-out tortures, both physical and mental—but I have. It's said that his dungeons rival the twenty-eight hells, and I believe it. I'm sorry. I'm not brave enough to risk such suffering.' She looked up, her eyes pleading. 'Please forgive me, my daughter, and let me make your life a little easier for you. I can force the guards—or persuade them with gifts—to treat you more kindly. That much power I do have—'

She stretched out her arms to embrace me, a terrible hunger in her face.

I jerked back in repugnance. 'I want nothing to do with your mad fantasy. I'm not the baby you sent off to her death somewhere. You can't use me to lessen your guilt. And most certainly I have no connection to your hateful husband—except for the fact that he abducted me by shameful trickery and ruined my life. I'd kill myself this very moment if I really thought rakshasa blood ran in my veins.'

I fisted my hands and hardened my heart against further pleading, but Mandodari said nothing. She left without making any more attempts to talk to me or touch me. She possessed a queenly dignity, I had to admit that. She didn't approach me again, although I had a feeling she sometimes watched me secretly from the night shadows of the ashoka grove.

I tried to purge her story from my mind, but disturbingly, it kept coming back. And with it came the questions. Wasn't it strange the way King Janak had found me wrapped in an expensive cloth the likes of which no one had seen in Mithila? People said the gods had left me in the field. But what if it had been a very different kind of being that had brought me to him? For a while I tried hard to remember the colour of the cloth, but it wouldn't come to me. Perhaps that was for the best.

I couldn't stop thinking about Queen Mandodari either, although it annoyed me. As the days passed, a reluctant sympathy grew in my heart, and this annoyed me further. It would have been so much simpler if I could have hated her. Now I kept imagining her in the dead of night, swaddling her infant daughter with loving anguish and handing her over to a grizzled retainer. I heard her whispering frantic instructions as she pressed a bag of jewels into his hand. Against my will, I felt her agony twist my heart as she watched them disappear into the inky ocean. Her agony over the years as she remembered that terrible, dangerous, guilty moment. And now, her greatest agony: watching me and wondering, unable to speak her suspicions to her husband, who was infatuated beyond reason with a woman who might be his daughter.

Twenty-one

THE VISITOR WHO CAME MOST often and troubled me most deeply was Ravan. Sometimes he came dressed in full royal regalia, displaying his ten heads, each topped by a sparkling crown. On these occasions he'd be accompanied by courtiers and musicians, dancing girls and vassals bearing precious gifts, caskets spilling over with jewels of many colours, the likes of which I'd never seen before, or stringed instruments from Indra's court that played, on their own, haunting celestial melodies. Gardeners carried shrubs whose names were unknown to me. Somehow Ravan had learned that I loved plants, and he filled the spaces around my ashoka tree with an embarrassing abundance of exotic and fragrant varieties, some of which, he told me, had been brought for me from as far away as the foothills of the Himalayas, or from Kusadvipa, which lay on the other side of the earth. Greater favours, he hinted, awaited me if I became his wife.

I'd close my eyes and turn my back on him. I'd press my face against the ashoka tree trunk, feeling it vibrate in helpless sympathy. I'd put my fingers in my ears, but even that did no good. His asura magic was such that his words travelled directly to my mind.

The visits always ended with him listing, in a calm and melodious voice, the dire consequences if I didn't agree to become his queen and bed-mate soon. He'd force me sexually; he'd give me to his guards to devour; he'd turn me over to Surpanakha to do whatever she wanted; he'd drown me, slowly, in the sea, while the monsters that guarded Lanka tore at my limbs; he'd chop me into pieces and send them to Ram as a gift. Each scenario, I confess, was terrifying, especially when described in Ravan's hypnotic tones. I tried to block them out by desperately repeating the chant I'd heard, on a long-ago happy day in the palace of Ayodhya, the day of the coronation that never happened. *SitaRamSitaRamSitaRam.*

At other times, though, Ravan came alone, dressed so simply that he could have been mistaken as a householder in some small town. He dismissed my rakshasi guards and sat on the ground, bareheaded. He didn't threaten or beg me on those occasions but told me, instead, stories from his life. How many hardships he and his brothers had suffered growing up, often going to bed hungry, his little sister crying, because his mother had been abandoned by his father, the sage Vishrava, who as a holy man should have known better. Her family didn't help them either because they'd been against the alliance in the first place.

Finally his mother put aside her pride and went with her children to the court of their half-brother Kuber to ask for help. Kuber was rich beyond measure, the treasurer of the gods. He could have turned their lives around in a moment. But he insulted her, calling her his father's whore, and the children illegitimate spawn. Looking at his mother's stricken face while his siblings cowered around him, not knowing what they'd done wrong, Ravan's heart broke into pieces. He called out in his sorrow to the gods to aid him, to punish Kuber for his cruelty. But they, too, ignored him.

'That was when the desire for revenge bloomed in my veins,' Ravan said, speaking meditatively, as though he'd forgotten I was listening. 'I decided to become stronger than Kuber, to wrest his kingdom and his wealth. The gods, too, I hated, for their indifference to my family's sufferings. I promised myself I'd make them beg for mercy and learn how it feels to have their pleas cruelly ignored. I went to the Himalayas to perform austerities. I meditated on Brahma the Creator, sitting neck-deep in freezing mountain streams, standing for years on one leg. Finally, despairing, I lit a fire and began to chop off my heads, one at a time, and offer them into the flames until only one head was left. That, too, I was ready to cut off. What use was life if I had to live it as powerless as a worm?'

I kept my face covered in my increasingly tattered sari, but I listened, fascinated in spite of myself. I imagined, as Ravan spoke, Brahma finally arriving in a shower of light, giving the emaciated young man with blazing eyes the boons he was ready to die for. Invincibility. Infinite power so that the gods would cower before him. Everything short of immortality. I visualized Ravan's invasion of the heavens, the great and tumultuous clash of the asuras and devas, until at last he wrested the celestial throne from Indra. I wasn't too displeased. In spite of the sudha he'd brought to me, I had my reservations about Indra's morality, his qualification to be the ruler of the heavens. Additionally, he hadn't sent me the dreams he'd promised.

'I could have remained in Swarga, on Indra's throne,' Ravan said. 'But I got bored. I missed our beautiful, imperfect earth—the trees and the clouds and the birds singing, the winds and the ocean, even the blazing sun. I came back to Lanka and took it from Kuber—it was like snatching a child's toy—and made it more beautiful than it had ever been under him. I became a good king, and a fair one. My subjects may have feared me at times, but they loved me too. I had more wealth and wives than I'd ever dreamed possible. The only times I left my beloved Lanka were when I went on conquests, or to see my dearest Lord Shiva, who was the only one in the pantheon that I revered, up among the icy peaks in Kailash.

'Ah yes. And once I went to Mithila, to try and win a bride.'

So he remembered that! But why was he telling me all these things? Did he want my sympathy? Was he, unbelievable as it seemed, lonely in this fabulous palace, amid all his loyal subjects, in spite of the beautiful females who doted on him? Or was it a rare opportunity for him to look back on this life and ruminate on the unusual trajectory it had taken?

And what was the enchantment in his voice that forced me to listen and—though I would have died before I admitted it to anyone—feel a strange sympathy for him?

Why, when he spoke like this, was I unable to hate him?

'Once, when I was in Kailash,' Ravan continued, 'visiting my dearest Lord, I decided I'd bring him to Lanka, so that I'd have him close by all the time. The weather's so much better here, I thought. He'd enjoy that as well. I decided to uproot the mountain, such was my ego, and carry it back on my head, along with Lord Shiva and Goddess Parvati. Well, I'd barely pulled up a corner of the mountain when the Lord, to humble my pride, pressed down with his little toe and trapped me under Kailash. Ah, the agony! I can't even try to describe it. None of my battle wounds came anywhere close. He was right to do it, of course.

'In my despair, crushed in that darkness, my bones pulverized by the monolith of the mountain, I began to pray. I composed a song to Shiva's glory as the cosmic dancer, and in his magnitude, he forgave me.'

Humming the words, Ravan drifted off into the night. He seemed to have forgotten my existence, but the words reverberated through me long after he had gone, forcing me into reluctant admiration of their pulsing images, their ecstatic beauty.

Jatatavigalajjala pravahapavitasthale Galeavalambya lambitam bhujangatungamalikam …

What a paradox the king of the asuras was.

I dreamed that night of the ecstatic dance of Shiva, his matted locks flying around his face, his serpent garlands, and the enchanting pulsing of his drum, which could create the world or destroy it. I remembered something I'd forgotten. Shiva's bow had promised me that in my darkest need, the Lord would come to help me.

Where are you? I called to him with all my heart's desperation. *I need you so much. Please come soon!*

TONIGHT, AFTER A LONG time there was a moon, full and golden. I don't know how it got past the rakshasa darkness, but I was thankful. I gazed at it longingly, remembering my nights with Ram in the forest, how the moonlight had rained down on our lovemaking, sometimes passionate, sometimes tender, in our little hut. How my husband's skin had glowed in its beams like shining honey. How afterwards—and this was just as precious—we conversed late into the night. We talked about everything: politics and statecraft, the roles of husbands and wives, what we'd eat the next day. When you loved someone, it didn't matter what you discussed; it was all fascinating. My heart ached for that companionship. My body, too—weaker each day in spite of the sudha Indra had brought me—ached with its many hungers.

How many months had passed since I was in captivity? I'd lost track. Surely it was almost year-end, when my fate would be decided.

Ram, I cried silently, because I did not wish to give my guards the satisfaction of seeing me weep, *will I ever see you again?* I didn't doubt that he loved me, but the odds of my rescue—as my guards reminded me mockingly each day—seemed insurmountable. He was just a man, after all, even if he were the best among men.

I heard procession-music in the distance. A wedding, I hoped. Because the other possibility was far worse.

But it was no wedding. It was, as I'd feared, Ravan, come to cajole me again. I turned my face and pressed it against the rough bark of the tree trunk. The ashoka shivered in response. Something, we both sensed, was worse than usual tonight.

I knew it as soon as Ravan spoke, his words slurring as he greeted me. He was heavily intoxicated.

I'd known, from overhearing the gossip of the rakshasis, that he drank. They'd spoken, admiringly, of the amazing amounts of sura he could consume without it affecting his sharp intellect, his battle skills, or even—they'd laughed slyly—his sexual prowess. Tonight was clearly an exception, and I could tell, by their uncertain greetings, that they weren't used to seeing him this way.

'Turn Sita to face me! How dare she ignore me while I'm talking to her!'

My guards were more than happy to oblige. Someone grabbed my shoulder in her claws and yanked me around roughly, not caring that she scraped my skin. Another rakshasi held my chin in a vise-grip, while a third parted my eyelids, forcing me to look at Ravan, dressed in all his finery and accompanied by a hundred wives and handmaidens. Even his yakshini guards were with him today.

The asura king's bloodshot eyes were fixed on me unblinkingly. The hot longing in them frightened me more than if he had railed at me in anger or hatred. I was intensely aware of my torn sari and how it barely covered my breasts.

'Sita,' he said, 'Sita, Sita, Sita! Who are you really? Because surely you can't be a mere human. Are you an enchantress, sent by Indra to drive me insane? Are you a witch from the dark caverns of the underworld? How have you managed to capture my heart like this? All day I can think of nothing but you. My kingdom suffers because I can't pay attention to matters of state. I've antagonized many of my counsellors—even my dear youngest brother—by refusing to give you up. And at night—ah, the nights are the worst. Even lying next to the most beautiful heavenly apsaras I keep imagining you. It pains me to think of you dressed in your rough bark, your hair uncombed and tangled, sleeping on the cold, hard ground. Why won't you accept any of my gifts? But even so, you're more beautiful than the best dressed damsels in my palace. Please end my misery. Become my queen—queen of Lanka and queen of my heart. One word from you, and I'll banish my other queens and never look at another female again. Imagine yourself, dearest, in my embrace, enjoying intoxicating pleasures of the body of which that callow youth you married knows nothing.'

Nausea rose in my throat at the images his words conjured, overcoming all caution. 'Ram is my entire universe,' I said, pronouncing each word deliberately. 'I've given him my heart, all of it, forever. Even if I wanted to, I could never enjoy another person, man or god or asura.'

I should have stopped there, but the moon-madness was in me, too. I spat on the ground. 'And you—what makes you think that I'd ever look at you willingly? That I'd endure your touch with anything other than disgust. If Ram is a lion, you're a dog. If Ram is fragrant sandalwood paste, you're gutter mud. If Ram…'

'Enough!' Ravan's voice was so loud, it sounded as though Earth herself was splitting in two. The rakshasis around me fell to the ground in terror. I looked up and saw that he'd transformed himself into his ten-headed shape. He'd grown to twice his size and was now clad now a dark, shining armour. Each of his heads scowled ferociously at me, grinding its teeth. He brandished a huge curved sword, its serrated edge glittering avidly. 'I've made my decision. If I can't have you, then no one else will. I'll kill you right now and throw your body to the jackals that prowl the cremation ground, and they'll tear it apart. Bereft of last rites, your spirit will wander Lanka forever, regretting your folly. And I'll be free of this torment.'

I closed my eyes. My body was stiff with fear. And yet, there was relief too. The moment I'd alternately dreaded and longed for had finally arrived. At least now I'd escape the constant heartache I'd suffered ever since I arrived here. And Ram wouldn't have to risk his life for me. My only regret was that I'd die without seeing my beloved one last time, that I wouldn't be able to tell him how much I'd suffered, and how, all through that suffering, had remained true to him.

They say that we're united, in our next life, with what we think of at the moment of death. I decided to focus my heart on Ram. Surely that intention would be more powerful than any last rites my body was deprived of. I called up his face, noble and stern but also, in our intimate moments, so vulnerable.

Ill-fortune tore us apart in this life, dearest, I said in my mind. But with all my strength I pray that the next time around I'll be your wife again—for I can't think of a better fate—as inseparable from you as a flame from its lamp.

Lost in my thoughts, I'd blocked off my surroundings. Now I became aware that I was still alive. That gruesome, serrated sword hadn't separated my head from my body. How could that be?

I opened my eyes to see Queen Mandodari struggling with Ravan.

Where had she come from? And why was she here today? Unlike his other wives, she never accompanied Ravan on his visits to me. And such was her power—and possibly his respect for her as his chief consort—that he never subjected her to that indignity.

'Please, my Lord,' she pleaded, her breath coming in gasps, her jewel-encrusted sari in disarray. 'You're a great warrior—it's unbecoming of you to kill a defenceless woman, no matter how much she's provoked you. Your reputation in all the three worlds—Swarga, Marta and Pataal—will be ruined. Even your dead ancestors would be ashamed of you. I call upon you to remember who you are—ruler of the greatest kingdom on earth, vanquisher of Indra, devotee of Shiva, learned in all the Vedas. Act with the dignity appropriate to your station. You've promised this woman one year of immunity—don't break your promise! At the end of the year you can sentence her to whatever punishment you see fit. As your greatest well-wisher and mother of your firstborn, I beg this boon of you.' She kneeled in front of him, hands joined in prayer.

Every single person in the ashoka forest, myself included, held their breath.

After a long moment Ravan handed his sword to one of the yakshinis standing near him. He inhaled deeply and transformed back to his usual appearance. Bending forward, he raised Mandodari from the ground. 'You've always been my best, most trusted counsellor,' he said to her tenderly. 'You know you have a special place in my heart. Led by my passions, I don't always listen to you. But today I will. Thanks to you, Sita is safe—at least for now.' He threw me a last, burning glare and left the grove, his arm around Mandodari's waist.

Mandodari, too, sent me a glance as she left. It was quick and covert and complicated, but I saw the mingled love and pain and horror in it, and I understood. Whatever the truth of my birth might be, in Mandodari's mind, I was her long-lost daughter, her cherished and guilty secret. She feared the havoc my presence would wreak on her kingdom and beloved husband. Yes, she continued to love Ravan, no matter how many women he brought to Lanka. Sometimes the river of love followed a complicated course. At the same time, she couldn't help doing everything she could to protect me. And she was horrified by the thought that if she failed, Ravan might well force his own daughter, unknowingly, to his bed. Would she, at that point, have the courage to confess what she had done and suffer Ravan's wrath?

Ah, love. Why had Vidhata made its nature so complex? Why did one love conflict, so often, with another?

Twenty-two

I'D HOPED FOR SOME QUIET after Ravan and Mandodari left, but that didn't happen. A new formation of rakshasi guards marched up. They must have received instructions to make my life additionally miserable, because right away they began to shout abuses, slapping and poking me until I was bruised all over. They were particularly angry because I'd humiliated their king and shunned what they must have fantasized about many times: Ravan's love. But finally, they tired of my silent endurance. It was like punching a tree or kicking the ground, one said in disgust. They arranged their pallets around my ashoka tree and went to sleep, snoring vigorously because we all knew there was no place I could escape to.

When they'd fallen asleep, I gave way to tears. I wept as silently as I could, but once in a while a sob broke out of me. 'Oh Ram,' I whispered. 'I'm so tired. I love you just as much as on the day of our marriage—no, more, because of all that we've been through together—but I don't have the strength to continue like this. I need a sign. Something to give me a little hope.'

There was a slight movement in the tree branches above my head, and when I looked up, two small, bright eyes gleamed down at me. I jumped up, startled, every muscle tight. What devilish new magic was this?

The creature above parted the branches a little. It seemed unafraid of me—in fact, it seemed more concerned with not frightening me away. Cautiously, I peered closer. It was the tiniest monkey I'd come across, with soft, greyish fur, quite harmless-looking. If I'd put out my hand, it would have fitted on to my palm.

I hadn't seen any monkeys in the ashoka garden until now. Was this some new trick meant to lower my defences?

The monkey laid a cautionary finger on its lips, a surprisingly human gesture.

I didn't trust it one bit. I drew in my breath to let out a loud scream. Unless it was a messenger from Ravan, or a god who could disappear at will, or (terrifying thought) Ravan himself in disguise, which I well knew he was capable of—it was about to get into deep trouble.

The monkey spoke, startling me. 'Ram, Ram,' it said, patting its chest gently as though my beloved resided there. 'Blessed be his name, the rightful king of Ayodhya and my beloved lord.' The blood thudded so loudly in my head, I had to hold on to the trunk of the ashoka tree to keep from falling. Was this the sign I'd begged for?

But how was it that a monkey could speak like a human? In all my years in the forest, I hadn't come across any speaking monkeys. In any case, a tiny monkey couldn't possibly cross the raging ocean that surrounded Lanka. This had to be another of Ravan's tricks.

My face must have indicated my doubts, because the monkey said a bit huffily, 'There's all kinds of magic in the world, Mother Sita, not just the clumsy asura kind. My people can speak—and not just human talk. We know how to communicate with the wind and rain and sun. And that's just for starters. You want to see what else I can do?' He changed into an orange-robed sannyasi so suddenly that I flinched away.

'Sorry!' the monkey said, contrite. 'Didn't mean to scare you, Mother.'

I liked how the monkey called me *mother*. I knew it was only a courtesy, but I felt an absurd desire to hold it close, as one would a baby. 'It's not your fault,' I said. 'I've been this way ever since Ravan disguised himself as a holy man to abduct me.'

Anger flitted over the monkey's face, and I was startled to see how fierce it could look for something so small. 'He'll get what's coming to him soon, don't you worry. Anyway, back to what I was saying. In our tribe, everyone has special powers. I, for instance, can grow as large as a mountain, or become as small as a pea.' Here, he shrank until he was almost invisible in the gloom, then began to expand so that the branch creaked painfully under his weight.

'Stop! I believe you!' I cried, terrified that the branch would break and my guards be awakened by the crash. And then surely they'd make a quick meal out of him, because even a magical monkey couldn't possibly elude an entire phalanx of ravenous rakshasis.

The monkey resumed its original size. 'By the way, my name is Hanuman. I can also leap huge distances. If you didn't know it, you'd think I was flying! That's how I got across the ocean, though there were gaggles of monsters everywhere, and it seemed like fresh monkey was everyone's favourite food! They were always jumping up and trying to grab me, but I managed to trick them all.' It gave a little hop of glee, then added, piously, 'By Lord Ram's blessing, of course.

'When I got to Lanka, though, it was a different story. Did you know the city has its own guardian goddess? She's black like the eclipse, and very fierce. She was standing on top of the gold turret of Ravan's palace, flames shooting from her eyes. Well, there's no tricking a real goddess, so I didn't even try. I just fell flat at her feet and told her who I was, and that I'd come to find you. I was afraid she'd burn me to a crisp, or maybe just squish me under her heel, but to my surprise she told me to go ahead. You know what else she told me? She said that the hourglass of Ravan's life had almost run out and it was time for her to leave Lanka. And then she vanished!

'So hold on for just a little while longer, mother. I'll go back and tell Lord Ram exactly where you are, and he'll come and get you out of this place.'

It sounded wonderful. Too wonderful. I'd learned, the hard way, to be suspicious. What if this was a part of Ravan's ploy to keep me foolishly happy and complacent until the time he'd promised me ran out?

Though my entire heart ached to believe the monkey, I said, 'If indeed you've been sent by my husband, Hanuman, he would have given you a token to present to me.'

The monkey slapped its head. 'Stupid me! I forgot.' It spat out something onto its palm, wiped it on its fur, and held it out to me.

I picked it up gingerly. Then my heart gave a great leap. It was Ram's ring.

THE SIGHT OF THE ring transported me to a happier time. Father Janak had presented it to Ram at our wedding. The priest had placed it on a copper plate and surrounded it with tulsi leaves because for some reason Ram loved the wild smell of tulsi. Pouring holy Ganga water over it, he asked me to place it on my husband's finger. I did so, fingers trembling with shyness as I touched Ram's hand. The ring was inlaid with the chandrakanta gem, the moon-jewel that represented our lineage, and it shone as though in sudden joy. All through my time in Ayodhya, whenever I saw it on Ram's hand, I was reminded of that special moment when I became his, and he became mine.

In our forest days, when we possessed almost nothing, I grew fond of the gem in a different way. On full moon nights, it gleamed with a special lustre, filling our simple hut with celestial light. And in that light, when we made love, I could see the eager passion on my husband's face.

Today, too, the gem shone equally brightly in the light of the full moon—but how different our circumstances were. How far we'd been pulled from each other.

Though seeing the ring had given me courage, I still knew nothing of Ram's plans for my rescue. And I had to send him word that time was running out.

But first I had to appease my starving heart.

'Is Ram well?' I asked. 'How does he look? What is he doing? Tell me everything!'

Hanuman said, 'By the time I met Lord Ram, he'd been on the road for a while, searching for you everywhere. He perked up a little bit when we showed him your jewellery. I guess you'd dropped it when Ravan was abducting you in that flying chariot of his. Smart thinking on your part, that was!

'Still, he was nothing but skin and bone, and burnt black by the sun. We offered him the best fruits and honey-sura that we had, but he refused to eat or drink anything. His brother Lakshman was in pretty bad shape too. He blamed himself for losing you. They both did, actually.'

'It was my own stupidity,' I confessed. 'First for wanting that cursed golden deer, and then for sending Lakshman away with the harshest accusations, and then for being duped by Ravan. I'm the one who's to blame for—'

Hanuman cut me off, a surprising sternness in his voice. 'Don't you be blaming yourself for someone else's wicked trickery, Mother. And don't ever let anyone else blame you for it either! Even the gods who've been around for so many ages don't know how to handle asura magic. How could you? You acted out of kindness, and because you thought a sadhu shouldn't leave your home hungry and unsatisfied. What happened after that wasn't your fault.'

I shot him a startled glance. I hadn't told him what had happened. How did he know? And his voice—it was sonorous and different, as though someone else was speaking through him.

There was more to this monkey than I'd guessed.

Hanuman continued calmly, as though there hadn't been an interruption. 'When I first saw Ram, even though he was all grimy and depressed, it was like there was a shining around him, so bright that I got dizzy, but in a happy kind of way—'

I broke in excitedly. 'It was like you forgot yourself. All you knew was that you'd been born for this moment, this meeting. I felt the same way when I first met him.'

Hanuman and I smiled at each other with a new understanding. Then he went on with the story.

'WE HIT IT OFF with the brothers right away,' Hanuman said, 'because our monkey tribe, too, had been banished from our homeland years ago. Our king Sugreev had a falling out with his brother and lost his wife in the process. We understood each other's pain and promised to help each other. Ram got Sugreev his kingdom back—it's a long story, he can tell it to you himself some other time. And Sugreev's put together a huge vanara army for Ram. They're just waiting to find out where you are before they start marching.'

'But how will they cross the ocean? They can't all fly over it like you did, can they?'

Hanuman scratched his head. 'No.' Then he brightened. 'I know what we can do! I'll take you back with me. I'll make myself big—no problem there. You can sit on my back and hold on tight to my fur, and before you know it, Lord Ram and you'll be back together. How about it? The only sad part will be, Ravan won't get what he deserves. But when he wakes up in the morning and finds you vanished—oh, I just wish I could be around to see his face!'

It was the perfect solution.

'You are so smart!' I cried. Hanuman bowed shyly, but I could tell he was pleased.

Then realization struck me like a giant hammer.

'I thank you for your valiant offer,' I said, even though my heart fought every word coming out of my mouth. 'But I can't accept it.

Then our action would be no better than Ravan's trickery. And it would deprive Ram of his glory. No, Ram must come here and rescue me himself and put an end to Ravan's wickedness forever. Isn't that what the goddess foretold? Perhaps that's the whole reason why I've had to go through all this suffering—so that the earth would be rid of his evil, once and for all, and the name of Ram be remembered by everyone in ages to come.'

Hanuman argued hard, trying to get me to change my mind. But finally he capitulated.

'I see what you mean, though I still hate to leave you in this hell,' he said. 'I'll describe to Lord Ram all the tortures you're putting up with, and how brave you've been. Also that time's running out. Don't worry, Mother. I'm sure he'll rescue you before this last month is over. Love's a pretty powerful weapon—it can cut through a lot of things. Now I've got to go—there's a couple of things I need to do before I get back to Lord Ram.'

'What things?' I asked, concerned. 'You aren't planning to fight the rakshasas on your own, are you?'

'Oh no, no,' said Hanuman. He blinked his eyes rapidly and looked so innocent that it made me suspicious. 'Just planning to eat a few fruits before I return. All that leaping around makes a body hungry, you know. Please don't worry, Mother. Just give me your blessings, and maybe point me in a good direction.'

I sketched a rough map of Lanka on the ground. Courtesy of Sarama, I knew quite a bit about the layout of the city, so I could tell him how to get to Ravan's favourite arbour, filled with all manner of exotic fruit trees—some of which, Sarama said, were brought from Indra's celestial gardens after the asura king's great victory over the gods.

I told him to be very, very careful.

'Indeed I will,' Hanuman promised. 'But first you must give me a token to take to Lord Ram. It'll do his heart good—he does miss you an awful lot, you know. Many times I've seen him sitting outside after everyone's gone to bed, just staring at the moon with a sad look on his face, and I know he's remembering you.'

His words were a balm to my heart, but they also wrung my entire being. Here was another paradox of love. I was deeply thankful that Ram loved and missed me—the opposite would have been unbearable—at the same time; I didn't want him to suffer even a moment of heartache because of me.

But time was passing and every moment brought greater danger to Hanuman. Already a couple of rakshasis were stirring and snorting as though they smelled something. I thought frantically. What could I give? I'd already thrown all my ornaments away. Then I remembered.

At our wedding, my mother had given me a little forehead-jewel. Her own mother had given this tikka to her at the time of her marriage, and she wore it always for good luck.

I, too, had worn it every day since then—partly because my mother had said it was lucky, but mostly because the jewel bore her touch. Several times Mother Kaushalya complained that it was too simple and wanted to give me one of her elaborate tikkas, especially when we attended state occasions, but on this matter I was firm, and Ram supported me. When Ravan was abducting me, I'd thrown all my other jewellery into the forest, but I couldn't bear to lose this one, my mother's blessing. Later, I'd tied it in a corner of my sari and hidden it from the rakshasis.

It cost me a pang to hand it over to Hanuman. Then I reminded myself where it was going. Whatever I gave to Ram wasn't lost to me; it would be with me even more fully.

I gave Hanuman the tikka and placed my hand on his head in farewell.

A shock went through me as I touched the monkey—because it wasn't a monkey I was touching. Who it was I couldn't clearly tell, but I sensed that his presence filled the ashoka grove, and the city, and even the earth. The light emanating from him was so brilliant that I had to close my eyes.

By the time I opened them, Hanuman had disappeared without a sound into the leaves of the ashoka tree.

I TRIED TO SLEEP, but due to excitement at having received news of my beloved, impatience at having Hanuman deliver my message, and anxiety that something might happen to the monkey before he had a chance to leave Lanka, rest was impossible.

Soon I heard distant crashes and shouts, gigantic thuds as though great buildings were coming down. The noise woke the rakshasis, who muttered fearfully. I gave up all pretense of sleep and paced around my tree, watching the sky. A white-hot comet sped through the air with a fearsome roar. I hoped it was Hanuman, escaping. But no, it was a missile. During my years in the forest, I'd listened in on the many conversations Ram and Lakshman had about astras. I recognized this one easily. It was the Brahmastra. There was no defeating it, not unless you had another Brahmastra. Hanuman was surely captured, perhaps even killed, by it.

Now Ram would never get my message. He would never know that Ravan held me captive. He would never come to rescue me.

I threw myself on the ground and wept. The rakshasis watched me suspiciously. One said, 'You think she knows what's going on?'

I didn't answer, but another said, 'I saw, in my dream, that she was whispering to a great yaksha warrior. Maybe it's him they're battling out there.'

A third cuffed my face—but carefully, so as to not disfigure me—and said, 'Where'd he come from? And what were you plotting? Tell us!'

'There was no yaksha warrior,' I said, truthfully enough.

'There was, too,' said the other rakshasi, and she cuffed me as well. 'Are you saying I'm lying? I saw his fangs in my dream. They were dripping blood. Maybe you put the thought to attack our city in his head.'

The others came closer, tightening the circle around me. 'Maybe he's your secret lover,' one of them hissed. 'Wouldn't King Ravan like to know that!'

I didn't care anymore what they did to me. Now that Hanuman had been captured or worse, I wanted to die. 'What if he was my lover?' I said. 'What would Ravan do if he knew that a yaksha was in the garden with me, doing whatever he wanted, while my fierce guards were all snoring soundly?'

The rakshasis growled their fury and rushed at me. I closed my eyes and stood still. No more flinching. No more weeping. Let them do their worst. *Death only comes once,* I told myself. *It might as well be now.*

Just then Trijata came running. 'Are you all crazy? Don't you know what King Ravan would do to all of you if you hurt her? In any case, it was no yaksha. It was a giant monkey—who knows how it entered Lanka city? Monkeys are not allowed anywhere on the island—you know why. I'm amazed it got in alive. No intruder has escaped our guardian goddess's razor-sharp gaze before this. They've caught it now, bound it and taken it to show the king, who was none-too-pleased at being awakened from his sleep. He was going to have it beheaded, but merciful as he is, he finally ordered the guards to set its tail on fire and parade it through the city.'

I held my breath, trying hard not to cry. My poor little Hanuman, to be tortured in this manner. I imagined his pain—he'd probably die from it. Oh Lord Agni, I prayed, you who control the heat of the flame, turn your cool and merciful eyes on Ram's messenger.

Just then one of the rakshasis screamed and pointed. Beyond the walls of the ashoka grove, the sky had turned an ominous smoky red.

'The city is burning,' someone said in a trembling voice.

Everything happened very fast after that. There was a lot of screaming, more explosions, and then the whole horizon lit up. I was terrified that Hanuman was dead, but a rakshasi, pale with terror, hurried up to say the monkey—who must have had help from the treacherous gods, or was perhaps a god in disguise—had set the royal buildings on fire and disappeared.

I lay down once again, covering myself with the tatters of my sari, hiding my elation. I held the ring tightly to my chest. Perhaps it had a special power, or perhaps it was the magic of hope, but I saw against my closed eyelids Hanuman flying over the ocean—huge now and glowing—in a great swift arc that rivalled the speed of the sun. I remembered Indra's words: when asking Brahma for his boon of invincibility over the different kinds of beings, Ravan had neglected to mention men and monkeys. And now men and monkeys had united against him.

Holding on to that happy thought, I fell into a dream where Hanuman landed at the southern tip of Bharatvarsha, where Ram waited. He bowed and handed my husband the jewel I'd given and recounted all he'd seen. Ram looked at the tikka. I waited for him to ask Hanuman about me. Even one question that showed his sympathy for my difficulties, his appreciation of my faithfulness would have satisfied me. One tear that expressed his tenderness and sorrow. But he said nothing, and his eyes were dry.

The pain of lost love had changed my husband. He'd closed off his heart in order to survive. Would he ever open it again?

Ram picked up his bow and aimed an arrow at the raging ocean. His face was implacable and emotionless, a stranger's face, carved from granite. Behind him stretched an army of monkeys so great in number that I couldn't see beyond them to the horizon. A voice devoid of emotion echoed across the waves. Was it my husband who spoke, or was it a god?

Mahakal awakes. Let the deaths begin.

Twenty-three

IT WAS, INDEED, THE TIME of death. I smelled it in the air, saw traces of it in the smoke and dust that filled the sky. Every day brought me deadly news. Some of the news was told to me by Sarama, whose eyes grew more and more haunted as the days went by.

Vibheeshan had been banished. Ravan had kicked him in the chest, the greatest insult an asura could imagine, in the presence of all the courtiers, and called him a traitor. Sarama had wanted to leave with him, but Vibheeshan refused to allow it.

'He's gone to join Ram,' Sarama told me. 'He wouldn't take me. He told me it was too dangerous. He told me that I needed to remain here so I could comfort you and support our son.' Her face was filled with sorrow, for no matter who won, forever to the asuras her husband would be known as Vibheeshan the Traitor.

'What will he do once he joins forces with Ram?' I asked.

Sarama didn't answer, but I guessed what she was afraid of. Vibheeshan knew all the asura warriors—their strengths and weaknesses, which astras would destroy whom. Would he divulge all this to Ram? Would he be willing to cause the destruction of his people, including his son, because of his belief in righteousness?

TIME CRESTED OVER US, a wave waiting to break. Against all possibility, a bridge was constructed over the ocean, stones that would not sink, as though the ocean god himself held them up with his thousand hands. Still, I doubted and feared. How could my husband—helped only by a band of monkeys—win against the hosts of asuras that had defeated even the gods?

But these monkeys were not like any other. With Ram and Lakshman leading them, they crossed the ocean and besieged the city. When the asura soldiers went out to meet them, they fell on them like crazed beings, slaying hundreds with nail and tooth, stone and tree. They refused to retreat, no matter how many of their brethren were killed by Ravan's army.

My guards huddled and spoke in frightened whispers, forgetting in their anxiety to torture me.

'They must be aided by the gods. How else could monkeys fight like this?'

'And how about those two brothers? Who knew that puny humans like them would have such powerful divine astras? That Ram, a single arrow shot by him can destroy a phalanx of seasoned warriors.'

And last of all, 'What's going to become of our beautiful Lanka? What's going to become of us?'

SOME DAYS, THINGS DIDN'T go well for Ram. On such days, Ravan came personally to see me and to enumerate my husband's losses. Twenty thousand monkeys killed. Who knows how many more wounded. Lakshman struck by a spear and carried off the field. Ram forced to call for a retreat.

'You can stop this massacre, you know,' he'd say. 'All you have to do is say yes to me. I'll send word to Ram that you've decided to become my wife. I'm quite sure he'll leave at that point. And here's my promise to you: I'll let him go safely, and with dignity.'

I'd keep my face turned away until he left. To his credit, since the night of his intoxication, he never tried to force me again. One day, when he was approaching us, a couple of my rakshasi guards started pushing me around, hoping for his approval. But he raised his hand to stop them.

'Ah, let her be,' he said. I tried to read his voice. Was it pity, or tiredness—for by now the war had stretched us all to breaking point—or certainty that it was just a matter of time before he had his way with me? I wasn't sure. Until the end, he'd remain an enigma, this asura king.

DAY BY DAY, THOUGH, Ram was gaining ground. His monkeys seemed to grow stronger as time passed. Maces thrown at their chest shattered. Arrows deflected off their bodies as though they'd hit iron. One by one, the great and noble rakshasa warriors—Dhoomrakshasa, Akampana, Prahasta—were sent out by Ravan to lead his army. They bowed to their lord, promising to bring him victory. None returned.

One morning I was awakened by a tremendous din, trumpets and the clash of cymbals, coming from one of the palaces. Trijata said, Ravan's brother Kumbhakarna is being awakened. He sleeps for six months and awakens for a day, but on that day, thanks to Brahma's boon, he is invincible.

'Is today that day?' I asked. My heart threw itself against the cage of my ribs.

'No. Ravan's been forced to wake him at the wrong time. Look, there he goes.'

The asura's enormous head rose high above the walls, obscuring the sun. He bellowed a deafening battle cry. My heart sank even as I prayed. Who could defeat such a monster?

But amazingly, he, too, didn't return. From the ashoka grove, I could hear the entire city mourning their fallen hero.

My rakshasi guards glared at me with hate and fear.

'Her husband must know big magic,' one said, 'to kill the great Kumbhakarna.'

I wanted to feel elation, but I only felt a deep tiredness. How much longer before the massacres ended?

TRIJATA CAME BY, BURSTING with news. The crown prince, Indrajit the undefeated, the commander of Ravan's forces, had been summoned this morning. Ravan had held off on calling upon him all this time because he was the heir to the throne and he'd promised Mandodari not to endanger him. But finally he'd had no choice.

'He should have done it earlier!' Trijata said. 'We all know that Indrajit is invincible, especially after he performs the Nikumbhila yagna and is blessed by the fire god.'

My heart was like a block of ice rattling in my chest. What ill news had Trijata brought now?

'Tell us what he did!' one of the rakshasis cried. 'We're the last to hear anything, stuck as we are here guarding this stupid human.' She kicked at me, but distractedly. They all gathered around Trijata to get news of Indrajit. Clearly, he was everyone's darling.

'Well, first he killed a bunch of monkeys, fighting so hard that they all fell back. Even their king Sugreev beat a retreat. But that wasn't enough for our Indrajit. He used his magic powers and flew into the sky, calling up an invisibility cloud around him. Then he travelled close to Ram and Lakshman and challenged them to battle with him. It was a glorious fight, the guards on the ramparts told me, each warrior using his best weapons, each cutting through the other's arrows. But finally, Indrajit called upon the powerful Naag astra. A million poisonous snakes exploded from it and bound Ram and Lakshman in their coils. And so the brothers fell.'

My rakshasi guards raised an outcry of joy.

'Glory be to our prince!' one of them said. 'Now this horrible war can end.'

'I don't believe it,' I said, with more bravado than I felt. Inside, my ice heart exploded into a million shards, each piercing me to the core.

'Ravan thought you might say that,' Trijata said. 'So he's instructed me to take you to view their bodies.'

TRIJATA LED ME TO Pushpak, the flying chariot. All along the way, rakshasas were celebrating. Dance, song, intoxicating drinks. Some spat at me but most ignored me. In their minds, I was no longer of importance.

The sight of Pushpak brought back so many terrible memories, I could hardly breathe. My hands grew clammy and my legs trembled. But I hardened myself and climbed in. I had to know the truth. Then I'd know what I needed to do.

The battlefield was a patchwork of blood, new and tragically bright, old and hopelessly dark. The stench hit me even though I was high in the air. There were so many bodies tangled together, I feared I'd never find my husband and his brother. But Pushpak knew where to go.

I looked down and there they were, Ram and Lakshman, bound together by writhing serpents unlike any I'd ever seen, other-worldly creatures born of darkest magic. The two brothers' faces were black and swollen with poison and pain. Around them lay several monkeys, also turning black. I figured that they'd valiantly tried to pry the serpents off Ram and Lakshman. The rest of the monkeys made a dejected circle around the fallen, not daring to approach the serpents. I looked for Hanuman—surely he wouldn't have given up—but I couldn't find him in the huddled throng.

I'd seen enough. The decision didn't take but a moment. I closed my eyes and leaped off the edge of the chariot. It was what I should have done the very first time I was in it. It would have saved so many lives—all sacrificed for me who did not deserve it.

Oh Ram, I thought, my dearest, my only beloved. I'm so sorry for bringing this death upon you. I don't know what evil karmas of mine separated us and caused us both so much sorrow. But at least we'll be together now. And your purpose will be fulfilled: I'll be delivered from Ravan's clutches.

I slammed into something hard almost immediately. Reeling, I opened my eyes and found I was still in the chariot. I put out my hand, but I felt nothing. Was Pushpak surrounded by some kind of magical wall?

Trijata gave me a shake. 'Wanted to get me into trouble, did you? No one gets away from Ravan that easily. And no one gets in or out of Pushpak unless its master—that's our king, in case you had any doubts—wishes it. Let's get you back now. Ravan said he's coming over to see you tonight.'

I fell to the floor of the chariot and lay dry-eyed. My sorrow was so great, no tears could express its death. So even death was beyond my reach? I would be Ravan's captive forever now. How long would I be able to hold out? Or would I, as Surpanakha had threatened, be given to her for slavery and torture?

I felt a deep hum rising from within the chariot, a throbbing that passed into my body. It was as though Pushpak sorrowed in my despair, though it had no power to go against its master's will.

When Pushpak landed, I refused to get up. Trijata gave an exasperated sigh. I thought she'd hit me again. I lay still, welcoming the pain. But she just hoisted me onto her shoulder and took me back to the grove. And that, too, was frightening.

My situation was so dire that even Trijata felt pity for me.

LATE THAT NIGHT, I heard the rakshasis whispering. Surprisingly, they sounded worried. I sat up to listen, but they gave me glances filled with hate and fear, and moved away. I had to wait until Sarama came to see me the next morning to find out what had happened.

Sarama looked harried. Her sari was askew, and her beautiful hair, which she took pride in braiding into intricate designs, was an uncombed tangle. She told me that soon after I left the scene, after the monkeys had lost all hope and begun their mourning wails, the sky filled with an enormous cloud. No, it was a bird, silver-white, huge beyond imagining, its curved beak large enough to swallow an entire rakshasa phalanx. It hovered over the brothers and flapped its wings, raising a blinding wall of dust. When the dust subsided, the snakes were gone, and the brothers sat up, blinking, as though waking from a dark dream.

'The bird hovered for a while over your husband, the guards reported later, as though speaking to him, though it didn't use words,' Sarama said. She stared at me, eyes narrowed. 'Who is Ram, really? He can't be a mere human because that was Garuda, the celestial bird-companion of the supreme god Vishnu, who came to rescue him.'

I wished I knew the answer to that. Instead, I said, 'You seem very disturbed today.'

'My son Taranisen has been asked to lead the army tomorrow,' she said.

I gripped Sarama's hands but she pulled them away and turned from me. I could only imagine the turmoil in her. On one side, her husband. On the other, her only child. And in front of her, the woman responsible for all her troubles.

For one of us, this day would end in tragedy. No, the death of Taranisen would wrench my heart, too.

Sarama said, 'I begged him not to go into battle, but of course we both knew that was impossible. Taranisen's loyal to the king, through and through, even though he loves his father and agrees with him. We knew, also, that he was doomed. He's a fine warrior, but no match for your husband.' She was weeping now. 'When he left, he smiled and touched my feet and told me to be of good cheer. He'd had a vision that Ram was the Supreme Being come to earth, to purify us and remove our sorrows. Death at his hand would be a glorious blessing.' She wiped her eyes and looked at me for confirmation.

Ram was the whole world to me. Everyone who knew him claimed he was special. But was he the Supreme Being? Was death at his hand a glorious blessing? I wasn't sure.

I breathed in the air, filled with the stench of carrion.

'Yes,' I said, to comfort Sarama, who had grown dear to me. A prevarication, a sacrifice at the altar of love.

TARANISEN HAD BEEN TRAINED by Vibheeshan himself. All day he fought marvellously. The greatest of the monkey warriors, Hanuman included, fled before his wrath. He wounded even Ram. But finally Ram called on the Brahmastra and killed him.

'Vibheeshan must have told him,' Sarama said. She had fainted at the news, but now she was calm, a statue of ice. 'Only Vibheeshan knew the secret of his death.'

I realized that even if Ram won the war and Vibheeshan was made king of Lanka and she the queen, Sarama would never forgive her husband for this betrayal.

ATROCITIES ESCALATED ON BOTH sides. The vanara army was being decimated. But even more rakshasas fell each day. All this death, for my sake. What a waste it was! Every moment I regretted that I hadn't listened to Hanuman and allowed him to carry me away.

After Taranisen's death, I did not see Sarama again. Trijata said, 'Ravan has ordered that no one except himself can see you from now on.' But I wondered if the real reason was that Sarama couldn't bear to look at me.

Thus I lost my only friend in Lanka.

I had to make do, now, with whatever gossip filtered to me through my rakshasi guard. The war wasn't going well. Ravan's ministers had advised him to send me out to Ram, to end the killing of his people. But of course he'd refused. I'd rather die with honour than live in shame, he declared.

The rakshasis looked uncertain as they discussed his decision. They were proud of their king's courage, of course, and too loyal to question him. But so many of their dear ones had died already. Lanka, once lauded as the most beautiful, most magical city in the three worlds, had become a charnel house.

'And the arch-enemy, Ram, and his brother also—even when you killed them, they refused to die,' one said.

'Look how Ravan struck Lakshman down,' added another. 'He pierced him in the heart with his magic spear, the shaktishel, given to him by the goddess herself. His death was certain, but then that monkey, the same one that burnt up our lovely city, flew far north and carried back an entire mountain of herbs and saved him.'

'They're being helped unfairly, by gods and sages,' a third rakshasi said. 'It isn't right.'

They glared at me, who was the cause of it all. If it wasn't for Ravan's strictest orders, they'd have torn me limb from limb.

I understood their fury. In their place, wouldn't I have felt the same way?

TIME FADED IN AND out of focus as I sat under my ashoka tree, its greyness pierced only by bereft wails. I held onto Ram's ring and prayed for an end to all the suffering around me. Surely it would come soon. After Lakshman's near-death, I heard, Ram fought with greater fury than ever before. The rakshasis whispered frantically.

Was it true that a mendicant had come to Mandodari and said, 'Have you hidden, carefully enough, the death-arrow created by the gods to slay Ravan, which he had wrested from Indra and given to you for safekeeping long ago?'

'Yes, I have,' the queen said.

'Are you sure the place is safe?' The mendicant asked. 'Are you sure the enemies will not guess where it is? Perhaps you should move it to a safer spot.'

'I am sure it is safe,' Mandodari said. But her voice quavered and involuntarily she glanced at the spire of the temple of the goddess, which had lain empty ever since the statue of the goddess had disappeared from it.

At once the mendicant metamorphosed into a giant monkey and leapt upon the temple roof. He punched at the spire with his huge, hairy fist, shattering it. Within was an arrow, coloured like lightning. The monkey grabbed it with both arms, pulled it free of the stones within which it was embedded, and shouting the name of Ram as though it was a battle cry, flew into the sky. Mandodari sent her guards after him immediately, but by then it was already too late. The monkey had disappeared.

When I heard the story, my heart seemed to expand until I could hardly breathe. My Hanuman! I was delighted by his trickery and its success. He would make sure the death-arrow reached Ram.

For the first time I believed that my rescue was possible. That it was close.

NEXT MORNING, THE WEEPING of my guards grew particularly intense. Indrajit had fallen—he, too, through treachery. The rakshasis cursed Vibheeshan, who had led Lakshman and a contingent of monkeys to the secret place where Indrajit performed the Nikumbhila yagna. They fell on him while he was praying and defiled the sacred fire. Indrajit duelled bravely with Lakshman, but he was unprepared, armourless. Lakshman killed him, and the monkeys kicked at his dead body until it was a shapeless mass of flesh.

The war had devolved from a righteous cause into gleeful carnage. Perhaps that's the way of all wars.

When they brought Mandodari her son's mutilated body, her cries rent the entire city. The very foundations of the city cracked with sorrow. Around me, the trunks of the ashoka trees split apart in distress.

Hearing her sorrow, Ravan knew what had happened: their valiant, blameless son, whose only flaw was that he'd obeyed his father without question, was gone. He swooned and fell from his throne to the ground. For an entire day he lay there, eyes unfocussed. When he finally returned to himself, he said, 'Now I know how it feels to have your heart torn from your body.'

There was only one thing left for him to do. He roused himself and called upon the remnants of his army. They rode out to war with their king, knowing they would not return.

Disobeying the explicit orders they'd been given, my rakshasi guards left me and rushed to the gates of the city to see their beloved king, one last time, in his terrible splendour. To offer him a hero's farewell. They, too, didn't return.

I could have walked out of the ashoka grove and gone anywhere I wished. I could have walked out of the city to the battlefield. Part of me longed for it, to see the final battle, Ravan's death at the hands of my beloved. My vindication. But I didn't. I waited for Ram to come to me, to see how I'd suffered for his sake. For the sake of love.

Twenty-four

DAY, NIGHT. DAY, NIGHT. AN acrid smoke covered the sky. Was the war over, then? Were they burning the bodies, rakshasas and monkeys all together, their differences erased by death?

I waited in the ashoka grove, my body afire with impatience—for a very long time, it seemed. Had they all forgotten me? Finally, exhausted, I lay down on the ground.

But no, at least one person had remembered. I awoke to hands squeezing my throat, furious fetid breath on my face. Surpanakha.

I pulled at her arms but, fueled by hate, she was too strong for me.

'Killed you! I should have killed you there in the forest, the very first time I saw you by yourself,' she panted. Crusty tears had left their tracks on her face. 'My first mistake. And my second one: I should have killed you right when you got to Lanka, no matter what they did to me afterwards. So many great warriors dead, my dearest brother dead, all for what? For a worthless creature like you!'

So Ravan had met his end. I tried to feel the reality of that fact, but I couldn't keep my mind on it. Why hadn't Ram come looking for me, then? Shouldn't he have done that first, before settling other political matters? Hadn't he missed me as much as I'd missed him?

But I couldn't think further. Couldn't breathe. In a moment I'd pass out, and then Surpanakha would choke me to death.

No! I hadn't endured the torture of this entire endless year for this, to be killed just moments before I had a chance to be reunited with Ram.

With the last of my strength, I focussed on my navel, on the manipura chakra, abode of power, seat of the goddess. From the depths of memory, I called up the martial moves I'd been practising, mentally, all these months. I let my body go slack and heavy, like a sack of potatoes, and as Surpanakha braced herself to accommodate the sudden weight shift, I twisted my head sideways, slipping out of her clutches. 'Ram!' I cried, bringing the side of my arm, held stiff as a dagger, onto her neck. She choked and staggered backwards, and I made use of my momentary advantage by delivering a couple of well-placed sidekicks. The second one landed where her nose had been. She clutched her face, screaming, and I noted, with some satisfaction, that black blood trickled from between her fingers. But I'd stopped her only for a moment. Unlike me, she was strong and well-fed. And she knew magic. In a moment she had transformed into full rakshasi mode, growing to twice my height. Her fingernails were sharp and curved like scimitars, and her fangs were sharp as well. I knew I was no match for her, but I was determined to do my best.

I balled my hands into fists and crouched low. 'Ram,' I whispered as I stepped backwards towards my ashoka tree.

Surpanakha rushed forward, hoping to pin me against the tree trunk, but she didn't know the ground here as well as I did. How could she? She wasn't the one who had spent night after night tossing on it, on a bed made only of the leaves the tree had let fall for my sake. These leaves still covered the ground—and the giant root that sometimes acted as my pillow.

As I'd hoped, Surpanakha tripped on the unseen root and went flying into the trunk. She threw out her hands to protect herself and her nails sank deep into the trunk. I was afraid she'd pull them out right away, that I'd gained no more than a moment's advantage, but they seemed stuck in there. The ashoka tree was helping me. I sent it my thanks and used this opportunity to kick out her legs from under her and, while she was off-balance, to deliver several punches to her stomach.

Having done all I could, I retreated behind a large bush.

Surpanakha wrenched her hands free from the trunk and came at me, bellowing her rage. Her jaws, wide open, had grown to a gigantic size. Her fangs were as long as knives, and as sharp. They dripped a greenish saliva—probably poison of some kind. I could see that she intended to sink them into my neck. My only hope was to dodge her with the quickest footwork I could manage. But my strength was fading. Months of starvation had taken their toll.

I won't give up, I said to myself. And I won't run. If Ram finds my dead body here, at least none of the wounds will be on my back.

How the fight would have gone I don't know, but at that moment a voice, edged with sharp authority, called from the corner of the ashoka grove. 'Surpanakha! What are you doing? Have you lost what little sense you had? I order you to stop.'

It was Sarama, but a Sarama so different that I had to look twice. She was attired resplendently in a gold sari and covered head to foot with ceremonial jewellery. Her face was expertly made up with sandalwood paste and her lips reddened. Her hair, which had been left carelessly uncombed the last few times I'd seen her, was tied in an elaborate design that looked familiar. Then I remembered. A long time ago, my hair, too, had been arranged like that, to accommodate a coronet.

Of course! Now that Ram had destroyed Ravan, Vibheeshan was to be the new king, and Sarama the new queen.

But her kajal-rimmed eyes were still filled with loss. I guessed that would never change.

What good is a kingdom when you have no one to leave it to?

Sarama clapped her hands regally and a phalanx of armed female guards, hidden behind the trees until now, stepped smartly forward and surrounded Surpanakha, lances at the ready.

'Behave, for once, like the princess you are,' Sarama said to Surpanakha. 'Haven't you done enough harm to Lanka already? Had you not come crying to Ravan, asking for revenge and describing Sita's beauty, tempting him, we wouldn't be seeing this day. Now at least think of the welfare of your people. If you harm Sita, what do you think Ram will do to the surviving rakshasas?'

Her stern tone would have cowed most people, but Surpanakha bristled. 'Look who's talking. The traitor's wife! Maybe you should ask yourself a few questions first. For instance, if your dear husband hadn't given away our secrets and told Ram exactly how to kill our greatest warriors, including my brother—and oh yes, I forgot, your own son—would we be seeing this day?' Having silenced Sarama, she turned to me.

'Don't think that you've seen the last of me,' she hissed.

She pushed her way past the guards, her ruined face held high, and disappeared into the shadow of the grove.

Sarama stood so still, I thought she'd been turned—like Ahalya—into stone. Only her eyes glittered with unshed tears. But she knew how to act like a queen, what the responsibilities entailed. After a moment, she took a deep breath and spoke to me with cool courtesy. She spoke as though we hadn't been friends and confidantes through all these months of shared grief, and I realized, with a twinge in my heart, that that part of our relationship was over.

'Ram wishes to see you. Vibheeshan will convey you to him in a ceremonial palanquin. My women will dress you appropriately. But first there is another request. From Mandodari. Her last request to you, she says. She asks that you meet her for a few moments.'

My whole being ached with impatience for my beloved. But a last request deserves to be honoured.

'Where is she?' I asked.

'On the seashore,' Sarama said. 'Ravan is near to death and in great pain. He wishes to draw his last breath under the open sky.'

'In great pain, did you say?'

'Yes. The astra that felled him must have had occult powers. Our medicine men can do nothing to reduce his agony, nor to hasten his death.'

I was surprised to discover that I no longer felt any hatred towards Ravan. Perhaps it was because he wasn't a threat anymore. Or perhaps we must all experience a moment of solemnity at the passing of great power, no matter how ill-directed it has been. And though he'd been my worst enemy, I had to admit that Ravan had been a mighty sovereign, a much-loved hero to his people, and a sincere devotee of Shiva.

I asked Sarama to wait. I hurried through the grove—grown so familiar over the months—and hastily gathered a few herbs that grew in the shadows of the trees. Perhaps they would ease Ravan's passing into the realm of Yama.

IT WAS THE FIRST time I had walked on the shore in Lanka. How beautiful the island must have been before the war, the pristine ocean and the glittering city, lying side by side like lovers, the waves kissing the shining fortress walls, the walls lending the water their elegant curvature. But today there was no shining. The blood-soaked sands were a dull red, the colour of decay. The sea and sky were both grey, though it was afternoon. The air, dense with the odour and smoke of the mass cremations, brought bile into my throat. I forced it down and walked towards where Mandodari sat with Ravan's head in her lap. She bent over him, running a hand tenderly over his ruined, bleeding body, while he held on to her other hand as though without it to anchor him, he might float away into the great void before he was ready for it. Seeing them like this, I realized something: although Ravan had countless wives and concubines, although he had been obsessed with me to the point of ruination, it was only Mandodari, wife of his youth, whom he truly loved.

I stood silent and still, reluctant to break this intimacy by announcing my presence.

Ravan's face was pale and crusted with whatever medicines his vaidyas had applied to his skin, and his lips, flecked with a bloody foam, moved slowly and uncertainly, as though they had forgotten what words were. The two of them hadn't seen me yet and continued with their halting conversation, punctured by Ravan's moans of pain.

'I'm sorry, my queen, my Mano,' Ravan was saying. 'I'm sorry for so many things—including the distress I've caused you all these years. I'm sorry I couldn't win this war for you. I'm sorry that I'm leaving you to suffer alone in a world that will be hostile to you because of me. But most of all, I'm sorry that I took your son Meghnad, the most magnificent warrior our lineage has known, from you. Because of me, he's dead now and you are childless.'

I could tell his strength was fading fast, the words tangling in his tongue.

Mandodari remained silent. I could tell she was trying to contain her grief, not wanting to distress Ravan further by breaking down in front of him. She would cry, I was sure, for days to come, for maybe the rest of her life, for her darling son. And for her husband, because—such is love's irrational pull—she loved him in spite of all the grief he'd caused her. But for now she was determined to be strong for his sake.

HAVING COLLECTED HERSELF, MANDODARI finally spoke. 'Meghnad was, indeed, the light of my eyes. But he died as a warrior should, defending his homeland. At least I have that consolation. And no, you didn't leave me childless. We have a daughter still.'

'A daughter?' Ravan rasped.

So this was why she wanted me to come here!

My entire being rose up in revolt, wanting to interrupt her, to shout that she was mistaken, that this was some crazy fantasy inside her head. But death when it swoops close imposes its own silences, so I held my tongue.

'Yes,' Mandodari said. 'Remember her, our beautiful baby whom you sentenced to perdition for no fault of her own? I made sure she wasn't killed. I bribed the asura to whom you'd appointed this task—as much with my tears as with the treasure I gave him. And so he left her far away, in a small kingdom in the north, where the king found her and brought her up. I should have told you this a long time ago, but I was afraid. I didn't know what you'd do to me in one of your terrible rages. Forgive me for that weakness. I didn't think it mattered, because I was sure we'd never see our girl again.'

Ravan's head jerked and he gasped in pain. Then he said, with effort, 'You—saw her?'

'You did, too,' Mandodari said. She turned and looked at me, and I realized that she'd known all along that I was standing there.

'Here,' she said, 'is your daughter. Sita.'

Ravan turned his head with great effort and stared at me. His eyes, once so terrifying, were glazed, barely open. Was that hope in them, or horror?

'That isn't true, Mandodari,' I said hotly. 'You're jumping to conclusions.'

'Didn't King Janak find you wrapped in a gold cloth unlike anything he'd seen before?' she challenged me. 'I sent spies to Mithila. They talked to people who remembered what the cloth had looked like. It was definitely woven here in Lanka.'

I drew in my breath to argue, to say that the spies had told her what she wanted to hear, but Ravan was speaking already. He had to make a great effort, and fresh blood stained his lips.

'Surely you're wrong, Mano. If Sita was my own flesh and blood, wouldn't I have known it as soon as I touched her hand that day in the forest? I might have still brought her with me, but not by force. I would have persuaded her with fatherly concern, so she could spend the rest of her banishment with us in love and safety. For although I never spoke of it, I've thought often, and with great remorse, of our daughter.

'But this much is true: I'm connected to Sita through some mystery. From the beginning I've felt that, and it's been part of the reason for my obsession.'

He lunged suddenly, before I could move, and grasped my foot with a trembling hand.

The hand had barely any power in it. I could have kicked it away without effort. Why then didn't I do so? Was it compassion for the dying? Or because I felt the truth in what he'd just said? That indeed we were connected.

Ravan gave a great shudder. Then he whispered, 'I see. I see it now.'

'What do you see?' Mandodari cried.

Ravan didn't seem to hear her. There was a smile on his face. 'How beautiful it is,' he said, his voice weak but ecstatic.

At his words, the world around me faded and another one opened up. It was the same world I'd glimpsed so tantalizingly when I'd first met Ram, but this time it no longer eluded me. I stepped fully into it and knew it for what it was: Vaikuntha, the abode of Vishnu. And even more surprising, I knew the beings that inhabited it.

Here was Vishnu himself, reclined upon the great serpent Seshnaag, effulgent with an otherworldly light. He looked strangely familiar. Glancing closer, I saw to my surprise that it was none other than Ram. More divine, and untouched by the lines that sorrow and hardship had etched upon his face, but clearly him! At his feet sat his divine consort Lakshmi. I tried hard to glimpse her face, but it was turned away from me. Standing in the corner, palms joined, was his loyal gatekeeper, Jaya.

'I need to rest, Jaya,' Vishnu said. 'Will you make sure I'm not disturbed?'

'With my life, my Lord,' Jaya replied, retreating to his post. Just before he drew the great golden gates shut, he raised his face, alight with devotion, for one last look at his Lord. With a shock that jolted me to my core, I saw who he was. Ravan.

How could this be? How could the furious Ravan I'd known, filled with hate for Ram, driven by revenge, determined to cause grief to him and all those closest to him, have been Jaya?

And who was I in this cosmic puzzle?

But there was no time to think things through, for there was a din at the door, the voices of children pitched high, demanding something. Jaya and his brother and fellow-gatekeeper, Vijaya, were trying unsuccessfully to quieten them.

How was it possible for children to reach Vaikuntha?

'We want to see Vishnu,' one of the children said, his voice surprisingly self-assured. 'We've come a long way to see him and we aren't going to be turned away by mere gatekeepers.'

'My Lord has just gone to sleep, after much celestial toil,' Jaya said. 'He's asked not to be disturbed. I can't go in there right now. Please, let me make you comfortable. He'll wake up soon.'

Another boy spoke up. 'Are you trying to trick us? Everyone knows that Vishnu's sleep lasts for eons. We can't wait that long. We have duties too. Cosmic ones. We're the Sanatkumaras, sons of Brahma, and more importantly, devotees of Vishnu. Vishnu has promised to always be available to his devotees. And now you, a mere gatekeeper, are telling us you won't let us see him?'

'I can't. I made a promise, too. I told Him that I wouldn't let anyone in until he wakes,' Jaya said. 'Hey! What are you trying to do? Vijaya, grab them.'

From the scuffling noises outside, I gathered that the children were trying to slip past the gatekeepers. I heard one of them cry out, 'Wake up, Lord Vishnu! See how your devotees are being mistreated by your servants.'

Vishnu stirred, but he was still deep in cosmic slumber.

Now another child spoke, his voice strong and resonant, echoing through Vishnu's chamber, 'Jaya and Vijaya, by the powers I've gained through meditating on my Lord, from whom you're forcibly separating me, I curse you both and send you to earth, to live seven mortal lifetimes with all their sorrows, the greatest of which will be your separation from Vishnu.'

In the blink of an eye, the gates opened and Vishnu was outside though I hadn't seen him rise from his bed. The children flung themselves at him with joy; he gathered them to him in a loving embrace. It seemed to last only a moment, but cosmic time is a slippery thing. Then the Sanatkumaras were gone and the gatekeepers lay at Vishnu's feet, weeping.

'I can't negate the curse of such great beings,' Vishnu said to them with sorrow, 'but since you were following my dictates, I can modify it. You can choose to spend seven lives on earth as devotees, remembering me with love, or three lives as my enemies, remembering me more intensely with hate.'

'Three lives,' Jaya said, without hesitation. 'You know that every moment we spend away from you is equal to the tortures of the deepest hell.'

'I give you this additional boon, then,' Vishnu said. 'I will come down to earth myself each time to deliver you from your mortal body. And before you die, you will know who you are and thus depart in peace.'

From behind him a melodious voice spoke. It was Lakshmi. 'Take me with you, Lord. I can't bear to remain in the emptiness of Vaikuntha without you.'

'If that's what you truly wish, I'll take you to aid me in my work,' Vishnu said. 'But remember, as a mortal, you'll suffer anguishes that you cannot even imagine now. Some of the time we'll be separated, even estranged. Such is the world of Maya, in which I, too, will be caught.'

'It's a price I'll gladly pay in order to be with you,' Lakshmi said. She turned her shining face, and I finally saw who she was. It was me.

A WEAK WHISPER BROUGHT me back to the present. It was Ravan. 'Ah, I didn't know! I didn't know! Forgive me, Goddess, my dearest Lady, for all that I've done to you in ignorance. I have no words for how deeply I regret it.' His face was racked with grief, and I knew that he, too, had experienced the same vision. 'I'm leaving now, but before I go, will you in your compassion, place your foot on my head?'

As though in a trance, I moved forward and did as he asked, feeling the blood, still warm and sticky from his wounds, on my sole. He held onto my foot with the last of his strength and gave a great sigh. His eyes closed.

THAT'S HOW THEY FOUND us, Vibheeshan and Hanuman and the other chieftains of Ram's army who had been searching for me through the city. I saw the shock in their eyes at coming upon this strange scene. Some of them wondered what it could possibly mean. Some, I could tell, questioned it. Some would gossip about it later.

It was Hanuman who finally broke the silence. 'Mother,' he said, bowing deeply, 'I've come to take you to Lord Ram. This is the end of your long sorrow.'

I walked away from he who had been Ravan—or was it Jaya? I'd have to tell Ram all this once we were finally alone. Would I also have to tell him who he'd been in the vision, the great Vishnu, or did he know that already?

I laid my hand on Hanuman's soft, furry head. Hard to imagine that he'd killed hundreds of rakshasas with a single blow. 'Bless you, my Hanuman, for all you've done to bring this joyful day to me. Bless you especially for coming to me in my darkest hour and giving me the hope that my sorrow would, indeed, have an end.'

Then we abandoned formality and grinned at each other gleefully, like truant schoolchildren.

I didn't know that, for me, a greater sorrow was about to begin.

Twenty-five

I WAS IN A FEVER OF impatience to meet Ram, but Vibheeshan, who liked to do things properly, said that first I had to be dressed the way the wife of a victor should be. That was what Ram wanted too, he added.

Perhaps Vibheeshan was worried that if Ram saw the way I'd been treated, he'd grow furious and order his army to wreak havoc on the city. He didn't know my husband. No matter how angry Ram was, he'd never let his emotions carry him away from the path of righteousness.

I could have insisted on going as I was, but vanity overcame me. I wanted my beloved to see me at my best, not in smelly rags, with matted hair and a face streaked with tears and dirt. I told Vibheeshan I would do what he requested.

'Please come to the palace,' he said. 'We've prepared the royal quarters for you and Ram. For we all know that without him there would be no victory. And thus, he is the real king of Lanka.'

But I'd made a vow never to step inside any of Ravan's edifices, and I told him that.

Vibheeshan sighed. 'It's going to take longer this way,' he pointed out.

'I can't break my word,' I heard myself saying. 'It is not the way of the House of Raghu.'

The words echoed inside my chest, reminding me of the terrible errors I'd made in the past. But this time they felt right. They made me realize that I, too, belonged to the House of Raghu and held to their creed.

A line of Sarama's waiting-women carried all I needed to the ashoka grove. I allowed them to bathe me in perfumed water and wash out my hair. I allowed them to oil and braid it with flowers, and to dress me in a splendid new vermillion silk coloured like the setting sun, and even to put gold jewellery on me. Beautiful though they were, the necklaces and bangles that I'd grown unused to hung heavy as chains.

'Are these Sarama's?' I asked.

The head attendant shook her head. 'They are from Mandodari's coffers, never worn. She insisted, saying she wanted you to have them.'

I didn't know how to decipher Mandodari's action. I looked at the clothes and jewels—and it struck me that they were what a mother would have given her daughter when she left for her husband's house. She'd stored them in her coffers all these years, hoping. But when the hope came true—or so she believed—it crushed everything else that she had loved.

A great pity rose up in me, but there was no time to feel it fully. I stepped into the decorated palanquin, curtained with silk, that Vibheeshan had readied, and we were on our way.

From behind the curtains I was surprised to see that the bearers were taking me towards the gates of Lanka, away from the gold-domed buildings where Ravan had held court.

'Where are we going?' I asked Vibheeshan.

'To the seashore,' he said. 'Ram wants to meet you there before he enters the city.'

It was a strange choice. But I was too excited to wonder why.

A DEAFENING CHEER ROSE up as soon as everyone saw the palanquin. I had to force myself not to flinch at its loudness. It had been a long time—fourteen years—since I'd been in such a large gathering, had heard my name being chanted like a mantra, *SitaRamSitaRamSitaRam.* The arc of my life was changing direction, swinging me back towards Ayodhya, to don the heavy mantle of queenship.

I said to myself, With Ram by my side, I'll surely handle everything perfectly.

But when the palanquin came to a halt, I was so nervous at the thought of all those eyes upon me that I froze.

'Mother,' Hanuman said, lifting the curtain. 'We're here.' He gave me a solemn, ceremonial smile, and extended his small, leathery hand. Gripping it, I stepped out. Excitement burst inside me, brilliant fireworks. But Hanuman sniffed the air uncertainly, as though he sensed something that wasn't quite right.

Ram was seated on a makeshift throne, a pile of stacked shields that must have belonged to the fallen rakshasas. There were wounds on his body, and his face was thin, its shining dimmed. Hanuman was right, he hadn't eaten or slept well in a long time. How much my husband had suffered for my sake. It made me feel at once sad and guilty, but also precious.

Beside him stood Lakshman, holding his bow and arrow in readiness, guarding his brother as always. I saw the great scar on his chest where Ravan's spear had struck him and felt a guilty pang. I was ashamed to look into his face, for I remembered the evil insults I'd shouted at him in my desperation on our last day together. Could I ever apologize enough for my behaviour? But Lakshman smiled at me with genuine delight and bowed, joining his palms in respect. In his magnanimity, he'd forgiven me.

I was thankful, though only for a moment. I couldn't focus my attention on anyone other than my beloved Ram.

The setting sun had formed a blood-red halo behind my husband's head, obscuring his expression. I was surprised that he hadn't stood up, that he wasn't rushing forward to greet me. I remembered how, in the forest, he would hug me unabashedly, and though of course he couldn't do that in front of so many individuals, his soldiers among them, I hoped that he would, at least, approach me and touch his lips—the lips I'd dreamed of for so many months—to my forehead in a ceremonial kiss of welcome.

But Ram didn't move.

I was disappointed, but mostly I was confused. Perhaps there was a protocol I was missing? Since he was the victor-king and I the rescued one, perhaps I was supposed to approach him, to thank him for rescuing me.

Very well. I would do it.

As I STEPPED FORWARD, a hush descended on the crowd. I could feel thousands of eyes on me like piercing darts as I walked to my husband. It was hard, after so many years of solitude, to be the centre of everyone's curious attention. But I took a deep breath and reminded myself of what was important: Ram, only Ram, my heaven, my bliss, my saviour, my refuge.

My husband stood up as I approached him. How tall he was, Ram, the invincible warrior, looming over me. I bowed before him and touched his feet. I wanted to thank him, to tell him how proud I was of him. But I was too overcome by emotion. I hoped that he'd see on my face the love I was unable to communicate. When I looked up, there was a deep and tortured tenderness in his eyes. I knew then how much he'd missed me, how much he'd suffered.

But he didn't touch me. And when I, pushing all shyness aside, not caring what the crowd might think, reached for his hands, he took a step back and crossed his arms.

Stunned, my head awhirl, I wondered if he was angry with me for having put him to all this trouble. For begging so foolishly for the golden deer and causing this war, this devastation.

But no, a voice inside me said. The devastation started before that, with a young woman being toyed with and then repulsed, her nose and ears cut off.

Foolish, insidious voice. I pushed it away.

When Ram spoke, there was no anger in his voice. There was no feeling at all. It was steady and impartial and uncaring, and so unlike my husband's that had I not been standing right in front of him I wouldn't have believed that it was him speaking.

'I have rescued you, Sita,' said the voice. 'I have built a bridge over the ocean and crossed over it with my allies of the monkey nations. My followers and I have suffered greatly in the process, for the rakshasa army was a powerful one. Now we have slain Ravan, and set you free. Here ends my duty to you, and my responsibility. Go where you will to live out the rest of your days.'

I stared at him uncomprehending. Had the yells of the crowd impaired my understanding? Perhaps the fact that I hadn't eaten for so long was making me dizzy and confused? Surely Ram couldn't have spoken the cruel words I thought I heard.

'What do you mean?' I finally managed to say.

'It was my duty to rescue you,' Ram repeated patiently, as though speaking to a child. 'But I cannot take you back to Ayodhya with me. Ravan abducted you from my home. You've lived in his palace for a year now. Who knows what kind of relationship you've had with him—'

I interrupted him, my voice shaking with fury. 'Is that the trust you have in me and in my love for you? Is that what you think of my virtue? Well, then, check with the inhabitants of the palace—or ask Hanuman, who saw me in the depths of my sorrow. I never set foot inside Ravan's palace. I never responded to him, no matter how much he threatened or cajoled. I refused to eat or drink a grain of food, or even a drop of water, so that I wouldn't be beholden to him in any way. Until today, when I was asked by Vibheeshan to follow court protocol, I wore only tree bark and didn't even comb my hair.'

'What you say may well be true,' the man who was no longer my beloved Ram said in his iron voice. 'But your words are not proof enough. Not for the citizens of Ayodhya. I cannot take back to them a queen whose virtue they'd question, whose purity they'd disbelieve. They will think that, like my father Dasharath, I swayed from the path of dharma, enchanted by a wife's charms. It will throw the entire kingdom in turmoil—and I cannot allow that to happen. I owe it to them.'

'And what about what you owe me, your wife?' I cried. 'Don't I have any rights?'

'I owe you safety and comfort,' Ram said, and his voice did not shake even in the slightest. 'And that I will provide. You may stay here in Ravan's palace. Vibheeshan will care for your needs. Or if the forest is more to your liking, you can go with Sugreev. He will be happy to give you a home. In any of these places, you can take another mate. I free you of all obligation to me.'

Ram's words, spoken so calmly, piled around me like ice. They froze my blood. Yet strangely, they gave me strength. Because what could happen to me that was worse than what Ram had just done by doubting my virtue in front of the entire populace? By rejecting me because of what his subjects might whisper? By shaming me by suggesting that I take another husband?

'It's not in your power to free me,' I said to Ram, and I, too, spoke calmly. 'The gods bound us at our wedding, with Agnidev, the holy fire, as witness, and they know that I am pure and blameless. Yes, I wanted the golden deer. But that was a mistake, a folly, not a sin. Yes, Ravan has touched this body, this bundle of flesh and bones and blood. Using his magic trickery, he took on the appearance of a sadhu and dragged me, against all my will and effort, into his chariot. I tried my best to stop him. I couldn't. Am I to be punished because he was physically stronger, because he used rakshasa guile?

'If you reject me now, word will travel all across Bharatvarsha, and men everywhere will feel that they, too, can reject a wife who has been abducted. Or even been touched against her will. Countless innocent women—as innocent as I am—will be shunned and punished because of your act. Is that dharma? Is that what you want?'

Ram looked stonily ahead as though he hadn't heard me.

'Ravan stole me away forcibly,' I continued, 'but even he didn't insult me as you've done here today. He respected me enough to not violate my body. And over my mind he never had control. But you—you've violated my heart, which I'd given to you in love.'

I paused, though I knew it was foolish to hope. Ram continued to stare at the horizon. The deepest pain of my heart, which I'd bared for him, didn't seem to touch him. There was no point in saying anything more to him.

I turned to Lakshman and said, 'Dearest brother-in-law, I ask your pardon for all the cruel words I said to you. I didn't mean any of them. I said them only so that you would go to your brother's aid.'

'I know,' Lakshman replied. 'I forgave you long ago. I knew you spoke only out of love for Ram.' He lifted his face and looked into my eyes for the first time since we were banished, and I saw that he was weeping. He, too, hadn't expected Ram to behave in this way. But he couldn't save me. We both knew that.

I wanted to sink into the ground, to become one with the earth from whose womb King Janak had once lifted me up with such hope and love. Surely his heart—and the heart of my mother Sunaina would have shattered into a million pieces if they'd known how Ram, into whose hands they'd given me, was treating me. How, for him, my needs came after that of even the lowest of the citizens of Ayodhya.

Goddess, I thought in my shame and desperation. What shall I do now? Where shall I go?

THEN, IN THE DARK hopelessness of my heart, a thought flashed like fire. Abandoned as I was by my husband, no one could save me. But I could save myself. Love and happiness might not be in my control, but at least my dignity still remained mine. I might not be able to have the life I wanted, but I could choose the manner of my death.

Thus I made my decision.

'Brother-in-law, I must ask you to do one last thing for me,' I said to Lakshman. 'Build me a fire. There's nothing left for me on this earth now that my husband, whom I love more than my own self, who has been in my heart and in my prayers every single day since I was taken by Ravan, has shamed and rejected me so cruelly—for no fault of my own—in front of this entire assembly. Therefore, I've decided to end my life today.'

Lakshman tried to stop me and so did Vibheeshan. Hanuman fell at my feet and beseeched me not to take this terrible course. They even called Sarama from the palace to reason with me. But the one person who could have swayed me stood still as a mountain crag. Behind the mask of kingship he had donned, I thought I saw pain in his eyes. I thought they brimmed with tears. But he said nothing.

Since no one would assist me, I began to gather pieces of wood from the battleground myself, pulling them from destroyed chariots or broken bows. Their jagged edges bit into my hands, making me bleed, but I went on.

When they saw that I wouldn't be deterred, Lakshman and Hanuman helped me, weeping all the while. Soon, there was a huge pile of wood in front of Ram. I asked for a brand and lit the fire. The flames leaped up avidly. Taller than the treetops, taller than Ravan's palace. Heat blistered my skin, burnt away my eyebrows. While everyone stared in horror or cried out to me to stop—everyone except my husband—I stepped into the blaze.

LATER, THE BARDS WOULD sing of the miracle that occurred. Agni, the fire-god himself, appeared and declared my innocence, putting my hand into Ram's as though this was our second wedding. And Ram—who'd fallen to the ground, crazed with grief, once I'd disappeared into the flames—embraced me, whispering apologies and love, begging my understanding.

'The virtue of the queen of Ayodhya has to be above all suspicion. You see how important that is, don't you, my dearest?' he said, his voice full of entreaty. 'And now you've proved it in a way that can never be questioned!'

And I, nestled against his chest after our long separation, dazed yet triumphant as the gods rained celestial flowers upon us and roar upon roar of jubilation rose from the crowd around us, focussed only on his dear, familiar heartbeat, *SitaRamSitaRamSitaRam.*

Truly love is the strongest intoxicant of them all, the drink of deepest oblivion. Else how could I have forgiven him so quickly for what he'd done?

No. Love is the spade with which we bury, deep inside our being, the things that we cannot bear to remember, cannot bear anyone else to know. But some of them remain. And they rise to the surface when we least expect them.

Here is one such thing: the terrible, maddening pain that engulfed my entire body when I entered the fire. I had to use every shred of willpower to keep myself from running out, screaming. The anguish with which I prayed for death to release me. The anger I felt that I, who was innocent, should be made to suffer in this way. My agony was timeless—I don't know, in terms of human measurement, how long it lasted. But I do know this: in that agonizing trial, I was transformed.

Perhaps that was why I had to endure pain—because true transformation can only happen in the crucible of suffering. All impurities fall away from gold only when it's heated to melting.

By the time the gods intervened, I was no longer just the Sita of old: daughter of earth, strong and silent, patient and deep, forbearing and forgiving. I was something else, too.

The fire-god himself acknowledged this change. Daughter, he called me.

Yes, I was now Sita, daughter of fire.

But I didn't know yet what this meant.

Twenty-six

THERE ARE TIMES IN OUR lives when the hours are an unmoving icy morass and times when they fly past us in a blur. How ironic that the joyous times we'd like to hold on to are the most fleeting, while the saddest ones clutch at us, refusing to let go. I'd been frozen by fear and anguish ever since I'd been dragged to Lanka. Now I was swept upon the wings of heady celebration so rapidly that it made my head spin.

It wasn't all merrymaking, though, because I had some important responsibilities. When Ram crowned Vibheeshan, I was the one who stood by my husband's side, pouring from a golden kalasha the holy water that would anoint him king. When Ram entrusted Vibheeshan with taking care of all his subjects, particularly the wives and children of all who had died in the great war, I met my husband's eyes in approval, for it was I who had requested Ram to make this stipulation.

'They have no protector other than you,' Ram told Vibheeshan. 'Remember, their husbands and fathers, though banded against us, fought bravely for their king and their motherland. Honour them accordingly.'

Vibheeshan joined his palms and bowed—cautiously, because he wasn't yet used to the weight of Ravan's giant crown. I knew he'd do what Ram asked—not only because of the reverence he had for Ram, but because Ram and he believed in the same things: righteousness and the sacred responsibility of kingship. For the sake of these, Ram had been willing to let me throw myself into fire. For the sake of these, Vibheeshan had told Ram how to kill his only son Taranisen, who would have been too strong to defeat otherwise. They'd both wept bitter tears afterwards, but faced with the same choice, they'd act in the same way again. The thought filled me with admiration—but admiration laced with anxiety. Such rulers were adored by the citizens they protected, but often their families had to bear the brunt of sacrifice.

Vibheeshan had begged us, over and over, to stay in the most luxurious of Ravan's palaces, but Ram refused, stating that he was still bound by the terms of his banishment. I was happy about that. I sensed that the palaces, though I'd never stepped in them, would be filled even now with Ravan's furious longings. So Vibheeshan set up a sumptuous silken tent for us in a pleasure-garden and spent much of his time there with us, consulting Ram on matters of governance. At one such moment, my husband said to him, 'Be sure to take special care of Queen Mandodari. Treat her gently. Among us all, her lot is the hardest, since she has lost both husband and son as well as all position and power.'

This, too, I'd urged him to ensure. Though I didn't believe she was my mother, I remembered that Mandodari had saved my life, and I was grateful.

'That is my intention, and Sarama's also,' Vibheeshan said. 'We've always held our sister-in-law in the highest esteem. But for her reining him back, Ravan would have wreaked a lot more havoc on the three worlds. But I don't know what to do. She refuses to return to the palace. She's still sitting by Ravan's funeral pyre, which continues to burn, for some mysterious reason, as strongly now as when his body was placed on it. Sarama tells me that she's still wearing her queenly clothing, and the sindoor on her forehead—though she's thrown away her crown—because according to the shastras she isn't a widow until the cremation fire dies. She refuses to eat or drink or answer any questions. Sarama thinks she's praying. I don't understand any of it.' He took off his crown and ran his hand distractedly through his hair, and I saw that he was going bald. It struck me that like Bharat, he, too, had never desired to be king. But fate had decided otherwise.

Ram looked distressed. 'I'm afraid I may be partly to blame for that. When Ravan was dying, I went to see him on the battlefield. I wanted to learn statecraft from him, as I'd heard that he was a great ruler. I wasn't disappointed—even with his failing breath, he taught me things that will be of great use when I return to my kingdom. I was overcome by sorrow that such an intelligent and noble being had fallen prey to revenge and lust and thus brought this fate upon himself. Ah, such is the paradoxical power of the mind. When we control it, it's our best friend, but when we allow it to control us, it becomes our worst enemy.

'As I left him, a woman came up, covered in a thick veil, and bowed, asking for a blessing. From her voice I could tell that she was distraught, and so I said, *May no new sorrows visit you.* From the bangles on her wrists, the only part of her body that was visible, I knew she was married. So I added, *May you never become a widow.*

'At this, the woman threw back her veil with a bitter laugh, and I saw that she wore a crown.

'"You are Queen Mandodari!" I said.'

'"Yes," she said, "and you are Ram, the great warrior"—here her voice dripped sarcasm—"who killed my husband and son, both by subterfuge. And now you've given me a blessing that is worthless."

'"Forgive me, Mother," I said. "I will think of a different and better blessing."

'But she said, "I am no mother of yours—at least for that I thank Providence. And I've no need of further blessings from you, you who have destroyed all that I held dear. Don't think that you can redeem yourself so easily. Now I'll give you something in return. A curse. At your most joyous moment, may your life be turned to ash. May the same heartbreak you've caused me break your heart, too."'

Ram ended, 'So perhaps I am the one who's responsible for subjecting Mandodari to this eternal torture.'

A shudder came over me when I heard Ram speak of Mandodari's curse. For wasn't his happiness intertwined with mine? If his heart broke, how could mine remain intact?

That night I lay awake, thinking of Mandodari, doomed to wait tragically by Ravan's funeral pyre, neither wife nor widow, until death claimed her. And then I realized something. For her, it wasn't a doom. Nor was it tragic. She'd wanted this fate—for when she went up to Ram in disguise, she must have guessed what he'd say.

Mandodari had chosen to wait by her husband's pyre for the rest of her life. She'd done this, giving up all worldly comforts and power, because she loved him in spite of everything he'd done. This final act was her declaration of this love, of her forgiveness.

Could I have done it? I wasn't sure if I was capable of such devotion. Of such total forgiveness for a man who'd betrayed my love, and who, in refusing my counsel over and over, had opened the gate for death to enter my home and snatch away my son.

OTHER MATTERS, TOO, REQUIRED our intervention.

'Lord Ram,' Vibheeshan asked, 'what should we do with the rakshasis who guarded Lady Sita? Your monkey soldiers want to slaughter them for the pain they caused her.'

'They must, indeed, be punished—' Ram started, but I interrupted quickly.

'They, too, were only doing their duty—no different from Ravan's armies on the battlefield. There was nothing personal in their mistreatment of me. Please pardon them, Lord, especially Trijata, who often sheltered me from harm. For the rest of my stay in Lanka, I'd like her to be my attendant.'

Ram and Vibheeshan stared at me in surprise.

The rakshasa king said, 'I've heard from Sarama of all the pain you were subjected to, Lady Sita. I can think of no other woman who would forgive her torturers so easily. That is indeed magnanimous.'

It wasn't magnanimity, though.

I bore the rakshasis no ill will because I'd never loved them, and they'd never pretended to love me. Forgiveness is more difficult when love is involved.

But that was too complicated to articulate, and perhaps harder for males to understand. So I said, 'Revenge doesn't help anyone.'

Vibheeshan nodded, but Ram shook his head. 'I applaud you, Sita. But justice must prevail, even if it is tempered with mercy. Otherwise the king will be perceived as weak, and his kingdom overrun by lawbreakers. The rakshasis must be whipped one hundred times each—except for Trijata, who did indeed protect you as best she could. She may wait upon you while we remain here. However, now that Vibheeshan has been crowned and my fourteen years of exile are almost at an end, this will be only for a short while.'

Lakshman had been waiting impatiently. Now he burst out, 'What of Surpanakha? Shouldn't there be a special punishment for her, in open court, or better yet, in the marketplace, for all to see? I'd be happy to deliver it myself. She's the one that caused this entire devastation. She's the one that needled Ravan, playing on his sense of honour and his greed. She's really the one who brought ruin upon her people—'

Vibheeshan bowed his head. 'I agree. That is why I looked for her as soon as I got to Lanka. But she's disappeared. No one knows where she has gone.'

My hand went, involuntarily, to my throat. Sometimes in the middle of the night, I awoke in a breathless panic, thinking that someone was choking me. Now I felt a stab of discomfort—and anger, I admit it—at the thought that Surpanakha, who'd brought so much suffering to so many, had escaped to wander freely around the world. It was unfair.

But a small part of me was also thankful that I didn't have to see her punished further. I still remembered the happy, trusting girl she'd been in the forest before Lakshman mutilated her, and I couldn't shake off the thought that if my husband and brother-in-law had been kinder and more forgiving of her innocent overtures on that day—or if I'd protested more quickly and loudly and stopped them from injuring her—all the tragedies that followed could have been averted.

Yes, I, too, had played my part in bringing about this destruction.

OVER THE NEXT DAYS, Ram and I gave many gifts to the monkey soldiers—jewels and armour and rare fruits from Ravan's gardens—and sent them off to their forest homes. All except Hanuman, to whom we were all greatly attached—Ram, Lakshman and I, each having our reasons—for he'd saved us all in different ways. We requested him to accompany us to Ayodhya and be with us for Ram's long deferred coronation. I secretly hoped he'd spend the rest of his life with us and planned to do my best to persuade him. I felt a powerful connection with him—perhaps because he called me Ma and followed me around wherever I went, his demeanour so docile that had I not known better, I'd not have believed what a fearsome warrior he was. I was certain that as long as he remained with us, we would be safe.

But why was I worried about safety? Our enemies were dead and we were returning in triumph to our home. Surely it was foolish to feel this way.

The monkey hosts marched away jubilantly across the ocean-bridge, all except Sugreev and his chief commanders, who wanted to see us off before they left.

Watching the line of monkeys grow smaller and smaller and then disappear, I felt a pang in my heart. This surprised me, for though I was grateful to them, I didn't really know them well. Perhaps it was because a crucial chapter in my life was ending—and in theirs also. I wondered if they felt, mingled with joy, a kind of deflation, for the most heroic days of their existence had now ended. I guessed that many among them would spend the rest of their lives retelling tales of this time of glory, a time when they'd achieved the impossible: binding the ocean, killing the mightiest rakshasas. Feats that even the gods had not managed to accomplish. But some of them—I'd glimpsed this in their eyes—were so greatly changed by their adventure that they'd no longer be satisfied with lives of domesticity. What would they do, then?

And what of me, once I returned to Ayodhya? Would the structured life of queenship with its myriad duties, its demands that I attend to every detail of palace administration, satisfy me?

But I had little time to wonder about all this. Even as the monkeys disappeared, Ram clasped my hand. A sense of urgency radiated from him, now that his tasks in Lanka were done.

'Ayodhya is calling to me,' Ram told me. 'She's weeping for my return. I have to get back as soon as possible and take up my kingship.'

His passion infected me. Suddenly, I was ready to return and be his helpmate and queen. It was time to put my house in order. To make my own mark on Ayodhya. Change a few things. And see my sister, my beloved, forsaken Urmila, whom I hadn't allowed myself to think about all this while, for I'd been afraid that one more sorrow placed on top of all the others I bore would break me.

Twenty-seven

'YOU SHOULD USE THE PUSHPAK chariot to return home,' Vibheeshan said to Ram, pointing to a mountaintop where we could vaguely glimpse a gleaming. 'It would be the safest and quickest way. The chariot knows all places in the three worlds. All you'd have to do is to speak your destination, and it would take you to Ayodhya.'

'Is it still here?' Ram asked in surprise. 'I thought it would have gone back to the heavens. Doesn't it belong to the gods?'

'It does, indeed,' Vibheeshan said. 'But for some reason it has remained in Lanka. Let's get it ready.'

Here, however, he ran into a problem. No one was able to get into the chariot. Vibheeshan's best men, the king himself, Lakshman—and even Ram—failed. The chariot would either vanish when they approached it, or it would give off a rapid vibration, along with a humming that sounded like thousands of enraged bees. The combination dizzied anyone who came close and left them with a severe headache. Even Hanuman, who made himself as small as a thumb and managed to reach the chariot, was stunned by a scalding burst of power that surged from it, flinging him off.

We were stumped. A whole week went by while Ram and Vibheeshan wracked their brains for a solution. Finally, reluctantly, they were forced to come to the same conclusion: we'd have to travel through the forests, retracing the path Ram had taken to come to Lanka.

It would be a risky journey. There were many rogue bands of rakshasas along the way, or admirers of Ravan, that were sure to attack us. Even the great seal that Vibheeshan promised us, to indicate that we were his honoured guests, wouldn't deter them.

But what other choice did we have? Vibheeshan began to put together a caravan—food, water, attendants, and a hefty contingent of guards. The monkey generals said they would accompany us as far as their lands in Kishkindhya, guiding us along the best paths through the rough terrain.

Still, Ram was not happy. Even at a punishing pace, it would take us months to reach home.

'PUSHPAK'S WAITING FOR SOMEONE particular to come to it, you know,' Trijata said to me one day when she was combing my hair. I'd been concerned that her new, domesticated role would have bored her, but so far she seemed quite content, helping me get dressed each day and attending to my few needs. In between, she stood guard outside my door and wouldn't allow anyone to pass until I gave permission. Even Ram, I noticed with some amusement, was made to wait.

'Pushpak will only obey someone with whom it has a connection,' Trijata continued. 'It had a bond with Lord Ravan because he had won it in battle. But clearly there's someone else here now towards whom it feels the same way. Or else it would have gone back to the gods. Perhaps that someone rode in it at some point. Touched it. Spoke to it. Someone to whom it feels it owes something.' She looked at me meaningfully.

She was surely mistaken. Still, the next day I decided to climb to the mountaintop. I didn't tell anyone, not even Ram. I was afraid he would laugh, thinking me fanciful.

Pushpak looked different from how I'd remembered it last time, when it carried me over the warring armies. Then it had hulked like a battleship. Now it was a beautiful palanquin, its lines elegant, glowing silver-white as I approached—just large enough for two, maybe three people. A sound emanated from it, but it wasn't the angry buzzing that others had reported. It was more like the purring of a large cat. My heart shook with excitement and fear as I walked up and placed my palm, tentatively, on its carved door. It swung open at my touch. I climbed into it and felt the purr change into a pulse, the beat synchronized with my heart.

'Will you take us home, Pushpak?' I whispered. In response, the chariot took off into the air with a burst of speed. Yet it moved so gently and smoothly that when it landed in front of our tent, not a single flower that Trijata had woven into my hair was displaced.

WHEN RAM SAW WHAT had transpired, he looked at me newly, with a different, considering gaze. Even as I basked in his admiration, I realized that until now, he had appreciated me only for qualities that he thought of as womanly: beauty, kindness, the skills to heal plants and animals and humans—and even rakshasas. The power to make him fall in love with me. He admired the fact that I'd repaired the relationship between Kaushalya and King Dasharath, bringing them closer. He was impressed because I created a beautiful home for us in the harsh wilderness. But he considered them all to be domestic skills. Now, for the first time, he looked at me with respect, the way one might gaze at an equal. It made me glow with satisfaction.

At the same time, though, I was saddened. What I'd taken as admiration all these years had really been a kind of indulgence, the way one might praise a child for her childish achievements. The womanly skills I'd mastered were important and intricate, and by no means easy. They required deep intelligence, an intelligence of the heart. But Ram didn't understand that. He didn't understand the complexity of the female existence.

Earlier, I'd have believed that I had the ability to alter that, to make him see the world in a different way. But my year of captivity had taught me much. I knew now that love—no matter how deep—wasn't enough to transform another person: how they thought, what they believed. At best, we could only change ourselves.

WE DECIDED TO LEAVE that same night, for it didn't matter to the chariot whether it was light outside or dark. It guided itself by a mysterious and invisible inner navigation. Vibheeshan gave us many coffers of gold and jewels as gifts—he wouldn't take no for an answer. We wondered where we'd place them in the slender palanquin, but the rakshasa king didn't seem to think that would be a problem. And indeed, when we approached Pushpak, we found, in the purple light of evening, that the palanquin was now a palace, with large white swanlike wings sprouting from every dome.

When they saw this, Sugreeva and the monkey commanders clamoured to come with us, because they wanted to be present at Ram's coronation. Then Vibheeshan decided that a rakshasa contingent, soldiers and courtiers carefully handpicked by him, needed to accompany us to declare their allegiance publicly on that special day and be acknowledged as our allies.

Ram was uncertain, especially about the rakshasas, but I whispered to him that it was a great idea.

'Let the citizens of Ayodhya, whose minds are filled with prejudices—as were ours when we lived within the tight boundaries of what we believed to be the sole civilized world—see beings of other races,' I said. 'Let them realize that these beings, though different, aren't necessarily evil or stupid or dangerous. That many are noble and admirable. Let there be goodwill between all creatures in Ram

Rajya. Then at least our fourteen years of suffering will have wrought some good.'

'Very well,' Ram said finally.

A cheer went up and we all climbed into Pushpak, rakshasas and monkeys and bears and us humans, now no longer enemies. Once on board, we were amazed, because Pushpak had expanded even further. Each one found that he had his own room, filled with all the luxuries his heart desired (for Pushpak, it seemed, had the ability to look into our minds). For entertainment, there were halls of crystal with divine musicians and dancers and performers of plays. Servants hurried back and forth, carrying unending platters of food and drink, heavenly items that none of us had tasted before. Or perhaps that was what I saw. From time to time, a shimmering light would run across the halls, so perhaps it was all an illusion, separate illusions that Pushpak created for each one of us.

A bent old woman, dressed simply in a cotton sari, shuffled up to me with a tray of food. I was about to wave her away when she raised her head to smile at me. Shocked, I realized it was my beloved nurse Malini, whom I'd been forced to leave behind in Mithila because Dasharath wouldn't allow us to bring our own retainers. How I'd longed for her wisdom and humour during my first year in Ayodhya, while I was learning the ways of my in-laws. I wanted to throw my arms around her, but I restrained myself, reminding myself that this was only a glamour thrown upon a serving woman by Pushpak. Could the vehicle look into our hearts, then?

I sent my admiration towards Pushpak, and my thanks. But I was in no mood to eat, even though the tray was filled with sweetmeats from my childhood. I hungered for only one thing.

In our tent in Lanka, Ram and I had had little privacy. Ram had many responsibilities as he oversaw the smooth transfer of power into Vibheeshan's hands. Additionally, we'd been constantly interrupted by messengers and visitors. Now I longed to be alone with my husband. I wanted one night of love and freedom before we reached Ayodhya. Before the royal crowns, together with all the responsibilities they carried, descended upon our heads. From the smouldering glances he sent me, I could tell Ram wanted the same thing.

But first he had to take care of our guests.

Ram went through the hall, touching a bowed monkey head in blessing, clapping a rakshasa chief on the shoulder. He spoke little, but he knew exactly the right thing to say to put our guests at ease, and always there was a genuine note of caring in his voice. Even after he'd moved on, they continued gazing after him, adoration in their eyes. All the difficulties of forest life, all his sorrows after we were separated, all the killing he'd had to do in the war had hardened Ram in many ways. A certain shining innocence had gone out of him. But this quality—his true love for all who were under his care, his sincere desire for their welfare, his wholehearted willingness to give of himself, to put them before his own needs—hadn't changed. If anything, it had grown stronger.

I watched my husband with an admiration so deep it was like pain. I thought, truly he is the perfect king come to earth to teach us all how a ruler must be.

As WE WALKED TO our chambers, I noticed Lakshman out of the corner of my eye. I hadn't realized it, but he must have slipped away early from the festivities. Now he stood at the far end of the ship, stern and solitary, having chosen to reject whatever comfort Pushpak must have offered him. In his right hand, knuckles tight, he held his bow ready, though I wasn't sure why. We all knew that Pushpak had the power to protect anyone it had chosen to carry. Perhaps, like some soldiers, Lakshman had a hard time letting go of the dangers he'd suffered. Such individuals, I'd heard, were unable to relax. They had trouble sleeping and often awoke in the middle of the night screaming and flailing out at whoever was close. I hoped for Urmila's sake that it wouldn't be so with him.

I paused for a moment to watch Lakshman. His face was hard and impassive, as it often had been on those nights when he guarded us in the forest. But when I looked closer, it seemed harrowed too. What was troubling my brother-in-law?

And suddenly I recognized the place where he was standing. It was the entrance to my balcony in Ayodhya, one of my favourite places—and Urmila's, too. I recognized the Mithilan flowers that I had planted in pots, white and purple blossoms that had filled the entire space. Urmila used to say that it smelled like our childhood there. She would escape to it whenever she could. Often, in the evenings, when he was done with work, Lakshman came there looking for her. Ram would join us, too. I'd have our maid bring them silver cups of mango juice, and we would laugh and joke and share news of our day, laying aside our royal responsibilities for a while.

Was Lakshman thinking of Urmila now, and how hard it might be to pick up the marital ties he'd discarded so ruthlessly in favour of his duty towards his brother?

I sent out a prayer for him and for my sister—and for myself. I, too, would have to repair my relationship with her, for hadn't I abandoned her too?

I pushed that troubling thought away from my mind. Not tonight, I said to myself. Tonight is for Ram.

WHEN RAM AND I entered our chambers, I was surprised and delighted, for Pushpak had transformed it into a forest grove, with the exact kind of leaf bed we used to sleep on. No, better, for soon I discovered that it was softer and smoother, with no hidden rock-lumps underneath to jab suddenly at our unwary bodies. Birds warbled from distant branches and a stream flowed by. A little breeze played around me and I could smell wildflowers. Around the corner was a pond, perfect for bathing. There were no maids to help me undress, for which I was thankful. Once we got to Ayodhya, I knew there would be retainers around us all the time, and as king and queen, we'd be expected to graciously use their services.

Thank you, I said silently to Pushpak, for giving my husband and me this one night to call our very own.

We lay down on the bed and held each other. Our bodies thrummed with a hungry urgency, but we knew that before we made love, there were things we needed to say.

RAM—ALWAYS A GENEROUS SPIRIT—WENT first. He apologized once more, holding me by the hand and looking deep into my eyes, his own beautiful eyes brimming like lotus petals filling with rain.

'I've failed you so many times, dearest,' he said, 'and in so many ways. I failed to anticipate Ravan's trickery, failed to protect you from him on that awful day in the forest. For an entire year, while you underwent sufferings I can't even imagine, I failed to rescue you. When I finally killed him and saw you face to face, I knew that your emaciated body was clear proof of your faithfulness. I should have praised you and embraced you. Instead, I failed again. I spoke the cruellest words, denouncing you in the harshest way I could think of, forcing you to walk into the fire. And the worst part is, even as my heart was breaking, that's what I hoped you'd do. I believed that a miracle would occur because you were innocent. But what if that hadn't happened? What if you'd died?' He gave a great shuddering sigh. 'When you disappeared into the flames, I started shaking so hard, I fell to the ground. In that moment I knew that without you my life wasn't worth living. If you hadn't stepped out, I was going to throw myself into the fire as well. I no longer cared about Ayodhya or its people—'

'Hush, hush,' I murmured, my heart beating joyously at this confession of love even as I was shocked to realize how close Ram had come to killing himself. I ran my fingers over his lips consolingly as I made my own confessions. 'I had my mistakes too. Blinded by desire, I sent you away for the golden deer even though you warned me. I chastised and accused Lakshman until he was forced to leave me alone. I, too, am responsible for what happened. And in the dark night of my despair when you seemed so far away, I sometimes lost my faith in you and considered killing myself. If I hadn't been guarded so vigilantly, day and night, who knows, I might have done it.'

Ram's arms tightened around me and he made a sound of misery deep in his throat. I, too, had to brace myself to keep from shuddering, for the pain of that time was still very real for me. I'd have to learn to lock the past away, to enjoy the bright present.

'Fortunately,' I ended, making my voice as cheerful as I could, 'all has ended well. Let's not think of it anymore.'

Ram nodded. 'I need to tell you something else. Something amazing that occurred as I wept on the ground in front of the fire. The gods appeared—innumerable hosts, covering every bit of sky. They spoke all as one, and only I was aware of them. Even Lakshman later said he'd only heard thunder.

'The gods told me something strange and marvellous: that I was Vishnu, come down to earth to rid it of Ravan's oppression. "Rise to the dignity of your own godly self, they said. Do not weep like a common man. Just like you, Sita is divine. She had her part to play in Ravan's destruction, and no matter what you fear is happening to her right now, she will be fine. You and she both still have to fulfil the rest of your destinies."'

Ram looked intently, questioningly into my eyes. 'Can this really be true, or did my mind just make it up to protect myself from my terrible grief? I certainly don't feel divine. Heroic, maybe. Someone who strives with his whole heart to do the right thing, yes. But no more than that. I don't even know what it means to rise to the dignity of my godly self!'

I could see in his tortured eyes that I was the only one to whom he could confess his doubts. I was the only one he trusted to tell him the truth. And that he would believe what I said. It was a great gift he was giving me, and a great responsibility.

I took a deep breath and told him part of the vision I'd had when the dying Ravan had touched my foot: the vision of Ram and myself in Vaikuntha, and of Ravan as his gatekeeper in that heavenly realm. I told him about the curse of the rishis that had sent us down to earth. 'You are exactly who the gods declared you to be,' I ended, 'though having taken on this human birth, you've forgotten what that is. That's how Maya works. But don't worry too much about it. Just be yourself. I don't think anyone—man or god—can be asked to do more than that. Do what your heart says is right. Then you'll find yourself naturally aligned with your own divine self.'

'Can gods really come down to earth?' Ram asked. 'Do you feel like a goddess?'

'Only when you kiss me!' I said. Then, more seriously, I added, 'But I believe in the vision of Vaikuntha I was allowed to glimpse. The world is full of divine mystery, dearest. You and I have been sent here to do something special. Something beyond the removal of the darkness that Ravan embodied. Maybe we're supposed to teach people how to live in peaceful times.'

'What if my heart tells me to live one way, and my head another?' Ram asked, a crease between his brows. 'That often happens to me—'

I sighed. Yes, he'd always be plagued with that, between acting as a king, upholder of dharma, and taking care of his family, whom he loved, but differently. Still, he was already looking more reassured, more confident and kingly, and I decided to let the matter be.

'The next step, after one destroys evil, is to re-establish the reign of the good. That I think is what you must do back in Ayodhya—show people how to live righteous lives.'

Ram nodded. Righteous was a word with which he was comfortable.

THERE WAS SOMETHING QUITE different that I wanted to share with Ram, something the fire god had told me when I was surrounded by burning flames, just before he took me by the hand and led me back into the world I'd thought I was done with. *He has come to teach the men, but you have come to teach the women. The lesson you teach will be a quieter one, but as important.* I didn't know what the god had meant. I hoped Ram would be able to throw some light on it.

But Ram had had enough of talk.

'The night is passing,' he said and reached for me, his eyes alight with passion. I reached for him, too, for he was right. This magical night, so precious and fleeting, when we floated far above the earth, balanced between the battles of the past and the duties of the future, wouldn't come again. I pressed my lips against his and felt his body come alive against mine. We made love in the moonlight, our limbs straining against each other. In my frenzy, I left my nail-marks on his chest. He bent my willing body into the positions that gave him most pleasure. Mad with love, we asked boldly for what we wanted and watched passion ripple across each other's faces as we were satisfied over and over, only to crave the joys of love again. Our hungry bodies came together with an almost audible click, two halves that had been torn asunder reuniting. The elation of it was so immense that I thought I'd break into pieces and dissolve into the silver moonlight.

At the height of my ecstasy, I felt something happening deep within me. It was as though a being—from where I didn't know—appeared and attached itself to my core and pulsed happily. Its presence filled me with excitement but also with a nameless worry and a fierce desire to protect. I wanted to tell Ram about this, but he was pulling me close to his chest, heaving a sigh of satisfied pleasure. He pressed his lips tenderly against my forehead. In the middle of kissing me, he fell asleep.

I pulled my discarded sari from the ground and covered us both with it. I snuggled into Ram's shoulder and I, too, slept.

In the morning when I awoke, the room was completely different, a formal palace chamber now, gold and silver everywhere, seats carved out of marble and studded with lapis lazuli. Handmaidens bustled around, beautiful with an unearthly glimmering around them. They carried scented water for my bath and stacks of silk saris and caskets of jewels. Ram was nowhere to be seen. One of my attendants told me he was in the main hall, speaking to the assemblage about what would be expected of them when they landed in Ayodhya, which was a scarce hour away. Yes, he was dressed in an appropriate royal fashion—and I needed to be, too.

I sighed and surrendered myself to the ministrations of the maidens, who washed and wiped, pulled and pushed, and painted and prodded me as necessary until I looked appropriately dignified. My sari shone with gold and studded jewels, my hair, tied back neatly, supported a sizeable coronet, and my arms were weighed down with bangles. I walked out, trying hard to feel appreciative. Pushpak had gone to a lot of trouble to procure me this beautiful attire. But I couldn't help feeling a twinge of regret for my old beaten-bark saris and the freedom that had come with them.

Stepping out onto a giant veranda that had not been there yesterday, I was surprised to find that dusk had descended upon us already. At some point, Pushpak must have slowed down to give Ram and me a little more time together. Looking down, I could see the spires of Ayodhya, tall and solid. My heart beat unevenly to think of the many responsibilities that awaited me there. Would I be a suitable wife to Ram, someone he'd be proud of?

I noticed something below: pinpricks of light shone all over the city, on balustrades and palace terraces and humble windowsills. The people had set out lighted lamps to welcome us—as they'd done long ago, when I first came to them as a young bride! As at that time, the lamps delighted and consoled me.

My time in the forest had been a wonderful adventure with Ram, thirteen years passing in a dream of love. My time in Lanka without him had been a nightmare that seemed would never end, something

I had to endure so that the cosmic drama of good and evil could be played out. But this, my life in Ayodhya, as Ram's helpmate, was my real life. My life as an adult. The purpose the fire-god had referred to. What I did here was what people would look at and remember and learn from. The way I lived now, the way I handled my joys and especially my sorrows, would leave a mark upon human civilization.

But, foolish me, why was I thinking of sorrow at this blessed moment in my life? How could there be any sorrow as long as Ram was by my side, his heart filled with love for me?

I took a deep breath and squared my shoulders. I was ready. I walked forward—with what I hoped was an appropriately regal smile—to join my husband as queen of Koshal.

Twenty-eight

PUSHPAK LANDED IN A LARGE field outside the palace walls. Ahead of us I could see the looming gates of the city, lit with smoky torches, and a huge, silent crowd that had assembled in front of it. They whispered and fidgeted and jostled each other impatiently, held back by soldiers who yelled at them roughly to keep order. I guessed these were Bharat's soldiers. I looked around, hoping to see Bharat, but in the milling dark I couldn't recognize anyone. Not Bharat, not Shatrughna, not even Hanuman, whom we'd sent ahead to inform them of our arrival.

I could feel anxiety pulsing through me. Why wasn't there a welcoming party? Why weren't the people chanting their new king's name? Was Bharat having second thoughts about returning Koshal to his brother? Fourteen years was a long time. Enough time to get addicted to power, which was stronger than any intoxicant. Beside me, Lakshman grasped his bow more tightly, his face grim. Only Ram's face was serene.

My husband descended from Pushpak and strode forward without hesitation. After a moment, Lakshman and I joined him, one on either side. We were followed by our companions. As we came into the circle of wavering light cast by the torches, there was a sudden, shocked silence. The rakshasas and mighty monkey warriors must have been a strange, even frightening sight for the city dwellers who hadn't ever ventured into the forest, who'd been brought up on terrifying tales of what lived within it. It didn't help that other shadowy beings—magically fabricated by Pushpak—carried out the treasure chests given to us by Vibheeshan and then disappeared, turning into wisps of fog. Or that Pushpak itself shrank, becoming as tiny as a bird, and flew away.

I felt a moment of pity for the Ayodhyans standing there, for all that they would never understand—and then a stab of worry. How would they greet our honoured guests? Had Ram been right in his reluctance to bring them, concerned that their presence would cause unrest, maybe even violence? Had I been too optimistic in thinking that we were ushering in a new age, a time when men and animals and rakshasas could coexist in peace?

OUT OF THE DARK, a horseman gave a loud yell and launched himself forward, shaking a great lance. The army took up his cry and rushed out behind him. I stiffened, wondering how to prevent the upcoming carnage. Behind me, I could hear the monkeys and rakshasas stirring restlessly, preparing to defend us. Surely our citizens were going to be slaughtered now.

But Ram laughed. It was a cool, unworried sound that seemed to clear the air and make the lamps burn brighter. Once again, he was right. For the horseman vaulted off his horse, handed the lance, which wasn't really a lance but a furled umbrella, to a follower, and threw himself into my husband's arms. It was Bharat, spare, almost emaciated, dressed in tree bark which, I'd learn later, he'd worn for our sake all through the fourteen years when we were gone.

Shatrughna joined them, and Lakshman ran up, too, and the four brothers laughed and cried and held onto each other as though they'd been separated for a lifetime—which in a way they had. But there was something more to this reunion. As I watched them, it seemed that their human outlines lost their shapes and became flame-like, and then the four flames merged to become one great shining. Its brilliance blinded me and its beauty brought tears to my eyes. Were they all part of Vishnu? Part of the divine play the fire-god had hinted at? As I watched, the shining spread across the entire crowd, though it was dimmer elsewhere, as though from small earthen lamps. Still, I could see that there was a little of the One Divine in them all.

After a moment the vision faded, and I became aware of the chant rising from the crowd. *RajaRamRajaRamRajaRam*. I was happy that they called for my husband, but a small cold hand clutched at my heart. They were not calling my name, as they had on that long-ago coronation day that never came to be. Why was that?

The brothers hadn't noticed anything amiss. They were clapping each other on the back, all talking at once. Bharat kept saying, 'Is this really happening? Or am I once again dreaming this reunion the way I've dreamed of it for all these years, only to awake alone in the grey morning?'

And Lakshman, punching him playfully, said, 'This is no dream. See, otherwise my fists would have awakened you by now.'

I stood back, willing to let the brothers have their time of intimacy, but Ram took me by the hand and brought me forward, saying, 'Here is Sita whom even the mighty Ravan dared not dishonour.' And the brothers all bowed to me with great reverence and addressed me as Queen.

Then a furry shape flung itself out of a tree and landed at my feet, crying, 'Sita Ma!'

'Hanuman!' I called out with joy, for his love was simple and unequivocal, unlike human love, and a powerful bond had been forged between us ever since he found me in the ashoka forest. He was the only one who really knew what I'd gone through, and having him here made my return to Ayodhya that much more of a victory.

Hanuman began a different chant now, *SitaRamSitaRamSitaRam*, and after the barest pause the crowd took it up, acknowledging me, along with my husband, as royalty.

And thus Ram and I rode in triumph at the head of the procession, the royal umbrella of red silk now unfurled above our heads, to the palace entrance where Kaushalya and Sumitra, aged now and half-blind with years of tearful sorrow, were waiting impatiently to greet us with platters of lamps and auspicious sindur powder and sandalwood paste and sweetmeats. And if their hands shook as they waved the arati plates, and if they wept more than they smiled, and if the palace they led us into was only a shell of what I remembered from Dasharath's day, none of it mattered.

I WAS AWAKENED IN the morning not by the playing of beautiful veenas or songbirds or the sounds of temple bells but my husband's sneezing. Ram's eyes were watering and his nose red by the time I got up. I could see why right away. I hadn't paid attention to it at night, in the dim light of the lamps, in the midst of my excited tiredness and everyone asking us questions about our years away.

Our rooms were full of dust, as though they hadn't been cleaned in a long time. I shooed Ram, who was still sneezing, out to the balcony for some fresh air and rang the bell for the attendant, but it was quite a while before anyone showed up. Meanwhile, I had ample time to examine our surroundings. I was dismayed to find everything in disarray. Our bedclothes were old and frayed, with tears along the creases, and smelled of mildew. It looked like they'd been stuffed inside a chest for all the years of our banishment. Our quilts were lumpy, with suspicious holes as though mice had chewed on them.

I remembered last night's dinner, and suddenly things that I hadn't noticed in the excitement of returning after the long exile began to strike me. Our dinner had been cold, only a few items, rice and lentils and a vegetable dish, left covered in an alcove in Kaushalya's chambers. Used to simple fare and then to fasting, I'd enjoyed it. Besides, I'd been distracted by all the news of the kingdom. But now I realized that it fell far short of the meals I'd had earlier in the palace—or even the food in my father's simpler household. In Dasharath's time, even at family dinners there would be several maids to serve the food, clear away the plates and bring bowls of scented water for us to wash our hands. Now there was no one.

I tried to piece together what must have happened. Bharat had moved out of the palace to the small town of Nandigram, refusing to enjoy any royal comforts until Ram returned home. He'd placed Ram's sandals on the throne there and held interim court as his representative. Shatrughna, ever dedicated to his brother, had gone with him. Their wives had accompanied them. How could they not? It was their primary duty. Kaushalya and Sumitra refused to leave the palace where they'd come as brides, but they'd been too grief-stricken and ill to attend to household details.

Over last night's dinner, Bharat had explained that, thrown as he was into a position for which he'd never been trained, he had his hands full. He faced internal strife, especially from the half-wild tribes at the edges of the kingdom. Neighbouring kings had taken this opportunity—with Dasharath dead and Ram gone—to invade what they perceived as a weakened kingdom. War upon war followed. Bharat and Shatrughna managed to defeat their enemies, but it took all their energy and seriously depleted the royal coffers. It hadn't helped that several years of famine had followed, the crops dying mysteriously in spite of ample rainfall. The people whispered that it was because such an injustice had been done to Ram.

I didn't blame anyone for the state of the palace. But I was surprised that Urmila, who had continued to live here, hadn't taken care of things. That she hadn't watched over Mother Kaushalya and Mother Sumitra's comfort more diligently. Surely my mother had trained her to be a better daughter-in-law and princess?

Where was Urmila, anyway?

She hadn't shown up at dinner last night, and when I asked, Mandavi and Shrutakirti had glanced at each other and said she was in her chambers. She wasn't feeling well. She'd gone to bed. The physician had instructed them not to disturb her.

'Let me take a look at her,' I said. 'I've been taking care of her ever since she was a girl. I know which herbs work well on her system—'

But at this my cousins and their husbands all insisted that I shouldn't trouble myself—or Urmila—at this time.

'She must be sleeping by now,' Mandavi said, avoiding my eyes. 'I'm sure you're tired after your long journey. Please rest tonight. You can see her in the morning.'

I guessed that Urmila was sulking, furious with Lakshman and me for abandoning her to loneliness and drudgery all these years while we went off on what she considered a marvellous adventure. She'd probably told my cousins that she wanted to see Lakshman in private, in her chambers, before she met with Ram or me. I feared there was going to be a fight, one involving fourteen years of stored up weeping and accusations. I glanced at Lakshman, who looked more worried than if he were about to face a phalanx of rakshasa warriors. I didn't envy him.

'Very well,' I said, yawning, suddenly tired, the long day's tensions hitting me all at once. I'd worry about Urmila's temper tomorrow. I'd faced enough of her tirades in the past and knew how to handle them. Once she'd vented her anger on me, she'd be ready for me to apologize. Then I could express how truly sorry I was about leaving her behind on her own. I hoped to make her see that I'd made the only choice I possibly could. Where Ram went, there I had to follow, like body and soul. I planned to tell Urmila about my trials in Lanka, how it felt to be forcibly separated from my husband. I had a feeling that when she learned about the depth of my suffering, my sister would forgive me.

A young maid had ambled up to my chambers by this time. I remarked with annoyance on the disgraceful condition of the palace, but she stared at me open-mouthed as though she couldn't see what was wrong. I could tell that no one had trained her. She probably thought that our rooms looked wonderful and I was merely being picky, in the way of aristocrats. When I pointed out the state of the furnishings and the layers of dust, and the fact that there was no clean water to wash in, and asked what she'd been doing all this while, she looked like she was about to cry.

I swallowed my exasperation and asked her who was in charge of the palace staff. She scratched her head for a moment, then told me that maybe it was Cook.

'Take me to him,' I said.

She led me along labyrinthine corridors and down several sets of narrow stairs that had clearly not seen a broom in months until I ended up in a cheerless, cavernous hall. At one time it must have been a bustling place, like the kitchens at Mithila, which I'd often visited. Today none of the fires were lit, except for a small one in a corner where a pot was being stirred unenthusiastically by an old man, unkempt gray hair falling into his eyes. The dishes from our dinner were stacked untidily on the floor, and vegetable peelings were strewn everywhere. I looked around for helpers—surely he had some—but none were to be seen.

'Cook,' I called.

He raised his head slowly, scowling his annoyance.

'What do you want now?' he said in a gruff voice. 'Can't you see that I have my hands full?'

Clearly, he had no idea who I was.

'I am Sita, Lord Ram's wife,' I said. 'Thank you for the dinner you cooked us last night. It was good to come home and eat some Koshalan food, after many years.'

His eyes widened and he joined his palms and bowed. 'Queen Sita! Pardon me, it's been so many years since I saw you last. You were a beautiful new bride, and I was just Sharav, a lowly kitchen assistant, peeling vegetables and washing pots. I still remember the wonderful feast that was prepared in this kitchen when you were welcomed into Ayodhya, though of course I wasn't allowed to cook any of it! It broke all our hearts when the old king was tricked into banishing Lord Ram and Lakshman to the forest and you went with them. I'm sorry I couldn't send a better meal to Queen Kaushalya's rooms last night, but that was all I could manage to put together. You see, I'm the only one left here, and the treasurer hardly gives me any money to buy food. Says things are very tight since the wars and the famines.'

'How about your pay?' I asked.

Sharav shook his head. 'That's why the others left. There's been no money to pay us for a while, and they have families to feed. But I stayed on. What would happen to the two old queens if I left? I thought. As it is, they don't ask for anything, don't seem to have any interest left in life. I cooked whatever I could forage for them, trusting that Lord Ram and you would return someday and things would get better.'

'How about Queen Kaikeyi?' I asked.

'Haven't seen her in years,' the man said. 'Lord Bharat—he was crazy with anger at her when he came back and found his father dead and his brother banished. He would have killed her if the holy sadhus who'd come to conduct the funeral hadn't stopped him, saying it was a great sin for a man to kill his mother. He threw out that hunchback Manthara, who'd been the cause of all the trouble, and he imprisoned Kaikeyi in her apartments. None of us know what goes on in there. Once in a while we see a maid or two go to the market for food, but they don't talk to us. Princess Urmila is another mystery. No one except her chief maid is allowed to enter her chambers, and she hasn't asked me for any food for the princess, not once in fourteen years.'

I was troubled by all this bewildering news, especially the part about Urmila, but I had to focus on one thing at a time. I took off the heavy gold bangles Mandodari had given me in Lanka and held them out to Sharav. 'Thank you for telling me what has been happening, Sharav. And thank you for your loyalty. Take these. Sell them in the market and keep some of the money for yourself—you deserve it for being such a faithful retainer all these years. Then buy all the ingredients you need, and cook a fine meal for the royal family. Send it up to Queen Kaushalya's rooms. Hire some people, too—under-cooks, washerwomen, cleaners. Get good, experienced workers, tell them that they'll be well-paid, and set them to work. I'm putting you in charge of all the domestic staff. Let's get this palace back in shape! And don't forget to send food to the guest quarters for our rakshasa visitors, and fruit to the royal gardens where I believe our monkey guests have been placed.'

Sharav stared incredulously at the gold bangles. 'You'll trust me with such expensive things?'

'Of course,' I smiled. 'And I'm ready to give you more if you need. Haven't you been taking care of the mothers all this time? Didn't you stay on here alone, even when there was no guarantee you'd ever get paid? Just be sure to get me a good price!'

Sharav touched the bangles to his forehead, his eyes filling with tears. 'I'll haggle with the goldsmith like my life depended on it, my queen. I'll make you proud!' He held his head high and set off briskly, a new spring to his step.

I went back to the chambers to tell Ram, who was getting ready for court, what had been going on in our absence. He, too, was shocked. 'I hadn't realized things had been so hard here. Thank you for taking care of things, dearest one, and for being so generous. You are my Lakshmi!'

I looked at him sharply. Did he believe the vision of Vaikuntha, which was already fading in my mind? Or was he merely paying me a compliment?

IN A LITTLE WHILE, a different maid, neatly dressed and efficient-looking, came by to call us to Queen Kaushalya's chambers, where the windows had been thrown open to sunlight and the floors cleaned. I found Kaushalya and Sumitra exclaiming in delight over the hot meal that had been sent up from the kitchen, freshly made rotis and vegetables, dals and sweetmeats. In the corridors outside, I could hear attendants scrubbing and dusting. Others were carrying out loads of clothing to be washed or mended. Sharav had done well, indeed.

I served the queens and my husband, but when they asked me to join them, I shook my head. First I had to accomplish the task that had been nagging at me ever since I awoke. As soon as Ram went off to the royal court, where a great many responsibilities awaited him, I hurried to Urmila's quarters.

Twenty-nine

THE DOOR TO URMILA'S CHAMBERS was massive, made of dark teak and carved from top to bottom with fierce looking mythical beasts, their mouths open and snarling. I didn't remember seeing them before. Had things changed magically in the palace while we were gone? Did the beasts symbolize the anger Urmila felt at having been abandoned by her husband and sister and imprisoned in this dungeon of sorrow and hopelessness? Or was it that I'd never noticed the carvings before because when we lived here, Urmila had always kept her doors open, along with her heart, for her beloved family?

Did the closed doors indicate that she'd closed her heart to me?

It was no use thinking like this. I rapped sharply on the nose of one of the beasts—but nothing happened. I knocked several times, shouting Urmila's name. Did anyone hear me? Was Urmila's maid—if she even had one anymore—as inefficient as the girl who'd meandered into my chambers? Or had Urmila given instructions that I wasn't to be let in? Had I been overly confident in believing that my sister would forgive me?

Finally, when I'd just about given up hope, the door was flung open. I was surprised to see that it was Lakshman himself who opened the door. I'd expected him to be at the royal court, assisting Ram. I was further surprised because he was disheveled and unkempt. Even in the forest, Lakshman had taken care to be as clean as possible, his hair tied up neatly, his bark-cloths regularly washed and stretched out to dry. But today he was still in his travel clothes, unbathed, chin stubbled, dark circles under his eyes as though he hadn't slept at all.

'Thank the heavens that you've come, sister-in-law,' he cried. 'I wanted to get you last night itself, but I hesitated to disturb you and my brother after our long journey. Urmila just won't wake up. I've been trying all night. I sent to the city for physicians, but they couldn't help either.'

I hurried after him to their bedchamber. The room was dark, the window coverings closed. Urmila lay stretched out on the massive bed. But whereas a person who was sleeping would have lain with her head on a pillow, covered with a comfortable quilt, my sister lay in shavasana, stretched out to her full length, her face peaceful but pale. She, too, was dressed in bark cloth.

Seeing her lying in the yogic dead man's pose alarmed me. I was further startled to see that she didn't look a day older than when I had left Ayodhya. And yet, in some way I couldn't define, she seemed like a completely different person.

Placing my fingers at her nostrils, I could feel Urmila's breath, steady but very slow, as though she were in a coma. My heart lurched in fear. There had been a man in my father's palace in Mithila, a groom kicked in the head by a horse. The palace physicians and I had worked on him for a long time until his vital signs were stable, but he never regained consciousness. His breath had been just like this.

I hid my fears from Lakshman and told him to join Ram in court. When he looked uncertain, I told him that Ram needed him. I knew that would persuade him.

'I'll take care of things here,' I said, with more confidence than I felt. 'Send her maid to me, if she has one.'

SOON AFTER LAKSHMAN LEFT, a woman appeared, looking frightened as though I might blame her for Urmila's condition. She told me that she was Urmila's chief maid—the only one who had remained with her. Her name was Saudamini, and from her, I finally learned what had happened after I'd abandoned my sister.

'For a long time, she sat on your balcony with those dead flowers strewn around her, so still that she might have been carved from the same stone. No one knew this except me. Everyone was gathered around the old king, who was dying. But I stayed close to her—I was afraid she might try to throw herself from the balcony. Finally, late at night, she came back to her rooms and locked the doors and lay in bed. She refused to eat or drink, and she refused to open the doors when, a couple of days later, Queen Sumitra finally remembered to check on her. The old king was dead by then, and the entire palace was in turmoil. I was getting really scared, afraid she'd die of starvation. She was getting weaker each day. But on the third night she sat up and told me to get her some bark-cloth to wear—"like my husband's," she said.

'I brought it, though it broke my heart to see her dressed like this. I begged her to drink some milk, at least, but she just told me to leave her. In the morning when I came back to check, she was lying on the bed, just like you see her today.

'Terrified, I called the mothers. We tried to give her water, but nothing would pass her lips. We called on doctors and priests—they couldn't do anything for her, either. Some said an evil spirit had taken over her body, but I didn't believe that. Finally a wise woman stopped by and said something beyond mortal understanding was going on. But it wasn't anything bad. We should leave Princess Urmila be the way she was. Keep curious people away from her and wait, hoping time would take care of things. So that's what I did.'

Saudamini looked at me as though afraid that I'd chide her. How could I? She'd done her best, while I—I had abandoned Urmila. I felt more guilt than ever, but I pushed it away. Guilt exuded negative energy, and right now I needed as much positive strength as possible.

I thanked Saudamini for her loyalty and gave her a gold chain from around my neck, for I was certain she hadn't been paid in a long time.

'Now let me be alone with my sister,' I said.

I climbed onto the bed and sat with Urmila's head in my lap. I placed my hands on her forehead, sending her love, trying to feel her spirit. It took a long time before I could sense the slightest stirring. The spirit had receded far away and was reluctant to return to this plane of sorrows.

'Come back, dear one,' I called to it. 'You've suffered a great deal, but now a happy time is about to start. Your beloved husband is back, and he longs to spend with you the hours of love that had been wrested away from you both.'

But the spirit, peaceful in its distant abode, would not listen. I tried over and over, to no avail. And now it seemed that my sister's breath was fading.

In my desperation I could only think of one thing. I would sing for her the song I'd made up when we met Ram and Lakshman. On that night, I'd sung it so she would calm down and sleep. But perhaps it would work in reverse today, reminding her of the excitement of love, how it was poised to re-enter her life. My voice trembled as I sang.

The wind blows through the forest
And comes to rest on the branches
of the pomegranate tree in our father's garden.
The day has come, it sings.
The heroes are on their way.
Faces of gold, eyes glimmering like mountain lakes,
Will they bear our hearts away with them
to our destinies?

THE LAST NOTES FADED away, but Urmila didn't move. Giving up, I lay down, cradling her as though she were a child, and tears of hopelessness seeped from between my closed lids.

Then I felt it, a cool, firm grasp around my wrist. My startled eyes flew open, and there was my sister, her head turned to look at me.

'Urmila!' I cried, embracing her joyfully. For a moment she lay unmoving, as though she didn't know who I was. Then her arms reached out, but slowly, as though she'd forgotten what such a gesture meant. And when I pulled back to look at her more closely, I saw that though her body had not aged, her eyes were different, at once wise and distant.

It took a whole day before Urmila would speak. This, finally was what she told me:

'On the day the three of you left, I made up my mind to die. What was the use, I thought to myself, of living on when I'd been rejected by the one man I had adored with all my heart since the day I met him? Ram took you with him. Why then did Lakshman refuse to take me? Was I so unworthy?

'Well then, I decided, I would free myself of this unworthy life.

'I sat in meditation, hoping to drop my body, hoping Death would come to me like he did to faithful wives in mythical tales. If that didn't work, there was always the balcony.

'I sat for a long time—days, perhaps—with my mind focussed on Death. I was able to focus purely and completely because nothing else mattered to me any longer. In time, the world around me faded, and in the darkness I heard a voice, gentle and reasonable, unlike what I'd expected. "I am Yama, lord of death. You have meditated on me with such intensity that I have been forced to come to you. What is it you want?"

'"Take me away from this misery," I cried.

'"I can end your life," Death said, "but it would benefit no one, not even yourself. For the suffering you seek to escape in this way is your karma, and you will have to undergo it in another life. Would you not rather help your husband?"

'"That's what I want more than anything in the world," I cried. "But Lakshman has refused to let me do it."

'"There are ways of assistance that lie beyond what you mortals can conceive," the voice said as it receded. "I will send my sister to you."

'I sat in the silent dark for a life-stretch, wondering if death had tricked me. I sat until time became a river and I a stone submerged in it. Finally, I heard a voice, so comforting that I wanted to wrap myself in it like a blanket on a cold day.

'"I am Nidra, goddess of sleep," it whispered. "Few humans are ever privileged to see me. I visited your husband earlier today, who asked me for a strange boon. He feels it is his duty to guard Ram and Sita through their fourteen years of exile. Thus, he begged that I should stay away from him during these years. His cause was just and exalted, and his heart pure, so I felt sympathy.

'"I said to him: I am willing to grant your desire, but I am like karma. I can be deferred but not escaped. If I do what you say, then, when you return to Ayodhya, I must descend on you, and fourteen more years of your life will pass before you wake again.

'"So be it, Lakshman said without hesitation, and marvelling at his dedication to his brother, I granted his wish.

'"But then he'll lose all the years of his youth," I cried in great distress. 'We'll never have the opportunity to enjoy our love, or delight in children. Is there nothing I can do to change your decree?"

'Nidra said, "My elder brother Death is impressed with your dedication to your husband and has asked me to take pity on your distress. Thus I offer you this choice—you may take on Lakshman's sleep for the next fourteen years. This will pay off his debt to me."

'A part of me was afraid. What would happen if I fell into fourteen years of sleep? Would people think I was dead and cremate my body? Then I thought, I don't care. If it helps Lakshman, I'll do it.

'"I agree," I cried.

'Even as I spoke, sleep, descended on me. My body fell, inert, onto the bed. I heard the distant voice of the goddess. "Sleep now, Urmila, whose sacrifice few will know and praise. But here is my gift to you:

I will not mire you in the blankness of common human sleep, but allow you to experience yoga nidra, where the workings of the world become available to the subtle intellect."

'As she spoke, my spirit rose out of my body and was suspended in a globe of light. In that state, I understood many things, though I'm not permitted to speak of them. Most of all, I understood that things happen to us for many complicated reasons, arising from both the past and the future. Thus I'm no longer sorrowful for all that has taken place in my life—or the things that are about to happen in yours.'

Urmila looked at me, a deep peace in her gaze, but a cold lump of fear filled my belly. 'What do you mean? What's about to happen?'

But now Urmila threw her arms around me as though she'd suddenly turned back into the little sister I used to take care of. It seemed that she'd forgotten everything she'd just told me. 'Didi, I'm so happy to see you!' she cried. 'Are you back from the forest already? Saudamini! Saudamini! Isn't there anything to eat in this place? I'm starving—and I bet Didi is, too!'

I summoned a delighted Saudamini, who ran down to the kitchen to fetch the food Sharav had saved for me. Urmila and I ate together, laughing and wiping away each other's tears, and I told her a little of my adventures. Then it was time for another task, the one I dreaded the most.

I'D EXPECTED TO WAIT outside Kaikeyi's chamber for a long time. In fact, I hadn't been sure if I'd be allowed in at all. But even before I reached the elegant doors carved out of ivory they swung open, and two maids, bowing, led me to an inner courtyard. Kaikeyi, at least, had kept a firm grip on her household affairs. The corridor I walked through was perfectly clean, not a speck of dust anywhere, the floor-stones shining.

Anger surged through me, though I tried to tamp it down. Intent on preserving her power, this woman had turned the palace upside down, insisting on having her own selfish way. She'd precipitated her husband's distressful death, caused immense sorrow to the other queens, and sent us into exile and war. If she hadn't banished Ram, we'd never have met Surpanakha. And I'd never have been abducted by Ravan. I remembered my unending year of grief in the ashoka van—grief that Kaikeyi couldn't imagine. Instead, here she was, enjoying life in her own little palace-within-a-palace, with everything just the way she wanted.

Rage rose up in me. Where was the justice in this?

I was additionally outraged when I stepped into the courtyard. Lined up against the walls in beautifully carved stone pots were all the flowers of Mithila that I'd grown with such care on my balcony, the flowers that had died on the day I left. How had Kaikeyi found out about them? Had she sent her spy, Manthara, to my chambers when I'd been busy with my mother-in-law? I imagined the hunchback snooping through my rooms. I imagined Kaikeyi using her wealth to have the plants shipped from Mithila so she could enjoy them while Ram, Lakshman and I trudged through the thorny forest. Fury flashed through me like lightning, and any thoughts I'd had of reconciliation were burned to ashes in it.

I turned to leave. Clearly, Kaikeyi was doing just fine. I need not have wasted my time coming to check on her welfare.

JUST THEN A GHOSTLIKE shadow detached itself from one of the pillars and knelt at my feet. It was a woman, so thin that the knobs of her bones showed through the thin white widow-sari she was wearing. It took me a moment to recognize the proud Kaikeyi in this woman who touched her forehead to the ground, meekly and wordlessly.

Was this another of Kaikeyi's dramas? Did she think that expiation for what she'd done to us was so simple? I wasn't going to fall for it. I hardened my face and stepped away from her towards the door.

One of Kaikeyi's maids came forward, palms joined. 'My mistress has taken a vow of silence, but with her last words, she instructed me to say the following: She knows she can never make up for the pain she caused you and your husband. She cannot understand what came over her, like a fever, forcing her to insist on the two terrible boons that destroyed your lives. She wants you to know that she hasn't had a day of peace since then. First to see her beloved husband, who held her so dear to his heart, die of grief, blaming her. And then to be berated and shunned by her son, for whose kingship she had risked all. She hadn't imagined either of these happening, but she understood why they did. Only ill-fortune can come out of evil.

'She has spent her days in penance since then, praying for your safety, waiting for Ram to return so she might express her repentance. She sent for all these plants and cared for them herself all these years, hoping that they can replace the garden you were forced to leave behind. She doesn't ask anything of either of you. Certainly not forgiveness. She merely wished to see you before she ended her life.'

The maid pointed, and I saw what I hadn't noticed before: on one side of the courtyard, a pyre had been readied, pieces of wood stacked, ghee poured on them for easy burning.

THE SIGHT OF THE pyre made me dizzy, taking me back to the battlefield at Lanka, scene of my supreme humiliation, my rejection by the man I'd loved with all my heart. I had to hold on to a pillar to keep from falling.

Ah, how difficult it was to know, in this world filled with grey shades, what was right and what was wrong. Ram had thought, in telling me to leave him and go away, that he was doing his duty as the future king of Ayodhya. Were Kaikeyi's actions, which sprang from love for her son and her desire to secure the kingdom for him, that much worse? She hadn't hurt me any more than Ram had.

If I could forgive him, could I not forgive her?

I BENT AND RAISED her up, the once-proud Kaikeyi now swaying like a faded flower in the breeze, bereft of all her beauty and her glory.

'Go to the court,' I told Kaikeyi's maidservant. 'Tell Ram that I am requesting his presence in Queen Kaikeyi's chambers, as soon as it is possible.'

When Ram arrived, I pulled Kaikeyi forward. She hid her face in shame, but I put her trembling hands in Ram's strong, callused ones. My sensitive, wise Ram. He looked at the funeral pyre, at the flowers. Even without a word of explanation, he understood.

'Kaikeyi Ma,' he said, embracing the woman who had caused him so much grief. His voice was full of affection, a balm for the wounded heart. And Kaikeyi, finally giving in to tears as he held her, knew she was forgiven.

Thirty

THE PROBLEMS WE'D FACED UPON returning to Ayodhya hadn't disappeared, but slowly they'd become manageable. Ram's policy of ruling firmly and justly but kindly, too, had improved the morale of all who brought their troubles to court. Our people were additionally struck by the fact that Ram freely used the treasure we'd brought with us to improve the run-down state of the kingdom.

He sent the welcome-back tributes of neighbouring kings directly to the treasury, with instructions that they be used to better the roads that connected Ayodhya to the other major cities around us. He made sure these roads were well-patrolled. This, as he'd foreseen, improved trade and made Ayodhya a favourite stop for merchants.

Ram reduced taxes, especially for the districts that had suffered worst in the famine, and gave free grain to farmers to start over. He ordered that organizations be founded all over the country to house, feed and teach work skills to the destitute. As a result, poverty and petty crime fell to an all-time low. He made sure the city was vigilantly patrolled by guards, day and night. Men and women could now go about their business safely, no matter what the hour. Tales of the vibrant night-life of the new Ayodhya, its music and dance concerts where world-famous artists performed, and its colourful bazaars with shops that never closed, enticed many visitors to our city.

I, too, had been busy. With the help of Sharav and the staff he'd hired, I made sure that the palace was efficiently and smoothly run, and that wherever we turned we were faced by beauty and prosperity. The gardens were, of course, my special joy. I'd taken care to choose plants and trees that would bloom or produce fruit at different seasons of the year, so that visitors would be greeted at all times by a riot of colours and sweet smells and singing birds. But, at the same time, I made sure to improve matters outside the palace walls. I took a special interest in the lives of destitute women in Ayodhya and established safe-houses for them. I opened the palace to female petitioners and made it known that the needy, as long as they were prepared to work hard, would receive money to start their own businesses. I rewarded employers who hired such women. I established free schools so that all Ayodhyan children would grow up to be educated, contributing members of our country.

Nowadays, when I accompanied Ram to the public balcony of the palace to greet our citizens, the applause was deafening. This didn't surprise me. But I was taken aback to hear people cheering me as well, because my work was done mostly behind the scenes.

Lakshmi, they called me, food-giver, queen of flowers, remover of sorrows. There were stories that the palace storehouses were brimful because grains flowed from my palms. Our gardens and lakes were as beautiful as in Indra's realm because flowers sprang up in my footsteps. Wherever I travelled in the city, people felt illness and grief receding, and peace filled their hearts.

I had a feeling that Sharav was responsible for some of these exaggerated tales, but I didn't mind. It was rather gratifying to know I was so popular!

Ram's old teacher, Sage Vasishta, visiting us from his hermitage, was delighted to see the new Ayodhya. 'You've turned out to be an even better ruler than I'd hoped for, Ram,' he said. 'No doubt it's because you have such a wonderful helpmate! It was good that you put the needs of your people before your personal celebration. But now it's time for your coronation.'

WHEN THE NEWS WAS announced, jubilation swept across the country. Hordes of people from distant corners of the kingdom began to make their way to Ayodhya to see their rightful king finally anointed. All of Koshal's allies accepted our invitation enthusiastically. Even Ram's sister Shanta, whom we hadn't seen in years, sent word that she was going to be present for her brother's special day.

Ram was particularly pleased about this. 'I have the fondest memories of my big sister playing with me,' he said. 'I only saw her a few times, because as I told you, my father let his dear friend adopt her. And after she got married and grew busy with her wifely duties, she rarely visited us. I'm so glad she's coming to bless us on this occasion. She's making a special effort. She lives very far away, and I know doesn't like to travel.'

I was excited about Shanta's coming, too. I hadn't been able to spend much time with her when she'd come to Ayodhya after our wedding—I'd just arrived from Mithila and was tired and homesick and disoriented by my many new duties. I looked forward to making friends with her this time. I hoped she'd approve of the changes I'd made around the palace.

For me, this was an especially happy time because I discovered that I was pregnant. My happiness was doubled by the fact that I'd been worried that I'd be too old for childbearing when I returned. When I shyly announced my news to Ram, he was overjoyed. I think he'd been worrying about the same thing. He gave me a beautiful pearl necklace as a gift of gratitude. At night when we lay in bed, he was careful of my comfort and asked me many times if I was eating right and resting enough. He kissed my stomach, which was just starting to develop a curve, and whispered tenderly to the baby, telling it all the things they'd do together—riding horses, practising archery, hunting in the forest. He was convinced it was a boy.

'What if it's a girl?' I teased him.

He looked a little taken aback. Then he rallied. 'I guess I can do all the same things with her too.'

I hugged him tightly, loving him even more for saying that. But deep down, I knew it was a male child I was carrying, the future king of Ayodhya.

We told only Kaushalya, Urmila, Lakshman, and the chief physician of the palace about my pregnancy. It wasn't hard to keep it a secret. Queens in Ayodhya didn't make many public appearances, and when I was visited by the wives of courtiers or neighbouring queens, I dressed myself carefully, arranging my sari in a loose and flowing fashion. Fortunately, I didn't have any nausea for the maids to gossip about.

Ram and I decided that we'd announce the pregnancy at the coronation. It would give the people another reason to celebrate, and another event to look forward to.

MY DAYS NOW WERE busier than ever, for I'd taken on the task of decorating the palace as well as the grounds where the ceremony would take place. I had also offered to take care of our guests, some of whom had already started to arrive. It was a big job, but I wanted to do it. So many times in the forest, people had welcomed us, even when they lived in a hut and had only a handful of rice to share. I wanted to do my part now. Fortunately, Urmila, Mandavi and Shrutakirti helped me with my tasks. Working together, laughing and joking as we used to in Mithila, I felt we were as close to our happy childhoods as we'd ever get.

In my rare moments of leisure, I'd retreat to my balcony. I'd accepted Kaikeyi's peace-offering of the Mithilan plants she'd collected, and they bloomed happily all around me. I'd put up my feet and sing to the baby in my womb. I sang of my joyous childhood in Mithila, and of my dear parents. I sang of the glories of Ram and my love for him, and my hopes for my child and the great king I knew he would become. I loved most to sing of my life in the forest and the many charming wild creatures there. Though I told no one, not even Ram, I missed the freedom of forest life, its many enchantments. The baby loved hearing me sing. He'd express his joy by kicking me. He was so active that sometimes I'd joke and ask, 'Are there two of you in there?'

But I never sang of the time I spent in captivity in the asura palace, or of the ten-headed king, magnificent and terrible, who had destroyed his beautiful kingdom because of his infatuation with me. That time was too painful. I couldn't bear to look at it. Perhaps I'd never be able to do so.

SHANTA ARRIVED THE DAY before the coronation. The long journey had tired her out. The swaying of the palanquin, with the men running double-fast to get her to Ayodhya on time, made her nauseous. A plump, cheerful woman who usually loved to talk and laugh, today she looked pale and wan. After the barest of hellos, she retreated into her mother's chambers, where Kaushalya made her drink lemon-water and lie down in a darkened room.

'I'll come by your rooms in the afternoon if I feel better,' she whispered to me apologetically. 'I'm so sorry—I'd been looking forward to chatting.'

I assured her that it wasn't a problem. I was planning to take a nap myself. I wanted to be well-rested for tomorrow.

'Come by if you feel up to it,' I said, though she didn't look like she'd be able to. 'I'll leave the chamber doors unlocked.'

Once I reached my room, I took off the heavy silk I'd worn to greet the guests. It was beautiful but stiff with gold thread and it made me sweaty and tired. My maid handed me a thin cotton sari which I draped around me with a sigh of relief. I dismissed her and lay down on the stone floor instead of the bed because it was cooler there. I was always hot nowadays, and often at night this made me restless. Ram would bring me water and sit up and fan me for hours, no matter how long a day he'd had, even though I told him not to. I wished he was with me now because he gave the best back rubs, knowing without being told exactly where my body ached.

AS THOUGH IN RESPONSE to my wishing, the door was pushed open. I sat up, yawning. Had Ram decided to take a break in the middle of his work? But to my surprise, it was Shanta.

'I couldn't sleep,' she explained. 'And it was so gloomy and dark in Mother's chambers. I decided I'd come and chat with you. Hear all about your adventures—stories about them have reached even my faraway home.'

I'd been looking forward to my nap because the evening was going to be busy again. A group of ascetics with strict dietary restrictions had arrived, and I needed to make sure that the cooks prepared the right kinds of food for them. But Shanta was making an effort to be friendly, and after all, I'd invited her to come to my rooms. So I smiled and asked her to sit on the cool floor near me, and began to tell her about the beautiful forests we'd travelled through, with their mountains and rivers and volcanoes, and the many amazing wild creatures I'd seen.

But Shanta, it seemed, wanted something more exciting. She asked me about the rakshasas we'd encountered and how Ram and Lakshman had destroyed them. When I said I didn't really know the details because I didn't like watching bloody battles, she seemed disappointed.

'Tell me about Ravan, then,' she said. 'Did he really have ten heads, like they say? Was he fearsome, or good-looking, or perhaps both? Tell me about how he stole you away, and how he kept you in his palace for months and months. Was his palace beautiful beyond compare, like the palaces of the gods? And is it true that though he abducted you to avenge his sister Surpanakha, he then fell in love with you?'

Anger flared in me at the questions. How could Shanta be so insensitive? Even Urmila hadn't asked me about these things. Didn't Shanta realize how painful these memories were? I wanted to ask her to leave my rooms, to leave me alone.

But she was my husband's only sister. He was so happy that she was here. I held on to my temper and said, 'I never really looked at Ravan, so I can't say much except that to me he was a monster who destroyed my happiness.'

But even as I spoke, my voice trembled. I hadn't looked at him, but I'd heard him. I'd heard him declare his love for me over and over, and that had disgusted me. But I'd also heard the stories he'd told me about his harsh childhood, and the years he spent in severe tapasya, up in the Himalayas, praying for special powers so he could relieve his mother of her poverty. I'd heard him sing songs that he'd composed on the glories of Lord Shiva, his beloved deity. And at the moment of his death, when he'd touched my foot, I'd seen him in his true form as the celestial gatekeeper of Vishnu.

Shanta must have heard the weakness in my voice, because she pushed on. 'It's not healthy to keep it all inside you, you know, pressed down upon your heart. If you don't feel like speaking about it, at least draw me a picture of Ravan. You can do it right here, on this stone floor. Look, here's a piece of chalk. Draw it and then together we'll stomp on his heads for daring to steal you away. I promise you, you'll feel a lot better after that.'

What persuasiveness in her voice made me take the chalk? What kind of spell did she cast on me? Did I really believe that drawing Ravan would help me exorcize him? As in a dream, I pressed the chalk against the floor.

'I can only draw his feet—I was forced to look at them plenty of times when he stood in front, threatening me,' I said.

'That's all right,' Shanta said. 'I'll draw the rest.'

When I looked surprised, she added, 'From my imagination, of course.'

The chalk glided over the stone. In a moment, I'd finished drawing Ravan's feet. I tried to hand the chalk to Shanta, but somehow it was stuck to my hand. Now it was moving rapidly by itself, pulling my hand along, drawing Ravan in his entirety.

'What's going on?' I cried. 'Sister, help me.'

But Shanta's face was changing. The nose caved in. Instead of ears, there were gaping holes. And the eyes—I knew those burning, hate filled eyes. It was Surpanakha! Somehow she must have come to Ayodhya and taken on Shanta's form.

'Oh yes, it's me,' she said. 'I followed you all the way from Lanka and waited patiently all this while for the right occasion. With all the hullaballoo of the coronation, it was easy enough to slip into the palace, taking on the appearance of one of the maids. And then, when Shanta arrived, my plan became clear and I took on her form.

'Tell me, Sita, did you think you'd get away so easily? Did you think I'd give up and forget about you after you'd destroyed my home and everyone I loved? Did you think there were no consequences? That you could put the devastation of Lanka behind you—my people killed or maimed, their spirits broken—and live happily ever after in Ayodhya, loved by your husband, your family, your subjects, your sons?

'Oh yes, I can feel those two alien hearts pulsing inside you. Maybe I'll kill you and your unborn babies right now and leave you here for Ram to find on the eve of his coronation.' She flexed her hands, from which nails as sharp as scimitars now jutted. I tried to move away, but her asuric powers had me pinned to the floor. I couldn't even curl myself into a ball to protect my stomach.

Not my babies, I prayed with all my heart. Goddess, I don't care how much I have to suffer—but let no harm come to them.

Then a dim corner of my mind registered what Surpanakha said and what I'd repeated unthinkingly. *Babies.* I was carrying twins!

With an effort, Surpanakha brought her hands down to her side. 'No, I'll not let you escape so easily. I have a better plan. Live on, Sita. Live without love, as I've been forced to. See how it feels to lose everything you cherish. I'll give you a little hint: you'll long for death.'

She grinned fiercely at me through tears, and then she was gone.

The portrait of Ravan opened its eyes and looked at me. It, too, grinned. It was dreadfully life-like, as though the asura king might rise up any moment from the floor. I tried to wipe it from the floor with the edge of my sari, but I couldn't. Whatever magic Surpanakha had used had etched it indelibly into the stones. And now my sari was stuck to the image. I pulled at the garment, panting with effort, but it wouldn't come loose.

Just then the door to my chamber opened and I heard Ram's voice.

'I thought I'd spend some time with you before—' He broke off and stared at me. 'What are you doing, Sita? Why are you lying on the floor half-clothed, panting? And what's that picture?' His voice rose, and I heard the anger and disgust in it. His face was cold and hard as granite. 'Is it—? Were you drawing—? What were you doing, Sita? And why?'

My face flushed with shame, although I wasn't guilty of anything. I was well aware, though, of how damning the entire scene appeared—just as Surpanakha had intended.

'I haven't done anything. It's Surpanakha's trickery, her evil magic,' I cried. Even as I said the words, I could see on Ram's face how unbelievable they sounded.

I forced myself to breathe deeply, drawing upon my inner strength even as my heart pounded in agitation at Ram's accusing tone. I am innocent, I said to myself. I am pure. I refuse to feel ashamed because I was made the victim of trickery. I refuse to apologize for something that is not my fault. I refuse to let Surpanakha win. I sat up straight, not caring that the sari fell away from my upper body, and told my husband what had occurred, and who had been here.

I prayed that he'd believe me, because truth was all I had.

Ram frowned as he listened. My heart sank at the incredulity on his face, his angry, fisted hands. After I'd finished, he closed his eyes. I could tell a battle was raging inside him. It seemed to take forever. I held my breath and felt it burning my lungs.

Finally, Ram opened his eyes.

'I trust you, Sita, life of my life,' he said. 'I don't know how Surpanakha could have entered this palace. It's heavily guarded, and special protections have been laid on every entrance. But if you say so, then that is what must have happened.' He dragged a heavy quilt from the chest and covered the portrait with it, and brought me a clean sari to wear. 'I'll get Vasishta to take a look and figure out how the evil brought in here may be exorcized. Meanwhile, let's move you to a guest chamber where you can rest.'

Relief made me burst into tears. I laid my head on his chest and hugged him tightly. As long as Ram's on my side, I thought, I can face anything. Anything in the world at all.

Only later, lying in the guest chamber, too shaken to sleep, did I think, I would have believed him at once if our positions were reversed. Why did it take him so long to believe me?

THE CORONATION CEREMONY WENT off perfectly, the kind of event bards would sing about for years. The largest grounds in Ayodhya had been prepared for the event, decorated with garlands hung from poles and covered with brightly coloured tents. In the centre of the grounds was the largest pavilion, decorated with silks and jewels. Here, kings and sages sat on elaborately carved gold and silver chairs. Behind them were placed the visiting dignitaries and the noblemen of our court. The queens and noblewomen sat to the side of the pavilion, behind a curved lattice wall that had been specially constructed so they could see without being seen—the Ayodhyan way. The rakshasas and monkeys each had their own sections, cordoned off carefully so that curious onlookers couldn't bother them. On another side were the great merchant families of the region. The rest of the field was filled to overflowing with cheering citizens, many of whom—I could tell by their simple clothes—had travelled from the distant countryside. I felt a powerful energy coming from the sky. The gods, too, were watching.

Amidst music and chants and flowers being strewn under our feet, we moved to the dais constructed for us. We walked side-by-side, Ram and I. My husband had broken tradition and insisted that my place was beside him and not behind. I tried to step with appropriate dignity and stateliness. The gold and jewels I wore were very heavy, but the lightness in my heart bore me up. How long my husband had waited for this day. How much he deserved it. I wanted to take his hand and squeeze it to show my support, but I knew he wouldn't think it appropriate for this formal moment.

No matter. We'd have our private celebration afterwards.

We were now seated on the dais, on thrones that seemed far too enormous. But Ram seemed perfectly comfortable in his, so I, too, made an effort to appear the same way. When Ram raised his arm to acknowledge the cheering crowds, I did the same, and the cheers grew even louder, *RajaRamRajaRam* interspersed with *SitaRamSitaRam*.

After so many years of deferment, it was finally happening, the ceremony that Dasharath had so eagerly planned but failed to execute! I could feel him looking down at us from the heavens, smiling. Were all the dead up there, then? Ravan, too? Or had he been transformed back to being the gatekeeper of Vaikuntha?

Stop! I said to myself in annoyance. I never want to think about Ravan again.

But of course, that only brought more uncomfortable thoughts: Of the image that had etched itself into the floor of my bedroom and wouldn't be erased, no matter how many maids—all sworn to secrecy—scrubbed it, until a powerful medicine-man performed a purification ceremony. Of Surpanakha, whom no one could find even though the palace was thoroughly searched. Of bewildered Shanta—the real one, lying next to Kaushalya—abruptly awakened by Ram, who'd come to check on her. She had sat up, rubbing her eyes and mumbling that she'd fallen into a deep sleep and had some very strange dreams. Of the additional protection charms that were placed that same day over all the doors and windows of the palace, but secretly, because Ram didn't want people to know what had happened and gossip about it. Of the guards now positioned twenty-four hours outside my chambers, which made me feel a little like a prisoner.

I forced my mind back to the ceremony, to the beautiful, grand (but rather lengthy) mantras being chanted for the prosperity of our kingdom, an abundance of rain and crops and cows—and progeny, may they come soon. (Here Ram and I exchanged a secret smile). Vasishta anointed Ram with waters from the five holy rivers and then took the large crown—which had been kept in the treasury since Dasharath's death—and placed it on Ram's head.

'May you be the best ruler Bharatvarsha has ever known,' he said.

Ram joined his hands in humble reverence. 'May that become true by your blessings.'

But I knew he needed no blessings, not for this. Whatever else in life he might have to strive or struggle for, he lived and breathed kingship naturally and effortlessly. He loved his people more than his own self.

Once he was crowned, Ram stood up. The gathering grew quiet with anticipation, wondering what would be the first thing that their king would say to them.

'My people,' Ram cried, 'I want to share some wonderful news with you. Soon there will be a little prince joining you.' He looked at me and added, with a smile which acknowledged our private joke. 'Or a princess. To celebrate this happy event, I declare a holiday tomorrow, to be spent in festivity. We will have food and drink for you, music and dancing and fireworks at night, and a gold piece as a gift for every citizen of Ayodhya, and a silver piece for all inhabitants of Koshal.'

The grounds erupted in cheers. I smiled and waved for as long as I could. The people wouldn't stop applauding. The musicians joined in with drums and trumpets, the noise cresting until I felt a headache coming on. I tried to catch Ram's eye to ask him if we might leave, but he was enjoying the moment, looking out at the assembly with so much love in his eyes that I didn't want to spoil it for him.

So what if I had to endure a little discomfort? I was happy to do it for Ram. Wasn't that what love was all about?

Then I noticed Vasishta. Standing next to my husband, he was running a hand over Ram's shoulders in blessing, the way a father might. I could feel how fond the sage was of his student, how he wanted the best of everything for him. I was glad he was there for Ram on this special day when King Dasharath could not be present.

But even while there was a genuine smile of joy on the sage's face, I noticed a frown of concern on his forehead.

What was it that worried Vasishta at this auspicious moment?

Thirty-one

AFTER THE CORONATION, THINGS QUIETED down in Ayodhya. The rakshasas left after vowing public allegiance to Ram. The monkeys stayed a little longer, but finally they, too, went back to their homes in the mountains of Kishkindhya. Hanuman was the last to leave. I felt a real pang when the day of his departure arrived. But he wouldn't let me be sad.

'Feed me, dear Mother,' he demanded. 'I'm going on a long journey, to meditate in the Himalayas, and I'm pretty sure I won't get any of your delicious cooking there!'

I decided to cook for him myself, in the little alcove of my palace chambers. I had the maid bring all the fruits and vegetables he liked, and milk for sweetmeats. I hadn't prepared any food since my forest days. I was surprised to find how much I enjoyed the chopping and cutting, the steaming and frying—and the happy memories they brought back of our carefree wanderings. I decided I'd do this regularly for Ram from now on.

I served the food to the two brothers and Hanuman with my own hands, and they kept me busy asking for seconds. Especially Hanuman. By the time I brought vegetables, he'd eat all the rice, and by the time I'd hurry back with more rice, he'd eat up all the vegetables! How amused Ram and Lakshman were at his antics. But

I had my revenge on him, too, though I'm not quite sure how the idea came to me. I sneaked up on him from the back and placed a few grains of rice on his head, then claimed that he'd eaten so much that food was bursting out of even his skull! Everyone laughed, Hanuman most of all, saying, 'Ah, Sita Ma, you've figured me out.' Was it only I who noticed that, even in the midst of merriment, his eyes were deep as a mountain lake?

WHEN IT WAS TIME for Hanuman to leave, I couldn't stop my tears. Ram and Lakshman moved away to give me a little privacy. Or perhaps they were uncomfortable with weeping women.

Hanuman had made himself small so that he'd be inconspicuous on his journey, so I had to bend down to speak.

'Will I see you again?' I asked.

'Not in this lifetime,' he said with regret. 'And therefore I ask for your blessing.'

As I stroked his soft head, a jolt went through me like lightning. The day grew dark, or maybe it was light from another world that surrounded us, paling everything else. I saw before me Lord Shiva standing with his matted locks and beautiful blue throat, arm raised in benediction.

And suddenly I remembered something from my long-ago, innocent girlhood. Something the magic bow had said to me, though I couldn't recall all the words. *Shiva the divine, the auspicious, bringer of happiness, he will come to you in your darkest hour.*

Has it been you all this while? I said in my mind, for words were no longer necessary.

Yes, he said.

Don't leave me, I begged. *The babies are coming. I want you to be there to bless and protect them.*

I am always with you—and with them. There is no living creature in whose heart I don't reside. You need only call upon me to feel my blessings.

Focus your mind on me, especially in your dark time. I will give you strength.

What dark time, Lord? I cried in fear. *Aren't our troubles over, aren't we all safe in Ayodhya now?*

But the vision was gone. There was only Hanuman, touching my feet, saying he'd better be on his way, the sun was past its zenith already.

WITH THE DEPARTURE OF Hanuman, the last of the shimmering magic of the forest seemed to fade from our lives. Though it saddened me, perhaps it was necessary. How, without detaching ourselves from the spell of the past, can we focus fully on the moment that faces us? We each had our duties. Ram and Lakshman took care of court matters, laws and judgements, trade and treaties with other lands. They sent out agents, carefully disguised, to wander among the common people and find out their troubles or concerns so these could be taken care of. Bharat and Shatrughna, by their own request, were posted at the far edges of the kingdom, to oversee the safety of the borders and keep an eye on the wild tribes. Their wives went with them happily. They'd grown used to being mistresses of their own households, where they could live the way they wanted, with few rules and less protocol. I didn't blame them for that. I would have liked such a free lifestyle myself.

As for me, with the help of Urmila I managed the palace, which was like a large and intricate machine. I made sure that the mothers were cheerful and comfortable and kept themselves busy, that the servants worked hard and were treated generously, and that all the palace animals—from the kitchen cats that kept the mice away to the ceremonial elephants that led our parades—were healthy and happy.

As in Mithila, I became known for my healing skills. The women who lived or worked in the palace, or were married to courtiers, soon began coming to me when they were ill. They often asked for advice with problems beyond the physical ones. The palace physicians—and even the city doctors—consulted with me when handling a strange or serious case. Sometimes they brought their most challenging patients to me. They said that when I placed my hands on them, these patients were healed. But I suspected it was that the patients were overwhelmed by the attention they received from a queen, and afterwards, when they went home, they followed their physician's instructions more carefully!

My favourite responsibility, the palace garden, was very different now from Dasharath's time, when everything had been planted in strict rows and tied to stakes so they stood at attention. My garden flowed along gentle lines, the way nature intended it to. It surrounded the palace on all sides, and a brook wound its way through it, babbling merrily. The entire side of the grounds that lay behind the palace I'd made into a little forest. I loved to sit there with my back against a tree trunk and watch the sunlight filtering through the leaves above my head. The fruit and berry trees and the honeyed flowers I'd planted attracted many creatures. I told the gardeners that they were not to be disturbed. Thus many kinds of monkeys (for whom I had a particular fondness) could be found swinging from branch to branch. Squirrels and birds chittered at each other. Swans floated elegantly on the small lake, their feathers white as springtime clouds. Bees built enormous, glistening hives. Butterflies of every colour flitted among blooms.

But no deer. I didn't allow a single deer in my sanctuary.

I loved my little wood, but some days a strange dissatisfaction would come over me, a longing to go walking in a real forest, a wild, unpredictable forest, the kind that had been my home for so many years.

Once, shyly, I told Ram about my desire. If anyone understood it, I felt it would be he. For hadn't he, too, spent time under the enchanting trees of Panchabati and Dandaka?

But Ram wasn't nostalgic like me. 'That time in our life is over, dear,' he said. 'We are now king and queen. We belong to the people. They count on us to be here for them, in good times and bad. Haven't you seen how many of them come to the palace each week, just to see us wave to them from the public balcony?'

I sighed. Thousands of people did come to see us, many of them having travelled from distant cities. Ram was right, although the silver pieces that the guards distributed among the crowd afterwards might have had something to do with it too!

I put my dream away in a secret chamber of my heart and focussed on being a good queen, a fitting consort for Ram, who was already known, far and wide, as the best king Koshal had ever seen.

ALTHOUGH RAM HAD INSISTED so strongly that our forest adventures were done with, they still haunted him. He would toss and turn in his sleep sometimes and call out names. Once I awoke to hear him crying, in a miserable voice, 'Tara! Oh Tara, I am so sorry!'

A little jealous, I shook him awake to ask who this Tara was, and why he was apologizing to her.

Ram sighed. 'Tara was the queen of the monkey tribe, a very wise queen. Her husband Bali was Sugreev's older brother. They'd had a big quarrel—that story's too complicated to go into right now. But as a result Bali, the king, banished Sugreev, taking everything he possessed, including his wife. When I met Sugreev he was destitute and in despair, ekeing out an existence with his small band of followers in a mountainous wilderness. I promised Sugreev that I would make him king, and in return he agreed that he and his entire vanara army would help me get you back. He promised to send out scouts to find where you were imprisoned, and then to fight by my side until your abductor was destroyed.

'But, for that, I had to kill Bali first. I was forced to use trickery because he was such a great warrior. He'd even defeated Ravan in the past. So because of me, Tara became a widow, and her son, Prince Angad, lost the love and protection of a father. Ah, how much misery did I create! I fear I'll have to pay for it at some point.'

I consoled him as best as I could. I told him the war had been in a good cause, for wasn't it his duty to rescue his wife? Most importantly, hadn't he rid the world of Ravan's tyranny? Surely the merit accrued from that would neutralize these other acts, which he undertook unwillingly, and only because there was no other choice.

But my heart was a dense ball of fear. The laws of karma were complicated, and ultimately, one never escaped them.

I SAT BY A shady copse in my wood, sharing a meal with Ram, listening to the tale of Shabari, a lone moment of joy in the midst of his desperate search for me. It was one of his favourite stories; he'd told it to me a couple of times. I, too, loved it, this tender story about an illiterate tribal woman who had been told by her guru that Ram-the-divine would come to her. Trusting in her guru, she'd waited for him all her life, gathering a basket of fruits for him each day, even though the people of her tribe mocked her for her blind faith. When, in the course of his search, Ram had stumbled upon her humble hut, she was old and near death. Delighted, she'd offered him the fruits she'd gathered that day. She'd bitten into each to make sure it was sweet enough. And Ram had happily eaten these and blessed her for her simple and deep affection.

But today, halfway through the story, a maid ran up to inform me that a woman had come to the servants' building, asking for my help. Would I please see her?

'We told her to wait until tomorrow, but she cried and cried and begged me to inform you,' she said apologetically.

I looked at Ram.

'Go on,' he said with a rueful smile. 'I'm done eating, and anyway, I know if you don't go you'll just sit here and worry.'

I apologized but he shook his head. 'You're doing the right thing. Your duty as queen is to take care of your people—especially the women. I know you've helped many, and I'm proud of you for doing that.'

'I'll be back as soon as possible,' I said, but Ram waved me away. 'Don't worry. Take your time. I have to go over some new trade levies with Sumantra and Lakshman. Sumantra is so particular about these things that we'll probably be up half the night.'

I got to my feet with a little sigh—the babies were getting heavy and I was often tired by the end of the day—and followed the maid. I could never turn down a call for help, even though I knew that people sometimes took advantage of that.

IT TOOK ME A moment to recognize the woman. She was one of the younger washerwomen who worked for us. A skilled worker, she was in charge of washing the queens' saris. I'd seen her several times when she brought back my clothing. The reason I didn't recognize her right away today was because her face was puffed up—from weeping, but also because someone had clearly hit her.

'My husband,' she said, in between sobs. 'He beat me and threw me out of the house last night and told me to never come back. I went to my father's, but he said he can't have me stay with him either. A married daughter who leaves her husband's home, he said, brings shame on her family. He'll never be able to get my sisters married if he takes me in.'

'What did you do?' I asked.

'Nothing! My husband—he's one of the palace washermen, too, and quite a bit older than me—has a suspicious nature. Because of that I'm very careful and hardly ever go anywhere. But one of my best friends was having a baby last night and asked me to be with her. She was scared because the midwife said the baby was turned wrong. The birth took a long time. I knew my husband would be angry, but how could I leave her? She was holding on to my hand, crying all the time.

'I got home well after midnight. My friend's husband had walked me home because it was so late, and when my husband saw him, he was furious. He said—' here she broke off and looked at me with fear.

'What did he say?'

She shook her head, looking at me with fear-stricken eyes. I guessed that she didn't want to repeat his curse-words. 'He accused me of unfaithfulness and told me to leave the house and never come back. When I tried to explain, he slapped me, and when my friend's husband tried to stop him, he called his brothers, who live in the same house with us, and drove him off. Then he hit me some more and threw me out of the house. And now my parents won't keep me either. I don't know what to do.' She broke into fresh sobs, throwing herself at my feet.

My heart ached for the girl. She was caught in a hard place. Suspicion is a terrible disease, a canker that can totally destroy a relationship. I'd felt its sting myself. It hurt worse when love was involved, even the kind of twisted love that made the washerman feel he needed to control his wife.

Was there any hope for this marriage?

It had been a long day. I was too tired to analyse the malicious intricacies of suspicion or figure out its solutions.

'Sleep with the maids for tonight,' I told the woman. They will bring you poultices and give you clothes to wear. Tomorrow we'll figure out what to do. We could send someone to talk to your husband—'

But at that, the woman wept more wildly. 'I don't want to return to his house. Even if he took me back, he'll bring up this night and accuse me all the time, and hit me whenever he feels like it. No one would stop him. No one would believe me even though I'm innocent. Please, can't I just stay here? I'll work really hard. I'll wash twice as many clothes—'

That might be the best solution, I thought. So many servants lived in the palace. One more would make no difference.

'Very well,' I said. 'Get up now'—for she'd thrown herself at my feet once again, thanking me over and over—'get yourself something to eat and get some rest. Remember, you're going to have to wash twice as many clothes tomorrow!'

'Yes, I will!' she cried. Then she saw that I was joking and a tremulous smile broke over her face.

That smile buoyed me up as I returned to my rooms. I wanted to tell Ram everything that had occurred, and ask him if some kind of law might be passed that didn't allow men to beat their wives or throw them out of the house so easily. But he was still busy with his trade levies.

I'll tell him tomorrow, I thought. I lay down, suddenly exhausted, and placed my hands over my stomach. The babies moved slowly, lazily in their sleep. They were a joy, a miracle. I couldn't wait to hug them, to see Ram holding them with a new tenderness in his eyes. Imagining that happy scene, I, too, fell asleep.

I TOLD RAM ABOUT the washerwoman the next night while he and I were having dinner. I was hoping that he'd be sympathetic to the girl's plight and follow up on my idea about changing certain laws to protect women in her situation. Generally, he was sensitive to the problems of women and often sent money from the treasury for my projects without my asking. But today he seemed distracted. I asked why, but he held up his hand and said, rather brusquely, that he didn't want to talk about it.

I was taken aback and a little hurt because Ram was always gentle in his speech with me.

Ram must have realized this, because after a moment he took a deep breath and said, 'I'm sorry. I have a lot on my mind today. I was thinking of what you'd asked for some time back, a visit to a nearby forest. Do you still want to go? Once the babies come, it won't be possible. So if you want to do it, we should plan it right away.'

This was a wonderful surprise, something I'd never have predicted! Ram had been overprotective of me since the pregnancy, sometimes annoyingly so. My heart spread its wings, soaring at this unexpected gift.

I spoke quickly before he could change his mind. 'I'd love to go—I can be ready right away, maybe even tomorrow. Why don't we go to Sage Valmiki's ashram? It isn't that far—just a two day journey, less if we have fast horses. This way, if something comes up and you need to get back to Ayodhya, you can return right away. I remember how kind he was when we last saw him. When we were leaving, he took my hands in his and said that I was welcome to come back there any time I wanted. I know I'll enjoy the break—and you will, too. We could go for long walks together in the forest again, remembering our happy—'

Ram cut me off abruptly. 'I can't go with you. I have to take care of some major problems here. I'll ask Lakshman to take you.'

I rubbed his back sympathetically. How many worries a king had, especially a good one like Ram. 'I understand. No problem. Lakshman will take good care of me. Maybe Urmila would like to come along, too. She's never seen a real forest and often asks me for stories of our adventures. I wish you'd tell me what is bothering you, though. I know I can't help. Still, sometimes sharing your troubles with someone who loves you makes you feel better.'

But Ram turned away. 'Urmila can't come with you. Who will take care of your palace duties, then? And I can't talk now. I have work to do. In any case, you should be getting ready for your journey.'

'Oh yes,' I said excitedly. 'I won't need to pack much—I only plan to go for a week. But I must take gifts for the ashram inhabitants. They were all so kind to us when we stayed with them. They'd surely like sweetmeats and spices, and maybe mats and quilts. Some strong metal cauldrons—I believe they only have earthenware vessels. A few large pots of ghee—I know they use it for yagnas. Can you think of anything else?'

But Ram replied, as though he hadn't really been listening to me, 'Yes, yes. Whatever you want. I'll talk to Lakshman. Go to sleep when you're done packing. I have to work late.'

When I wished him good night, in spite of being so busy he held me for a long moment. There was a stricken look in his eyes. It amused me that the thought of being away from me for just one week distressed him so. How lucky I was to have a husband who loved me so deeply even after all these years.

Looking into his unhappy face, I almost told him that I was carrying twins—he didn't know that yet. It would cheer him up, give him something joyful to occupy himself with until I returned. No. I'll tell him when I return. We'll celebrate this double happiness together.

Thirty-two

I COULD BARELY HOLD MY EXCITEMENT in check as I climbed into the chariot that was to take me to Valmiki's ashram. It was a light vehicle, made for speed, just large enough for myself and Lakshman—who was to drive me there and return the next day—and the many boxes and pots stacked behind our seats. The morning was chilly and Urmila tucked a shawl around me.

'I wish you were coming with me. You would have loved the ashram,' I said as I hugged her.

'I wish I were too,' she said, throwing a reproachful glance at Lakshman because he, too, had insisted that she needed to stay in the palace and look after the mothers. I had to admit that he had a point. The mothers had grown frail and forgetful. They needed someone around to spend time with them, to make sure they ate their meals and took their medicines on time.

'Maybe you can come with Lakshman to fetch me,' I said.

'That's what I'll do,' she said, cheering up. 'In the meantime, I'll train Saudamini carefully so she can take care of the mothers while I'm gone.'

I looked back at the ramparts of the palace one last time as Lakshman cracked his whip, setting the chariot in motion. I wished Ram had been there to wave goodbye to me. But he'd left before sunrise, while I was still half asleep. Apparently there was some kind of trouble at the border. He'd left even before I could say *I love you.* A needle of unease pricked my heart at that thought.

THE HOUSES AND HALLS and marketplaces and even the massive gates of the city soon fell behind us, obscured by the dust of our passing. Lakshman drove fast, answering only in monosyllables when I tried to engage him in conversation.

'Why so glum, Brother-in-law?' I joked. 'Are you missing Urmila already?'

I'd hoped to make him laugh and blush because he'd fallen deeply in love with my sister since he returned to Ayodhya. But he only bowed formally and said, 'Please forgive me. I have a lot on my mind today.'

He was probably concerned about the trouble at the border, and about the fact that Ram was there alone, handling it without his help.

'Don't worry,' I said. 'Ram will be fine. Bharat and Shatrughna are not too far away—they'll help him if necessary. For all you know, he'll be back in the palace before you return.'

'I'm sure you're right,' Lakshman said gloomily.

I refused to let his despondence infect me. This was my last chance to enjoy the forest before I was plunged into the responsibilities of motherhood, and I was determined to make the most of it. I watched the many greens of the trees and bushes flowing past me, speckled with bright dots of flowers. They were like a balm to my eyes. I hadn't realized how much I'd missed nature in its wildness. I took great gulping breaths of the fresh, wild-smelling air and loosened my hair to allow the wind to blow through it. It seemed to me that the babies were enjoying the ride, too, for they kicked and somersaulted energetically.

In the afternoon, I took out the food that Urmila had packed and offered some to Lakshman. But he said he didn't want anything.

I shrugged and ate it all myself—the delicious rotis stuffed with vegetables, and cool buttermilk to wash it all down. Because of the pregnancy, I was constantly hungry. The rest of the trip, I watched for different kinds of birds and was delighted that I could still recognize them. I pointed them out to Lakshman, telling him their names. He didn't appear too interested, but that didn't dampen my enthusiasm.

It was almost evening when we reached the beautiful Yamuna River. I remembered that Valmiki's hermitage wasn't far from here. There was a rickety bridge that Lakshman had to navigate carefully. Clearly, not many chariots came to the sage's ashram. When we were on the other side, I asked Lakshman to pause. I wanted to tidy myself before meeting the sage and his wife. I stepped into the stream to wash my face and drink the fresh, clear water. It was cold, and the current pulled hard at my feet, but I couldn't resist splashing around a bit. It had been a long time since I'd played in a river.

'Do you remember, Lakshman, how in Panchabati, Ram and I—' I started, turning to him. But what I saw made me forget my words.

Lakshman was weeping, his face streaked with tears, his body racked by silent sobs. He kept his eyes on the ground.

In my entire life, I'd never seen Lakshman cry. My hands began to shake. I tried to ask him what was wrong, but the words froze in my throat.

Finally, Lakshman said, 'Sister-in-law, I ask your deepest pardon, though I know you'll never forgive me for this. Please keep in mind I'm only doing what Ram asked—no, commanded me, not as my brother but as my king. I am to leave you in Valmiki's ashram.'

'Yes, I know,' I said, still not understanding why he was so upset. 'That's why we've come here—for me to spend a week in Valmiki's ashram.'

'Not a week,' Lakshman said. 'The rest of your life. Ram is banishing you from his kingdom.'

My head spun. I had to sit down on the muddy riverbank to keep from falling. Was this some kind of a recurrent nightmare I was having? It happened every once in a while. I'd wake up, gasping, hearing again his voice in my head, *Now I have slain Ravan, and set you free. Here ends my duty to you, and my responsibility. Go where you will to live out the rest of your days.* Inside me, the babies somersaulted, agitated by my fear.

I said to myself, I didn't hear Lakshman correctly. Or maybe he was the one who'd misunderstood Ram.

'What do you mean, banishing me? I haven't done anything wrong. Are you sure that's what Ram said? He's the most righteous person I know. He wouldn't do such an unjust thing—especially when I'm carrying his children. No, Lakshman! Don't look away. Explain to me what's going on.'

I got the story in reluctant pieces from Lakshman as the sun sank below the horizon. There were rumours in Ayodhya, people whispering about my chastity. *How did Ram know Sita wasn't raped by Ravan, or worse still, didn't give in to his persuasions? She was with him in Lanka for an awfully long time. How do we know that there really was a trial by fire? None of us were there, nor our priests or courtiers. Only Ram and Lakshman—and you can't quite call them unbiased, can you? And the child she's carrying—how do we know it's Ram's? She got pregnant so quickly, didn't she? She was already showing at the coronation. How do we know when exactly it happened?*

And then came the attacks on Ram himself: *Maybe he's just like his father. Remember how old Dasharath was blinded by infatuation, doing whatever that Kaikeyi asked, no longer knowing or caring what was right and what was wrong? When Dasharath banished Ram, we went through years of bad luck. Famine. With Ram bringing Sita home, impure as she is, who knows what will befall us now?*

And how about our wives? They're going to start expecting the same kind of submissive behaviour from us. They'll be doing whatever they want, going wherever they want. Anything we say to them they'll shrug away, saying, if Ram can accept Sita after she lived with Ravan, surely you can put up with this little thing. Or do you think you're better than the King?

Everyone talks about Ram Rajya, heaven on earth. But it's becoming a place of lax morals. Maybe we should be thinking of moving somewhere else!

A huge boulder pressed down on my chest. I had difficulty speaking, even breathing. Finally I managed a whisper. 'And all this time I thought the people loved us because of how hard we were working to improve their lives, to make Koshal the best-governed kingdom ever. Was it all a sham, the crowds cheering us when we appeared on the palace balcony?'

'No,' Lakshman said. 'Many people still worship Ram and think you are a kind and wonderful queen. But the gossip is growing. And as you know, Ram has very high standards for kingship. He feels that there must never be an occasion for anyone to point a finger at him.

'The agents whom Ram sent among the people in disguise have been hearing these mutterings for a while. Loving Ram, they kept it to themselves, but it got to the point where they felt they had to tell him. I was with him when he got the news. I've never seen him so distressed—not even when the battle with Ravan was at its worst. You know how important his kingship is to him, how crucial it is for him to do the right thing. But he loved—loves you, too, with his whole heart. Additionally, he's well aware of his duties as a husband. It was torture for him, caught in the middle of these different conflicting duties, trying to figure out what was the right action. A day and a night he suffered, unable to focus on anything at court. He wouldn't talk to anyone about it, not even me.

'Finally he decided to go for a walk around the royal lake to clear his head, and there he overheard two washermen arguing. Listening, he realized they were a father-in-law and son-in-law. The father-in-law was begging the younger man to take back his wife, whom he'd thrown out of the house. But the son-in-law was adamant.

"I'm not like Ram," he said. "I don't take back a wife who comes home late in the night, having spent her time doing who-knows-what."

'"How can you say that? You know she was with her friend who was having a difficult childbirth," the father-in-law protested.

'"Women will say whatever suits their purpose," the son-in-law said. "All I know is that she came home with another man. Why are you worrying about her, anyway? I hear she's gone running to Sita, who's taken her in. Birds of a feather. I tell you, we're well rid of her. And if Ram had any backbone at all, he'd get rid of Sita, too."'

Pieces of the puzzle began to come together for me. Ram's distracted air, which I thought was due to state matters. The way he cut me off brusquely when I tried to tell him about the washerwoman. The way he was suddenly willing to let me go off to Sage Valmiki's.

My body trembled, but this time with anger. 'So he banished me because a few people are gossiping? People always talk. Should an elephant turn around and run away because dogs are barking?'

'You know Ram,' Lakshman said sadly. 'He's always believed that the reputation of a king should be above reproach, and even more so the reputation of a queen. It's what he's built his whole life around. He can't change his nature—no more than a leopard can change its spots. Believe me, I tried everything I could to make him decide otherwise. Finally he said that if I didn't obey him, he'd banish me to the forest, too.

'I considered it seriously. Would it be so bad if Urmila and I—for surely she'd come with me—lived a simple forest life by your side, with a clear conscience? But then I thought, Ram would be left all alone, without either of the two people who truly love him, and whom he loves most. Alone in that dark, stone-cold cave of a palace, for that's what it's going to be now without you.

'I couldn't do that to him, Sister-in-law.'

Rage had receded from me. My teeth were chattering. I felt cold. Cold and defeated. 'But why didn't he tell me any of this?' I said. 'Why didn't he explain what was going on? I would've understood. I would've been angry, yes, but I would also have sympathized with him. Don't I know how important his reputation as king is to him? Together, we might have come up with a better plan. And even if we couldn't have come up with a solution, at least I would've been part of the decision, not a victim of it.' I choked up with tears. I tried to swallow them, but they kept coming.

'But he didn't trust me, Lakshman. My husband, whom I trusted from the very moment my father put my hand in his. My husband, whom I believed in through the darkest nights of my despair in Lanka. My husband, whom I forgave even after his harsh words on the battlefield in Lanka gave me no choice but to throw myself into a fire. My husband, to whom the gods themselves proclaimed my innocence. That husband has now discarded me like an old sandal.

'You go back and tell him this, Lakshman: He sentenced me to banishment because people were whispering that I might have betrayed him. But he's the real betrayer. Who's going to sentence him?'

I turned and started pushing my way blindly through the bushes, not sure where I was going. Behind me I could hear Lakshman calling out frantically, urging me to stop, but that only made me hurry. Brambles tore at me. I didn't care. When I'd stepped into the fire in Lanka, I'd believed that nothing could hurt me any worse, body or soul. How wrong I'd been! The pain was so excruciating now that if it hadn't been for the babies, I would've thrown myself into the Yamuna and ended the burning.

My babies. The most innocent. The most wronged. I could feel them inside me, trembling, clutching at each other, sensing that something terrible had happened.

'Don't be afraid, little ones,' I whispered, pushing my way determinedly into the dark, even though I had no idea of what it held. Hot tears scalded my cheeks. 'I'm going to live for you. I'm going to guard you with my last breath. I'm going to love you enough for mother and father both, so you feel no lack. I'm going to teach you everything you need to know to be princes. But more than that, I'll teach you what you need to know to be good human beings, so that you'll never do to a woman what your father has done to me.'

Thirty-three

THINGS DID NOT GO QUITE the way I'd declared so optimistically. In my agitation and ignorance I walked in the wrong direction, away from Valmiki's hermitage, deeper into the forest, into the night. It was only by luck that I wasn't attacked by a wild beast. Or perhaps it was fate. It's hard to tell them apart, what we bring upon ourselves and what destiny determines. They're as difficult to disentangle as love and sorrow.

Finally, I fell to the ground in a deep sleep or a swoon, so exhausted that I no longer cared what happened. I don't know how long I lay there. When I awoke, it was to the flickering of smoky torches, and a man with a long white beard calling my name. It took me a moment to recognize Valmiki—he looked a lot older than I remembered. He told me that Lakshman had searched for me for a long time. Finally, giving up, he'd made his way to the ashram and explained what had happened. Valmiki sent him back to Ayodhya, saying he would take over since he knew the forest better. He gathered his students and came looking for me. Fortunately, they'd thought to bring a pallet, for I couldn't have walked another step. They placed me on it and hurried back to the ashram, where Valmiki put me in the care of his wife, Indira.

The first few days in the ashram, I was numb. The determination I'd experienced the night I walked away from Lakshman had vanished, its place taken by a thick, sticky depression that mired me so that both past and future seemed unreal and disconnected. I swallowed, without complaining or enjoying, enough of whatever food the wives of the sages brought me to keep them from getting concerned. When they walked me around the ashram, because Indira-Ma insisted that I needed exercise, I shuffled along. At every opportunity, I welcomed the opaque lake of sleep and fell into it until shaken awake. I lost sight, for periods of time, of who I was. When someone called my name, I often didn't answer because I didn't recognize it. Looking down at my distended stomach, I was sometimes startled because I'd forgotten I was pregnant.

THEN ONE MORNING I woke up and everything was devastatingly clear again. I remembered my life from girlhood onwards, how each important moment had felt. How excited I'd been when I first met Ram, how I sensed that I'd known him in another dimension. I felt again my excitement when he strung Lord Shiva's bow, my consternation when he broke it into pieces. My elation when I put the wedding garland around his neck. The long journey to Ayodhya with him riding by my side, and how at night, in our palace chamber, our bodies came together in ecstasy. My determination to follow him into exile, and his consternation, followed by joy because he wouldn't be separated from me. Our wanderings through forests dangerous and exciting. Our simple life with its simple joys. I remembered the terror of my abduction, the endless nights under the sorrow tree in Ravan's garden, where even in the midst of despair I trusted that Ram would save me. And then his heartless rejection of me, the fire into which I stepped, hoping to end the burning in my heart. The gods exonerating my innocence, and Ram contrite yet joyful beyond measure to get me back, ready to start our life anew. How willing I'd been to start over even though he'd wronged me. That's what you do when you're in love. I remembered our desperate, hungry lovemaking in the magical chamber created by Pushpak as we flew back to Ayodhya, and the moment I felt life enter my womb. Our return to a dispirited and dilapidated country and helping my beloved husband, my king, to fashion it anew, filling it with abundance and hope. I remembered that ill-fated day when Surpanakha had crept into the palace and forced me to draw Ravan's image.

Was that when a seed of doubt that had somehow remained in Ram's mind all the while, began to sprout? Was that when the whispers became so important to him?

And then he'd sent me away without even having the courage or the consideration to tell me to my face what he was doing to me and why. Without asking me, his helpmate and queen, what I thought should be done, he'd banished me and his babies, all three of us equally innocent, because he believed that was his duty to his people.

But weren't we his people, too? Didn't he have a duty to us?

I WEPT AS THESE thoughts raged like a whirlwind through my mind. I tried to harden my heart towards Ram, but I didn't know how. I wept especially bitterly for my children, deprived of their inheritance, fatherless in the world. How would I ever take care of them?

I cried hysterically until I threw up and my stomach hurt so much that the women had to call Indira. I was curled on the floor when she arrived. She helped me get up and wash myself off, and then she spoke to me kindly but firmly, in a tone that reminded me of my own mother, Sunaina.

'You know that if you behave like this, you'll hurt the babies, don't you? And you certainly aren't helping yourself, either.'

I nodded, silent and shamefaced. 'I can't stop myself.'

'Pull yourself together,' she said sternly. 'You aren't some weak-willed wench. You can control your emotions. Remember all that you've survived. Behave like the queen you are. No one can take your dignity away from you. You lose it only by your own actions.'

Before she left, she gave me a hug and said, 'Remember also that you're not alone. Valmiki and I are happy to have you stay with us as long as you want. For the rest of your life, if you wish. Your children will be part of our ashram family.'

I TRIED VERY HARD after my talk with Mother Indira to do what she said. I no longer allowed myself fits of weeping. I avoided being by myself, for it was then that the world seemed darkest. I repeated to myself what Mother Indira had told me. But they were only words. I didn't know how to touch the truth that was inside them.

Finally, I decided to go into the forest. Perhaps I'd be able to think more clearly under its majestic trees. The women in the kitchen packed food for me. Indira whispered prayers as she waved me goodbye. 'Come home before sunset,' she cautioned. 'That's when the creatures of the night take over the forest.' She asked the ashram boys to point out a path that would take me to a honey-grove. 'It's a good place,' she said, though she didn't elaborate further.

I found the honey grove without much difficulty. How different the forest was by day, compared to the menacing wilderness I'd thrashed through in the panicked dark. Was that how life, too, seemed when we flailed around in desperation? I ate my food, simply cooked vegetables and coarse-ground rotis. The grove was filled with dripping honeycombs. I cupped my hands under one and licked the honey that pooled in them. For the first time since my banishment, I tasted what I ate and found it satisfying. But my heart was still heavy. I lay down, pressing my cheek to the earth. Help me, I whispered. You are my first mother. You kept me safe when there was no one to take care of me. Help my babies now.

Was it my imagination, or did I feel warmth seeping into me?

I turned over and regarded the leafy canopy. Flecked golden by the sun, the leaves rustled peacefully. Watching them, I fell into a dream.

In the dream, too, I lay in the forest, but now I was surrounded by women. They walked around me with soundless measured steps. They looked at me with wise and compassionate eyes, eyes that had known suffering. Some I recognized: Sunaina, Ahalya, Mandodari, Sarama, Kaikeyi. Some I guessed at: a monkey with a diadem on her head who must be Tara; a tribal woman holding a half-eaten fruit who must be Shabari. Why, even Surpanakha was among them, a rare calm veiling her mutilated face.

Endure, they seemed to say. *Endure as we do. Endure your challenges.*

The words resonated through me.

I stood up slowly, holding on to a tree trunk for support. I still felt anger towards Ram. His memory was a bruise that might never fade from my heart. But I was ready to focus my energies elsewhere.

Living in the forest wasn't what I'd planned for myself or my babies. But then, had I planned that Ram should come into my life like a tidal wave and sweep me away? Had I planned to be banished to the forest on the eve of our coronation, to be abducted, or even rescued? Had I planned on the rumours upon our return, or Ram's harsh decision? All these had happened without my choice, but I'd survived them. Wasn't that all we could do as imperfect human beings?

I started home—it was time for me to start thinking of the ashram as home—with a more resolute step. I couldn't control what was done to me. But my response to it was in my control.

All the way back, I pondered the word *endure,* what it meant. It didn't mean giving in. It didn't mean being weak or accepting injustice. It meant taking the challenges thrown at us and dealing with them as intelligently as we knew until we grew stronger than them.

That was what I'd work on.

Over the next few days I evaluated my newfound community, trying to figure out how best I might be of use to them. In my current state, I was no good at cleaning or cooking or carrying heavy pots of water back from the river. But their medicine woman, Dharini-Ma, who was old and half-blind, was glad for my help, more so when she realized how much I knew about healing herbs. She'd tell me where to find the ones she used most commonly and send me off with a basket. I enjoyed my jaunts into different parts of the forest. I was delighted to discover some of the herbs and berries I'd used in Mithila—including those that aided childbirth. I brought them all back and ground them into powders and unguents until our stores were full.

I worked side by side with Dharini, helping the people of the ashram. Mostly their troubles were minor ones, for they followed a healthy lifestyle, waking at sunrise to bathe in the river, then spending long hours in study or prayer, followed by daily chores, simple meals, storytelling or singing at night, and early sleep. At most a child might break a limb, or an elderly resident suffer from a stubborn, hacking cough, or one of Valmiki's students get stung when he tried to get a honeycomb.

But often the forest tribes came to us with more serious problems: a leg gashed while hunting, now infected, or a child born with a breathing disease. Under Dharini's guidance, I learned how to clean an infected wound by dousing it with spirits that burned and made even the strongest of men yell in pain, and to stitch it up afterwards, or to cut out a tumour that made a woman's stomach swell like she was pregnant.

I often stayed with our patients afterwards, holding their hands until they slept, and it seemed that this made them heal faster. Word travelled through the forest that the pregnant woman who had suddenly appeared at Valmiki's ashram had the touch, and more and more tribals came to us for help.

I welcomed the work. It kept me busy all day and tired me out at night so that I fell asleep as soon as I lay down on my bed of leaves.

This way, I didn't lie staring at the moon, remembering my happy times with Ram on a similar bed in Panchabati.

DHARINI-MA WOKE ME UP, shaking my shoulder gently. 'You've got a visitor.'

My heart careened. I had to press down on my chest to calm it. Some of my wild hope must have shown in my eyes, because she shook her head sadly. 'No, it's not him.'

Outside, two women sat on the porch, leaning exhaustedly against the posts. They must have travelled a long way, because the bottoms of their peasant-saris were crusted with mud. Looking closer, I recognized them.

'Urmila!' I cried, shocked and worried and delighted at the same time. 'What are you and Saudamini doing here?'

She struggled to her feet and threw her arms around me in a desperate hug. 'Oh, Didi, I was beginning to think I'd never find the ashram—or you. Thank God you're all right.'

Over a meal of milk and puffed rice, which she devoured ravenously, Urmila told me her story. She'd started growing suspicious as soon as Lakshman had returned to Ayodhya because he acted so unhappy and guilty, refusing to meet her eyes at mealtimes and sleeping by himself in an alcove every night, no matter how many times she called him to bed. Even her most passionate kisses failed to make him change his mind. He wouldn't answer when she asked about me, and when she said she wanted to go with him to fetch me from Valmiki's ashram, he scowled darkly and snapped at her to leave him alone.

Ram was acting strange, too. He'd shut himself up in his chambers, not eating or bathing, refusing to see anyone except Lakshman, who'd spend his whole day in there with his brother.

'Ram didn't even attend court,' Urmila said. 'Can you imagine that? That's never happened since he returned to Ayodhya, not even that one time, you remember, when he was so badly injured boar-hunting. I was sure that something dreadful had happened to you. Perhaps there had been an accident on the way, and you were dead. Or maybe some other rakshasa had snatched you away. That would explain why Lakshman acted so guilty. And why, even after two weeks, he made no efforts to return to Valmiki's ashram to fetch you back.

'I asked Saudamini to check in the servant's hall, which as you know is a great source for news and gossip. But there, too, no one knew anything. The chariot and horses that Lakshman had taken to Valmiki's ashram were in good shape, which proved that he hadn't been attacked. Nor had there been an accident.

'What then could it be?

'Desperate for an answer, I stopped eating and took to my bed. For three days, I starved myself. Believe me, it was no easy task. My stomach ached all day with hunger and I felt dizzy.

'On the fourth morning, Lakshman came in with a bowl of milk. If I drank it, he said, he'd tell me what happened.

'That's how I learned of the terrible injustice that was done to you.

'I said nothing to Lakshman after he told me your story. I was angrier with him than I'd been with anyone in my entire life. How could he have agreed to be the agent of Ram's unjust folly? How could he have just left you like that in the forest? But I stitched a smile on to my face and went on with my daily duties. I didn't want him to guess my plan and imprison me in our chambers, with his soldiers at the door. I told Saudamini to ask Sharav for help. We needed a guide who could take us to Valmiki's ashram. He would, I promised, be richly rewarded.

'Sharav did his best, asking around secretly, but no one seemed to know exactly where the ashram was. Finally he brought a woodcutter to see us. The woodcutter said he could get us to the vicinity. But there was something odd about the ashram, he warned us. Sometimes one could see the roads that led to it, and sometimes they disappeared.

He'd leave us at the river, he said. After that, we'd be on our own. I agreed and gave him enough gold to make him happy.

'I told Lakshman that I was worried about you and wanted to visit a goddess-shrine that brought good luck to pregnant mothers—but the rule was I had to go incognito and on foot, with no more than one female companion. He didn't like the idea, but he was so relieved that I was eating and talking to him that he didn't protest. Moreover, he was preoccupied with a new project. Ram's ministers, realizing that he'd sent you away, and seeing how depressed that had made him, had begged him to marry again. But Ram had flown into a rage and ordered them to get out of his sight. So now they were building a life-sized gold statue of you, a golden Sita that would be placed next to Ram in court. That was the only way, they felt, that he might get over his melancholy and take up his kingly responsibilities again.

'Ridiculous, I thought. Nothing could remove Ram's sorrow and guilt for abandoning his innocent, pregnant wife the way he did. And nothing should. But let him have his statue. It'll be a good reminder of the terrible decision he made.

'Anyway, here I am, after three excruciating days of being lost in the forest. I think every mosquito that lives in this area has made a meal out of me! And don't you dare tell me to go back. Because I absolutely won't do it.'

I cried as I heard Urmila's tale, overwhelmed by her fierce loyalty towards me, for the sake of which she'd risked both life and happiness. I cried thinking of Ram and his grief. I cried for the love we'd shared and which now festered in our hearts. And finally I cried—for the last time, I hoped—for the cruel way in which he'd sent me and his innocent babies away.

Then I forced my sorrows to the back of my mind so that Urmila and I could spend three beautiful days together. We laughed like girls, remembering childhood incidents, staying carefully away from subjects that could cause us grief. I showed her around the ashram, where she tried her hand at various tasks—such as milking cows and husking grain—most unsuccessfully.

On the fourth day I sat her down and said, 'I love you for coming all this way, through all these dangers, braving your husband's anger to be with me. But you have to go back now. You know that. You've seen me. You've seen that I'm well taken care of. It's my destiny, for whatever reason, to be here now. But yours is to go back to the palace. Go and do what I can't: make it into a true home for your husband. You love him and he loves you. What has happened to me shouldn't ruin that, otherwise it'll be an added sorrow for me to bear. Go and be a comfort to the mothers. And bring your children up—for I foresee several in your future—according to his or her royal heritage.'

The last words almost made me break down, for they reminded me once again of all that my own children would be deprived of.

Urmila protested and raged and stomped her feet, but I was adamant. I did a good job of hiding how hard it was for me to let her go, and finally she gave in. Valmiki managed to procure a palanquin, along with bearers, from a nearby village so that she and her maid could make the journey back in comfort and safety. As I watched Urmila climbing tearfully into the palanquin, an odd thought came to me: I would see my sister only once more, and that would be on the day of my death.

Valmiki sent two of his senior disciples with her, along with a letter he'd written to Lakshman. I'm not sure what the letter said, but when the disciples came back, they told me that after he read it, Lakshman hadn't been angry with Urmila, only grateful that she'd returned to him.

Thirty-four

I AWOKE WITH RACKING PAINS AND knew it was time. Indira and Dharini tended to me along with a couple of younger women, while outside the hut Valmiki and the other rishis chanted prayers. I asked Indira if they did this for every child born in the ashram, but she shook her head.

'Valmiki has meditated on these boys and knows they have a great destiny. They'll be even greater warriors and kings than their father. That's why they must be welcomed with the proper auspicious prayers.'

The contractions came faster now. I cried out partly in pain and partly in sorrow that my children wouldn't be welcomed to this earthly life by their father. But when I saw them, red and wrinkled, swaddled tight in the soft white cloth woven by my friends, I forgot all sadness. Indira placed them on my chest, where they didn't cry but listened, wide-eyed, to my voice calling to them.

Then Valmiki came in and blessed the boys and named them Lav and Kush. I'd never heard such names, but the sage said they'd come to him in meditation. These boys would be raised like no other. Their greatest teacher would be their mother. Their world would be that of the hermitage. Their playground would be the forest. Because of this, their strengths would be unique. It stood to reason, then, that their names had to be unique too.

I took comfort in what Valmiki said, though in the back of my mind I worried. How would I—or even Valmiki, sequestered as we were in the forest, educate them in the right way? How would we teach them all that worldly princes needed to know?

Valmiki was asking me a question. Lost in my thoughts, I hadn't heard it and he had to repeat himself. 'Shall we send news to Ram?'

Ah, his name. I hadn't heard it since Urmila left. No one in the ashram mentioned him because they didn't want to upset me. I thought I'd grown an armour strong enough by now to deal with it. How wrong I was. His name sent a sharp stab of pain through me, worse than anything I'd experienced during the birthing.

I turned my face away so Valmiki wouldn't see my foolish tears. 'No,' I said. 'He doesn't deserve to know.'

But inside, my traitor heart still hoped. Surely he'd send a messenger asking for news? After all, he knew when the babies were due. Surely, even if he didn't want me, he'd take his sons back to the palace, bring them up royally, as they deserved to be. I longed for that to happen even as I dreaded it.

But no one came, and finally I was forced to face the truth.

Ram no longer cared for me. Or if he did, it was pushed deep down inside him, suffocated by kingship. And since the children came from my body and were subject to the same gossip and doubts, he couldn't afford to care for them either.

AFTER THE BIRTHS, THE entire hermitage rallied around me. Though they never spoke of Ram's continued silence, they were outraged by it and did whatever they could to keep me in good spirits. Lav and Kush, being the first babies born here in a long time, were the darlings of the ashram, passed around from lap to lap, kissed and cuddled and so dearly loved that they never learned to cry. They may have lost their father, but they'd gained an entire community to love them unreservedly and teach them and spoil them and, thankfully, give them a scolding when they needed it—which was often, because they were always landing in some mischief or other. They called Valmiki and Indira Grandfather and Grandmother, while all the others became their uncles, aunts or cousins.

Compared to Ram, alone in his splendid, loveless palace, we were the lucky ones.

As soon as they were old enough, Valmiki made sure Lav and Kush received a proper education. In the mornings, along with all the boys that were sent for study to Valmiki's gurukul, they learned the Vedas with all the rituals that brought blessings to humanity. In time they were taught the wisdom of the Upanishads. They learned to chant and sing, and their voices were so clear and melodious that even the denizens of the air, gandharvas and apsaras, paused to listen. After lunch, they did chores with the other rishikumars, taking the cattle out to graze, or bathing the cows, or repairing the thatched huts, or learning to collect the right kind of wood to build a yagna fire that wouldn't smoke.

In the evenings, though, Valmiki took them aside for private lessons. This is where they learned about wartime strategies and peacetime statesmanship: how to direct an army into intricate formations and inspire them to fight with everything they had; how to be a good ruler and make the right decisions when people brought you complicated disputes; how to interweave justice with mercy. At first I was astonished by the breadth of Valmiki's knowledge. How could a simple rishi possibly know such complicated statecraft? Then I remembered that Ram himself had learned all that made him into a great warrior and king from Sage Vasishta. Furthermore, Valmiki explained that much of the information he needed to impart to the boys came to him in meditation.

What really took me aback was when, after those lessons were done, Valmiki tied up his long hair and beard, knotted his dhoti tightly around his waist, and taught the boys how to fight with sword and staff. In spite of his age, he was strong and wiry and moved fast, often disarming the boys in minutes. He grinned at my astonishment and said, 'I wasn't born a rishi, you know! One of these days, I'll tell you about my colourful past.'

Lav and Kush loved these lessons—and the fact that they were secret and not to be spoken of. Their favourite, though, was archery. A twinge went through me as I watched them, for the bow was their father's favourite weapon too. Soon the boys had learned to fashion their own bows and arrows, great intricate ones that looked far too big for them. But they had no problems handling them and spent all their free time running off into the forest to practice. I'd forbidden them to kill any creature unless it threatened their lives, but they had great fun competing with each other, shooting stone chips off distant mountains and dislodging berries that dotted faraway hedges.

I, too, played my part in the education of the boys. We went on long walks through the forest, where they learned to recognize medicinal herbs—particularly the ones that staunched wounds and healed injuries—and how to use them. At night, when we retired to our little cottage at the edge of the ashram, I taught them self-defence, all that I'd learned in Mithila. How to fight calmly when no weapons were available. How to fight without hatred or vengeance, turning the attacker's rage against him. Or her, I told them, remembering Surpanakha. Putting my pain aside, I focussed on remembering the evenings in Panchabati, Ram and Lakshman arguing excitedly about weapons, and wrote down all I could recall about summoning magical astras. I didn't think they'd work because I was sure I'd forgotten some crucial detail or other.

So I was astonished when the boys chanted the words of power I'd given them and shining astras materialized. The boys didn't seem taken aback. I watched in wonder and trepidation while they held, with confidence and a certain strange familiarity, weapons that could blast through mountains or vaporize entire armies. They spoke gently and respectfully to the astras, bowed to them and sent them back to their realms, requesting them to return in the moment of their need. Clearly, they were their father's sons.

And mine, I thought, remembering the special relationship I'd had in my childhood with Shiva's bow.

Most of all I loved my children because they were kind to all around them, humans as well as animals. They weren't perfect, by no means. They had tempers that flared up at seemingly small things, and they could be maddeningly stubborn. They also tended to boss over the other boys they studied with, even ones that were older. But with me they were particularly gentle, perhaps because they sensed my sorrow which, although I tried to shake it off, clung to me as stubborn as a shadow. They brought me little gifts from their trips into the forest: pretty stones, a garland they'd woven, a chunk of honeycomb, a colourful feather.

They hugged me often, not caring who might be watching, and at night they lay on either side of me, with their arms around my neck, asking for stories. Their hunger for stories was insatiable, and they wouldn't allow me to repeat a tale. I had to search deep into my childhood memory and was often forced to use my imagination.

Sometimes I thought, it's true what people say: every darkness is edged with light. In a palace, bound by my royal duties, I'd never have had so much time for my children. We'd never have been so close to each other, known each other so well. Motherhood taught me something new about love. It was the one relationship where you gave everything you had and then wished you had more to give.

But here was a strange thing: even though Lav and Kush were curious about everything, they never asked me a single question about their father. Was it because they believed what Valmiki had implied, though he never actually told them an untruth: their father, a member of the ashram community, had travelled to a faraway land to practise austerities and was never heard from again?

Or was it because they knew the question would pierce me to my heart's core?

Thirty-five

For a while now, Valmiki had been composing his life's work, the Ramayan, the story of Ram's adventures as hero and king. He'd started it long before I arrived at the ashram, so I didn't take it personally. I was afraid he might ask me for details of our life together, but he never did.

Once I asked him how he knew the information he was putting into the book—after all, he hadn't been with us on our forest journey, nor observed the terrible battles in Lanka. He told me that visions of all he needed to write came to him at the oddest moments, forcing him to abandon other activities and write them down. The resulting work, he said, would be an inspiring epic and a powerful poem, teaching readers and listeners in centuries to come how to lead a virtuous life. He was very secretive about it and never allowed anyone, not even Indira-Ma, to take a look. If someone asked him to recite even a few lines from it, he refused.

'You'll hear it at the right time,' he'd say, 'when it's all done.'

Except now he was stuck. The visions had dried up for some reason. Was it because he was now embroiled in the story himself? He walked around the ashram, glowering and muttering. Indira massaged his head with Brahmi oil to cool the brain and increase creativity, but it was of no use. She consulted with me and dosed him with triphala and ishabgol, but though it cleared out his stomach, his brain remained constipated.

FINALLY, VALMIKI DECIDED TO travel to Chitrakoot Mountain to meditate. Chitrakoot was known for being a holy mountain. It clarified confusion and shed light on darkness. It was also one of the places where Ram, Lakshman and I had spent a significant amount of time. Perhaps Valmiki felt that walking in our footsteps would inspire him.

The entire ashram was highly excited because Valmiki hadn't travelled anywhere in a long time. His students—and even the other rishis—begged to go with him. It would be an amazing experience, they said, to meditate with him on a holy mountain. But I think they mostly just wanted an adventure to break the monotony of ashram life. Indira urged him to take them along. They'd make sure he ate and took his medicines and bathed at the right times. She had reason to be concerned. Once, long ago, he'd meditated for so long that a huge anthill had grown all around him, covering him completely.

Lav and Kush clamoured to go, too, but when Valmiki whispered something in their ears, they nodded thoughtfully and didn't ask again.

After the entourage had left, I asked them what the sage had said.

'Grandfather told us we needed to stay and protect the ashram,' Lav told me.

'He chose us because we're the best warriors he has,' Kush added proudly.

'We're going to patrol the borders of the ashram every day with our bows and arrows,' Lav said.

'One never knows what kind of danger might come hurtling through the forest,' Kush explained kindly. 'It's best to be prepared.'

I nodded, hiding my smile because the ashram was the safest place I'd ever lived in. Probably the meditative aura that exuded from it created a shield. But the wily rishi had said exactly the right thing to appease my children. 'I know you'll do a great job,' I said.

'Naturally, we can't do our other chores, like cleaning out the cow-stalls or cutting wood,' Lav said.

'We have to patrol full time,' Kush added. 'Will you pack food for us every morning?'

'Lots of food,' Lav said. 'It's hungry work, patrolling.'

Indira-Ma told them they were excused from cow-stall cleaning and woodcutting until Valmiki returned. I agreed to provide all the food they needed. They went off, whistling happily, to put new strings on their bows and sharpen their arrows.

A WEEK PASSED UNEVENTFULLY, and then another. We didn't hear from Valmiki, but Indira said that was a good sign. The boys grew nut-brown as they wandered the forest every day, coming home ravenous in the evening. They wouldn't let me comb or oil their hair, which now formed shaggy manes around their faces. They told me they needed to look fierce.

'What do you do out there all day?' I asked them.

'We practise fighting,' Lav said.

'We summon new astras,' Kush said.

'How do you know to do that?' I asked, intrigued.

The boys shrugged as though summoning astras was the most natural of activities.

'We send out a call and they come,' Kush said.

'They tell us their names and their powers,' Lav said. He counted on his fingers. 'There's Aishik, which turns into thousands of lions. Just its roar is enough to frighten enemies to death. And Brahmajaal, which falls on enemies like a huge net of fire.'

'Don't forget the Paashupat,' Kush said, 'the snake astra which comes from Lord Shiva. It told us that only a few people on the entire earth are able to use it. But my favourite is Akshayjit. You have to be careful to give it the right instructions, though, because used at its highest power, it can destroy the three worlds. It has the ability to bring down even the greatest warrior in the world.'

There was a conviction in their voice that made me believe what they said, impossible though it seemed. I stared at them in amazement and some trepidation, these two beings that had come from my body. They were still boys, not even as tall as I was. I wondered what their destiny was to be when they were fully grown. For what heroic role was the universe preparing them?

But meanwhile, it was my job to guide them.

'Don't you hurt anything as you're practising,' I warned.

'What about in self-defence?' they asked.

'Well, you do have to protect yourselves, but try not to kill anything.'

The boys nodded.

'And don't be late for dinner,' I said, but they'd run off already.

TONIGHT THE BOYS WERE very late. They always returned before dark—I'd made them promise they would—so all of us women worried, pacing up and down. At night, the jungle turned into a different place, wilder, not to be trusted. We lit all the torches we had and placed them at the edges of the ashram boundary so the boys would see them and make their way to us, but still there was no sign of them. We beat gongs and blew into conches so they might follow the noise home. Still nothing. Finally, we heard a sound coming towards us, but it wasn't their footsteps. It was something large, tramping loudly along the dark path, brushing against the hedges as it got closer. My heart beat unevenly as I listened. I grabbed a torch, ready to fling it at the creature, whatever it was. But when he appeared, I stood open-mouthed because there in front of me was the most beautiful horse I'd ever seen, white as moonlight, with a long silky mane and muscles that rippled under his shiny skin. His great black eyes looked at me with deep intelligence. There was a red star on his forehead. He wore a thick gold necklace but no saddle or bridle.

And my boys, their faces and bodies dark with grime, were grinning at me from his back.

'Where did you get this horse?' I said suspiciously. He was so beautiful that I would have taken him to be a creature of magic, except that no magic could enter the hermitage.

'He came up to us while we were protecting the ashram and nuzzled us,' Lav said. 'We thought he was hungry, so we gave him some fruit and soft new river-grass. He really enjoyed that.'

I doubted that the horse had been hungry. He looked very well taken care of. But clearly he liked my boys. Otherwise he would have shaken them off his back a long time ago.

'But why were you so late coming home?'

The boys jumped off the horse and hugged me. 'Sorry to make you worry, Ma,' Kush said. 'But we had to defend our horse. People were trying to take him away from us.'

'What people?'

'It was some kind of army, actually,' Lav said. 'They told us the horse belonged to a king. He was a yagna horse and had travelled all over Bharatvarsha. They wanted to take him away, but we could see he wanted to stay with us. I think he's tired of travelling.'

'What happened to the army?' I asked. The boys were probably exaggerating. It must have been a small group of grooms. Still, I looked around cautiously, wondering if they were about to rush in upon us any moment to claim their rightful property.

Kush grinned. 'We defeated them, of course.'

I looked closer at my boys. It wasn't grime on their faces but blood. My heart gave a shuddering leap.

Behind me, Indira said, 'This must be a horse for the ashwamedh yagna. Only the greatest kings perform this ceremony. The horse runs free wherever it wants to go. Any kingdom it runs through has to accept the horse's master as its overlord. If a king stops the horse, he must fight the army that accompanies the horse. If he wins, he keeps the horse and is praised as the stronger ruler. If he loses, he becomes a vassal of the horse's master. Clearly, this horse has never been stopped. I wonder whose horse it is.'

I barely heard her. With shaking hands, I was busy examining the boys' bodies for wounds, but there were none.

Lav touched my face gently and said, 'Don't worry, Ma. They couldn't hurt us. We prayed for your blessing and conjured a shield of magic arrows around us. We know nothing would get through it.'

Kush added, 'We could have killed them all easily, even the four generals, though they were quite good at fighting and had some fine astras of their own. But we remembered what you told us, so we didn't. Instead we called on our unconsciousness astra and our binding astra, and—'

The blood pounded in my ears. 'What four generals?' I whispered.

Lav creased his brows. 'They said they belonged to the Raghu dynasty. They added a lot of stuff about how great it was. We couldn't hear everything. It was noisy there, with all those soldiers that kept rushing up, trying to kill us.'

'Their names are on the necklace,' Kush said, holding it up for me. 'Mother, are you all right?'

I grabbed the horse's neck to keep from falling. Even before I read the embossed plaque that hung from the necklace, I knew what it would say. *The great monarch Ram, son of Dasharath of Raghu Vamsa, is performing* … The rest of the words faded away.

'Take me to the leader,' I cried. 'He's your father.'

THE DARK MEADOW WHERE the battle had taken place was full of bodies and slippery with blood. Lav and Kush held my arms and guided me. I kept my eyes on the single flaming torch we carried with us into the black night. I was glad I couldn't see the grimaces of horror that must have frozen on the men's faces. I hoped the boys were right, that the soldiers were unconscious and not dead. I didn't want my children to suffer the heavy karma of so much killing. Even though by the rules of war they were innocent, having only responded to being attacked, I knew that karma worked in strange ways. Why else would Ram—Vishnu himself come down to earth—have suffered so greatly throughout his life? Why else would he have been forced to condemn himself to a life of royal, arid loneliness?

Even before Lav and Kush pointed him out, I sensed his presence and rushed forward. I fell to my knees and held his still, blood-streaked face in my hands. He was bound with cords that sparkled and crackled as though they were made of lightning. They must have hurt—from time to time his body convulsed—though when I pulled at them, they didn't harm me. That was the way of divine astras. I tried, with all my strength, to loosen them—but I wasn't able to do it. I glared at Lav and Kush through my tears, too overwhelmed to speak. But they'd started chanting already, and in a moment the bonds faded away—not only from Ram but also from his brothers, who had fallen around him.

Dharini-Ma had followed me, along with a few of the women. They poured water over Ram's body so I could wash it and handed me my basket of healing ointments. The boys held the torches steady as I applied ointments and whispered prayers. How handsome Ram was, even with a bloody gash on his pale cheek. But he'd aged. There were lines of worry on his forehead, and a downturn to his lips as though life had disappointed him. I touched his wounds—he had many—and shuddered as though they were my own.

All this time I'd believed that I'd successfully steeled my heart against him, but ah, that wasn't true. I still loved him as much as when we'd been forest-dwellers in our little moonlit hut in Panchabati. And remembering how he'd sent me away without a word still hurt me as much as the night I'd arrived in Valmiki's ashram.

WHILE WE WERE WALKING to the field, I'd told the boys their history.

A distraught Lav had asked, 'But why didn't you explain this to us earlier, Ma, instead of letting us think we were rishikumars? Then we'd never have done something so terrible today.'

'What would I have told you?' I said sadly. 'That your father, though a great and valiant king, had banished me for no fault of my own, because of frivolous gossip? That he cared more for the stability of his kingdom and the brilliance of his reputation than he did for his innocent, unborn children? Wouldn't you have hated him if I'd done so? Wouldn't you have grown up angry and resentful and dissatisfied with the ashram—and perhaps blaming me, thinking that you should be in a palace instead?'

'We'd never have wanted to leave you, Mother,' Kush cried, hugging me tightly. 'We'd never have blamed you. But yes, you're right, we would have been furious with Ram. We might have gone searching just to battle him.'

I noticed that neither of the boys would call Ram *father*. But they observed him intently. No doubt they were seeing what I'd noticed earlier—and Valmiki, too. My sons looked just like Ram, with only a soft touch of me around their mouths.

But why weren't the ointments and the chants working? Why was Ram still lying there, pale as a corpse, his breath so shallow that I could hardly feel it? I tried again and again—and Mother Dharini tried with me—until the moon was low in the sky and the stars began to disappear one by one. Still Ram was caught in a place between life and death. Finally, in exhaustion, I threw myself down on the ground by him and prayed. Was it to the goddess or to the earth, my mother? Or to the divine being I'd been in the otherworld? Or were they all the same?

Help me. Please help me.

Praying thus, I fell into a trance. I don't know how long it lasted, only that the torches had sputtered out by the time I came back to myself. And when I opened my eyes, I knew the answer. The herbs and chants weren't working because of my anger towards Ram. In some dark part of my soul, I wanted him to suffer.

I took a deep breath and focussed on the faces of my children. They hung anxiously over me, holding back only because Dharini insisted that I shouldn't be touched when I was in the process of healing someone. I focussed on the flow of love between us and the fact that, more than anything in the world, I wanted them to be happy and fulfilled. But for that to happen, they had to develop their gifts to the utmost and then use them for the world's good. They'd already learned whatever Valmiki and I could teach them. They'd already learned whatever they could teach themselves. The best place for them now was their father's court. Ram had to be their teacher now. And to accept his teachings fully, they needed to love him.

They couldn't do that as long as I held onto anger, for anger gives out a powerful vibration even when it's wordless.

I concentrated as deeply as I could on my heart centre. I spoke to my inner self—or to the universe, which was, ultimately, the same thing.

For the sake of love, I give up my anger.

For the sake of love, I give up my anger.

For the sake of love, I give up my anger.

I felt a tingling in my palms and then a burst of energy surged through my body. I didn't know where it came from: the earth, the sky, or my own heart. Perhaps it didn't matter. My body grew light, almost as if it would lift off the ground. I placed my hands against Ram's chest and repeated the healing chant.

This time, even as I finished, he took a deep, jagged breath. Under his lids, his eyeballs moved. I waited, holding my breath, for him to open his eyes and see me. What would he say? What would he feel? Would he be grateful? Would he ask for forgiveness? Would he say he loved me?

I imagined him opening his arms wide and gathering us close, myself and the boys. I imagined how it would feel to rest my head against his heart once more.

SOMEONE TOUCHED MY SHOULDER, startling me. To my surprise, it was Valmiki.

'I saw in meditation all that was happening here,' he said. 'I returned immediately, using my yogic powers. You are to be commended for saving Ram's life. I hadn't thought it could be done.' Then his face grew sad. 'But this is not the right time for him to see you—or your sons. That occasion will come, I promise. For now, though, you must take your children and go.'

I wanted to protest. To refuse. To be so close to my beloved and not converse with him, not enjoy even a moment of his touch? Not see the admiration in his eyes because I'd raised his sons so well? I confess: I wanted also for him to know that I'd saved his life. I'd let go of my anger, yes, for the sake of my children. But I wouldn't have minded a little gratitude, the look of shame in his eye, an apology.

But there was a ring of truth in Valmiki's voice that made me pull the reluctant Lav and Kush to the shelter of a big banyan tree a little distance away. From behind its hanging roots, we watched as Ram gained consciousness and sat up—too quickly, for he had to brace himself with his arm. He looked around, disoriented. There was confusion on his face and also disappointment. He hadn't noticed Valmiki yet.

'I think he's looking for Lav and me,' Kush cupped his hands and whispered in my ear.

I was sure he was right.

From behind him, Valmiki cleared his throat meaningfully. Ram spun around and put a hand to his head, as though the sudden movement made it hurt.

'Revered sage,' he said, bowing to the rishi, 'have you seen the two young boys who detained my ashwamedha horse and did what no one in all of Bharatvarsha has been able to do? They defeated our entire army and then took on my brothers and myself as well. One by one, they brought us low. Ah, the way they called upon the most complex and powerful astras! I've never seen it done before. Even as I lay paralysed on the ground, I marvelled at their skill and wondered if they were children of the gods.'

Lav stifled a laugh. 'Did you hear that?' he whispered in my other ear. 'He thinks we're gods!'

I scowled at him to be quiet. I didn't want to miss even a word this conversation.

'Do you know who they are, rishi?' Ram asked plaintively. 'I'm not sure why, but even as they were battling me, I felt a great fondness for them. As though—' He shook his head. 'Are they from your hermitage, by any chance?'

'I have no idea who you could be talking about,' Valmiki said, straight-faced.

'Did you hear that, Mother?' Lav exclaimed, scandalized. 'Grandfather's lying!'

'I didn't know sages were allowed to do that,' Kush said with prim disapproval.

'Sometimes they are, when it's in a good cause,' I told them. 'Hush and listen carefully. I think Grandfather has a plan.'

I wondered why Ram couldn't guess who Lav and Kush were. He'd sent his pregnant wife to Valmiki fourteen years ago—and now, here were two boys who looked just like him. But perhaps guilt keeps us from seeing things that are otherwise as clear as a cloudless sky.

'My disciples and I were away,' Valmiki said, all innocence. 'We were meditating and didn't keep track of worldly things. I've only returned right now and am shocked to find that a great battle took place here.' He chanted some mantras and sprinkled holy water from the pot he was carrying in every direction. Ram's brothers sat up, glancing around in confusion. No doubt they, too, were looking for my sons. Slowly, the soldiers were also beginning to stir.

'The women tell me that last night a horse wandered into our compound,' Valmiki said. 'Ah, here it is.' He gestured and a couple of his disciples pulled the yagna horse forward. They had to struggle because the horse dug in its hooves and snorted menacingly and looked towards the banyan tree, where the boys were.

'Mother, see, he doesn't want to go,' Lav said. 'He's looking for us.'

'He wants to stay with us. He likes us better,' Kush said.

But they had to watch helplessly from behind the banyan while Ram walked over to the horse and patted its neck. The horse tossed its head a couple of times, but finally calmed down and Lakshman led it away.

IT WAS TIME FOR Ram to leave, too, but he was delaying, for some reason. 'There was another thing,' he said to Valmiki, speaking so softly that I had to strain to hear. 'In my swoon, I thought I saw—I thought I heard her voice. She was taking care of—'

I clasped my hands tightly together. He was talking about me. Somewhere in the depths of his being, he'd felt my presence.

Valmiki looked at him blank-faced. 'Who could you be thinking of?'

'Ah, no matter, it was probably just a fever-dream,' Ram said, shaking his head as though to clear it. 'Revered sage, thank you for restoring our horse. Now the yagna can be completed. I invite you, most humbly, to come to Ayodhya with all your disciples to bless the yagna on this holy occasion.'

'I accept your gracious invitation,' Valmiki said magnanimously. He sent a triumphant flash of a glance towards the banyan tree, where he knew we were hiding. 'But how will you conduct the yagna? I believe a king has to have a wife by his side when he makes the final offering. Has there been a wedding in Ayodhya that, sequestered as I am in the forest here, I didn't know about?'

I twisted my sari so tightly in my fists that it tore. Lav and Kush stared at me in astonishment.

Ram's face was pained but also resolute. 'No, great sage, I have not married again. I've been true to the vow I made at my wedding to take only one life partner. I have a golden image of'—here he stumbled over his words—'my … wife by my side. The priests have said that would suffice.'

When I heard that, I wanted to both laugh and cry. Was it only because he felt he must be true to his vow that Ram hadn't remarried? Or was there another reason?

'I am glad to know there will be no impediments to the yagna,' Valmiki said. 'I look forward to attending the ceremony. It is a rare king who manages to perform this ritual. But then, you've always been an exceptional monarch, haven't you?'

Ram lowered his head modestly. But I could tell he was pleased with the rishi's praise. Was I the only one who heard the irony in Valmiki's voice?

'I'll bring my senior disciples with me,' Valmiki added. 'They will chant auspicious mantras to bring prosperity and happiness to your kingdom—and to you.'

Ram sighed. 'I thank you. I would greatly appreciate your prayers. For some reason, though Ayodhya's treasury is fuller than ever before, and its citizens healthy and prosperous, it's lacking something. Some kind of life, some joy, has gone out of the city—no, the entire kingdom.'

'I wonder how that could have happened,' the sage said.

Another man might have grown suspicious at his overly innocent tone, but Ram only sighed again and said, 'I hope your blessings will bring us some peace.'

'I am sure it will,' Valmiki said piously as he walked Ram to his chariot. 'And joy, in addition, if God wills.' As Ram was about to drive away, he added, 'In fact, to enhance your joy, I will bring three special gifts for you when I come to your court. No, no, don't ask me what they are. You'll just have to curb your curiosity until the day of the yagna.'

He stared after the chariot thoughtfully for a long while, even after the sounds of the marching army faded and the dust settled and the forest creatures that had been frightened away returned to forage and feed.

Then he turned to us and put his arms around Lav and Kush.

'I know now what I must do,' he said. 'I will take the boys to the yagna. There in the court of the king, after the ceremony is ended, they will sing his life story, my Ramayan, which I am now ready to complete, having envisioned clearly how it is to end. When the king sees Lav and Kush, he—along with the entire court—will recognize that they are his sons. And he will accept them as his heirs.'

'And our mother?' Kush asked. 'Will he accept Ma too?'

'He'd better,' Lav said belligerently. 'Otherwise I'm not staying in Ayodhya.'

But Valmiki had hurried on ahead—perhaps so that he wouldn't have to answer them—and I followed his lead.

Epilogue

IT IS THE MORNING OF the journey to Ayodhya. Lav and Kush are excited beyond measure. They've made me wash their clothes—the simple dhotis that all of Valmiki's disciples wear—twice. They've sat, impatient but compliant, while I oiled their shoulder-long hair and combed the knots out of it. They've polished their necklaces of tulsi beads until they shine. Now they've come to say goodbye.

I hug them hard, suddenly panicking, not wanting to let go. I have no reason to be afraid. I know Valmiki will take excellent care of them. Plus, they've proved that they are eminently capable of protecting themselves. But there's a bad feeling inside me.

I can tell the boys are itching to be off, but they hold still in my embrace. Lav kisses me on the cheek. Kush pats my back. They tell me there's nothing to worry about. They'll be careful and not take any risks. They'll obey every word of what Valmiki tells them.

'We'll be back before you know it,' Kush says.

'We'll bring you gifts from the big city and tell you all about the court,' Lav says.

I nod and place my hand in blessing on their heads, too overcome to say anything.

Then they're gone, running and laughing with all the disciples, kicking up dust, ignoring the remonstrations of Valmiki's assistants.

MY LIFE FEELS LIKE a hollow gourd, scraped empty of seeds. I wander aimlessly around the ashram. With the men and children gone, it's too quiet. I try to busy myself, but there's hardly any work. I try to join the other women's conversations, but they can't hold my attention. I can't eat. And at night I lie on my sleepless mat in a hut that seems vast as a desert and watch the moon making its lonely way across the sky. I look desultorily for my Sitayan, wanting to add a few lines, hoping it will distract me, but it isn't where I thought I put it, and I don't have the energy to search.

So I'm at the mercy of my memories, which break upon me, endless as waves. The boys when they were born, their tiny reddish-brown faces, their puckered lips searching for my nipples, the sweetness that went through my whole body when they found them. I would've died for them then. Killed for them. I see them older, running through the forests with me following, urging them to be careful as they clambered up trees or pushed their way into thorny bushes, searching for berries. Or hid in the tall grasses, breathless with silent laughter, waiting for me to find them. Childhood ailments, fevers when I sat up through the night, placing cool poultices on their brows. The pride with which I listened to them chanting hymns, or watched them sparring with Valmiki, bringing him down to the ground so that he laughed and said, '*Now you are ready*.' And in our hut, late at night, their intense eyes when I told them about the astras, their lips silently repeating the words of power.

Every morning I wait for hours at the gate of the ashram, hoping for news. What are the boys doing now? I wonder. Have they sung the Ramayan yet? Has their father recognized them? Will he really accept them, like Valmiki thinks? I want that so much for them, and yet I dread it because that will mean that they'll never come back.

What will happen to me, then?

ONE MORNING INDIRA-MA INTERRUPTS my prayers. A messenger has come from the court. He tells me that after the yagna was successfully completed, Valmiki asked Lav and Kush to sing his great composition. Ram listened intently, tears running down his face, and at the end he embraced the twins and accepted them as his sons and declared, in front of the entire assembly, that they would be his heirs.

I'm weeping so hard—happiness for the boys, a dreadful emptiness for me—that I don't hear what else the messenger is telling me until Mother Indira says, 'When does she have to leave?'

'Today,' the messenger says. 'The king wants her in the court as soon as possible.'

I wipe my eyes and look, and there's the palanquin, huge and glittering and embossed with the seal of the House of Raghu, sixteen bearers standing ready to carry me away. Extra bearers, the messenger tells me, are waiting along the way so we'll not have to stop anywhere. And before I've fully taken in what's happening, Indira and Dharini are walking me to the palanquin, which the other women are filling with simple ashram gifts. I try to thank them—an impossible task—for saving my life. No, it was my spirit they saved, and thus my soul. We're all weeping, all the women of the ashram, but this time it's tears of happiness.

All the way back to Ayodhya, my heart swaying in time with the palanquin, I think of many things—seeing my dear Urmila after all these years, and my sons, now that they are officially princes. But most of all, this: *He loves me he wants me he loves me he wants me.*

AT THE LION-HEADED MAIN gate of the palace, a woman is waiting for me. I recognize Urmila's maid, Saudamini, older and comfortably plump now. She stops the palanquin bearers imperiously, even though the messenger protests that he's supposed to take me straight to the court, those were the king's orders.

'Are you crazy, man?' Saudamini barks. 'The queen can't go to the court looking like this. I'm taking her to Princess Urmila's quarters. When she's properly dressed, we'll bring her. You just go and tell King Ram that.'

Urmila throws open the doors to her chambers herself and hugs me so hard, I think she'll never let me go. We weep a few happy tears, but mostly we look at each other. I touch the silver strands in Urmila's hair, the lines radiating from the edges of her eyes. She takes my face in her hands and says, wonderingly, that I look as young as ever.

'Must be all that clean ashram living!' I quip. I don't believe her completely. Love does that to you, makes you see everything through a golden veil. But a part of me is happy to think that Ram might find me more beautiful than he expects.

Urmila's children run in, a beautiful boy and girl that have her eyes and Lakshman's stubborn mouth. They hug me and tell me that they've already become great friends with Lav-bhaiya and Kush-bhaiya. Lav is teaching them how to shoot arrows, and Kush is teaching them to sing. It makes me happy that my sons already have so many loving relatives around them.

I hand them chunks of honeycomb that they stuff greedily into their mouths, claiming that it was the most delicious thing they've eaten. Urmila shoos them off. 'Go play with your brothers,' she says. But they tell her that Lav and Kush are busy in the court, singing something very long and difficult for Uncle Ram.

He must really like the Ramayan, I think, if he's making them sing it again. I'm happy for Valmiki because he worked very hard on the epic, even though he didn't get it quite right. I think of my own Sitayan, wondering where I'd left it. Perhaps if I send a messenger to

Indira, she'll be able to find it and send it to me. Even if no one else ever sees it, it'll comfort me to possess a record of the truth.

'Many times I thought of leaving the palace, going to the ashram to be with you,' Urmila says. 'What was done to you was wrong, and I felt guilty that by remaining in Ayodhya I was condoning that.' She sighed. 'But I couldn't leave the children, and I couldn't leave Lakshman. He would be so lonely without me because I'm the only one to whom he can confide his doubts and sorrows.'

'You don't have to explain,' I say. 'That's love—golden ropes that bind you and pull you in different directions.'

Urmila's maids take over now, washing my hair and massaging me with turmeric paste. They pour buckets of scented water over me and wipe me with the softest cloths. My undergarments are as soft and light as a baby's breath and smell of sandalwood. Urmila has set out the most beautiful saris for herself and me, in complementary colours, parrot green for her and hibiscus red for myself. I protest that it'll make me look like a bride, especially with all the jewellery she's taken out of her coffers for me to wear.

'That's the idea,' she says with a mischievous grin. 'I can't wait to see the look on Ram's face when he sees you.'

We hug again. It's a joy to hold each other after such a long separation. A foolish memory comes to me: how I'd believed, when I said goodbye to her in the ashram, that I'd only see her again on the last day of my life.

I'll have to tell that to Urmila sometime, I think. How she'll make fun of me for having such strange fancies!

THE WOMEN HAVE ALMOST finished dressing me when Saudamini comes rushing into the room. Her face is pale. Her lips tremble. She whispers something into Urmila's ear that makes my sister sit down heavily on her bed.

'Saudamini heard that Ram is planning another agni-pariksha for you. She didn't believe it at first, but then she crept into the alcove behind the hall with one of the court servants and saw it, a great pile of wood in the middle of the hall, surrounded by large pots of ghee. All ready to be lit.'

I walk slowly and carefully across the room, holding onto furniture because a sudden movement might make my body fall apart. The end of my beautiful red sari trails after me like a slash of blood. I sit down next to my sister.

'He wants me to go through another test by fire?' I ask. I want her to tell me, *That's ridiculous!* I want her to say, *You heard it wrong*. But she's silent, eyes lowered.

'After the pain and humiliation I suffered last time?' I ask. 'After the gods themselves proclaimed me innocent? After all his apologies? This is why he wanted to bring me to Ayodhya?'

Urmila raises her eyes. They are bright with anger and tears. She says, 'Don't do it. Return to the ashram and preserve your dignity. Saudamini will get us a carriage. We'll leave by the back gate. Before anyone knows it, we'll be in the forest. Oh yes, this time I'm coming with you and so are my children. Lakshman can do what he wants. I've given him enough of my life already. And I bet when Lav and Kush find out what their father is planning, they'll go right back to you.'

Her plan sounds very tempting. To return to the peaceful forest, its healing green canopies. To return to the ashram community, where everyone trusts and accepts me, with my sister by my side. To have my dearest children with me the rest of my life, to bring them up, along with their cousins, to be the kind of people I want them to be.

I take a deep breath.

'No,' I say. 'I will not run away. I'll meet Ram, just as he wishes. But not like this, dressed up as a queen. Because I'm not a queen any longer. I'm Sita, the forest dweller, Sita, daughter of earth. And yes, Sita, daughter of fire as well.'

I begin to remove my ornaments and unbraid my hair. I ask the maids to bring back my simple ashram sari.

Urmila falls at my feet, begging me to reconsider, but I raise her up and kiss her gently. 'Be strong for my sake,' I say. 'Take care of Lav and Kush when I'm gone. They're shy, you know, underneath all that young-man bluster. They'll have a hard time asking for anything. They love milk sweets. Will you make them some on their birthday?'

'What do you mean *gone*?' Urmila asks, her face pale with shock. 'What are you going to do? You're not planning to walk into that fire, are you?'

'No,' I say.

'Then what?' Urmila asks.

I don't answer because I'm not sure myself. I don't know what will happen when I'm face-to-face with Ram, my greatest joy, my greatest sorrow. I only know that I cannot—will not—do what he asks.

THE FIRST THING I hear when I enter the royal court is my boys singing, their high clear voices that lodge in my heart. Their tones, innocent yet powerful, rise all the way to the high ceilings of this ancient room that has seen so much already, both tragedy and triumph. They are seated on Ram's right, on silver thrones that indicate their princely stature. They're the only ones who see me. No one else notices because every single person in the room is mesmerized by the purity of their singing, their passion and their conviction.

I, too, listen. I listen with my whole body because this may be the last time I'll hear them. Their beautiful voices pierce my entire being. I struggle to hold in my tears, my pride, my joy. Ah, love is the sharpest, sweetest weapon of all.

Then I recognize what they're singing. It's not Valmiki's great epic! They're singing the pages I'd written in my lonely darkness, out of the need to give voice to all of us who were pushed to the edges.

Misjudged, misunderstood. My truth, and the truth of the women whose lives touched mine for better or worse. Their laughter and tears, their triumph and suffering, their blessings and curses.

Lav and Kush must have conspired and taken the manuscript from our hut when I was busy elsewhere. They must have practised singing it in secret. They must have decided to perform it in my honour, risking the anger of their guru as well as their new-found father to tell the world my story.

I'm weeping as I listen to them sing the Sitayan. Their eyes meet mine, and they're weeping too.

And this is one of the final things I learn about love: it's found in its purest form, on this imperfect earth, between mothers and young children, because there's nothing they want except to make each other happy.

The song ends. The last immaculate notes float away. As though they are released from a trance, people blink and wipe their eyes and look around. That is when they see me.

A whisper goes around the hall until it reaches Ram, who is even now lost in the world of the Sitayan. He raises his eyes, which are still unfocussed, and I see that his face is wet with tears. His face, so stately, is the face of a true king, bearing nobly the marks of sorrow and care that life has left on it. But when his gaze falls on me, it changes and a wild hope, shimmering with excited joy, leaps in his eyes. For a moment he is my Ram, my beloved, my own, the young man I vowed to love and follow all my life. The husband who washed and bandaged my blistered feet and held me close to his heart all night in the forest. The king who, after we returned and struggled together to bring back prosperity to Ayodhya, clasped my hands tightly and said, '*You are my Lakshmi! I couldn't rule this land without you.*'

'Is it really you?' he cries now. He puts out a hand towards me as though he is afraid I might vanish.

I want to run and throw my arms around him. I want the sorrows of the last ten years to dissolve as our breaths mingle. I don't care what people will think. I don't care about anyone except him.

I start forward. But the piles of firewood block my path, forcing me to stop, reminding me of the reality of my situation. Lav and Kush begin clambering down to me. I know what they're planning: they'll help me navigate the barrier and bring me to their father. Finally we'll be together, the family they've longed for all their lives. They don't know, in their innocence, that an invisible barrier far higher than these pieces of wood rises between us.

I shake my head slightly, a subtle signal. They're confused, but they've always trusted me. So they obey and return to their seats.

Ram is speaking now. He has controlled whatever emotions shook him a few moments ago and uses his regal, official voice. 'I commend you for bringing up Lav and Kush so well—with the help of Maharshi Valmiki, of course. You will be happy to know that I have accepted them as my sons and have declared that they will inherit my kingdom. As you surely understand, from now on they must live with me in the palace so I can train them appropriately, preparing them to be great kings. They—we—have lost so much time.'

He pauses and swallows, and I recognize—though probably no one else in the court does, because none of them know him as I do—that he is nervous.

He continues, 'I would like you to come back to Ayodhya and live with us so that we can be a complete family. The children need you—and I do too. As you know, I have never taken another wife. But there's one thing you must do first—you must go through a test by fire here in the courtroom, so that the sages and attending kings and ministers of the court can witness the fire-god vouching for your innocence and purity. In this way, the citizens of Ayodhya will be satisfied for good.'

Rage rises up in me until my whole body is scorched, for some kinds of burning don't require a fire. Not a word of love, not a word of apology for the sorrow he has caused me. Not a word about the unjust and cruel way in which he sent me away. He hasn't even called me by my name.

It's clear to me now, what I need to do. Anger and self-pity are useless emotions, so I push them away and speak calmly, even though my heart is breaking all over again.

'O King of Ayodhya! I address you in this way because you've always placed your role as king ahead of your role as husband. In this court, which has been set up to dispense justice to all citizens, I ask you this, for I've been a citizen of Ayodhya too: Did you act justly when you sent me away to the forest, knowing I was innocent of what gossip-mongers whispered? Did you stop to think—as a wise king would—that there would always be people who gossip, even in the best-run kingdoms, for it's their nature? Were you compassionate, the way a king is meant to be, when you banished me without telling me what you were about to do, without allowing me to defend myself or choose my destiny? Were you fair to your unborn children when you sentenced them to a life of hardship, perhaps even death, in the wilderness?

'And if you were not, shouldn't someone be judging you today?

'You who care so much about the citizens of Ayodhya, did you think of the impact your actions would have on the women of the city? That men would punish their wives harshly or even discard them for the smallest refractions, saying *King Ram did so. Then why shouldn't I?*

'I accept your priorities, and I understand why they are so important to you. You're compensating for the mistake your father King Dasharath made when he gave in to the demands of his favourite wife and banished you, even though he knew it was bad for his kingdom. It left a deep mark on you. But I don't agree with you that the private life must be sacrificed for the public one. And that is the final advice that I leave for my children: my dearest boys, balance duty with love. Trust me, it can be done.

'O king of Ayodhya, you know I'm innocent, and yet, unfairly, you're asking me to step into the fire. You offer me a tempting prize indeed—to live in happiness with you and my children. But I must refuse. Because if I do what you demand, society will use my action forever after to judge other women. Even when they aren't guilty, the burden of proving their innocence will fall on them. And society will say, why not? Even Queen Sita went through it.

'I can't do that to them.

'For the sake of my sons, I made myself live when it would have been much easier to give up and die than to go through the pain of having the person you love most in the world abandon you. For the sake of my daughters in the centuries to come, I must now stand up against this unjust action you are asking of me.

'I wish you all happiness with my dearest Lav and Kush. I bless this land, its men and women. I bless my sons. And finally, I bless my daughters, who are yet unborn. I pray that, if life tests them—as sooner or later life is bound to do—they'll be able to stand steadfast and think carefully, using their hearts as well as their heads, understanding when they need to compromise, and knowing when they must not.

'And that is why, O King Ram, I must reject your kind offer to allow me to prove my innocence again. Because this is one of those times when a woman must stand up and say, *No more*!

'I call on my mother earth and my father fire—for both have shaped me into the woman I am today—to come to my aid. O Mother, O Father, all my life I've suffered and endured and been wrongly accused. If I am indeed blameless of what the gossipmongers whispered, give me a sign.'

As I speak, I feel a powerful energy course through me. Underneath my feet, the earth cracks open with a deafening roar. The wood around me ignites. Leaping flames surround me, forming a protective barrier. Beyond them, I can see Lav and Kush struggling mightily to get to me. But Ram's brothers hold them back. My heart wrenches at the anguish in their voices as they call to me. *Mother, please. Don't go. Don't leave us alone here.*

Ah, my dears. I hope someday you'll understand why I had to do this.

Ram is running towards the fire, his arms outstretched, his crown falling, unheeded, to the floor. But he can't pass through the flames.

'Sita!' he cries desperately. 'Sita, Sita, Sita.' But he's saying something quite different with his heart. And because I'm no longer fully in this mortal world, I can hear it. *Forgive me, dearest. No matter what I did, no matter what I prioritized, through everything, I've always loved you. Forgive me, though I don't deserve it.*

Is that a golden chariot, rising up from the darkness of Pataal to carry me away? I step forward and set my foot on it. Around me celestial flowers are falling in a crystal shower. Or are they the tears of the gods who crowd the skies, looking down in sorrow and admiration at my final act of self-respect? The flames crackle and leap higher, blackening the ceiling of the royal sabha. But when I focus my gaze on them, they grow still and clear, like a wall of crystal. Through them I can see the otherworld that has come to me only in tantalizing glimpses until now. The pristine ocean of milk. The jewelled palace of Vishnu sparkling with all the colours of the rainbow. It is more real than the royal court of Ayodhya, which is beginning to recede from me, its finery turning into dust. Far more beautiful. Unearthly music, played by gandharvas, rises in a crescendo, calling.

Come, it is time. You have done your duty. You have suffered enough. It is time to return.

Am I the only one who can hear it?

I have one last thing I must do before I turn back from woman to goddess, before my new world—no, it is my original, forever abode—envelops me in pristine bliss, obliterating all complicated, contradictory human emotions. One last, crucial thing I must tell my husband.

'I forgave you a long time ago,' I say to Ram. 'Though I didn't know it until now. Because this is the most important aspect of love, whose other face is compassion: It isn't doled out, drop by drop. It doesn't measure who is worthy and who isn't. It is like the ocean. Unfathomable. Astonishing. Measureless.'

Acknowledgements

MY SINCERE THANKS TO ALL the people listed below for their support, encouragement and suggestions as I wrote *The Forest of Enchantments*.

My American agent Sandra Dijkstra and her team, especially Elise Capron and Andrea Cavallero.

My British agent Caspian Dennis.

My editor at HarperCollins India, Diya Kar.

My writer friends Sreya Chatterjee, Philip Lutgendorf, Auritro Majumdar, Keya Mitra and Oindrila Mukherjee.

My family: Murthy, Anand and Abhay.

My spiritual teachers, Baba Muktananda and Bhagawan Nityananda.

I am deeply grateful to each one of you.

About the Author

Chitra Banerjee Divakaruni is an award-winning and bestselling author, poet, activist and teacher of writing. Her work has been published widely, in magazines and anthologies, and her books have been translated into twenty-nine languages. Several of her works have been made into films and plays. She lives in Houston with her husband Murthy and has two sons, Anand and Abhay. Chitra tweets @cdivakaruni and she loves to connect with her readers on her Facebook page: https://www.facebook.com/chitradivakaruni/.

Divakaruni teaches at the highly acclaimed Creative Writing programme at the University of Houston.